D0032728

After a few minutes, her sobs began to slow and he became uncomfortably aware of the effects of holding her so closely. The incredible softness of her breasts crushed against his chest made his blood fire. He felt the weight come over him. The heavy pull in his groin. The hardening. It had been too long since he'd had a woman, and it had caught up to him—at the wrong time.

She sniffled and gazed up at him with watery eyes, her long lashes clumped and spiky. Her face was bathed in tears and moonlight, with an opalescent glow that seemed almost unworldly. For a moment, it was just the two of them, man and woman, in a realm untainted by blood feuds. In a world where a Campbell heiress might welcome a MacGregor suitor. Where deception was unnecessary. Where kissing her seemed the most natural thing to do—the only thing to do.

Her mouth—with her soft pink lips parted only inches below his—tantalized. A sweet, sugary confection for a man starved with bitterness. Aye, she was ripe for seduction. He just hadn't anticipated how strong the urge would be for him to do so. He ached to kiss her, to take her lips beneath his and slide his tongue deep in her mouth until her breath came fast and hard. Until she moaned for him. He could almost taste her honey sweetness beneath the saltiness of her tears. His entire body felt possessed by desire. The primitive call was bone-deep, encompassing every part of him.

Also by Monica McCarty

Highland Warrior

Highlander Untamed
Highlander Unchained
Highlander Unmasked

Books published by The Random House Publishing Group
are available at quantity discounts on bulk purchases for
premium, educational, fund-raising, and special sales use.
For details, please call 1-800-733-3000.

HIGHLAND OUTLAW

A Novel

MONICA McCARTY

BALLANTINE BOOKS • NEW YORK

Sale of this book without a front cover may be unauthorized. If this book is coverless, it may have been reported to the publisher as "unsold or destroyed" and neither the author nor the publisher may have received payment for it.

Highland Outlaw is a work of fiction. Names, characters, places, and incidents are the products of the author's imagination or are used fictitiously. Any resemblance to actual events, locales, or persons, living or dead, is entirely coincidental.

A Ballantine Books Mass Market Original

Copyright © 2009 by Monica McCarty
Excerpt from *Highland Scoundrel* copyright © 2009 by Monica McCarty.

All rights reserved.

Published in the United States by Ballantine Books, an imprint of The Random House Publishing Group, a division of Random House, Inc., New York.

BALLANTINE and colophon are registered trademarks of Random House, Inc.

This book contains an excerpt from the forthcoming edition of *Highland Scoundrel* by Monica McCarty. This excerpt has been set for this edition only and may not reflect the final content of the forthcoming edition.

ISBN 978-0-345-50339-8

Cover illustration: Aleta Rafton

Printed in the United States of America

www.ballantinebooks.com

OPM   9   8   7   6   5   4   3   2   1

To Reid, my strapping lad in training.
May you grow up just as strong, handsome, and loving
as the heroes in my books
(okay, and your dad, too, but don't tell him!).

Acknowledgments

I'm fortunate to have two doctors in the family "on call" for personal medical clinics on battle wounds. It was my brother-in-law Sean who answered the phone this time for digging out musket balls in the thigh. (Nora, you need to get to the phone quicker—I think Sean is pulling ahead in the "getting ink" department.)

A special thanks to my editor, Kate, for her always quick and insightful feedback and support. It's been so fun working with you. (Go, Sox!)

Thanks to my agents, Andrea and Kelly, whose patience with my questions and occasional neuroses-filled phone calls about "the business" is much appreciated.

Jami and Nyree, my two CPs extraordinaire and my personal cheering section. I feel so fortunate to have found you guys—I shudder to think what I would do without you. Neither of you is ever permitted to move.

My Scotland travel buddy, Veronica—Mommy Abandonment Tour 2008!

Dave, Reid, and Maxine, the good news is that I love you and appreciate all your support; the bad news is we're having Mommy's pasta again for dinner.

HIGHLAND OUTLAW

The moon's on the lake, and the mist's on the brae,
And the Clan has a name that is nameless by day;
Then gather, gather, gather, Gregalach!
Gather, gather, gather, &c.

Our signal for fight, that from monarchs we drew,
Must be heard but by night in our vengeful haloo!
Then haloo, Gregalach! haloo, Gregalach!
Haloo, haloo, haloo, Gregalach &c.

Glen Orchy's proud mountains, Coalchuirn
and her towers,
Glenstrae and Glenlyon no longer are ours:
We're landless, landless, landless, Gregalach!
Landless, landless, landless, &c.

But doom'd and devoted by vassal and lord,
MacGregor has still both his heart and his sword!
Then courage, courage, courage, Gregalach,
Courage, courage, courage, &c.

If they rob us of name, and pursue us with beagles,
Give their roofs to the flame, and the flesh
to the eagles!
Then vengeance, vengeance, vengeance, Gregalach!
Vengeance, vengeance, vengeance, &c.

While there's leaves in the forest, and foam on the river,
MacGregor, despite them, shall flourish forever!
Come then, Gregalach, come then, Gregalach,
Come then, come then, come then, &c.

Through the depths of Loch Katrine
the steed shall career,

O'er the peak of Ben-Lomond the galley shall steer.
And the rocks of Craig Royston like icicles melt,
Ere our wrongs be forgot, or our vengeance unfelt!
Then gather, gather, gather, Gregalach!
Gather, gather, gather, & c.

"MacGregor's Gathering"
SIR WALTER SCOTT

Prologue

God can not be appeasit ... unless that unhappie and destable race
be extirpat and ruttit out, and never sufferit to have rest or remaning within
this cuntrey heirefter ... they salbe prosequte, huntit, followit, and
persewit with fyre and sword....

—Edict for Extermination of Clan Gregor
Commission given to the Earl of Argyll by the Privy Council
February 24, 1603

Inveraray Castle, June 1606

One of these days his cousin was going to get them
killed. Patrick MacGregor could only hope that day wasn't
today. But Alasdair never could resist a challenge, even one
that took them deep into the devil's lair—in this case Inveraray Castle, the Highland stronghold of clan Campbell.
The thick stone walls of the austere keep jutted high above
the trees to disappear into the gray sky, a forbidding reminder of the dominance of their enemy for more than a
hundred and fifty years.

Today, however, the gates of the impenetrable fortress
had been raised in welcome, and the glen that stretched
from the castle to the line of thatched cottages nestled
along the shore of Loch Fyne teemed with hundreds of
clansmen who'd descended on Argyll from all across the
Highlands. A whiff of excitement hung in the drizzly morning air. The games were about to begin.

As they left the sheltering shadows of the forest and
approached the field of play, Patrick's senses flared, heightened by years of evading capture. Wariness and distrust
were ingrained in every fiber of his being, and right now
every instinct screamed caution.

His gaze darted through the crowd, keeping him well apprised of the situation. But no one had taken undue notice of the three newcomers . . . yet.

The MacGregors were once again at the horn—thanks to the Campbells, being outlawed was an all-too-common occurrence in the last seventy-odd years. Nonetheless, his cousin Alasdair Roy MacGregor, Chief of the MacGregors of Glenstrae, had insisted on attending the gathering this year to enter the archery competition. Known as "the Arrow of Glenlyon," Alasdair was a bowman of repute. But he wasn't the best. That title belonged to Rory MacLeod. It was the opportunity to face MacLeod and best him that had forced them out of hiding. The fact that the gathering was being held this year at Inveraray—home to their fiercest enemies—only heightened the danger.

The three men had reached the edge of the muddy field. His cousin turned to him. "You know what to do?"

"Aye," Patrick replied. He'd better, since it was his plan. "But are you sure you want to do this?" Despite the steel knapscall that covered his cousin's distinctive red hair—a trait the MacGregors shared with their Campbell enemies—and the hood he wore against the rain that shadowed his features, if anyone recognized him before their plan was set in motion, the chief was a dead man.

His cousin's eyes lit with anticipation. "Absolutely." He looked to Patrick's brother Gregor for support. " 'Tis time Rory MacLeod faced a wee bit of competition, and the opportunity to do so right under Argyll's pointed nose . . ." His mouth slid into the familiar roguish grin that had endeared him to the heart of their clan. " 'Tis a temptation too great to ignore."

"We'll be gone before they realize what happened," Gregor added.

"Not too soon," the chief said, "I want everyone to know who won."

Patrick leveled his steely gaze on his bold cousin. "So you can claim the golden arrow from Maid Marian?"

Alasdair chuckled and clapped him hard on the back, well aware of his Robin Hood reputation. Nor had he missed the allusion to the archery contest held to trap the famous outlaw. "Behind that black façade is a wry wit, cousin. I've no intention of meeting any Campbells today, but you can be assured that I'll leave them with something to talk about."

Patrick didn't doubt it. His cousin had a streak of daring in him that at times bordered on foolhardy. The head of clan Campbell—Archibald the Grim, the Earl of Argyll—was not a man to prod: He had a crushing bite. But knowing Alasdair would not be dissuaded, Patrick nodded. "Good luck, then, cousin. And take care. If anything goes wrong, be ready."

"With my two fiercest warriors at my back, what could go wrong?"

Patrick cocked an eyebrow. "You don't really want me to answer that, do you?"

His cousin chuckled and bounded off toward the line of contestants.

Patrick admired his cousin's easy confidence, even if he couldn't share it. He'd been on the wrong end of a hagbut or arrowhead too many times in his life not to recognize the scent of danger. And right now it fairly reeked.

As his cousin approached the field of play, he and Gregor moved stealthily into position. Patrick did his best to blend into the crowd—not an easy feat given his height and build, but one perfected over years of practice.

Though his face was not as recognizable as his cousin's—and his hair black, not the characteristic red—he was grateful for the hood and knapscall. They'd bargained for rain, and the skies had not disappointed. Cold rain in spring was an occurrence of such regularity these past few years, it could almost be counted on. The brown woolen cloak helped cover the tattered, dirt-encrusted *leine* and *breacan feile,* but no amount of dunking in the loch could fully hide the evidence of a man who'd lived in the wild for months.

He helped himself to a tankard of ale and stood at the back corner of the crowded pavilion that had been set up for the spectators. As had been popular in tournaments of old, a large tent had been erected to give the principal members of the clan a comfortable—and somewhat dry—position from which to watch the competition.

The tent formed the basis of their plan. They'd been scouting the area for a few days from the safety of the forested hill of Duniquoich overlooking the castle and village to come up with a way to create a distraction. When the tent went up, Patrick knew he'd found it.

After Alasdair won the contest, he would give the signal by removing his hood to reveal his bonnet trimmed with a sprig of pine, *Giuthas nam mòr-shliabh,* the badge of the MacGregors. Then Patrick and Gregor would knock down the poles erected to hold up the canvas tent. Normally, it would take more than one man to knock over each of the substantial wood posts, but he and Gregor had unusual—or, as his cousin like to jest, inhuman—strength.

As soon as the tent was down, a handful of MacGregor guardsmen waiting in the forest would send a barrage of arrows toward the castle, raising the cry of an attack. Disturbing the peace of the games was a great offense and a serious breach of Highland custom and tradition, but Patrick figured that since it wasn't a real attack, their clan honor—what was left of it, anyway—was intact.

With the crowd rushing to get to the safety of the keep through the *barmkin* gate, the stables and horses would be cut off. Taking advantage of the ensuing chaos, the three of them would make for the forest, where a handful of their men were waiting with horses to enable their speedy escape. Certainly they would be followed, but once they were in the trees and hills, the MacGregors had the advantage.

They were used to being hunted.

From his position, Patrick had a clear vantage point of the line of archers readying to take their first shots at the butts—the targets fixed to the mounds of earth. All that was left to do was wait and watch. With each round the risk would grow, as the crowd's curiosity grew about the skilled stranger. Once his cousin pushed back his hood, there wouldn't be much time.

Until then, it was important that he do nothing to draw attention to himself. One false move . . .

He glanced over at the small rise a short distance from the castle, a wooden structure just peeking through the gray mist. The infamous executioner's hill. All three of them could be hanging from the Campbells' well-used gallows by sundown.

As the competition got under way, the boisterousness of the crowd increased with the flow of ale. One group of men in particular was difficult to ignore. Patrick recognized the man with the loudest voice as John Montgomery, brother to the Earl of Eglinton. The earl was rumored to be seeking an alliance with Argyll to garner influence in his deadly feud with the Cunninghams.

Apparently there was truth to the rumor. From what he could tell, Montgomery had recently become betrothed to Elizabeth Campbell, Argyll's cousin and sister to both Campbell of Auchinbreck and Argyll's Henchman, Jamie Campbell. And from the unflattering remarks offered by her betrothed, if the lass weren't a Campbell, Patrick would almost feel sorry for her. She must have a stammer because they referred to her pejoratively as Elizabeth Monntach, Stammering Elizabeth.

"But I thought you intended to wed the fair Bianca?" one of the men said. "The Campbell mouse will surely pale in comparison."

"She's pretty enough. For an alliance with the Earl of Argyll I'd wed a horse missing half its teeth," Montgomery replied defensively.

A hearty round of laughter ensued.

"But what about conversation?" another man asked. "A-a-ren't y-o-o-u w-w-worried that it will take all day to get past 'Good morrow'?"

Patrick could tell from Montgomery's reaction that the other man's jest embarrassed him, but Montgomery masked his discomfort with crudeness. "I'll just have to keep her mouth busy with other things."

The ribald humor found an appreciative audience as the other men snickered.

Asses. Doing his best to ignore them, Patrick glanced down at the field, noting that the number of competitors had lessened to only a handful, including, among others, Alasdair, Rory MacLeod, and the Campbell Henchman. He hoped to hell his cousin was being careful. Jamie Campbell was a formidable enemy—more dangerous than even his cousin the earl. Thankfully, Alasdair was on the opposite side and had yet to attract the Henchman's notice. But as the field of play narrowed . . .

Patrick caught Gregor's eye from across the way and nodded at him to be ready.

Just as he was about to turn his attention back to the field, he caught sight of a young woman making her way through the south *barmkin* gate toward the tent. He didn't know what it was about her that drew his eye—perhaps the lightness of her step or the tentative smile on her face that he could just make out beneath the hood of her cloak. She seemed so young and carefree, practically bubbling with excitement. But there was an uncertainty to her expression—as if she were not accustomed to the feeling—that made his gaze linger.

He glanced back to the competition, saw that his cousin had moved on to the next round, and then inexplicably his gaze turned back to the lass. From the richness of her clothing, he knew she must be of considerable fortune. He could see glimpses of a court gown beneath a fine, dark blue velvet cloak—the edges of which were embroidered with jewels. But she was a tiny thing and seemed to drown in the wide skirts and layers of heavy fabric.

She was heading right for him, and as she drew closer, he had a better look at the face beneath the hood.

Big blue eyes dominated an elfin countenance that was older than he'd first assumed—at least a few years past twenty. But it was her eyes that startled him, so light and crystal clear as to almost seem unreal. She was fair, with pale skin, slight features, and a delicate pink mouth. He couldn't see the color of her hair tucked up in the hood, but he would guess it was light. She wasn't beautiful precisely, or even striking, but pretty in a quiet, understated way that he found strangely arresting. It was the type of face that grew more beautiful on study. The tilt of her head, the view of a profile, could bring an entirely new perspective and appreciation.

She stopped not five feet from him, and her soft feminine scent wrapped around him. She smelled like spring, as fresh as dew upon a rose. It had been a long time since he'd smelled anything so sweet and unspoiled.

Her gaze was fixed on the men he'd overheard earlier. It was only because he was watching her so closely that he saw her smile falter as she listened to their conversation.

"But how did you convince Elizabeth Monntach to agree to your suit?"

She flinched as if struck. Her face drained of color, taking with it all the tentative excitement he'd noticed only moments earlier.

Montgomery laughed, puffing up like a peacock. "With her stammer, it's not as if suitors are storming the castle gates. It's amazing how easy it is to lie with a tocher of twenty-six thousand merks and land to look forward to."

Patrick would have choked if he'd had a mouthful of ale. Twenty-six thousand merks! A fortune. *And* land? Though not unheard of, it was unusual for a woman to possess land in her own right.

"All it took was a few compliments and whispered endearments," Montgomery boasted. "The lass lapped them right up like a grateful pup."

The woman made a strangled sound in her throat. Her eyes were wide and horrified. From the stricken look on her face, it wasn't hard to figure out who she was: It had to be Elizabeth Campbell.

Damn. Given his avowed hatred of anything Campbell, the twinge of sympathy was unexpected.

Her betrothed had heard the sound as well, and his head jerked around to meet her gaze. Patrick saw Montgomery's shock and then dismay as he realized he'd been caught in a trap of his own making. It was the look of a man who knew he'd lost a prize and perhaps earned himself some dangerous enemies at the same time.

The humiliation and raw hurt on her face were almost too hard to watch as the group of men standing with Montgomery quieted, realizing what had happened. She looked heartbroken, as if a world of illusions had just been ripped away from her. It was a feeling he knew only too well. Her chin trembled, and Patrick feared she was close to tears.

He took a step toward her but faltered, wondering what the hell he thought he could do. It wasn't his problem. The lass was Argyll's cousin and the Henchman's sister, for heaven's sake.

The silence was thick and uncomfortable. The men with Montgomery began to shuffle.

Elizabeth Campbell stood stone still, her gaze still pinned to Montgomery. Patrick experienced an unfamiliar tug in his chest at the raw vulnerability she was fighting so hard to mask. He found himself silently rooting for her as she mustered her pride, straightening her back and lifting her quivering chin. She might be a wisp of a thing, but there was strength in those delicate bones.

Her face was a mask of alabaster, devoid of expression and as fragile as glass. One tap and he feared she would crack. "Not so grateful that I will m-m-mar-r . . ." Her voice fell off as the word stuck in her mouth. She covered her mouth with her hand, her eyes round in horror. One of the men smothered a laugh, and Patrick could have killed him. Cheeks aflame, she spun on her heel and started to run up the path toward the *barmkin* gate. But she'd taken only a few steps before disaster struck.

One foot skidded out from under her in the slippery mud and she lost her balance, falling backward on her rump and landing with an emphatic splash in a soupy brown puddle.

One of the men muttered, "It seems her feet are as tangled as her tongue."

There were a few nervous chuckles, and Patrick prayed that she hadn't heard but knew from the way her shoulders slumped that she had.

It was the final straw. He'd had enough. The role of champion was unfamiliar to him, but he could stand aside no longer. He knew what he risked, but something compelled his feet forward. No lass—even a Campbell one—deserved such cruelty. And Patrick, perhaps more than anyone, understood being beaten down and left to flounder in the mud. He understood injustice.

He closed the gap between them with a few long strides. Her hood had shifted with the fall to reveal a single heavy curl of flaxen hair, shimmering with light even in the gray mist. The simple beauty of it struck him. Though he couldn't see her face, he could tell from the soft shake of her shoulders that she was crying. He felt a tight burning in his chest and something that he'd no longer thought himself capable of twisting deep in the bowels of his blackened soul: compassion and an inexplicable urge to protect.

He'd gladly strangle those men with his bare hands for hurting her. Perhaps he would. "Here, lass," he said softly, holding out his hand. "Take my hand."

At first, he didn't think she'd heard him. But then she turned her head slightly so that he could see the sparkle of a single tear sliding down her pale cheek. The tiny bead ate like acid through the steel forged around his chest. Slowly, she raised her hand and slid it into his. It was so small and soft, he almost pulled back in shock—and then embarrassment when he thought of his hard, callused palms caked with dirt.

But she didn't seem to notice.

Gently, he pulled her to her feet. She was such a wisp of a thing, he could have lifted her with a finger. He held her hand, feeling an odd reluctance to let her go, until she tugged it gently from his.

She kept her gaze down, too embarrassed even to look at him. "Thank you," she said so softly that he almost didn't hear her.

"They're fools, you are well to be rid—" he started, but she was already hurrying away. From waist to hem, the back of her fine cloak was soggy and dripping with mud.

He took a step after her, then stopped, setting his feet solidly in the mud. He let her walk away. Even if it were possible, comforting a lass wasn't anything he knew how to do. The idea of a MacGregor outlaw consoling a Campbell heiress was so improbable, he would have laughed if the ability to do so hadn't died in him long ago.

He turned his gaze away from the solitary figure disappearing through the gates of the castle.

Just in time to see Jamie Campbell, Argyll's Henchman and the most dangerous man in the Highlands, headed right for him. The Henchman must have seen his sister stumble and had decided to investigate. And by helping her and drawing attention to himself, Patrick had made himself the center of that investigation.

He cursed, and his gaze shot to Gregor. His brother was looking at him as if he were half-crazed, and in truth, Patrick had begun to wonder the same thing himself.

What could he have been thinking?

He knew they had to act fast. Campbell was closing the distance between them, recognition flaring in his eyes.

Anticipation surged through his veins with the promise of a battle long overdue. There wasn't a MacGregor alive who didn't want to see Jamie Campbell dead, and Patrick would like nothing more than to have the honor of sending the Henchman straight home to the bloody devil.

His hand flexed around the hilt of his dirk. One throw . . .

God, he was tempted. More than tempted—eager, even. But reason interceded. It would be a death knell; three men against a hundred were odds he wasn't inclined to test.

His gaze shifted quickly to his cousin. Three contestants remained on the archery field, but there was only one thing he could do. The chief would have to wait to best the MacLeod, just as Patrick would have to wait to face Jamie Campbell.

Revenge would hold for another day; the sands of vengeance never ran dry.

Mouthing "Now" to his brother, he pushed hard on the pole. It wobbled and started to fall, slowly at first, swaying like a pendulum, then coming down hard with a mighty crash.

The distraction worked as pandemonium exploded throughout the crowd. Patrick ran toward the forest, joining his brother and cousin, but something made him look back to the tower keep of Inveraray Castle.

Regret, perhaps, for something that could never be his. For the life that had been stolen from him. A life where a MacGregor warrior and a Campbell lass were not separated by fortune and hatred.

With one last glance at the mighty fortress, Patrick slipped into the trees and disappeared into the mist.

Chapter 1

O Castle Gloom! thy dark defile
Throngs not with Scottish story;
On other towers, O proud Argyle
Sits crowned thine ancient glory.
But little have we of the past,
As up the dell we ramble,
To figure, floating on the blast,
Thy banners, Castle Campbell!

"Castle Campbell," by WILLIAM GIBSON

Near Castle Campbell, Clackmannanshire, June 1608

Elizabeth Campbell lowered the creased piece of parchment into her lap and looked out the small window, watching the hulking shadow of Castle Campbell fade into the distance with a heavy heart. No matter how many times she read the letter, it did not change the words. Her time, it seemed, was up.

The carriage bounced along the uneven road, moving at a painstakingly slow pace. Recent rain had made the already rough road to the Highlands treacherous, but if they continued like this, it would take a week to reach Dunoon Castle.

Lizzie glanced across the carriage and caught the furtive gaze of her maidservant, Alys, but the other woman quickly shifted her eyes back to her embroidery, feigning a concentration belied by the ill-formed stitches.

Alys was worried about her, though trying not to show it. Hoping to divert her questions, Lizzie said, "I don't know how you can sew with all this bumping—"

But her words were cut off when, as if to make her point, her bottom rose off the seat for a long beat and then came down with a hard slam that rattled her teeth, as her shoulder careened into the wood-paneled wall of the carriage.

"Ouch," she moaned, rubbing her arm once she was able to right herself. She glanced at Alys, who'd suffered a similar fate. "Are you all right?"

"Aye, my lady," Alys replied, adjusting herself back on the velvet cushion. "Well enough. But if the roads do not improve, we'll be a heap of broken bones and bruises before we arrive."

Lizzie smiled. "I suspect it will get much worse. Taking the carriage at all was probably a mistake." They would have to switch to horses when they passed Stirlingshire, crossed into the Highland divide, and the roads narrowed— or, she should say, became more narrow, as they were barely wide enough for a carriage even in this part of the Lowlands.

"At least we're dry," Alys pointed out, always one to see the positive side of a situation. Perhaps that was why Lizzie enjoyed her company so much. They were much alike in that regard. Alys reached down and picked up the letter that had fallen to the ground with the tumult. "You dropped your missive."

Resisting the urge to snatch it back, Lizzie took it casually and tucked it safely in her skirts. "Thank you." She could sense Alys's curiosity about the earl's letter, about what was taking them to Dunoon Castle so suddenly, but she wasn't ready to alleviate it. Alys, like everyone else, would find out the contents soon enough. It would be no secret that her cousin the Earl of Argyll intended to find Lizzie a husband.

Again.

Apparently, three broken engagements weren't enough. It was her duty to *marry*, and marry she must.

Her chest squeezed as the humiliating memory of her most recent broken betrothal returned to her in an unwelcome flash. The pain, even with the passage of two years, was still acute. "Elizabeth Monntach," they'd called her. And she so eager for compliments that she'd "lapped them right up like a grateful pup."

The humiliation still burned. Worse, John was right. She'd been far too eager, far too ready to believe that a handsome man like him could care for her for reasons beyond clan alliances and wealth. Her best friend had found happiness; she'd desperately wanted it, too. Enough to ignore what her gut was telling her—that beneath the handsome exterior was a man of weak character and strong ambition.

Hearing the man she'd given her heart to speak so cruelly of her would have been bad enough, but then it got worse. Much worse. She closed her eyes but could not shut out the memories of stammering. Of slipping in the mud. Of their mockery. "Her feet are as tangled as her tongue." The sounds of their laughter still echoed in her head. She could almost taste the hot, salty tears that had burned in her throat and eyes. She'd wanted to crawl under her bed and never come out.

Only one man had helped her. She'd been too embarrassed to look at him, but she remembered the kindness—not pity—in his voice and the comforting strength of his callused hand. She frowned. Strange to think that her gallant knight had been a MacGregor.

She'd missed the chaos that had followed her departure from the pavilion, but later her brother had told her what had happened. Alasdair Roy MacGregor and his men had escaped right out from under his nose, and Jamie had been none too happy about it. What Jamie couldn't understand was why the outlaw had risked discovery to come to her assistance in the first place. She didn't know, either, but she would be forever grateful for his act of kindness.

She sensed that Jamie knew more about the man who'd helped her than he'd let on, but perhaps because he could sense her interest, he'd held his tongue, refusing to satisfy her curiosity about the gallant outlaw.

She'd put an end to the betrothal with John Montgomery immediately, too ashamed to tell her family the particulars. But when he'd been maimed in an attack not long afterward, losing an ear and part of his sword arm, Lizzie wondered if her family had discovered something on their own. She had not wished him ill but knew that nothing she could have said would have stopped her family from exacting retribution. They were much too protective of her. Perhaps that was part of the problem—the Campbells were an intimidating lot.

Lizzie had put the unpleasantness behind her and tried to forget, but sometimes, like now, it would come back to her in a vivid wave as if it had been yesterday. And when word spread that once again the Earl of Argyll was seeking an alliance for his oft-betrothed cousin, the whispering would start all over again.

She dreaded the conversation with her cousin, knowing that she would no longer be able to keep secret the extent of her foolishness with John.

Though her cousin Archie hadn't come out and said marriage was his intent, Lizzie had read between the lines of his letter. She lifted the parchment to the window once again, the bold black scratches of ink revealing far more than what was written.

My dear cousin,

Summer is fast upon us. I request the pleasure of your company at Dunoon as soon as possible to discuss a matter of some import. As we discussed last winter, for your kindness following the death of the countess last year and your attention to little Archie and the girls, I've gifted you with a sizeable parcel of land.

Archibald, 7th Earl of Argyll

More land. How humiliating. Despite her cousin's claim, Lizzie knew that her help following the death of the countess wasn't the real reason for the gift. Archie obviously thought he needed to sweeten the pot to get someone to marry her. No doubt he was only trying to help, but her tocher was already one of the richest in the land; wasn't that enough?

Her shoulders sagged. Apparently not.

Part of this was her own fault. *Summer,* she'd promised. Could it be June already? When her cousin had broached the subject of another betrothal all those months ago during the Yule celebration, the days were still short and the snow blanketing the moors of Inveraray Castle still comfortably deep. Summer had seemed so far away. There had seemed plenty of time to find a suitable man on her own. Plenty of time in which to fall in love.

After the travesty of her last betrothal, she'd vowed to marry only for love—what she thought she'd found with John. But it had been a foolish girl's vow. A vow made when her emotions were still raw and tender from his cruelty.

Now, two years later, Lizzie had to be practical. At six and twenty, love probably wasn't for her.

Probably.

She sighed at her own foolishness. Even with reality staring her in the face, she could not completely shed the possibility from her mind. But it was well past time to give up that particular fantasy. She didn't want to live her life alone. Taking care of her cousin's and brother's households would not be enough forever, and as much as she loved little Archie and the girls, the children were not hers. She wanted a home and family of her own—enough to accept a new betrothal brokered by her cousin.

She felt a twinge of regret, thinking of her friends' happiness, then quickly pushed it aside. Her two closest friends, Meg Mackinnon and Flora MacLeod, had both been fortunate enough to find love with their husbands. Ironically, Meg had married Flora's brother Alex. Meg had two young sons, and Flora had recently given birth to twins. Lizzie was happy for them, but it made her deeply aware of all that she was missing.

But as much as she wanted what her friends had found, she had to accept that she could not wait any longer for something that might never happen.

It doesn't matter, she told herself, determined as always to make the best of every situation. *I will make my own happiness. Arranged marriage or not.*

"Is something wrong, mistress?"

Lost in thought, Lizzie hadn't realized that Alys had been watching her again. She lifted a brow. "I thought you were embroidering?"

This time Alys would not be put off. Curiosity, it seemed, had finally overridden discretion. "You keep staring at that letter as if it's an execution warrant."

A wry smile curved Lizzie's mouth. "Nothing as dramatic as that, I'm afraid." The earl would be angry, but not with her.

"Are you worried about the travel with all those horrid MacGregors scurrying about the countryside?" Alys leaned across and patted her knee. "There's nothing to worry about. My Donnan will see that we come to no harm."

Alys's husband was captain of the earl's guardsmen at Castle Campbell, and she was fiercely proud of the formidable warrior.

"No, it's not the travel," Lizzie assured her. They were well protected by a dozen guardsmen, and not even the outlawed MacGregors would dare attack the Earl of Argyll's carriage. Besides, they were still in the Lowlands, well away from the Lomond Hills, where the proscribed clan was reputed to have fled following the battle of Glenfruin. Even as news of the atrocities committed by the Mac-

Gregors at Glenfruin spread through the Highlands, it was hard for Lizzie to reconcile the man who'd come to her aid with the band of ruthless outlaws who'd perpetrated a massacre on the field of Glenfruin. In this, however, she was alone in her family. Her cousin had been charged by King James to bring the MacGregors to justice for their crimes and for the past few years had made it his mission. A mission in which her brothers Jamie and Colin had joined. It was only a matter of time before the outlaws were all hunted down.

What would happen to her warrior? Knowing the answer, she tried not to think about it.

Lizzie met the other woman's gaze, seeing the concern brimming in her warm brown eyes. She sighed, knowing that Alys was truly worried about her.

She would have handed her the note, but Alys, a Highlander to the core, did not read Scots, only a smattering of the Highland tongue. Lizzie read the words aloud as the coach bumped along a particularly rocky patch of road, her voice reverberating with each jolt.

When she was finished, Alys frowned. "Why would you be upset about getting more land?"

"Don't you see? The land is only the bait. My cousin intends to find me another husband."

Alys snorted. " 'Tis about time, if you ask me."

Having suspected that this would be the older woman's reaction, Lizzie had hoped to avoid the subject altogether. A wry smile turned her mouth. "Your sympathy is overwhelming."

"Bah," said the other woman with disgust. " 'Tis not sympathy you need but a husband and bairns. You're a beautiful lass with a loving heart, and you've locked yourself away because of some arse . . ."

Lizzie gave her a sharp look.

"Because of some overstuffed peacock," Alys continued.

"I don't know what that man did to you, but he wasn't worth a halfpenny of the tears you spent on him."

Lizzie knew it was useless to try to make her loyal maid-servant understand. By no stretch of the word could Lizzie possibly be considered beautiful, but try explaining that to anyone in her family and they looked at her as if she were addled.

Her family just didn't see her the way other people did. To them she was a prize. A woman any man would be proud to have by his side.

They loved her too much to view her stammering as anything other than a minor inconvenience. Usually, they were right. Lizzie stammered only in large groups or when she was nervous or anxious, and now almost not at all. She supposed there was one reason to be grateful to John. The past two years, she'd devoted endless hours to speaking softly and slowly in the effort to further control her stammer, determined never to allow herself to be made the butt of anyone's mockery again.

"Perhaps not," Lizzie agreed, anxious to avoid the subject.

"Then what is it? Are you worried that your cousin will betroth you to a man you cannot abide? The earl loves you too much to ever see you unhappy."

"He would never do that," Lizzie agreed. She was lucky. Not only did she have the love of her family, but they also respected her in a way that was hardly typical of the position of most women in today's world. She'd been educated by tutors alongside her brothers before they went to Tounis College, and was as knowledgeable about Highland politics as any man.

Indeed, it wasn't her cousin's choices in husbands that had proved the problem. John Montgomery had actually been her choice. The two men her cousin had picked for her would have been infinitely better choices, but circumstances beyond her control had forced them apart.

Her first betrothal, to James Grant, had been arranged when she was a child, but it had been broken by Duncan's treason.

Duncan. The brother she'd idolized, lost to her almost ten years ago. God, how she missed him. Despite the proof against him, Lizzie had never believed him guilty of the betrayal that had cost the Campbells the battle of Glenlivet and ultimately their father his life. She hoped one day to see him return to prove it. She'd begged him to do so many times in the occasional letter she managed to smuggle to him. Their communication was the one secret she kept from her family. But she was enormously proud of the name he'd made for himself on the continent after having it erroneously blackened at home.

Lizzie had also welcomed her second betrothal. She'd known Rory MacLeod since she was a child, and would have been hard-pressed not to have been at least a little besotted with the handsome chief. Unfortunately for her, he'd been ordered by the king to handfast with Isabel MacDonald and had fallen in love with his beautiful bride.

"Then why are you so upset?" Alys asked. "Do you not wish to be married?" She sounded as if the very idea were unfathomable.

"Of course I do. It's just that I want . . ." Lizzie stumbled over the words, embarrassed. It sounded silly, particularly after her disappointment with John. Women in her position married for duty, not for love. Feeling the telltale rush of anxiety that precipitated a stammer, she took a deep breath, counted silently to five, and then forced herself to speak slowly and softly. "I want what you have."

Alys's eyes widened with understanding. It had probably never occurred to her—or to any of Lizzie's family, for that matter—that she would wish for something so fanciful and not be content simply to do what was expected of her, as she always did. She would do her duty, of course, but that didn't mean she could completely quiet the whispers in her heart.

The maidservant studied Lizzie's face for a long moment before answering. "Aye, I want that for you, too, lass. But you've nothing to worry about. The earl will find you a good husband, and once he gets to know you, the man won't be able to stop himself from loving you."

Alys said it with such conviction, Lizzie realized that arguing was futile. It sounded so much like something her mother would have said that tears blurred her eyes, and she had to turn away. Not a day went past that she didn't miss her mother. Her death only months before that of Lizzie's father had been a cruel blow that Lizzie felt every day.

She gazed out the window to distract herself from the memories, the countryside rolling by in a vivid panoply of green. The heavy spring rain had reaped its munificent bounty, turning the glens thick with grass and the trees dense with leaves.

The light dimmed as the hours passed and they moved deeper into the forest, sending shadows dancing across the walls. The carriage slowed, and an eerie quiet descended around them. It felt as though they were being swallowed up. Like a sponge, the canopy of trees took hold, soaking up the noise and light. Unconsciously, Lizzie's fingers circled the hilt of the small dirk she wore strapped to her side, as she silently thanked her brothers for insisting that she learn how to use it.

The coach jerked hard to the side, knocking Lizzie from her seat once again. But this time the carriage did not right itself, and they came to a sudden stop.

Something didn't feel right. It was too quiet. Like the still before the storm.

Her pulse quickened. Tiny bumps prickled along her skin, and the temperature seemed to drop as the chill cut to her bones.

They'd come to rest at an angle so that both women had

settled on the right side of the carriage opposite the door. It took a bit of maneuvering to get themselves up.

"Are you all right, my lady?" Alys asked, giving her a hand. Lizzie could tell from her quick, high-pitched tone that the maidservant was nervous as well. "A wheel must be stuck—"

A primal cry tore through the shrouded trees, sending an icy chill straight down Lizzie's spine. Her eyes shot to Alys's in shared understanding. Dear God, they were under attack.

She could hear the voices of her cousin's guardsmen outside, shouting orders back and forth, and then the name clear as day: "MacGregors!"

Lizzie couldn't believe it. *The outlaws must be mad to risk . . .*

Her blood went cold.

Or so desperate, they have nothing to lose.

Fear started to build along the back of her neck. A whispery breath at first, then an icy hand with a tenacious grip. She fought to catch the frantic race of her pulse, but it kept speeding ahead.

A shot fired. Then another.

"Donnan!" Alys cried, lurching for the door handle.

"Don't!" Lizzie stopped her, the maidservant's rash act finally wrenching her from her shock. "He'll be fine," she said more gently, knowing she had to calm the other woman's rising panic. "If you go outside, you will only distract him. We need to stay inside where they can protect us."

Alys nodded, fear for her husband rendering her temporarily mute.

Lizzie's heart went out to her; she was unable to imagine how difficult it must be to sit and do nothing while outside the man you loved was in danger. "It will be all right," she said as much to calm Alys as herself. *If only Jamie were here.* Argyll's guardsmen were well trained, but the Mac-

Gregors were reputed for their battle skills. Even her cousin had hired the proscribed warriors at times, before relations between the clans had splintered. But no one could defeat her brother. He was the most feared warrior in the Highlands.

The two women put their faces to the small window, trying to see what was happening, but the smoke from the musket shots was thick, and the fighting seemed to be in front of the carriage, beyond their field of vision.

The noise was deafening, but the most horrible part was imagining, trying to match the sounds with what might be happening. Unfortunately, there was no mistaking the sound of death. It surrounded them like a tomb in their small carriage, closing over them until the air was thick and difficult to breathe.

Alys began to weep softly. Lizzie took her hands and, unable to find words, hummed a song to soothe her. The music worked its magic, and the older woman began to relax.

"Oh, my lady. Even in the midst of hell, you've the voice of an angel," Alys said, tears glistening in her eyes. The fine lines around her eyes etched deeper.

Lizzie managed a small smile, having always found it ironic herself that the girl with the stammer had been gifted with song. While she was singing, her voice had always been miraculously free of fumbling.

She put her arm around Alys and they huddled together, listening and praying.

Lizzie had never been so terrified. It felt as if every nerve ending, every fiber of her being, were honed to a razor's edge on what was happening. Everything felt as if it were moving too quickly: her mind, her pulse, her breathing. But strangely, at this moment of extreme danger, she'd never felt more alive.

But for how long?

The handle to the door rattled, and she jumped. A menacing face appeared in the window, and her heart lurched forward, slamming into her chest, and then came to a complete stop.

Alys screamed. Lizzie wanted to, but though her mouth was open, the sound wouldn't come out. She couldn't breathe; all she could do was stare at the face in the glass. At the wild man. His hair was long and unkempt, his features hidden beneath the dirt and hair that covered his face. All except for his eyes. They were glaring at her with hatred. It was like looking into the face of a feral animal. A wolf. A beast.

For the first time, it occurred to her what these men might do to them if they were taken. The thought of him touching her . . . Bile rose at the back of her throat. She would slit her own throat first.

The door started to open. Lizzie grasped the handle from her side and pulled hard, finding an unexpected burst of strength as she engaged in a battle that she was sure to lose. "Help me!" she yelled to Alys.

But before Alys could move to do so, another shot rang out, and the man jerked and froze in a state of momentary suspension. His eyes went wide, then wider, right before his face smacked hard against the glass with a horrible thud. As the dead weight of his body pulled him down, his nose and mouth dragged against the glass, stretching his features into a hideous mask of death.

The muscles she'd been clenching released. Her breathing was hard and quick as air once again tried to get into her lungs. The immediate threat was past, but Lizzie knew it was far from over.

Her heart was still racing, but her mind was oddly clear, focused on one thing: keeping them alive.

That an attacker was able to get so close to them did not bode well for their guardsmen. She looked out the window again, trying not to think about the dead man lying right below them, and weighed their options. They had only two: Stay put or try to hide.

The carriage that had felt safe a few minutes ago now felt like a coffin waiting to be lowered into the ground. It was worth the risk. She turned to Alys. "We need to go."

"But where?"

"We'll hide in the forest until it is over."

Alys nodded, too shocked to argue. It was clear to both of them that even without deference to rank, Lizzie had taken charge.

"Are you ready?"

The older woman nodded dumbly.

Lizzie could tell that Alys was hanging on by a very thin thread—ready to slip into panic at any moment. "Stay close and follow me." She paused. "And whatever you do, don't look." Tears of understanding swam in Alys's eyes. "Promise me," Lizzie said more forcefully, taking her shoulders and giving her a hard shake.

"I promise."

"Good." Taking a deep breath, she lowered the handle and pushed open the door. When it was wide enough, she poked her head out to get a look around. The acrid smell hit her first—of gunpowder and the unmistakable metallic scent of blood. It filled her nose and burned the back of her throat. She coughed, covering her mouth and nose with her hand against the urge to retch.

Though she wanted to follow her own advice to Alys, Lizzie knew she had to look.

She braced herself, but it wasn't enough to prepare her for the shock of what she saw. Dead men littered the forest floor, strewn in awkward positions. Bellies slit open. Holes torn in chests. Unseeing eyes. Blood. *So much blood.*

The horror would have paralyzed her if she'd allowed herself to look at their faces, for some were men she knew. Instead, she forced her eyes from the dead to the living. To the men still engaged in battle.

It was as she feared. The Campbells were outnumbered. The surprise attack had worked to immediately lessen her guardsmen's numbers, giving the MacGregors the advantage. She counted only a handful of Campbells and almost twice that many MacGregors, who were easily identified by their Highland clothing and barbaric appearance. Unlike the leather doublets and breeches worn by her cousin's men, the MacGregors wore *leines* and dirty, tattered plaids belted at the waist. Their hair and beards were long and unkempt. Only a few wore the added protection of a cotun, and none had armor. They were armed with pikes, swords, and bows, and she even saw an old ax, but they carried no guns. Not that it would help her cousin's men. Though they were well armed, when the battle drew close their guns had become virtually useless against the great Highland *claidheamhmór*.

The clang of steel on steel rang in her ears. She was just about to turn away when she stilled, catching sight of Alys's Donnan. He was holding off a particularly large MacGregor, but it was clear that he was overmatched. The MacGregor warrior didn't let up but kept striking and striking, wielding his sword with vicious brute strength, if not finesse.

She knew what was going to happen, but she couldn't tear her gaze away. When the MacGregor finally connected with flesh, slicing Donnan across the belly, she choked back a sob in her throat.

Though she knew it was impossible, it was as if the MacGregor heard her. His gaze locked on hers, and everything inside her froze as she stared into blackness. Into the eyes of a man without a soul.

His mouth curved in a menacing smile, and he started moving purposefully toward the carriage.

She dared to breathe only when one of her cousin's guardsmen stepped in his way.

"What is it?" Alys said from behind her.

"Nothing," Lizzie said, trying to keep her voice steady, though inside every inch of her was shaking. "We need to go. Now."

Taking hold of Alys's hand, Lizzie stepped carefully out of the carriage. Anticipating Alys's instinct, Lizzie looked back at her and reminded her, "Don't look."

The ground was spongy under her feet with dirt and moss still damp from the earlier rain. The thin leather slippers she wore had little traction, so she had to move cautiously. They stepped around the disabled carriage, heading toward the woods.

All of a sudden, Alys cried out as her hand was ripped from Lizzie's hold.

She spun around, gazing right into the obsidian eyes of the man who'd slain Donnan. Despite the chill in the air, her skin dampened with fear. He was even bigger and more fearsome-looking up close. And dirt seemed to fill every line and crevice of skin that wasn't covered with hair.

"Going somewhere?" He spoke in the Highland tongue, his voice thick with a heavy brogue.

Alys struggled against the massive circle of his arms, but it only made him squeeze her harder, until the older woman winced in pain.

"Let go of her," Lizzie demanded, taking a step toward him, finding courage she didn't know she possessed.

"Or what?" He sneered, lifting the dirk he was holding to Alys's throat. "I don't think you are in any position to be issuing orders, Mistress Campbell."

Lizzie sucked in her breath, never taking her eyes from the blade at Alys's throat. He knew who she was. Out of the corner of her eye, she could see her clansmen still fighting, trying to get to her, but they were overwhelmed. "Let us go. You don't want to do this. You'll die if you hurt us."

"I'll die anyway," he said flatly. "But I shall have some fun before the devil bids me welcome." He took a step toward her, loosening his hold on Alys.

Lizzie saw her opening and didn't think but simply re-acted. In one smooth motion, she grabbed the dirk at her side and threw it as hard as she could. His eyes flew open in surprise. He let out a strangled gasp when the blade sank into his belly with a satisfying thud.

She was out of practice. She'd aimed for his black heart.

He sank to his knees, clutching his stomach in pain. "To hell with it—I'll kill you for this, you little bitch." He yelled to one of his men nearby, "Get her!"

She was about to grab Alys's hand and tell her to run when she heard the sudden thunder of hooves coming toward them.

The MacGregor scourge heard it, too.

Neither of them had time to react before the riders were upon them. Warriors. Perhaps a half dozen strong. But who were they? Friend or foe?

Her pulse raced as she waited to find out, horribly aware that their fate likely hung in the balance.

She could just make out their faces. . . .

She sucked in her breath, her gaze locked on the man a few lengths in front of the others, tearing through the trees at a breakneck pace toward them. Every nerve ending prickled as she beheld the fearsome warrior. She prayed he was a friend. One look was all it took to know that she would not want him as her enemy. The man had the look of a dark angel—sinfully handsome but dangerous. Very dangerous.

The shiver that swept through her was not from fear but from awareness. Awareness that made her skin tingle just to look at him. Enormous warriors armed to the teeth and clad in heavy steel mail did not usually provoke such a dis-tinctly feminine reaction—except that he wasn't wearing mail. The hard lines of his formidable physique were all him. She sucked in an admiring breath, noticing the way the black leather of his cotun pulled tight across a broad chest and snugly around heavily muscled arms, tapering neatly over a flat stomach.

He was built for destruction, his body forged into a steely weapon of war.

But it wasn't just his physical dominance that set him apart from the others. It was the ruthlessness in his gaze, the hard, uncompromising bent of his square jaw, and the strength of his bearing. He wore a steel knapscall, his jet black hair just long enough to show below the rim. Thick and wavy, it framed his chiseled features to perfection. A strong jaw, high cheekbones, and a wide, sculpted mouth were set off by deeply tanned skin. Only a nose that had been broken more than once and a few thin, silvery scars gave proof to his profession. He was a Greek god carved not from marble, but from hard Highland granite.

He met her gaze for an instant, and a charge shot through her with all the subtlety of Zeus's thunderbolt. It rippled through her like a warm current from her head, down her spine, extending to the tips of her fingers and toes, shocking her with its intensity.

Green, she thought inanely. In the midst of the most terrifying experience of her life, she noticed the striking color of his eyes. Not the obvious skill with which he wielded his sword or the way he ordered his men with the barest gesture into formation or even—God forbid—whether he intended to finish the job that the MacGregors had started, but that his eyes blazed like the rarest emeralds sparkling in the sun.

He held her gaze for another moment before shifting to the man she'd stabbed.

The situation came back to her in a staggered heartbeat and she froze, waiting to see what he intended. One beat. Two. Her heart rose higher in her throat.

Relief washed over her when an arrow shot by one of his men landed in the tree inches from the MacGregor's head. *A friend. Thank God!*

"Help us! Please help us!" she shouted. But her words were unnecessary. The warriors had already drawn their swords and started to attack the outlaws. It didn't take long to measure their skill and see their superiority. Her cousin's remaining guardsmen fought with renewed vigor, energized by the additional sword arms.

It was as if the wind had shifted; the attackers had become the attacked.

The dark knight dismounted, his horse an encumbrance in the narrow clearing, and came to the aid of one of her clansmen, swinging his sword down hard to fend off an attacker. The steely clash reverberated through the dense forest, and Lizzie could have sworn the earth shook with the force of the blow. He fought with savage grace, wielding his sword with skill and ease.

Forsooth, this was a swordsman who might give her brother Jamie a challenge.

A small cry drew her attention from the dark knight. *Alys!* Frantically, the other woman was searching the fighting men with her gaze, looking for her husband, and Lizzie knew she had to do something.

"Alys, come." She grabbed her icy hand. "We must get out of the way."

"But Donnan . . ." She turned to Lizzie, her face crumpled with such despair that Lizzie's heart broke for the pain she would suffer. "I don't see my husband."

"The men are spread out, I'm sure he's fighting up ahead," Lizzie lied. "We can't look for him now. It will be over soon and then we'll find him."

She started to lead her away, only to find her path blocked. The MacGregor ruffian she'd stabbed had managed to get to his feet and unsheathe his sword. He held it with one arm, as the other was wrapped around his waist to stanch the flow of blood streaming from the wound in his stomach.

The rage in his expression shook her to her toes. He raised his sword above his head . . .

Everything stopped. Time. Her heart. Her breath. She didn't feel anything. For a moment, it didn't seem real. She could have been standing on a balcony watching players on a stage below. The girl was too young to die. She'd barely lived. There were so many things still before her. A family of her own. A man to love. A child to hold in her arms. All that she'd yet to do was reflected in the shimmer of steel poised precipitously over her head.

I don't want to die.

The urge to live broke through the shock of impending death, and Lizzie started to back away, ready to do whatever it took to protect herself and Alys.

The sword started down . . .

"Don't," a man boomed from across the path. His deep, husky voice held the cool ring of authority. Lizzie knew it was the dark knight even before she looked. When she did, she saw him still a good distance away, but he'd exchanged his sword for a bow and had it aimed right at the MacGregor warrior's heart. "I won't miss." Cold certainty made it a promise and not a threat.

Her heart stilled.

The two men squared off in a silent battle. Tension stretched between them, thick and heavy. Finally, the MacGregor brigand lowered his claymore.

One of his men appeared at his side with a horse. "We must away."

The MacGregor looked as though he wanted to argue, but with one last glance at Lizzie that promised future retribution, he mounted his horse and let out a fierce cry: *"Ard Choille!"* The Woody Height, Lizzie translated from her childhood memory of the Highland tongue. Probably the clan battle cry, she realized.

His warriors responded immediately. Like wraiths, they vanished into the forest as suddenly as they'd appeared.

Only the flutter of leaves trailing behind them gave proof to their existence.

That and the dead bodies of her clansmen littered across the forest floor.

She muffled a dry sob in her mouth.

It was over. But she was too numb to feel relief. She was too numb to feel anything at all. She closed her eyes and inhaled deeply, letting air fill her lungs. *Breathe. Just breathe.*

When she finally opened them again, it was to search for the man to whom she owed her life.

Chapter 2

The battle was over, but the hot pounding of blood surging through his body had yet to slow. Patrick was too damn furious.

He lowered his sword, wincing as a sharp pain bit his side. Blood wasn't just rushing through his body, but also out of it. He could feel the unmistakable warm dampness soaking the linen of the shirt that he wore under his leather cotun. It wasn't a new wound, but an old one, suffered weeks—nay, months—ago at the battle of Glenfruin. And now reopened.

Thanks to his damn brother.

Patrick tugged off his steel helmet and raked his fingers through newly shorn hair, surveying the senseless destruction before him. His gaze slid over the battlefield, over the dead bodies, a sick feeling twisting in his gut. He had been reared on a battlefield. With all the death he'd seen, he was surprised that it still had the power to affect him. Perhaps it was because this time the loss of life was so unnecessary.

No one was supposed to get hurt.

At least that had been the plan, before Gregor had taken it upon himself to decide otherwise. His damned hotheaded brother had gone too far. Gregor had all the boldness of their cousin without the charm and fortune—and added a dangerous streak of recklessness.

Patrick swore with even greater fury when his gaze fell on the mutilated body of one of his clansmen. Bitterness soured his mouth. Conner had been a bonny lad who

smiled more than not—a rarity among the outlawed men—
though you wouldn't know it by looking at him. A musket
shot had hit him in the cheek, blowing half his face off.
Patrick's fists clenched. Not yet eight and ten and look at
him.

The senseless waste of a young life made him want to
lash out. If Gregor were here right now, he'd feel the weight
of Patrick's anger.

It was little comfort that his brother was paying for his
sins—if the wound in his belly felt anything like Patrick's
side right now. What the hell could Gregor have been
thinking to attack the lass like that? He hoped that the
lass's dirk hadn't done lasting harm, but Gregor had much
to account for.

By his count, four MacGregors and twice as many
Campbells had died today. He did not mourn the lives of
his enemy, but neither had he intended their deaths. Today
wasn't supposed to be about killing Campbells. He'd
thought Gregor had understood that the risk was too great.
With the king and his Campbell minions hunting them
down, there were too few of them left as it was. Even one
lost MacGregor was too many. Depriving them of their
land wasn't enough: the king wouldn't be happy until every
last MacGregor was rooted out of the Highlands.

They'd been hunted before, but nothing like this. The
battle of Glenfruin might prove to be their undoing.
Though the MacGregors had won the battle against the
Colquhouns, it had mobilized the king and the Earl of
Argyll—the king's authority in the Highlands—against
them with ruthless intent. Of course, the Colquhoun the-
atrics hadn't helped—who could have foreseen the widows
riding on white palfreys while parading the blood-soaked
sarks of their dead husbands on spears before the notori-
ously squeamish king? False rumors of MacGregor atrocities had only added to the furor against them, and the

broken men were being pursued with a vengeance never before encountered.

It had become harder and harder to hide. Though there were plenty in the Highlands who were sympathetic to the MacGregors, the penalty for harboring the clan was death—something not many were willing to risk. And those unsympathetic to the clan were only too eager to collect the bounty hanging over their heads—or perhaps he should say *on* their heads, as the Privy Council was offering the bounty to anyone who could produce a severed MacGregor head.

And he was the barbarian?

Patrick pushed aside his anger at his brother—he would deal with Gregor later. Right now he had a job to do. One that promised retribution and would help even the score.

For years, the Campbells had systematically been trying to destroy them. They'd stripped them of their land, turned them into a broken clan, and now pursued them with fire and sword as outlaws. But their enemy hadn't counted on the tough, tenacious spirit of the warrior clan. Like the mythical hydra, every time the MacGregors lost a head, one grew back stronger in its place.

Patrick and his clansmen were determined to do whatever it took to reclaim their land. Land was their lifeblood, and without it they would die—as so many of them already had.

He clenched his jaw in a hard line and turned his thoughts from the dead to the living. To the lass.

Elizabeth Campbell was kneeling over one of her injured guardsmen beside the other woman. As if sensing his scrutiny, Elizabeth turned and lifted her gaze to his.

He flinched. He'd thought it a fluke the first time, but there it was again. That strange jolt he'd felt before when their eyes had met across the battlefield. Though it didn't

concern him, he didn't like it. Particularly in light of his uncharacteristically rash behavior the first time they'd met.

On first glance, she looked exactly as he remembered
her: pretty and fresh as a spring flower. But on closer inspection, he could see the strain of the battle etched on her
face. He recognized her shock in the pallor of her skin and
the glassiness of her eyes. Still, it hadn't prevented her from
seeing to the comfort of her men and tending to the
wounded.

Most women would have fainted by now or at the very
least dissolved into a fit of tears, but clearly Elizabeth
Campbell was not most women. She had strength hidden
beneath the lithe exterior. Her bravery impressed him. As
did her skill with a knife. The expert toss of the blade had
shocked the hell out of him—and his brother.

Perhaps there was more of her brothers and cousin in
Elizabeth Campbell than he'd anticipated. The thought
was enough to wipe away any twinge of conscience.

With a quick word of reassurance to the injured man,
she got to her feet, only a slight sway betraying her weariness, and started to walk toward him. There was grace not
just in her bearing, but also in the rhythmic sway of her
hips as she walked. And now, without the elaborate court
clothing she'd been wearing last time, he could actually see
the soft curve of her slim hips. She wore a plain woolen kirtle and jacket of brown wool. The simple clothing suited
her dainty figure.

But it was her hair that took his breath away. It had
come loose, and tumbled down her shoulders in a magnificent cloud of spun gold. He didn't think he'd ever seen
anything so soft and silky.

His body hardened as she neared—a remnant of the battle surging through him, he supposed. She was smaller than
he recalled. Not short, but slim. Delicate. With a bone
structure so finely carved, it could have been wrought from
porcelain.

Too small for him. He would crush her. Not that it would stop him from imagining all that softness underneath him, his hands twisted in the mass of flaxen curls, as he buried himself deep inside her. Heat and heaviness pulled over him so hard, he almost groaned.

Hell, he was a damn animal. Having been treated like a dog for so long, he was beginning to act like one. But living on the edge did something to a man. It made his base instincts simmer close to the surface. And right now he felt two of them in full force: hunger and lust.

The primitive desire to claim what would belong to him.

For a lass of otherwise unremarkable beauty, she managed to rouse his lust well enough. Too well.

She stopped a few feet away and gazed up at him uncertainly. Her eyes unnerved him—so light and crystal clear, he felt as if she could see right through him.

Ridiculous. By all that was holy, he should despise this girl. Hatred, bitterness, and anger were all emotions he was familiar with. Her fine clothing, her jewels, and her refined, pampered loveliness had been forged from the blood of his clan. He should resent her. Should see the dirty, starving faces of his clansmen reflected in her gaze. Should see her as an instrument of revenge.

But all he could see was the lass, who looked as harmless as a kitten but fought like a tiger and gazed at him as if he were some damn hero.

She would be cured of that notion soon enough.

"I must thank you," she said softly. She had a slow, musical lilt to her voice that would have made a bard weep with envy. He recalled her stammer but didn't hear any evidence of it now. "I don't know what would have happened had you not arrived when you did."

Apparently thinking of the possibilities, she stopped, and her face turned an even starker shade of white. He ignored the prick of conscience.

"I wish it had been earlier," Patrick said truthfully.

Wanting to keep the conversation going, he asked, "What happened?"

"We were ambushed." She pointed to the carriage. "My men believe the trench was intentionally dug to snap the wheel and covered with tree branches so that the driver would not see it. When the guardsmen stopped, the Mac-Gregors attacked."

"How can you be sure they were MacGregors?"

She tilted her head to the side, gazing up at him thoughtfully. "Who else would they be? And they wore the pine sprig in their bonnets." Her gaze slid over his bare head and freshly shaven face. Washing away the months of living as an outlaw had felt better than he'd imagined. "I'm sorry, I have not introduced myself." She held out her hand. "I'm Elizabeth Campbell."

The courtly gesture disarmed him momentarily. It had been a long time since someone had mistaken him for a gentleman. He stared at the dainty, perfectly formed hand, the delicately shaped fingers, the ivory skin unblemished and as smooth as if she'd never known a day's work, not quite sure what to do. Finally, he enfolded it in his, feeling an unwelcome urge to warm her icy fingers. Instead, he bowed over it awkwardly. "Patrick," he said. "Patrick Murray of Tullibardine."

It was the truth . . . mostly. Murray was the surname he'd assumed when the clan was proscribed—even using his own name was punishable by death.

She tilted her head and looked at him with an odd expression on her face. "Have we met before?"

He tensed but covered it quickly with a smile. "I don't think so, my lady. I never forget a beautiful face."

She looked uncertain, as if the compliment didn't sit well with her. "Are you and your men returning home?"

He shook his head. "Nay, we travel to Glasgow and then across the sea to the continent."

She looked as though she wanted to ask more, but politeness prevented her from inquiring further.

He'd piqued her curiosity, and that was enough . . . for now. "And where is your destination, Mistress Campbell?" He said her name, as if to remind himself who she was.

She bit her lip, her tiny white teeth pressing firmly on the lush pink pillow of her bottom lip. A charming, feminine gesture that fascinated him far too much. Desire stirred his already-heated loins. He ignored it, lifting his gaze back to her eyes.

This girl had already caused him enough trouble. Coming to her aid two years ago had been so unlike him, he still didn't understand why he'd done it. Once Alasdair's anger had faded, his cousin had teased him mercilessly, referring to her as "Patrick's Campbell." Not realizing how prophetic it would prove to be.

The fate of his clan was tied to this girl, and he'd better damn well remember it.

"We were traveling to Dunoon Castle"—she paused—"in Argyll." As if it needed explanation. There were few in the Highlands who did not know where the strategically important castle was located—or that the keeper of that castle was the Earl of Argyll. "But we must return to Castle Campbell to get help for the wounded. It's a good thing we have only just begun our journey. The castle is only a half day's ride."

Patrick motioned toward the man she'd been tending. "Your man. He's badly off?"

She nodded, tears glistening in her eyes. "But alive for now. I saw him fall and thought he'd . . ." Her voice fell off. "He's my maidservant's husband and captain of the guardsmen. We need to get him back to Castle Campbell, but he can't ride."

"What about the carriage?"

She shook her head. "The wheel snapped off the axle. It will need to be repaired before it can be moved."

"So what will you do?"

"Take a few guardsmen and return to Castle Campbell for help. The remaining men will stay with the injured."

"And your maidservant?"

She smiled wanly. "I'm afraid I couldn't pry her from her husband's side. Alys won't hear of leaving her Donnan."

He frowned, counting the remaining guardsmen. "That will leave you with only a few men as escort."

"There's no help for it. We'll manage. It's not that far."

He lifted his gaze to the sky meaningfully. "It will be dark in a few hours."

Her eyes shot to his as a thought suddenly occurred to her. "Do you think . . . ?"

"They won't be coming back." Instinctively, he moved to calm her fear and took a step toward her. Close enough to inhale her sweet perfume. To reach out and slide his hand over the milky soft curve of her cheek. But he didn't. He kept his damn hands to himself.

Unaware of his thoughts, she asked, "How can you be sure?"

"From the looks of their leader, he will have other matters to attend to. Namely fixing the hole in his belly."

A strange look crossed her face, part embarrassment and part uncertainty. "I know it's silly, but I've never had to hurt anyone before." She bit her lip again, a habit he was becoming too fond of. "He meant to abduct us."

Patrick cursed his blasted brother once again. "You defended yourself well. Very well. Where did you learn to throw a blade like that?"

"My brothers. I was about twelve or thirteen when they taught me. They said one day I might have need of it." He saw the small shudder that racked her. "I guess they were right."

He stanched the reflexive spark of anger at the reminder of his enemies and instead focused on the lass. On his mission. "You were very brave."

The observation surprised her. She tilted her head and studied his face as if she weren't quite sure whether he was jesting. "Do you really think so?" Her voice dropped. "I've never been so scared in my life."

"That's precisely why you were brave."

"I don't understand."

He tried to think of a way to explain. "A lad will train for years to become a warrior, learning to use his weapons, training, becoming stronger. But it isn't until he goes into battle for the first time that you can know what kind of warrior he will be. Bravery and courage are easy to find on the training field, it's not until you are tested in battle that your true character emerges. It's not that you were scared that matters, but how you reacted to that fear." A corner of his mouth lifted. "I'd say you have the heart of a warrior."

Her smile started out slow and tentative, then spread to her cheeks and eyes with brilliant intensity. It took his breath away. It felt as if the sun had just broken through the clouds and shone a ray of sunlight on a place inside him that had been buried in darkness for a very long time.

"I think that is the nicest praise that anyone has ever given me."

The way she was looking at him was dangerous. A man could get used to being looked at like that. He shifted uncomfortably, turning his gaze back to the guardsmen readying the horses. "My men and I will escort you back to Castle Campbell and see that you are safe."

She shook her head. "No, you've done so much already. I couldn't ask you to do that."

"You didn't, I offered."

"But what about your journey to Glasgow?"

A shadow fell over him at the reminder of the deception. "It can wait."

He wasn't Elizabeth Campbell's hero and would do best to remember it.

*　　*　　*

Lizzie peeked out from under her lashes at the man riding beside her, more relieved than she wanted to admit that he'd agreed to accompany her and her guardsmen back to Castle Campbell. Night was falling, and the realization of what had nearly happened had only just begun to hit her. She didn't think she'd ever forget the MacGregor scourge's face. His cold, bleak eyes devoid of humanity. She'd seen more compassion in a snake. But Patrick Murray's presence helped. He made her feel safe. She couldn't explain it, but he did.

More than once she'd found herself studying him, not knowing quite what to make of the formidable warrior. Undoubtedly, he was one of the most handsome men she'd ever seen. The kind of handsome that made your belly flutter and your knees weak. The kind of handsome that inspired allusions to Greek gods and dark angels.

Her first impressions had only improved on closer study. On the battlefield, she'd noticed the thick black hair cut short to frame perfectly chiseled features, but it was only up close that the full magic of the combination was revealed. And his eyes . . . surely the most brilliant green eyes she'd ever seen. A dark, mossy green that made her think of pine trees in the afternoon. Of glens rich with grass. Of the Highlands.

Physically, he was impressive as well. Broad in the chest and shoulders, with powerfully wrought legs and the thick-muscled arms of a man who lived with a sword in his hands. She was used to tall, muscular men—her brothers certainly qualified. But never had she been so deeply aware of a man's strength. His raw masculinity made her feel her own femininity in a way that she never had before.

He surely must have his pick of beautiful women falling at his feet. But Lizzie could have sworn she detected something beyond politeness in his gaze—something hot and intense. Something that made her pulse race and her skin feel too tight.

It was probably just her imagination. She was hardly the type of woman whose countenance inspired anything beyond a polite smile. It didn't bother her. What she lacked in beauty she made up for in other ways—she'd had the benefit most women didn't of an education, and had made good use of it. She was admired, but that admiration usually came with time and acquaintance, not with first glances.

She ventured another peek. There was something about him that she just couldn't put her finger on. An air of danger and mystery. It was as if he were a puzzle she could not quite figure out. But it intrigued her . . . he intrigued her.

He seemed so hard and remote, every inch the fearsome warrior. A Highlander to the core. Not at all like the smooth, polished men she was used to speaking with at court. Yet their brief conversation had touched her unexpectedly. His simple praise was more meaningful than the hundreds of practiced compliments she'd heard before. One minute he was terrifying in his intensity, the next more gallant than a practiced courtier.

Who was this man?

From the serviceable but plain leather cotun and trews he wore, she could tell he wasn't a man of wealth. But his sword was fine and his horse exceptional. He was outfitted as a typical man-at-arms, but he fought like a champion. He appeared to be the leader of the half dozen men he'd arrived with, but he had not identified himself as a laird or a chieftain. Yet there was no disguising the pride and authority of his manner.

Though she'd been around guardsmen—the warriors charged with defending her cousin—she had surprisingly little interaction with them. Truth be told, she'd always found them a bit rough and a lot intimidating. Patrick Murray certainly qualified on all counts, but she'd never realized how attractive such raw physicality could be.

He'd saved her life; it was only natural that she was fascinated by him.

His voice gave her a start. The easy, husky lilt was so unexpectedly sensual and at odds with his hard-edged appearance. "Are you feeling all right? There is a place up ahead where we will stop and water the horses if you need to rest."

Had he noticed her watching him? A hot blush crawled up her cheeks, and she was grateful for the semidarkness. "I'm fine," she assured him quickly. Eager to change the subject, she said, "It's been some time since I've seen Sir John and Lady Catherine."

He gave her a hard look. "Do you know the Laird of Tullibardine and his lady well?"

She frowned. His question was odd given her frequent visits over the years. Then again, she wasn't all that memorable. "Fairly well, though I haven't seen them in some time. The earl, countess, and I were guests at Balvaird Castle about three years ago." She tilted her head. "Were you not there?"

"I must have been away at the time."

She smiled. "How old is young John now? I don't think I've ever seen the arrival of a child so celebrated." Her smile fell. Except for her cousin's son last year, but that was marred by death.

Lizzie felt the tears gather behind her eyes; she still missed the woman who hadn't been much older but had become almost a mother to her. The earl, too, had taken the countess's death hard.

His face darkened. "Five, I believe."

Lizzie counted back. "That sounds about right, although I thought he was a year younger."

"He'll be sent to be fostered soon."

She nodded matter-of-factly. "I imagine it will be hard on his mother."

"I should think it would be difficult for both of his parents."

She eyed him a bit more intently. Once again, he'd surprised her. Most men wouldn't think twice about sending their child away to be fostered. It was the way of things. Patrick Murray might be hard on the outside, but there was unexpected depth to him. "Are you traveling to Glasgow on business for your laird?"

"No."

The abruptness of his response took her aback. "I'm sorry, I didn't mean to pry."

They rode in silence for a while, so long that she didn't think he was going to speak to her again. Eventually he said quietly, "I'm leaving the Highlands for a while."

Her heart did a funny tumble. "Leaving . . . ? But why?" she blurted before she could take it back.

He paused. "A change of scenery."

She clamped her mouth closed so as not to ask the question on the tip of her tongue and dropped her gaze, focusing on the gentle sway of her hands holding the reins. Despite the quick wash in the burn, dirt and blood still smudged her fingertips.

"The place is too filled with memories."

She looked back at him, meeting his gaze, silently encouraging him to continue.

"I lost my wife a few weeks ago. She died giving birth to our first child."

She gasped. Her heart immediately went out to him, thinking of the pain he must have suffered. It certainly explained the dark look on his face when she'd mentioned Sir John's child. "How horrible. I'm sorry for your loss. You must have cared for her deeply."

He nodded once and then turned his eyes back to the road, avoiding her gaze. Except for the grim set of his mouth, his expression gave no hint of his emotions, but Lizzie could feel the darkness simmering under the surface.

"What will you do?" she asked softly.

He shrugged. "I don't know. Fight, I suppose. It's what I know. There is always a position for a man with a sword."

A mercenary. Like her brother Duncan. She didn't know why it bothered her. A man could make his fortune—and his name—in such a manner . . . Duncan certainly had. But it just seemed wrong.

They fell into a comfortable silence until a few minutes later, when the group veered off the road and followed a much narrower path that wound through the forest to the edge of a small loch.

Lizzie sucked in her breath at the beauty of the natural splendor laid out before her. The loch was almost perfectly round and encircled with towering trees, their branches heavy with leaves, hanging over the water like a lush protective canopy. It was only twilight, yet the full moon could already be seen reflected like a disk of alabaster on polished onyx.

He must have noticed her reaction. "It pleases you?"

He'd dismounted and stood beside her, his hand raised to help her down. She accepted the offer and slid her hand into his. Even with the protective shield of gloves between them, she felt the strange crackle. The spark that slipped into simmering awareness.

Their eyes met. Her heart started to flutter like a bird with its wing caught in a trap. Dear Lord, he was gorgeous. *A face to make a woman forget herself.*

No! Never again.

She shifted her gaze and dismounted quickly, sliding her hand from his while trying to control the blush heating her cheeks. He must think her a complete ninny allowing such a commonplace occurrence as help down from a horse to send her into a feminine tizzy.

The state was so unlike her, she didn't know what to do. Lizzie knew her strengths, and usually acted with ease around men, but for some reason she found herself wanting to impress Patrick Murray, and her natural confidence appeared to have deserted her.

He was looking at her oddly, and Lizzie realized he'd asked her a question. She swallowed hard, trying to recall. . . . Ah, yes, the loch. "It's charming. How is it that Castle Campbell is but a few miles away and I've never been here before? And yet you, who are not from these parts, know of it?"

"There are few acres of forestland in these parts with which I am not familiar." There seemed to be something behind his words, but before she could question him further about his meaning, he added in a clipped voice, "See to your needs, but do not wander too far. It will be dark soon enough and difficult to see where you step."

He turned abruptly and moved off toward the trees, leaving Lizzie staring at his back and the hard set of his broad, muscular shoulders. Her breath caught. The man was a rock.

Wondering what she'd said to anger him, she wanted to call him back, but she let him go, cognizant that others were watching her. He was a stranger. A mere guardsman. Not someone she should be interested in, no matter what the circumstances. But . . .

No. She shook herself free from the dangerous path of her thoughts. Lizzie knew her duty. She sighed, watching as the handsome warrior slipped out of view. But it didn't hurt to dream.

Time was running out, and it was all Patrick could do to keep himself upright on his sodding horse. Rather than felling Elizabeth Campbell with charm, he was losing blood, and needed to see to the wound before he was the one who ended up flat on his back. He doubted that fainting would impress her into hiring him as a guardsman.

He didn't know what had possessed him to think that he could be charming. Perhaps he had more charm than most of his clansmen, but that wasn't saying much. The Mac-

Gregors were a brutal lot—hardened and toughened by years of relentless persecution.

But it was more than acting that failed him. Something about Elizabeth Campbell disarmed him. There was such an easy, unaffected way about her that he found himself wanting to talk to her. *Really* talk to her. When she gazed up at him with those wide blue eyes in that pale, serious little face, she looked so damn vulnerable that it made him feel like a brute for deceiving her.

She was a woman to protect and cherish. A fragile piece of fine porcelain in the hands of a ruffian.

He'd slipped into the trees out of sight, but not before he glimpsed her talking to his men and passing out food. As he'd noticed before on the battlefield, she saw to others' needs before attending to her own. She did her duty well. A true lady of the castle born.

Knowing he had to act quickly before someone spied him, he shifted his thoughts from the lass and moved to the loch. After divesting himself of his weapons and leather cotun, he started to peel away the sopping linen that had worked its way into the crevice of blood and mangled skin. It was as he'd thought. The sutures of animal intestines they'd used to stitch the wound closed had torn apart, revealing a wide gap of raw, bloody flesh. If he had the time to build a fire, he'd take a hot blade to the wound just to stop the bleeding—even if he trapped the poison inside.

The pain was considerable, but it did not impede his motions. He'd endured worse. The memories made him grimace. Far worse. Discomfort was what he knew—constant cold, damp, hunger, pain . . . it was only the level that differed. The simple comforts of a hearth and home had been denied him for too long.

But that would soon change.

He moved swiftly and deliberately, tending to the wound as best he could. After rinsing it with clean water, he tore a piece of his newly purloined linen shirt—the cost of which would have fed his men for a week—and bound it tightly around his waist. The waste almost hurt more than the wound. He'd traded in his *leine* and *breacan feile* for the clothing favored by Lowlanders to further mask his identity.

He knew it was a risk to leave the wound as it was, but there was little he could do about it now. He dared not risk questions about how he'd received it.

When blood did not immediately stain the linen bandage, he considered his efforts a success. At least he wouldn't fall off his horse from loss of blood. After replacing his cotun and weapons, he rejoined his men, who had already seen to the horses.

He looked around, keeping well apprised of the location of their enemies. The handful of Campbell guardsmen who had accompanied them were sitting near the edge of the loch, still eating the bits of beef and oatcake that he'd seen Elizabeth pass out. He didn't think he'd crossed paths with any of the men before, but he knew he had to be careful. There was one man in particular—Finlay was his name—whom Patrick didn't like the look of.

Robbie, who was one of the youngest of his warriors at nine and ten but had been with Patrick since he'd fought with Alex MacLeod on Lewis almost three years ago, gave him a hard look as he approached. "Has it opened again?"

"It's nothing."

Robbie swore. "You could have both legs cut off and be dragging your insides behind you and still claim, 'It's nothing.' Your sister will string me up by my bollocks if I let you die from a fever."

"I didn't realize Annie had sent love-struck lads to spy on me."

Robbie fought to stave off the color that rose high on his cheeks. The young warrior's infatuation with Patrick's younger sister was well-known. But equally well-known was that the hardheaded Annie had given her heart away long ago to Niall Lamont. Patrick liked Niall well enough, but the Lamont of Ascog's second son was an ambitious man intent on making his name as a warrior. When he married, it would be to further his clan's alliances. An outlawed MacGregor wife would not be his choice. Poor Annie was doomed to heartbreak and disappointment, but the chit wouldn't listen to reason.

"Since it was Annie who stitched you up in the first place, she simply didn't want to see all of her hard work go to waste," Robbie pointed out.

"My stubborn sister should mind her own blasted business."

Robbie snorted. "Runs in the family," he added under his breath.

Patrick eyed him, brow raised. "What's that?"

"Nothing." He looked around and lowered his voice. "At least your plan seems to be working."

"So far."

"No problems?"

"One," he admitted. He should have realized that she would know Tullibardine and his lady. It was lucky that Patrick's memory of the child's age had proved close enough. He'd met the laird only once, and that was some time ago. "It was nothing I could not handle."

As he'd intended, the invention of a dead wife and bairn had played upon her sympathies, deflecting further questions. But the deception didn't sit well with him, even if it was necessary.

Robbie nodded and looked around. "Where did she go?"

He glanced through the trees and frowned, seeing no sign of Lizzie. "I don't know. Ready the horses. I'll fetch the lass."

He started walking in the direction he'd seen her leave. She'd been gone for no more than ten minutes, but even allowing for the inordinate time women took to tend to personal matters, she should have been back by now. Although he was loath to disturb her privacy, a private conversation in the secluded forest might help further his cause.

He took a few steps in the direction in which she'd disappeared and called her name. The sound that came back to him sent ice storming through his veins. Drawing his dirk from the scabbard at his side, he plunged into the darkness.

Chapter 3

Lizzie sat on her knees at the edge of the loch, dipping her hands in the icy water, removing the last stains of the battle from her fingers. If only the memories were as easily washed away. She mourned the men who had died today, and pitied the suffering their families would endure when she brought them the news. She would never shirk her duties, but some were harder than others. She sighed, thinking of the conversations before her. Much harder.

At first she thought the rustling sounds she heard behind her were leaves being tossed about by the wind. But then she felt the distinct weight of eyes upon her. The hair at the back of her neck stood on end, like tiny sentries alerting her to danger, but she forced herself to stay calm.

It was probably nothing.

She dried her hands in her skirts, got to her feet slowly, and turned around. Her entire body went perfectly still, frozen with fear. It wasn't "nothing." Standing not twenty feet from her in the shadows of the trees stood a lone wolf. His golden yellow eyes were fixed on her with cold calculation—not unlike the MacGregor warrior's gaze had been earlier. It was the look of a hunter. It was a look that promised no mercy.

He was close enough for her to see the dampness shining on his black nose and the gray streaks in his black coat. His mouth was pulled back in a sinister impression of a smile, revealing long, sharp teeth. Was it possible to see hunger in a gaze? Because the wolf was looking at her as if he were starving and she were a tasty feast. Though from his immense size, he certainly didn't appear to be suffering from any lack of sustenance. His head came up to her waist, and he was built thick and solid, easily outweighing her.

Her heart was beating so fast that it hurt, straining against the tight confines of her chest.

She heard Patrick call her name, and the wolf howled in response. She wanted to scream for help but dared not do anything to startle or provoke the vicious beast.

Hearing the sounds of footsteps coming toward them, the wolf growled and his fur bristled. Spit slid in heavy sheets from his mouth as he crouched low to the ground, ready to pounce.

She held her breath, praying that someone arrived—

"Don't move."

The sound of Patrick Murray's deep, steady voice was the sweetest thing she'd ever heard.

Move? She couldn't even if she wanted to. Her feet seemed to be stuck in a bog. "I w-won't," she whispered, fear carrying her past caring about her stammer. Patrick tossed a rock in the wolf's direction. Rather than scare him off, however, it seemed only to make him angrier, thinking that Patrick was infringing on his territory. The beast had claimed Elizabeth as his prey and wouldn't let her go without a fight.

Tiring of Patrick's efforts, the wolf attacked without warning, leaping forward and closing the distance to Lizzie in a matter of seconds. She didn't even have time to breathe, let alone get out the scream that strangled in her throat, before two front paws hit her square in the chest and knocked her harshly to the ground, taking the air from her lungs.

For one terrifying second, she felt his suffocating weight on top of her; the horrible stench of his fur and breath enveloped her in a sickening noose. His teeth were so sharp. They were going to hurt. . . .

Suddenly the snarling beast was ripped off her.

Patrick had wrestled the wolf to the ground, one arm wrapped around his neck. The animal's long teeth gleamed in the moonlight as he twisted wildly, gnashing and snarling at his captor. Lizzie knew from his size how strong the wolf must be, but he was no match for the fierce warrior. Patrick's eyes were cold and determined, not a hint of fear in their dark green depths.

She stared in awed wonderment as he subdued the ferocious animal as if he offered no more fight than a rabbit. She'd never seen anything like it—his strength was extraordinary. His arm squeezed around the wolf's neck, the muscle in his arm bulging against the leather of his cotun like a boulder, until the wolf hung limp.

Lizzie swore she saw regret on his face as he tossed the lifeless animal to the side and came quickly to her.

"Are you all right?"

She nodded dumbly as he helped her to her feet. "I—I'm fine." She struggled to control her stammering tongue. But the strain of what had just happened, added to the horror of the earlier attack by the MacGregors, proved too much. She didn't care. Her carefully wrought composure dissolved. She could barely stand, her legs felt so weak. Her body began to shake uncontrollably, her throat tightened, and hot tears stung her eyes.

He was standing so close to her, all six feet plus inches of masculine strength. So solid and safe. Her valiant protector. It seemed only natural to seek the safe enclosure of his embrace. She ran into his arms, burying her head against the hard wall of his chest. He smelled . . . wonderful. Warm. Of leather and pine needles and strength. Savoring the distinctly masculine scents, she closed her eyes. Only then did the tears start to fall.

Patrick MacGregor, a man known for his cool authority, for his decisiveness in battle, for his strength and toughness in the most extreme conditions, was at a complete loss. He looked down at the flaxen head of the tiny feminine bundle against his chest and didn't know what to do, having little experience with comforting weeping women. He felt a hard twinge in his chest. A flood of warmth that almost bordered on . . . contentment. An emotion so foreign to him, he didn't know what to make of it.

After a moment's confusion, he relaxed and acted on instinct, allowing his arms to come around her and snuggle her closer to him.

He figured it was the right thing to do—despite the fact that it seemed only to make her cry harder—when every muscle in her body seemed to heave a sigh of relief and she collapsed limply against him.

He felt a surge of protectiveness. An overwhelming urge to keep her safe. Ironic, given his task.

Still, it pleased him that she'd turned to him so easily. He knew not to read too much into it; he was convenient, nothing more. And she'd been pushed to the end of her rope by the day's events. But it didn't mean he didn't like it.

Holding her like this, it felt . . . nice.

More than nice. He couldn't help but notice how well they fit together. Her head tucked neatly under his chin, and his arms wrapped perfectly around her. Her hair smelled like lavender, and was so silky soft that he couldn't resist the urge to touch it. He let it slide under his palm as he stroked her head soothingly, his own pulse beginning to slow.

Her weeping did not diminish his opinion of her strength. The lass had been through a lot today; she'd earned the right to her tears. She wasn't the only one reeling from what had nearly happened.

He didn't know how to describe the feeling that had shot through him when he'd heard the wolf howl. His heart had seized for one paralyzing second. If he didn't know better, he would think it had been a flash of panic—laughable under ordinary circumstances.

But these were hardly ordinary circumstances. If anything happened to the lass, he would have only himself to blame. He'd put her in this position. She was his responsibility.

Unlike the attack on her carriage earlier, the wolf had not been planned.

After a few minutes, her sobs began to slow, and he became uncomfortably aware of the effects of holding her so closely. The incredible softness of her breasts crushed against his chest made his blood fire. He felt the weight come over him. The heavy pull in his groin. The hardening. It had been too long since he'd had a woman, and it had caught up to him—at the wrong time.

She sniffled and gazed up at him with watery eyes, her long lashes clumped and spiky. Her face was bathed in tears and moonlight, with an opalescent glow that seemed almost unworldly. For a moment it was only the two of them, man and woman, in a realm untainted by blood feuds. In a world where a Campbell heiress might welcome a MacGregor suitor. Where deception was unnecessary. Where kissing her seemed the most natural thing to do— the only thing to do.

Her mouth, with her soft pink lips parted only inches below his, tantalized. A sweet, sugary confection for a man starved with bitterness. Aye, she was ripe for seduction. He just hadn't anticipated how strong the urge would be for him to do so. He ached to kiss her, to take her lips beneath his and slide his tongue deep in her mouth until her breath came fast and hard. Until she moaned for him. He could almost taste her honey sweetness beneath the saltiness of her tears. His entire body felt possessed by desire. The primitive call was bone-deep, encompassing every part of him.

He lowered his head.

And stopped.

It was too soon. One wrong move could ruin everything. She was a frightened lass; he couldn't take advantage of her vulnerability. Not yet, anyway.

He knew he'd been right when her eyes widened, as if all of a sudden realizing what she'd done, and she pulled away. "I'm sorry. I shouldn't have . . . I didn't mean . . ." There was a long moment of awkwardness, where she fumbled with her skirts and took great efforts to wipe away the dirt and leaves that still clung to the wool where she'd fallen. "What must you think of me?"

He knew from the way she avoided his gaze that she was embarrassed. "I think that you were scared. I was here. There is nothing to explain."

Her gaze met his uncertainly, as if trying to convince herself of the same. She managed a tentative smile. "It seems I am doubly indebted to you and owe you thanks again for saving my life. If you hadn't called out when you did . . ." She shivered, her gaze falling on the dead animal.

Her gratitude weighed uneasily upon him. "I would never have allowed you to come out here on your own if I'd suspected. But it's unusual to see wolves in these parts." He looked with regret at the fallen beast. "Stranger still to see one on its own."

She made a face. "I'd rather not see any."

"Soon enough you will get your wish." His words came out harsher than he'd intended, and he explained. "If the king has his way, there will be no wolves left anywhere in the Highlands. Forty years ago, it was necessary to build spittals on the roads for travelers to take refuge. Today, it is rare to see a wolf at all."

Perhaps that was why he felt such a strange kinship with the wolf. The king sought the extinction of them both. The laws enacted to eradicate the race of MacGregor did not differ much in language from those to eradicate the wolves.

"You sound as if you have sympathy for their plight. But

you saw what happened. Surely we must do something to prevent further attacks."

"It isn't usually in a wolf's nature to attack man. It's only because we leave them no choice that they are forced to fight back."

"I don't understand."

"Cutting down their forests, encroaching on their land. They have an ancient right to roam this land, and it's been taken from them. What else can they do but fight?"

He realized he could have been speaking about his own people. Like the wolf, the once-proud race of MacGregors, whose badge proclaimed their descent from kings—*S Rioghail Mo Dhream*, "Royal Is My Race"—had been stripped of their land, backed into a corner, turned wild and ferocious in their effort to protect what was theirs. Fitting, then, that they were known as "the Sons of the Wolf."

Her head tilted as she studied his face. He feared his impassioned speech had revealed more than he'd intended.

"Ancient right? It's an interesting concept." Her mouth lifted in a half-smile. "One that my cousin would take umbrage with, since he holds the charter for this land."

She said it in jest, but truer words could not be spoken. It was upon the same basis that the Earl of Argyll and his kinsman "Black" Duncan Campbell of Glenorchy had deprived the MacGregors of their land. Hundreds of years of ownership ignored for the failure to produce a piece of parchment.

Her words also served as a harsh reminder of why he was here: land.

When his gaze fell on her again, it was with cold resolve. No matter how sweet, he would not forget who she was and what she would bring him. He'd waited too long to get back what was his.

Ripe for seduction, he reminded himself. *A means to an end.*

"We should return. The others will be waiting and wondering what has happened to us."

Lizzie gave him a knowing smile, her eyes twinkling with a shared understanding. "We shall have much to tell them. I fear that your exploits this day are in danger of taking on heroic proportions."

He didn't know whether it was that smile, the twinkle in her eye, or the resilience with which she'd weathered a trying day and managed to find humor, but Patrick realized that his mission was going to be more difficult than he'd ever imagined.

Thief, brigand, outlaw, scourge: Those were names he was familiar with, not hero. Yet for a moment, this wee lass could make him want to believe that it was a possibility. Make him believe that there might be a flicker left in the embers of his blackened soul. That maybe there was still something inside him that hadn't died.

He regretted that one day soon he would have to prove her wrong.

Chapter 4

Not long after they left the loch, the great shadow of Castle Campbell came into view, its austere gray stone walls rising high on a hill surrounded by dense woodlands.

Like its Highland counterpart of Inveraray Castle, the Lowland stronghold of the Earl of Argyll served as an imposing reminder of the strength of the clan. The fortress had once been called Castle Gloom, and from its steep, imposing setting and stark stone walls, it wasn't hard to see why. But to Lizzie it was home.

After all that she'd been through this day, she should feel relieved to reach the safety of the formidable keep. To smell the familiar pungent aroma of ramsom that filled the steep ravines; to hear the rush of the Burn of Sorrow and Burn of Care, which flowed below to the west and east of the promontory upon which the castle stood. But for some reason, she was reluctant for this part of her journey to be over. She suspected that it had something to do with the man riding beside her.

A man she barely knew, but whom she'd thrown herself at like . . . like . . . She blushed. Like a common strumpet.

The poor man was still mourning the loss of his wife and unborn child for pity's sake!

Was she so desperate for romance that she could fall for the first handsome man who was kind to her? Apparently so.

Despite his gallantry, she was mortified by what she'd done. With that face he was probably used to women falling into his arms, but Lizzie had never done anything so remotely improper. Had never so completely abandoned decorum to seek comfort from the embrace of a stranger.

Yet it had felt incredible. Warm. Safe. Secure. And so much more. She'd felt a connection. An awareness that went beyond simple attraction but seemed to take hold of every part of her body. In his arms she'd felt alive. As if her body had woken from a long sleep and tingled with pleasure at the wakening.

Something had come over her, and she'd felt an intense urge to touch him. To slide her hands over his arms and feel the heavy muscles beneath her fingertips, to trace the hard lines of his chest and back. To absorb his strength.

Her body had flooded with heat. With heaviness. And then for a moment her heart had stopped, thinking he was actually going to kiss her. His mouth had been only inches away. The wide, sensuous lips, the dark stubble along the hard lines of his jaw, the spicy warmth of his breath on her head.

But he hadn't. Whether she'd only imagined it or he had simply thought better of it, she didn't know. She had had no business encouraging him in the first place, but she could not deny the twinge of disappointment.

She told herself it was for the best. Now that he'd seen them safely home, he would be leaving, continuing on his journey across the sea to escape the memories of the past. It was ridiculous. The poor woman was gone, but Lizzie felt a twinge of envy. His wife had been a fortunate woman indeed to have a man care for her so deeply. Enough to drive him far from his home when he lost her.

That he'd not yet recovered from the loss was obvious. Though on the surface he was friendly and charming, Lizzie sensed the sadness lingering underneath. And there was a hard bleakness in his gaze that came with pain and suffering.

After all he'd done for her, Lizzie wished there was something she could do to help him.

She'd hoped to have the opportunity for further conversation, but as they neared the castle they were forced to ride single file as they negotiated the treacherous narrow path that wound around the castle from the north, fording the Burn of Care on the east.

All too soon they rode under the shadow of the great Maiden's Tree—the old plane tree near the entrance that dominated the approach—and under the spiked iron yett of the castle.

She lost sight of him temporarily in the furor that followed their arrival, when the reason for their unexpected return became known. It seemed all at once the *barmkin* filled with people as efforts were quickly under way to rescue those they had been forced to leave behind after the attack. Only after additional men and a cart to bring home the wounded had been dispatched and she'd finished the difficult conversations with the families of the men killed did Lizzie have the opportunity to ensure that Patrick and his men had been taken care of.

She scanned the courtyard, still teeming with people. Though it was dark, torches lined the perimeter, providing just enough light to make out the faces of her clansmen flickering by. But there was no sign of Patrick and his men.

They seemed to have disappeared.

Her pulse started to pick up pace as her chest grew tight with increasing anxiousness. They couldn't have left already . . . could they?

She stood on her toes, trying to look over the heads of her clansmen. But when that didn't work, she stopped one of her guardsmen as he walked past her toward the hall. "Finlay . . ."

Finlay was one of her cousin's most trusted guardsmen. She didn't know him very well, but she sensed ambition in him. With Alys's Donnan—the captain of the guardsmen—

injured, Finlay would probably be made interim captain. He was a rough, coarse man, and his features matched his disposition. The round dome of his bald head seemed to meld seamlessly into a very thick neck, reminiscent of the seals that roamed the waters of the Western Isles. His nose was flat and crooked from being pounded too many times by a fist. Though not a tall man, he made up in width what he lacked in height. He was built like an ox, his chest as wide and round as a cask of ale.

"My lady?" He smiled, a gaping grin of yellow flecked with brown.

Lizzie repressed the distaste that she knew was unwarranted and managed to return his smile. "Have you seen the men we rode in with?"

"The Murray men?"

She nodded, trying not to look too eager.

"The last I saw them, they were in the stables."

Relieved that they had not yet left, she managed, "Thank you," before hurrying off.

The door was opened and the earthy, pungent smells hit her as she swept through the doorway, the hay strewn on the floor clinging to the hem of her skirts.

"It's something to consider," she heard one of her cousin's men say. "We could use the extra sword arms." She didn't hear the reply because another man, seeing her, cleared his throat and the conversation came to a quick stop. An uncomfortably quick stop.

There was nothing worse than bringing a room to dead silence, unless it was a roomful of men who were then staring at you.

She fought a blush, feeling distinctly out of place. They were obviously surprised to see her. The lady of the keep—the role she'd assumed on the death of the countess—did not usually visit the stables to see to the comfort of guardsmen. But these weren't ordinary circumstances, she reminded herself.

Knowing that with all eyes upon her like this she would be prone to stammer, she paused and took a deep breath before she spoke. "Food and drink have been set out in the great hall." She turned to Patrick. "And pallets are being readied for you and your men in the garret."

"A meal is much appreciated, but we don't want to put you to any trouble. We should be on our way."

Lizzie frowned, her eyes narrowing on his handsome face. Was it her imagination or did he look a little pale? "It's no trouble. After all you have done for us, the least I can do is see that your men have a good night's rest." She smiled. "Surely there is no harm in waiting to continue your journey until morning?"

"No, but—"

"It's the least I can do," she interrupted, not wanting to give him the opportunity to refuse. She had that sick feeling in her gut again, just as she had when she'd thought they'd already left. It was somehow vitally important that he not leave. Not yet, at least. She looked to the young, dark-haired man at his side for help. "I'm sure your men would welcome a dry night on a comfortable pallet, wouldn't you?"

Her encouraging smile succeeded only in further discomforting the younger man. He was probably just a handful of years younger than her own six and twenty, but compared with the broad-shouldered, heavily muscled Patrick, his long, lean build looked practically boyish.

"I . . ." He looked helplessly to his captain, caught in the impossible position of wanting to please her and not wanting to oppose his leader.

Patrick took pity on him. He bowed in mock surrender; a crooked smile played upon his mouth. "How can I argue with such a pretty request?"

Lizzie gave him an uncharacteristically impish grin. "You can't."

"Then it seems we will be happy to accept your hospitality for the night."

She clapped her hands together. "Wonderful."

Their eyes met, and she felt it again. That strange current of awareness that started at her head and shimmered all the way down to her toes. It made her feel warm and syrupy and a little bit drowsy.

"Was there something else, my lady?" he asked politely.

"No, I . . ." She dropped her gaze, her cheeks heating, realizing she'd been staring. Thankfully, there wasn't a roomful of men to witness her embarrassment, as most of the others had started to drift away to finish tending to their mounts and then heading to the hall. She swallowed and started over, slower this time. "You seem anxious to leave."

He'd taken a brush from the bag tied to his saddle and began to slide long, hard strokes over the shiny black coat of his stallion. It was impossible not to notice the impressive breadth of his shoulders and the powerful muscles of his arms as he worked. Very muscular arms. She doubted she could span one with both her hands.

Her mouth went a little dry, and she had to lick her lips to finish. "Is there a job waiting for you on the continent?"

His gaze leveled on her, and her belly fluttered. "Nothing in particular, but there is always a market for good sword arms. Why?"

She cleared her throat nervously. "I just wish there was some way I could thank you for all you've done."

He brushed aside her gratitude. "I did no less than any man would have done in the circumstances."

She shook her head. Never had she met a man so uncomfortable with praise. "At least let me pay you for your—"

His gaze went cold. "That will not be necessary."

Lizzie's eyes widened as she realized she'd unintentionally offended him. He was a proud man, and her offer of recompense had impinged his honor—an odd reaction, she thought, for a man intent on selling his sword to the highest bidder.

She reached out and grabbed his arm. It was hard and unyielding under her fingers, with all the give of steel. "I'm sorry, I meant no offense."

His eyes were black, as dark and impenetrable as his granite-hard body. He looked down at her hand.

She released it self-consciously.

He lifted his gaze to hers and then turned back to resume his task, finishing a few minutes later. "Is there someplace we can wash before the meal?"

"Of course. I can show you to where you will be staying." She motioned to the bag tied to his saddle, which he'd removed and hung on the stable wall. "Bring your things if you like."

He nodded and proceeded to remove the bag and sling it over his shoulders. A few of his men did the same and followed her out of the stables and into the *barmkin*. She led them across the courtyard and into one of the many wooden outer buildings constructed beside the keep that housed the castle's guardsmen—though right now it was empty. It was one large room with a wooden floor and a fireplace burning at the far end. Simple accommodation, perhaps, but at least it was warm and dry.

"One of the serving maids will bring you water." She looked over the tired, dirty men, seeing the scrapes and bruises on some of their faces. "I will also send the healer with some salve if any of your men have need of it."

He seemed about to argue, but she stopped him with a look and folded her arms across her chest. His mouth curved, and instead he said with a nod, "Thank you."

She turned to leave but stopped suddenly to look back at him. Something niggled at her. The hard lines etched around his mouth seemed a little deeper. Her gaze slid over his face. "Are you sure you are feeling all right?"

"Nothing a good night's sleep and a meal will not cure."

Deftly, he turned the conversation back to her. "What of you? You've been on your feet for hours, tending to everyone's needs but your own."

"There is much to be done," she said unthinkingly.

"Surely not all of it must be done by you? You must be exhausted, yet I have not seen you sit down. Is the lady of the keep not allowed to rest?"

He'd been watching her, she realized, and seemed genuinely concerned. No one had ever worried about her before. A warm glow settled somewhere in her middle. "It's been a difficult day," she admitted. "So many lives lost. But it would have been much worse without you."

Worse without you . . . Something she'd overheard one of her men say when she'd walked into the stable came back to her. The answer was so simple. Why had she not thought of it sooner?

She opened her mouth and then hesitated. What did she really know about him, other than that he'd rescued her . . . twice? "I . . .".

"Yes?"

She straightened her spine, knowing all she needed to know. "I have a proposition that might be to both of our benefit."

"What kind of proposition?"

"I know you are intent on leaving Scotland, but Castle Campbell is a good way from your home."

"It is."

"You and your men are looking for employment, and with the MacGregors on the loose and the men we lost today, we are in need of added protection."

His eyes met hers. "You are suggesting that we stay and work for you?"

"It seems a perfect solution."

He didn't seem convinced. "I don't know," he hedged.

"Will you at least think about it? You don't have to give

me your answer right away. Stay for a few days, take a look around, meet some of the other men, and then decide."

He considered her for a moment, his expression inscrutable. Finally, he nodded. "I'll think about it."

Lizzie beamed, unable to contain the burst of excitement. It *was* the perfect solution. She was so glad she'd thought of it.

It was easier than he'd expected, and what he'd intended all along, yet even more perfect because she believed it was her idea.

As Patrick watched Elizabeth Campbell leave the barracks, he knew he should be pleased. Not only had he achieved the first part of his mission by wheedling his way into her household, he also sensed that she was far from indifferent to him. But it wasn't satisfaction that he felt. Instead, it was something akin to guilt—ironic for a man known for his ruthlessness both on and off the battlefield.

Unfeeling. Cold. Remote. He'd heard them all, and usually from the fairer sex. But he never made any promises. On the contrary, he was crudely blunt about his needs. It wasn't his fault if women didn't want to believe the truth.

Distancing himself from emotion had never been a problem, and in this it would be no different. Any attraction he felt for Elizabeth Campbell would never get in the way of what he had to do.

Robbie came to stand beside him. The younger man shook his head. "I have to hand it to you, Captain. You work fast. And not appearing too eager is a stroke of brilliance."

Patrick heard some loud grumbling coming from another one of his men and gave a look in his direction. "Have you something to say, Hamish?"

The older man glanced around to make sure they could not be overheard. "Not as fast as taking her." He shook his head with great sadness. "In my da's day, a man saw a lass he wanted and he took her."

Patrick bit back a smile. "Hard to see what's objectionable in that. Cattle don't mind lifting, why should a lass?"

His sarcasm was completely lost on the old warrior. "Exactly. 'Twas good enough courtin' for my ma. None of this trifling about with wooing and seducing."

Robbie put his arm around the other man consolingly and met Patrick's gaze with laughter twinkling in his eyes. It was hard to imagine anyone courting the sour-faced old woman who was Hamish's ma. "Aye, Hamish," Robbie commiserated. "Those were the days. But the times they are a-changing. Remember what the captain said: A forced marriage brings too many problems, and would be easy to set aside. We want to hold the land, and for that we need the lass willing."

Patrick could see Hamish's point. There was a certain simplicity in the old ways, whether it be abducting a bride or claiming land by right of sword. But if they were to have any chance of success, the MacGregors could not afford to be impetuous. They had to adapt to the changing world— one where the king's authority could not be denied—and employ a bit of strategy in getting their land back. So rather than kidnap Elizabeth Campbell and force her to marry him, he'd suggested a more subtle method of persuasion.

The older man was not pacified. "Put a babe in her belly and she'll not be so quick to object—kidnapping or no kidnapping."

Crude, Patrick thought, but true. He'd reached a similar conclusion. A child would help ensure that they stayed wed—and that the land in Elizabeth Campbell's tocher stayed with its rightful owners.

"Our captain will woo the lass and she'll marry him soon enough," Robbie said confidently.

Hamish shook his head again. "These modern lasses are a demanding lot. I still say my way is easier."

Patrick chuckled at the old warrior's stubbornness, but he admitted that Hamish might be right. His own plan had seemed much simpler a few weeks ago. Then again, at the time he and two score of his clansmen had been running for their lives following the battle of Glenfruin, holed up deep in MacGregor country on Eilean Molach—one of the tiny islets in Loch Katrine—with Campbells breathing hard down their back, and hadn't exactly had time to analyze every permutation.

It had been a gut decision brought on by their desperate circumstances and the chief's determination that the kinsmen should separate. Gathered together on the tiny tree-lined isle were the remaining chieftains and principals of Glenstrae: Alasdair, their uncle Duncan of the Glen, Patrick, Gregor, and their younger brother, Iain.

Four hundred MacGregors had fought at Glenfruin against a Colquhoun force of twice that size, and though they'd lost only two men, one of the losses had been particularly costly—Black John of the Mailcoat, Alasdair's brother and, as Alasdair's wife had yet to give him a son, his *tanaiste*. A position that now, temporarily, at least, belonged to Patrick. He had no desire to be chief of the band of renegades. The MacGregors—including some of his kinsmen—were a wild, uncontrollable lot.

By separating, Alasdair was trying to protect them, but also the future of the clan. If they were caught together, there would be no one left to lead—no matter how unenviable such a position was.

Word had reached them on the island that the king had called for every man between sixteen and sixty in Lennox to root out the MacGregors in Loch Katrine. Apparently they were undaunted, this time, by the difficult terrain that the MacGregors relied upon to hide in. The shores of Loch

Katrine were virtually inaccessible, steep mountains on one side and rocky, forested banks on the other.

The chief and his *luchd-taighe* guardsmen had gathered around a fire to decide what was to be done. They were a motley group. Dirty, exhausted, and hungry. Some, like Patrick, still suffering wounds from battle. Even the chief looked tattered and worn down.

They were discussing where to go. The options were few, to say the least. Not many would be willing to take on the wrath of the king, who'd made harboring MacGregors punishable by death. Worse, Argyll had put his Henchman, Jamie Campbell, in charge of hunting them down. Patrick had crossed paths with the Henchman enough times to know that he was relentless and would not rest until they were found.

He regretted the missed opportunity of ridding his clan of their bane two years ago at the games.

Patrick bided his time as names were bandied about and quickly discarded. Even MacAulay and Murray, who'd sheltered them before, would be unlikely to risk doing so at this time.

Finally, he spoke what had been on his mind from the first. What was always on his mind. "My brothers and I will go to Balquhidder."

Alasdair gave him a long look, guessing at Patrick's motives. "Glenorchy is no friend of ours. And at least for now, he holds those lands. Though not for long, I warrant."

Patrick went completely still. "Explain yourself, cousin."

"Argyll and Glenorchy are squabbling again."

The two branches of clan Campbell were often at odds—a state that suited the MacGregors just fine. As long as Argyll and Glenorchy were fighting, they would not unite against them. "What does their squabbling have to do with my land?"

Alasdair hesitated. He knew Patrick's determination to reclaim his father's lands. Knew how even mentioning the subject would send him into a black mood for days. "Argyll is claiming the land for his cousin's tocher."

Patrick's fists clenched at his side. Claiming *MacGregor* land. Land that had belonged to his clan for hundreds of years. Land that had been stolen from them twice—first by Argyll, who'd turned them into tenants on their own land, and then by Glenorchy, who'd purchased the superiority from Argyll and refused to recognize them even as tenants and burned them out.

The haunting images assaulted him, but he forced them aside, leaving only the familiar hatred and bitterness coiling inside. The Campbells had paid for their injustice, but it would never be enough. Some things could never be replaced.

But taking back his land would help.

All of a sudden, Patrick stilled. His gaze shot to his chief. "You said cousin. Which cousin?"

Alasdair and their uncle Duncan exchanged looks, as if realizing the reaction his pronouncement would effect. "Elizabeth."

"Patrick's Campbell?" Gregor asked.

"Aye," Duncan said.

Patrick held his expression impassive, masking the turmoil burgeoning inside. The lass he'd once helped now held his land. Fate or irony? He didn't give a damn either way. It was an opportunity.

The crackle of the fire seemed to accentuate the tense silence.

"Who is she betrothed to this time?" Patrick's youngest brother, Iain, finally asked.

"No one," Alasdair replied. "Yet. I suspect that Argyll has added the land to the gel's tocher to pique interest in her. I'd marry the lass myself—if I didn't think Maihri would object."

"She'd cut off your bollocks and serve them to you for

dinner for even suggesting it," Duncan said in all seriousness. The men laughed when Alasdair paled.

Patrick's mind was racing as he realized that the chance
he'd been waiting for might have just arrived. Not only
would he have the personal satisfaction of seeing his land
returned to his family, but it could also be a godsend to his
clan. Without land, they'd been forced to steal and scav-
enge for food. But never had the situation been so dire as
after Glenfruin. The people were starving, and he didn't
know whether they could survive another cold winter like
the last.

They couldn't ignore the opportunity. If they didn't do
something, someone else would.

"I'll do it," Gregor proclaimed boldly.

"No!" Patrick boomed. The men were silenced by the
forcefulness of his outburst. Hell, it had surprised even
him. But the thought of his brother with that delicate
lass . . . He moderated his tone. "I will."

Alasdair met his gaze. The chief did not look surprised
by Patrick's pronouncement. "You have a plan?"

"Aye." His mouth thinned to a hard line. "To get my
land back."

Alasdair frowned. "You will take the lass?"

It was his first instinct, and one that would exact further
revenge, but Patrick shook his head. "Nay. 'Twould be too
easy for Argyll to set aside." And only cause them more
problems. He needed Elizabeth Campbell to *want* to marry
him—and stay married.

"The Campbell devil will hardly allow a MacGregor
near his precious cousin," Duncan pointed out. "How do
you intend to marry the lass if you do not take her?"

"I'll have to persuade her," he said with grim determination.

"And how do you intend to do that?" Alasdair asked.

"Seduce her," he replied flatly. "As old as she is, the lass
is surely ripe for it." Elizabeth Campbell was vulnerable.

He knew it. Not just from the broken engagements and the fact that she was still unmarried, but because he'd seen it. He'd seen her disappointment, seen the heartbreak when Montgomery had hurt her. Almost as if she'd been expecting it. Patrick knew he could take advantage of it. A few kind words. Compliments. Shower her with attention.

The lass was ripe for seduction, and he would be the one to do it. He felt it with an intensity that he could not explain. He recalled her pristine beauty, her fragility. The longing he'd felt for something beyond his reach, something he shouldn't touch.

He wanted her, and now he could have her.

The chief didn't look convinced. "If anyone discovers who you are . . ."

"I know," Patrick said. *I'm a dead man.* "It's a risk. But my face is not as recognizable as yours."

"True," Alasdair agreed. "But won't the lass recognize you? Maybe Gregor should be the one. With my brother gone . . . you are my *tanaiste.*"

"Temporarily," Patrick said. He didn't look at Gregor, but he could feel his simmering resentment. "The lass won't know me. She didn't see my face."

Alasdair grinned. "From what I hear, one look is enough for most lasses."

He didn't bite. His cousin loved to prod him about his damn face. As if something so ridiculous mattered to a warrior. Not that he was very nice to look at right now. He'd have to "find" some new clothing, a bath, and a razor if he was to have a chance at deceiving her as to his identity. "Whatever it takes," Patrick answered.

He didn't delude himself that it would be easy, but frankly, a chance in hell was better than none.

The chief nodded. "If you are willing—"

"I am. The risk is nothing compared to what we might gain." Not only the land, but possibly influence with Argyll. Because of his success in charming King James into pardoning him a few years ago, Alasdair hoped to find it again with the king, but Elizabeth Campbell presented another possibility.

"Godspeed, cousin," Alasdair said soberly. But his somber expression was soon broken by a wide grin. "I wish I could see Argyll's face when he discovers one of the barbarians he's tearing apart the Highlands to find is hiding right under his nose."

Patrick returned the smile but knew Alasdair was offering him a subtle warning to be careful.

The details of the plan had come later. It had been decided that Patrick, Gregor, and half of the men would head to the Lomond Hills, while Alasdair, Iain, Duncan, and the rest of the men went to the Isle of Bute to seek refuge with the Lamonts. The Lamont wouldn't like harboring the outlaws, but Alasdair intended to call in an old debt.

From the Lomond Hills, Patrick had organized scouting parties to see what they could discover of Elizabeth Campbell's movements. Castle Campbell, with its position high in the hills of Ochil, surrounded by steep ravines and trees, was impenetrable. When they'd learned from a loose-lipped Campbell guardsman who liked to drink his ale in the nearby village of Dollar that she would be traveling to Dunoon Castle, Patrick knew it was their chance.

Gregor, like Hamish, had wanted to take the lass, but Patrick had come up with another plan. Instead of attacking the coach to abduct her, they would use the attack—and his riding to the rescue—as a way of gaining her trust. No one would have been hurt had Gregor not taken matters into his own hands, attacking before he was supposed to.

"The chief was right," Robbie said, returning Patrick to the present. "The lass seems entranced by your pretty face." He saw Patrick's dark expression, but it didn't deter him from adding, "I can't say I see what all the fuss is about. Guess there's no accounting for taste."

"Which is why someday a lass might look on you with favor."

Robbie grinned. "One lass? And break all those other hearts that teem with hope? Nay, unlike you, I'll not be looking to wed for some time."

Marrying hadn't been on Patrick's mind either—but he would do what he had to do for his chief and clan. He wished it felt like more of a sacrifice.

All of a sudden, Robbie's expression changed.

"What is it?" Patrick asked.

The younger man frowned. "The Campbell lass. She isn't how I thought she would be."

Patrick tensed. "What do you mean?"

Robbie looked at him uncertainly. "She seems . . . well, kind. On the road she made sure we had enough to eat, sharing the beef and oatcakes she had for her guardsmen. Are you sure—"

"Save your sympathy for our people, who will be starving and freezing this winter if we don't do something to help them," Patrick snapped.

"I didn't mean—"

"She's a Campbell," Patrick swore. "When you find yourself losing heart while staring at her pretty face, picture her brothers and cousin instead."

Robbie took a step back, staring at him with a peculiar expression on his face. "Aye, Captain. I'll remember that."

Patrick felt the eruption of temper cool just as suddenly, realizing what had happened—and what he'd been reacting to. Robbie had done no more than voice Patrick's own qualms—qualms that he hadn't anticipated. "It's better than the alternative," he said, more to convince himself as Robbie walked away.

Patrick yanked off his shirt, using the water brought by the maidservant to wipe away the sweat, blood, and grime from his body. He balled up the ruined shirt and tossed it in the fire, then pulled a fresh one from his bag, silently thanking the merchant he'd stolen the clothing from for being thoughtful enough to have a spare.

Tucking in the shirt, he flinched as his fingers scraped the wound at his side. But he ignored the pain as he pulled on his cotun and strode out the door, heading to the great hall. He tried to blink, but could not clear the black spots in his vision. With some food and a good night's rest, he would be good as new.

He made it as far as the staircase.

Chapter 5

[faint offset text from facing page, partially legible]

Lizzie lingered over her food, taking another piece of brown bread and slathering it with fresh, creamy butter, even though she'd had her fill. She sat at the dais beside the bailiff and the *seannachie* along with other high-ranking men of the clan, the room buzzing with the loud voices of the guardsmen who'd decided to drown the hardships of the day in a hearty amount of *cuirm*. Her gaze shifted more than once toward the door, wondering what was keeping them.

It was only the concern that the lady of the keep would feel for her guests, she told herself. But the longer the delay, the more obvious the lie. Her concern was for one man.

Patrick Murray fascinated her. Everything about him seemed intense—larger than life—from his impossibly handsome face to his strength to the darkness and turmoil she sensed simmering just below the surface.

As the minutes ticked by, she became even more convinced that something was wrong. So when the young Murray warrior she'd spoken to earlier—Robbie, she recalled—appeared at the entry to the great hall, his eyes frantically scanning the room, she practically leapt to her feet and hurried across the crowded room.

"Is there something wrong?" Her fingers clutched the wool of her skirts, already anticipating the answer.

Robbie nodded. "It's the captain, my lady."

Her heart plummeted. "What's happened?"

She could tell that Robbie was uncomfortable—as if he weren't sure he was doing the right thing.

"Please tell me. I only wish to help," she urged gently.

"He's unconscious, my lady." He lowered his voice, and she could see the worry in his roguish gaze. "I thought he was dead. He's lost a lot of blood."

"He's wounded?" Lizzie couldn't control the high pitch of her voice.

"Aye."

"But how?" Her mind shuffled through the day's events. She'd known something was wrong. How could she have missed it? "Was he shot?"

The young warrior shook his head. "Nay, he took a blade in the side."

Surely she would have seen an injury of that magnitude? "But when? How is it possible?" When Robbie started to look even more uncomfortable, she said, "Never mind. It doesn't matter."

Not wanting to waste a minute, she motioned for a serving girl and gave her orders to have the healer meet them in the barracks right away with her medicines. Thinking of what else they might need, she told the girl to find hot water and fresh linens and bring them as well. And some broth. And plenty of whisky.

A few minutes later, she entered the barracks with Robbie. Patrick's men had laid him on a pallet and were gathered around, staring at him indecisively. Lizzie waved them out of the way and knelt beside the unconscious man, feeling a strange tightness in her throat and chest—as if the swell of emotion inside her had suddenly grown too large to hold.

Why he should affect her so, she didn't know. Perhaps it was the shock of seeing such a big, powerful warrior blazing with life suddenly cut down. His face was bloodless. Fear trickled down her spine. It was easy to see why Robbie had feared he was dead: He looked it.

She put her hand on his cheek, shocked by the cold clamminess of his skin. Leaning over him, she put her cheek
next to his mouth. Her chest heaved with relief when she
felt the warmth of his ragged breath sweep across her skin.

Though faint, it was a sign of life—one that she intended
to hold on to.

He would not die. Not if she had anything to say about it.

Fionnghuala, the healer, arrived, and with the help of
Robbie and another of Patrick's men, they removed his
cotun and shirt, slowly revealing the broad shoulders,
heavily muscled arms, and powerful chest that looked as if
it had been ripped from steel.

Jesu!

The shock was like a lightning bolt running through her
body. Her mouth went dry and she stared at him, utterly
transfixed by the naked display of blatant masculinity.
She'd never seen his like—his arms and chest could have
been chipped from stone. The shape of each hard muscle
was carefully honed to lean precision, not an ounce of fat
to mar the sharply defined edges.

His skin was dark and smooth but for the smattering of
warrior's marks that gave testament to his profession. He
was a man who lived by the sword, and his body bore
the scars to prove it.

Her palms itched to feel him, to lay her hands on the hard
muscle, to trace her fingers across the ridged bands that
were packed in tightly formed lines across his stomach.

Magnificent. Her body flooded with awareness. With
heat. With desire. With a sharp yearning that gathered with
the intensity of a maelstrom inside her.

Until the healer peeled back his shirt enough to reveal
the gaping wound at his side.

She gasped, and her stomach rolled in revolt. How could
he have stood, let alone ridden for hours, with such an injury?

The cut sliced across his side from back to front, starting

at his shoulder blade and ending a few inches above his waist. It was splayed open, red and raw like a side of beef, the edges crusted with thick globs of blood and tissue, and so deep that she could see the white of his bones. The meal she'd just eaten threatened to return, but she swallowed it back. A steady stream of blood trickled down his side, gathering in a pool on the pallet. His side and stomach were streaked with the stains of blood that he'd obviously made a recent attempt to clean away.

Her eyes sought the grim gaze of the healer, silently asking the question she dared not put to words.

"The blood still runs red, my lady," the old woman said, offering some ray of hope.

It hadn't festered . . . yet. But they could both see that he'd lost too much blood.

The healer started peppering questions to his men and soon grew impatient with their vague responses. It made Lizzie wonder if the Murray clansmen had something to hide. Eventually, however, they were able to determine that Patrick had received the injury weeks ago. A rudimentary attempt had been made to stitch the wound closed, but it must have reopened during the fighting today.

He'd been bleeding for hours.

Her chest tightened, thinking of the wolf's attack. Of how the added struggle must have sapped Patrick's strength—yet he'd hidden it well. She'd never guessed.

Why hadn't he said anything?

Her mouth tightened. Patrick Murray was clearly a man who would not ask for help. What was the fascination with Highlanders and invincibility? Something in the blood, she supposed, along with a healthy dose of stubborn pride.

She squared her shoulders, determination set across her face. "What can I do?"

"We'll clean the wound as best we can and stitch it closed again. I'll apply a salve, and then 'twill be in God's hands." The healer's voice did not hold much promise.

"Nay," Lizzie said with a fierceness that shocked her. "It's in my hands." She felt the weight of all eyes upon her, and heat rose in her cheeks. Despite the blasphemy, however, his men looked at her approvingly. Embarrassed by the outburst, she explained to the healer, "This man saved my life twice today, I can do no less."

The healer gave her a look that said she understood more than Lizzie might want her to, then she turned to Patrick's men. "I'll need a few of you to hold him still while I work."

The men did as they were bid, and the healer began her preparations. Once everything was in place, they began. Using damp swathes of linen, they carefully washed the blood from the wound. Anxiety made Lizzie's heart pound erratically. She was trying to be careful, but when he flinched at her touch, she gasped and pulled her hand back.

"You're doing fine, my lady," the healer encouraged her.

"But it's hurting him."

"Aye, and it will hurt much worse before this day is done. If you've not the stomach—"

"I'm fine." Lizzie gritted her teeth and kept swabbing the red, angry cut, steeling herself for his flinches of pain. She wiped her hand across her forehead when they were done, relieved, until she saw the healer lift the flagon.

"What are you doing?"

"The whisky will help wash away the poison."

Lizzie had heard of this but never seen it done. Having splashed claret on an open cut before by accident, she couldn't imagine . . . it would be excruciating. "Are you sure this is necessary?"

"I've seen it help, my lady," Robbie added.

Lizzie swallowed and braced herself. "Do it."

Patrick's eyes opened as a guttural cry emitted from deep in his lungs. The sound cut her to the quick. His guardsmen held him down, but it was horrible to watch as his body twisted with pain. Finally, after what seemed an interminable time, he stilled.

The healer took out the needle and fine silk thread. "This is going to take a while. I need you to hold the wound closed as I stitch it together." She looked to the guardsmen. "You'll need to keep him very still. The tissue around the wound is tender and will cause him a great deal of pain."

Lizzie felt as if she didn't breathe for an hour, every inch of her body on edge as the healer worked down the gash methodically. It was a long, painstaking process that taxed every ounce of her strength. When the healer was finished, they applied a salve and a fresh linen bandage over the wound.

"I don't understand how he walked around for weeks with a wound like that. It must have pained him something fierce," the healer said, shaking her head.

"The captain doesn't feel pain like most men," Robbie said admiringly. "He's endured far worse."

"Aye," added one of the older warriors. "See that right there?" He pointed to a round scar on Patrick's shoulder. "Took a hagbut shot in his sword arm and fought for hours afterwards."

Lizzie clamped her lips tightly together. "Everyone feels pain," she said. "Some are just too blasted stubborn to admit it." *Now* the men gaped at her as if she'd blasphemed. "I'll make sure to tell your captain exactly that when he wakes up."

Gazing at the handsome but incredibly pale face of the man lying on the pallet, she prayed she had the opportunity to give him that piece of her mind.

He didn't want to remember.

Patrick struggled against the images, against sleep, but the dream kept coming. Faster now. Barreling toward him with the force of an avalanche. There was nowhere to run. Nowhere to hide. He couldn't escape the memories . . .

Of a deep sleep and the sweet sound of his mother's voice sifting through his dreams.

Except that it hadn't been a dream.

"Wake up, Patty! Get dressed. Hurry, my love."

His mother's voice, he realized, except that it didn't sound like her at all. His mother was happiness and light, not anxiety and terror. He opened his eyes. Her pale face lit by a single candle appeared like an apparition floating in a sea of black.

He knew from her expression that something was wrong. Terribly wrong.

A cry tore through the night from outside: "They're coming!"

Campbells. The Campbells were coming for them.

He remembered the bitter taste of fear. And the shame. He was ten years old. Almost a man. He shouldn't be scared. He was a warrior like his father. And like his father one day, he would be chieftain to his cousin Alasdair Roy.

He could still feel her hand cradling his face with tenderness. Could still see the green eyes that mirrored his own, gazing at him so lovingly. "I need you to be brave, my love." She'd known—she always knew what he was feeling. "Take your brothers and run deep into the forest. Hide there until someone comes to get you when it's safe."

He didn't want to go. The forest was haunted and rife with faeries.

But he hid his fear and nodded. "But what about you?"

"I'll not leave your father. Don't worry." She pressed her hand on his face. "Annie and I will be safe."

His mother was a Campbell born. Sister to the Laird of Glenorchy, the man who'd sworn to clear the MacGregors from their land.

He shook his head mulishly. "I won't leave you."

"You must," she said sternly, more sternly then she'd ever spoken to him. "I need you to take care of your brothers. I'm counting on you."

And he could not—would not—disappoint her.

In his dream he wanted to argue, wanted to beg her to

come with them, but his dream wouldn't listen. So he'd left his mother behind, taking the sword that she'd given him— a real one of steel, not of wood like he normally used—and ran, leading the seven-year-old Gregor and five-year-old Iain into the trees until he thought his lungs would burst.

He'd gone about a mile before he remembered his badge. The chieftain's badge his father had just given him. The badge that had been passed down in his family for generations. "Guard it well, my son." His legacy. The symbol of his clan. He wanted to throw up with shame. How could he have forgotten it? His father had trusted him; he couldn't let him down.

It doesn't matter! Patrick shouted to the boy in his dream. But the boy couldn't hear him. The boy thought nothing was more important to him than the badge.

God, how wrong he was.

Patrick left his brothers with a stern warning for them not to move and turned back for his treasured badge.

He smelled the smoke first. It filled the night with a black, thick haze, burning his throat as he ran toward the keep. He was running harder now, the heavy sword etching a deep line in the dirt beside him.

Breaking through the trees, he saw the flames. They filled the night sky with flickering shards of orange along the banks of Loch Earn, engulfing everything in their wake.

His eyes blurred, stinging with smoke and disbelief. His home was . . . gone.

People were everywhere. Running. Screaming. Trying to escape the fire and the Campbell swordsmen who'd over-run the village.

He knew what it meant but didn't want to believe it.

He knew his father would never let this happen . . . not while there was a breath left in his body.

Patrick raced toward the keep, not heeding the flames.

As he drew closer, the bodies of his father's guardsmen confronted him like angels of doom at the gates of hell.

Bile rose in his throat, but he didn't stop running. Not until he saw the familiar plaid in a bloody pile at the foot of the stairs. "No!" He threw himself on the still body, burying his head against the powerful chest, not caring that tears were streaming down his cheeks. "Father!"

Someone tried to pull him off and he reacted, slashing his sword in an arc but connecting only with air.

The man who'd grabbed him swore, holding him by the neck in a viselike grip. Patrick thrashed wildly, trying to break free from the Campbell warrior's hold.

"What should we do with him?" the man asked.

"Kill the whelp," another man said. "If he's old enough to carry a sword, he's old enough to die by one. Besides, MacGregors are a vengeful lot. Look at his eyes. He'll be back for us one day."

Patrick hit the ground hard and saw the blade flashing above his head.

He wanted to stop the dream. Wanted to change the memory. He tried to thrash away, but it wouldn't let him go. . . .

"No!" His mother's voice came from out of the darkness. "Don't hurt my . . ."

Patrick's chest burned as the images assaulted him mercilessly. His mother jumping in front of him. The Campbell unable to stop the sword. Her chest splayed open instead of his.

". . . son."

The sound echoed in his head relentlessly—the gurgle of death. He would never forget that sound for as long as he lived.

"Mother!" The cry that had torn from his lungs had not been human. It had been twisted with agony and rage and helplessness. He'd gone berserk, lifting the heavy sword he'd dropped at his father's side with strength he didn't *know he possessed. It was strength born of hatred. The strength of a boy thrust brutally into manhood.*

He remembered the surprised expressions of the two dead men as he'd left them before he'd escaped into the forest. But it would never be enough to replace the parents he'd lost.

Killed by Campbell greed.

A soothing hand on his forehead eased the haunting memories. The dream faded, and he slept.

Patrick woke to the sound of an angel. Or perhaps he'd died and gone to heaven, for he seemed to be floating on clouds so soft was the surface upon which he lay.

He tried to open his eyes, but they resisted; his lids seemed to be weighted down with lead. He attempted to lift his head, but when the tiny movement caused an ax to split through his skull, he thought better of it. Content to float on the cloud a little longer, enfolded in soft linen and warm furs, his cheek pressed against a pillow of feather, the subtle scent of lavender filling his nose, and the angel's song lulling him back to sleep.

His eye cracked open. Cloud? Pillow? Angel? What in Hades . . . ? He wasn't floating in the heavens, but lying in a bed. It had been so long since he'd slept on anything other than dirt and brush, he almost didn't recognize it.

Where am I?

He tried to remember, but his brain wouldn't work properly. Everything was disjointed . . . fuzzy.

Until the bedclothes were pulled back and a velvety soft hand skidded along his bare chest. The gentle touch was like a firebrand, startling him awake—fully awake. His eyes snapped open and he grabbed a delicate wrist, looking into the crystal-clear blue eyes of his angel, Elizabeth Campbell. A very shocked Elizabeth Campbell.

She gasped and the heavenly song came to a sudden stop. "You're awake!"

"Where am I?" he demanded, his voice as dark as his head, hating this feeling of confusion. He was lying in a strange bed half-naked, his head splitting apart, more thirsty than he'd ever been in his life.

What had she done to him? Had she discovered who he was? Had he been imprisoned?

For the first time, he looked around the room. If this was a prison, it was the most luxurious one he'd ever seen. The room was enormous, perhaps twenty feet square, with an unusual vaulted stone ceiling and plastered walls painted a soothing yellow. Two large leaded-glass windows enabled an abundance of sunlight to spill across the polished wooden floors. There was a large stone fireplace at the opposite end, and fine furniture scattered across the room. In addition to oil lamps, he counted two silver candelabra. Above his head, he saw a canopy of heavy silk curtains between intricately carved wooden bedposts. The bed, the decoration, the furnishings . . . all were rich enough to house a king.

He squeezed her wrist a little more tightly and repeated roughly, "Where am I?"

"I heard you the first time you bellowed at me," she reprimanded him with a sharp glance, not perturbed in the least by his burst of anger. Anger that had cowed many men. Hell, he must be getting soft. "You are in the tower of Castle Campbell," she explained. "In my cousin's bedchamber, actually."

Fit for a king all right: King Campbell. He—an outlawed MacGregor—was sleeping in the Earl of Argyll's bed. The world must have come to an end. He swallowed the irony and looked around again, trying to remember. "How did I get here?"

Carefully, she pried his fingers from her wrist and stepped away from the bed. Standing with her back to the sunlight like that, her hair caught in a golden halo of light, and her skin as delicate as alabaster . . .

The air shot from his lungs as if he'd just been socked in the gut.

She didn't just sing like an angel, she looked like one. *My angel.*

Her delicate brows gathered together across her nose. "You don't remember anything?"

He shook his head, the small movement making him wince with pain.

She was at his side again, touching him. Her hand on his forehead. "Are you all right?"

She sounded . . . concerned, as if she were worried about him. "As long as I don't move my head."

"Then I suggest you lie still," she said with a teasing smile. She poured a glass of water from a pitcher at the table beside the bed and handed it to him. "Drink this. You must be thirsty." He drained it quickly, the cool liquid sliding down his parched throat like ambrosia.

Handing the empty glass back to her, he asked, "Now tell me how I happen to find myself asleep in the Earl of Argyll's bed."

A pretty pink blush crept up her pale cheeks, and once again she stepped away from him. "You were very ill, and the healer said you needed to be kept warm." She motioned to the fireplace. "As this is the only private chamber with its own fireplace until the new tower and range is completed, it made sense."

He frowned. "Ill?"

"Your men found you in the *barmkin* unconscious from the wound you received in your side." She gave him a long look. "A day and a half ago."

Damn. Apparently his injury had finally caught up to him. Normally the sign of weakness would annoy him, but not this time. If he'd known blacking out would get him half-naked in a bedchamber alone with her he might have tried it sooner. And from the way her eyes were avoiding his chest, he sensed that she was no longer thinking of him as a patient.

"You'd lost so much blood, we thought you'd died," she added. "How could you say nothing of your injury?"

He shrugged. "I didn't think it was that serious."

Her expression changed from concerned to irritated—angry, even. "Not serious? How can you say that? You were walking around with an open gash in your side about a foot long. Surely you must have felt it? Surely it must have pained you?"

Her anger—and the hint of sarcasm—momentarily took him aback. "A bit," he admitted reluctantly, not quite sure what to make of this side of Elizabeth Campbell. His delicate little kitten, it seemed, had claws. "But it feels much better now." A little sore, but he felt better than he had in weeks.

"Of all the stubborn . . . foolish . . ."

Her eyes flashed, and he thought she was the most beautiful thing he'd ever seen. The ferocity hinted at the strong, passionate woman burning behind the paragon of duty and virtue.

God, he wanted her. As he'd never wanted anything before in his life. With an intensity that should have alarmed him, if he hadn't been so consumed with other matters. Like covering her with his body and lifting her hands above her head so that she was stretched out beneath him as he eased himself slowly inside her.

"You could have died," she seethed. "*Would* have died were it not for the healer's help."

"And yours," he said, holding her gaze intently. The idea of her caring for him . . . he liked it.

She dropped her eyes. "I did very little."

She lied. It had been her soothing his dreams with her songs and gentle hands.

Avoiding his gaze, she approached the bed, once again the dutiful lady of the keep. "I've come to check on your wound," she said briskly. "I can come back if you'd rather do it later."

"Nay." The idea of her hands on him . . . "Now is fine," he said, his voice unmistakably husky.

She hesitated, her gaze sweeping over his bare chest to the bedcoverings slung low across his stomach. Apparently he was feeling much better, because he stiffened like an untried lad under the weight of her gaze.

He sensed her nervousness but made no effort to cover himself. He liked her skittish, liked that she was aware of him.

"Very well."

He lay back on the pillow and watched her as she worked. She leaned over him to examine the bandage, and her delicate scent hit him. Damn, she smelled good. Fresh and flowery. Like the lavender that scented his pillow. She wore a simple brown wool kirtle and fitted jacket that hugged the gentle curves of her breasts. Lush, round breasts that he was painfully aware were only inches from his mouth. He could lift his head and bury his face in their softness.

A lock of her hair fell forward on his chest. The feathery brush of flaxen silk on his skin nearly made him groan.

"Sorry," she mumbled, quickly tucking the errant lock behind her ear. Still bent over him, she lifted her eyes to his. "I have to pull the bandage back to check beneath. It might hurt a bit."

He was in pain all right, but not from his wound.

His cock felt as if it might explode. She was so close. He couldn't breathe; every inch of his body was honed to a razor's edge. Somehow he managed a strangled, "Fine."

Gently she pulled back the bandage, and he could see the carefully stitched wound. It looked good. Surprisingly good. Annie would have nothing to complain about—not that it would stop her from trying.

Elizabeth took a damp cloth from the basin and gently

wiped away the dried blood. He closed his eyes, his skin flaming when she touched him. Her hands on his body were maddening. Torturous. An exercise in restraint for a man who had none.

Take her.

His pulse raced, his breath jagged, his patience run out.

Her fingers skimmed over his ribs to his stomach, to the waist of his breeches.

Too damn close. But not close enough. He was hard as a rock, primed for her touch, and all he could think of were those velvety hands closing around him.

Lizzie's heart pounded in her chest. Her hands were shaking as she ministered to the wound, as she'd done for two nights and a day.

But this time was different.

This time he wasn't unconscious, but fully awake. The skin that she touched was warm and pulsing with life. Tension crackled in the sultry air between them. She could feel the weight of his eyes on her, watching her intently as she ministered to his wound. There was something wickedly satisfying about the knowledge that her touch affected him. It made her feel . . . desirable.

She dabbed the damp cloth along the bottom of the cut near his stomach, trying not to notice how hard it was. How defined the muscles were. The problem was that she *was* noticing and her hands weren't following direction. She accidentally brushed the edge of the bedsheet slung low over his hips, coming into contact with his manhood. His very prominent manhood. For just an instant, her gaze lingered on the bulge underneath the sheet.

Mother Mary.

His hand whipped out to clasp her wrist. "Enough!"

His voice was ragged and raw with pain. Her gaze shot to his face, despair plummeting through her chest. "I'm sorry, did I hurt you?"

His eyes locked on hers—the brilliant green so dark, it appeared almost black. She could see the tension coiled in him, the strain, in the slight flare of his nostrils and the tiny white lines etched around his mouth. "Not in the way you think," he said roughly. "You'd best leave. Send someone else to finish."

Lizzie sucked in her breath as the wallop of hurt hit her hard across the chest. Her eyes widened in horror. She'd thought he was attracted to her. God, what a fool she was. Despite what had happened with John, she was far from experienced. She tried to look away, but there was nowhere to hide. He was holding her so close, the hand wrapped around her wrist as rigid as a band of steel. "Of c-course."

Stammering. Her humiliation was now complete. With a choked sob, she tried to jerk away, but he pulled her against him with a harsh curse. The hand she instinctively braced against his chest to break her fall was the only thing preventing her from collapsing on top of him.

She gasped, the breath knocked out of her—not from the harshness of the movement, but from the force of the awareness that crashed over her at being held so close to him. So close that her breasts grazed his chest and only inches separated their mouths. The warmth of his breath swept over her lips. She could taste the hint of spice on her tongue, and all she could think about was pressing her mouth against his.

What would it feel like to kiss him? Were his lips as impossibly soft and velvety as they looked? Would he be gentle or hard? Entreating or demanding?

The temptation was torturous. His dark, masculine scent filled her senses. And he was so warm, his skin almost hot to the touch. Her body felt flush and prickly, engulfed by his heat. She could hear the pounding of his heart—or maybe it was hers.

She gazed at him, wide-eyed, trying to read the thoughts behind the implacable façade. His expression was tight, unyielding. His eyes were dark and hard. He looked as though the last thing on his mind was kissing.

She was a fool, allowing herself to get caught up like this. Hadn't he just made very clear that he wanted nothing to do with her?

"Don't," he said harshly. "What you are thinking is wrong."

Hot tears pricked at the backs of her eyes. "You don't need to explain. I should go." She tried to lever her body off his, but it was like trying to bend steel. The hard, muscular wall of his chest didn't budge, nor did the arm holding her.

He uttered another oath, muttering something about her being too damn innocent.

In that he was wrong.

"Look at me," he ordered, his fingers gently tipping her chin. Reluctantly, she complied. "I don't want you to touch me, because it feels too good." The muscle below his jaw pulsed. He leaned closer, his mouth a hairbreadth from hers. Her heart fluttered wildly—erratically. Startled, she felt the slightest brush of his lips against hers, like the whisper of a feather—so soft that she wondered whether she'd imagined it—before he pulled back with a groan. "It's all I can do right now not to pull you down on top of me and kiss you until you beg for me to take you."

The heat in his voice left her no doubt that he meant what he said. The idea of ravishment didn't frighten her as much as it should. Two spots of color burned high on her cheeks. She swallowed hard. "Oh."

"Yes, oh." He dropped her wrist, releasing her, but she didn't move right away. Couldn't even if she wanted to. Her body seemed to have a mind of its own—being near him like this felt too good.

His confession shouldn't have made her so absurdly pleased . . . but it did. A flush of pleasure rushed up her cheeks. She bit her lip and said shyly, "I didn't realize . . ."

"I know." His gaze deepened. "But now you do. I want you, and I'm not gentleman enough not to do something about it."

Her eyes widened again, taking in the dangerous-looking man lying half-naked beneath her. He was right about that—he didn't look anything like a gentleman. He looked like a warrior. Like a man hanging very close to the edge of civility. Why wasn't she frightened? "I see."

"So if that makes you change your mind about your offer—"

"I'm not changing my mind," she said firmly. The look that passed between them in the silence that followed was so thick with intensity, it was almost palpable. She felt the connection, the cinch that was pulling them closer and closer. Tighter and tighter.

She realized her words might have sounded like an invitation. Blushing, she pulled away. "I mean, well, these are unusual circumstances. There's no reason to think something like this will ever happen again. One of the maidservants can tend to your bandage from now on."

He gave her a look that suggested it might not be so simple, but she chose to ignore the implications.

She moved toward the door, stopping suddenly and turning to give him one last glance. "So you'll stay?"

Their eyes connected with an intensity that told her she was a fool. What sparked between them was not confined to this room.

"Aye, lass, I'll stay."

She smiled, more relieved than she wanted to acknowledge. But a small part of her wondered whether she'd just opened Pandora's box and invited in more than she could handle.

Chapter 6

Two days later, Patrick could no longer contain his restlessness. To hell with what the blasted healer said, he would not stay abed for one more hour, let alone one more day. He was a chieftain, a warrior, not a bloody invalid. Every minute that he and his men spent in the bosom of their enemy increased the danger of discovery. Time was of the essence, and he'd not waste it abed—alone.

Bathed, fed, and dressed in clothes that had been thoughtfully cleaned for him, he fastened his dirk and sword at his waist and tossed his bow over his shoulder, leaving behind the luxurious accommodations of the Earl of Argyll as he went in search of his men. It was amazing what simple comforts could do to revitalize a man. For the first time in years, more than he wanted to think about, he felt civilized. A strange occurrence for an outlaw, and one he'd best not get used to.

His stay at Castle Campbell was not likely to be a long one. As soon as he could convince Elizabeth to run away with him, they would leave for the Highlands. It might be some time before she was welcomed back into her home.

The realization of all she would unknowingly be leaving behind pricked at him like a swarm of pesky midges in August. He didn't like deceiving her, but Elizabeth would be more likely to throw one of her dirks at him than she would be to entertain the suit of a MacGregor.

Even with the deception, however, she was avoiding him.

Not surprising given what had—and what had nearly—happened between them.

He couldn't recall ever having something come over him like that. The all-consuming, almost violent urge to possess. His need for her had filled every pore, every fiber, every bone of his body. He rarely lost control—even in the heat of battle—and certainly not with a woman. No one had penetrated the shell that had surrounded him since the murder of his parents. That this tiny, serious lass should do so now surprised him. It had been the truth when he'd told her that he was moments away from pulling her down on top of him and ravishing her senseless.

Perhaps he should have. Then she would be in no doubt of what she did to him.

He couldn't believe she'd actually thought he wasn't attracted to her. His blunt appraisal to the contrary had unsettled her. Unsettled, but not discouraged. A subtle but important difference.

It was all the encouragement he needed. The challenge would be in finding time alone with her. Perhaps he shouldn't have warned her away from his sickbed, but the thought of her tending him, of her hands on his body and him not being able to do anything about it . . . there would be nothing "slow" about his seduction at all.

What happened to his vaunted control? It sure had picked a hell of a time to desert him.

His shoulders bumped along the walls of the narrow staircase as he wound his way down the three flights to the great hall. Though he knew they'd been built for protection—to prevent attackers from storming up the stairs—he vowed one day to build a keep with doors high enough that he did not have to duck his head, and stairs wide enough not to have to walk sideways. Still, despite his size, he was used to moving stealthily through confined areas, and habit made him do so now. The soft leather of his boots was nearly soundless on the narrow stone treads as he exited the dark stairwell.

He took one step into the great hall and stopped for a long, bloodcurdling instant before retreating silently back into the safety of the stairwell.

He leaned against the cool, solid stone, allowing the fierce pounding of his heart to slow. A cold sweat had formed on his brow and down his back. Still in shock, he listened to the voices of the two people he'd seen, knowing that he'd been one step, one chance glance, away from certain death.

For standing with Elizabeth before the big stone fireplace was the man charged with hunting the MacGregors to extinction: Jamie Campbell.

Years of hatred erupted inside him. Faces sped by like cards shuffling in a deck. He thought of his family, of all the clansmen he'd lost at the hands of the Campbells.

The promise of vengeance hovered in the air, so strong that he could almost taste it.

Ignoring the stab of pain from his wound, he reached behind him and with cold deliberation plucked an arrow from the quiver at his back.

If he did this, he'd have to flee. The opportunity to reclaim his family's land would be lost, and Elizabeth Campbell would be forever beyond his reach.

Jamie Campbell's voice rang out loud and clear. "Alasdair MacGregor has gone too far. I'll see every one of their damn heads on pikes."

If he had any doubt, the Enforcer's words erased it. Patrick's mouth clenched in a grim line as he notched the bow and raised his arrow to the back of the man who'd hunted his clansmen like dogs. Who'd been responsible for the countless deaths of his kinsmen. Whom every MacGregor wanted dead.

An opportunity like this might never come again.

His eyes narrowed as he drew back the string and took

steady aim, intending to rid his clan of its ruthless pursuer once and for all.

A movement caught her eye, and Lizzie glanced over her brother's shoulder to the stairwell. Seeing nothing, she turned back to Jamie, trying to calm him down with a tempering smile. But she knew her fierce brother would not be so easily pacified. News of the attack had thrown him into a rare rage. Reasoning with him when he was like this was like trying to soothe a bear roused from his winter's bed.

"I know you are upset, Jamie, but—"

"Upset? God's wounds, Lizzie! That doesn't begin to describe what I'm feeling right now." His voice lowered and he pulled her into his arms. "If you'd been harmed—"

"But I wasn't."

"From what you've described, only by the narrowest of margins. If Tullibardine's men had not arrived when they did . . ." His voice trailed off.

He gazed down into her face, his handsome features twisted with the deep emotion he so rarely revealed. It was strange to see her big, strong brother shaken. "You don't know what these men are capable of, Lizzie."

Remembering the look of hatred on the MacGregor warrior's face before he left, she shivered and rested her cheek against the cold steel of his chest plate. "I'll be forever grateful for Patrick Murray and his men for saving me from finding out."

"As will I, little sister. As will I." He hugged her close for a moment longer, then gave her a hard squeeze and released her. "Patrick Murray . . ." He shook his head. " 'Tis a common enough name, but not one that rings familiar. From what you describe of his skills, I'm surprised that I haven't heard of him. No matter, I should like to offer him my own thanks."

She'd mentioned Patrick's injury and that he was resting in their cousin's room when she'd first relayed the details of the attack. "And so you shall. Perhaps this evening, if he feels up to entertaining visitors." She smiled up at her brother, still not believing that he was truly here. She hadn't realized how much she'd missed him until she'd seen him riding through the gates as if the devil were nipping at his heels. "I still can't believe you arrived so quickly. I haven't even had time to pen a note to Archie explaining my delay."

Jamie shrugged. "It's not often that Colin and I are of the same mind, but when you did not arrive as planned, we both had the same bad portent."

Lizzie regretted that Colin and Jamie were not closer, but Colin kept himself apart. She knew he resented Jamie for his closeness with their cousin—closeness that Colin felt was his due as the elder brother and chieftain.

"The MacGregors are out of control, but still . . ." Jamie shook his head. "I never thought that Alasdair MacGregor would be so foolhardy. Surely he had to know that attacking you would bring the full force of clan Campbell down upon him."

"Perhaps he felt that they already were," Lizzie said soberly. "Desperate men are not known for their caution. Besides, from what you say of the MacGregors, they are a wild and uncontrollable lot. The chief might well have had no part in it."

Jamie gave her a wry smile and dropped a fond kiss on her forehead. "Always so sensible, little sister. You are probably right. This attack does not have the markings of Alasdair on it. But if Glenstrae has lost control of his men, it makes the need to bring the outlaws to justice even more imperative."

Jamie took his charge to heart. Lizzie knew he'd traveled to the Isle of Bute to follow their trail. "Did you have any luck on Bute?"

A strange look crossed her brother's face—if she didn't

know him better, she would say that it was regret. "No. There was no sign of them."

There was something in his voice. "But?"

"But I'm almost sure they are there."

Lizzie thought for a moment, recalling what she knew of the Lamonts. "How did you find the Laird of Ascog's daughter? I've heard it said that she is very beautiful."

There it was again. The look of regret, but this time tinged with something else. Something she'd never seen on her brother's face before: a raw mixture of hurt and anger. Her gaze turned assessing. Could it be that a woman had finally gotten under his steely skin?

"Beautiful? Aye, she's a beauty. But sharp-tongued and spoiled as well."

Lizzie's mouth quirked. "So she wanted nothing to do with you?"

Jamie chuckled. "I see your wit has not softened any, sister of mine. But nay, that is not the problem."

"What is the problem?"

"It seems my reputation preceded me."

"And if she didn't see that reputation for exactly what it is—rubbish—then she's not worthy of you."

Jamie smiled. "I'm afraid it's not as easy as that, Lizzie."

Seeing from his expression that she'd gotten as much out of him as she would, she turned the conversation. "How long will you stay?"

"A day or two, no more. Our cousin is probably awaiting our arrival at Dunoon right now."

Her heart stopped. "Our?"

"I shall escort you there myself."

"But . . ." Her thoughts flew instinctively to the man resting in the chamber above. He was not ready to travel. If she went to Dunoon, it would be without Patrick Murray. There was no good reason for her not to travel with Jamie, except the increasingly strong urge to delay the talk of marriage.

"I won't let anything happen to you," Jamie said, assuming that the possibility of another attack was bothering her.

"I know that, but we lost so many men. You have only a handful of guardsmen with you. A large traveling party will leave the castle woefully underprotected."

Jamie thought for a moment. "Aye. We will need to hire more guardsmen right away. I will have Donnan see to it as soon as he is able."

She opened her mouth to tell him that she'd already done so, then slammed it shut again, knowing how overprotective her brother could be. Instead she took a deep breath and ventured, "I think it would be best if I stayed here. At least until this situation with the MacGregors is resolved."

He rubbed his chin, thoughtful. "Are you sure you are not trying to avoid a certain conversation with our cousin?"

Lizzie bit her lip, heat crawling up her cheeks. "You know about that?"

He shrugged. " 'Tis no secret."

There was something in his voice that did not bode well. "Does Archie have someone particular in mind?"

"Aye, I thought you knew. Robert Campbell."

Campbell of Glenorchy's second son. It made horrible sense. The two branches of clan Campbell had been at odds for years over power and land. She should have guessed when her cousin wrote about the new addition to her tocher. If she wasn't mistaken, that parcel of land was the subject of their current dispute.

She swallowed, feeling the noose of duty tightening. "I see."

Jamie frowned. "I thought you'd be happy. But if Campbell is not someone you would consider, we'll find someone else."

Even her brother's choice of words made her feel horrible. She knew how lucky she was. Most women would not be so fortunate as to even be allowed an opinion on their choice of bridegroom, let alone one that mattered.

She'd met Robert Campbell at court a few times and because of the conflict between the families had never considered him, but he was a man any woman would find herself fortunate to marry. Handsome, strong, charming—completely at odds with his terrifying father. The stories she'd heard of Glenorchy's rages would chill even the hardest heart.

She had no reason to object, yet quite uncharacteristically that's exactly what she wanted to do.

"Lizzie?"

She forced her mouth to curve upward, but she could not lighten her heart enough to put any feeling behind the effort. "Of course I shall consider him."

Jamie nodded, as if he'd expected that she'd say nothing else. "I will inform our cousin."

"Then I can stay?"

"I will consider it, but if things are as you say, it might be for the best." He paused, searching her face. "Is there something wrong, Lizzie?"

"You mean beyond my almost being kidnapped by a band of outlaws?"

Jamie grinned. "Yes, beyond that. Do you not wish to marry? I've always wondered whether there was something you didn't tell me about Montgomery."

There was much she hadn't told him, and much she never would. She stood up on her toes and kissed him on the cheek. "There is nothing wrong. Of course I wish to marry."

It was the truth, but sometimes the truth didn't tell everything.

Robert Campbell. Glenorchy's son. His damn cousin—though the murder of his mother had severed all kinship to the Campbells of Glenorchy in his mind. Patrick felt as though he'd taken an arrow in the back.

Glenorchy was the man responsible for his parents'

deaths, for evicting his clan from their land and burning down his home. For turning him into an outlaw. And now Glenorchy's son would have it all—Patrick's land, the life denied him, and Elizabeth Campbell. The injustice ate at him, churning like a pool of acid inside his blackened soul.

Shoot him.

His muscles started to twitch from the force of holding the bowstring taut for so long. He should have taken his shot right away. But he'd been surprised to see a touch of humanity in the man he'd thought a ruthless Enforcer. "Lizzie," he'd called her, for Christ's sake. Though Patrick hadn't thought Jamie Campbell had it in his black heart, clearly he loved his sister. And just as clearly, she loved him. That perhaps more than anything else stayed his hand.

He gritted his teeth, sweat running down his temple. The loss of blood had made him weaker than he'd realized.

The Enforcer's broad back loomed before him, an easy target. There was no one else around. He could make his escape before anyone realized what had happened. There was nothing in his way. . . .

Take the damn shot.

Patrick lowered the bow.

Damnation.

He couldn't do it. No matter how much he hated him, he couldn't shoot a man in the back. The Campbells might have forced him from his home, turned him into an outlaw, and hunted him with bloodhounds, but Patrick had not lost all honor. No matter how slippery the reins of civility had become, he was not yet a cold-blooded murderer.

Besides, if he was forced to flee, there would be no one to prevent Lizzie from marrying Robert Campbell and Patrick's land would be forever in Glenorchy's hands. He couldn't let that happen.

Self-doubt was not something that normally troubled him, but he couldn't escape the feeling that in not killing Jamie Campbell, he'd failed his clan.

What part did honor have in the life of an outlaw?

He hoped to hell he did not live to regret it. For the blood of every MacGregor killed by the Enforcer from this day forward would be on Patrick's hands.

Upon further consideration, Lizzie was not particularly eager for the meeting between her brother and Patrick to take place. She feared that her astute—and annoyingly overprotective—brother would see more than she wanted him to. Lord knew she'd never been very good at hiding her feelings, and there was no denying that Patrick Murray roused a maelstrom of "feelings" inside her. Just what they were, she didn't know. But she didn't want Jamie to reach any conclusions before she did.

Thus, she felt some measure of relief when Patrick left word that he was not to be disturbed. Worried that he'd taken a turn for the worse, she sought out the healer, who informed her that though he'd appeared well enough that morning, he'd weakened considerably by the afternoon. The older woman had given him a posset to ensure a good night's rest, and had every hope that he would be better in the morning.

By morning, however, Patrick was still not feeling well enough to appear.

"I thought you said he'd all but recovered?" Jamie asked idly, washing down the herring he'd chosen to break his fast with a long drink of *cuirm,* the strong ale preferred by Highlanders.

Lizzie's brows wrinkled. "I thought so as well." She plopped a piece of buttered bread in her mouth and chewed it slowly. "He seemed much better a few days ago."

"If I didn't know you better, Lizzie, I'd think you were hiding your knight from me."

Blast her fair coloring. Lizzie knew her brother could no doubt see the flush heating her cheeks. The last thing she wanted was Jamie curious. Once he sniffed trouble . . . he had a streak of doggedness in him that defied belief.

Her brother's attention, however, was shifted from her pink cheeks to a disturbance in the entry and then by the timely arrival of a messenger who burst into the great hall and demanded to see Jamie immediately. From the harried looks of him, he'd ridden all night.

The young guardsman bent to whisper something in Jamie's ear, and whatever he said provoked a reaction unlike anything she'd ever seen in her brother. His face turned white and every muscle in his body went taut. Rage she recognized, but this was different. If she didn't know better, she might think it was fear.

"I'll kill him!" Jamie said, exploding up from the table and slamming his drink down hard.

"Who?"

"Our cursed brother."

Colin. Oh no, what had he done this time? "What's happened?"

But Jamie wasn't listening to her. He had a far-off look in his eyes, his mind consumed by the news he'd received. "I have to go. Immediately."

"Where?"

He turned to look at her, for a moment seeming to remember where he was. "I'm sorry, Lizzie. There's no time to explain. It seems I will be unable to see you to Dunoon after all. You will be safe here."

"Of course I shall."

"I will leave instruction with Donnan about the hiring of more guardsmen. I want a man with you at all times." Anticipating her objection, he added, "Even near the castle, Lizzie. I'll take no chances until the MacGregors are subdued."

Lizzie nodded, one guardsman's face coming to her.

"I must ride with all haste to Bute."

His voice was cold and emotionless, yet Lizzie thought she'd never heard her brother sound so tortured. Whatever or whoever it was that had a hold on him was much worse than she'd thought.

She put a hand on his arm. "Godspeed, brother."

His eyes were bleak. "Have care, Lizzie."

But it wasn't herself she was worried about. If the look on her brother's face was any indication, it was Colin who should be worried.

Chapter 7

A few days after Jamie Campbell's fortuitous departure, Patrick strode outside for the first time in nearly a week. The brightness of the sun surprised him, and he had to squint for a few minutes to allow his eyes to adjust.

His short—and nearly catastrophic—sojourn out of bed a few days ago had hit him harder than he'd expected. The pretext he'd come up with to avoid coming face-to-face with Jamie Campbell had proven more real than he wanted to admit.

He'd sent word for Robbie and warned him to keep clear of the Enforcer, who would recognize him from their time together on Lewis. They'd come up with a plan to leave for a few days if it proved necessary, but his luck, it seemed, had turned when Jamie had been called away.

Though he was still appallingly weak, Patrick knew that he could delay no longer. Tonight would be one week after the attack, and he would meet his brother as originally planned—if Gregor dared show his face after what he'd done.

The persistent mist clouding his mind since the attack had cleared. Whatever personal qualms he'd been feeling about deceiving Elizabeth—Lizzie, her brother's nickname, suited her—had to be put aside. The thought of Glenorchy getting full possession of his land was like *uisge-beatha* poured on an open wound. He'd die before the son of the man responsible for his parents' death married her. Nor could he allow Argyll and Glenorchy to join forces against his clan.

The *barmkin* was crowded with clansmen going about their daily activities. Children playing shinty in the yard, a group of women standing around the well filling their buckets and gossiping, a few more with baskets in the garden, gathering vegetables, herbs, and the fresh flowers that he'd noticed filled every room of the gloomy old keep. Yet despite the grim, austere façade, the inside of the keep was warm and comfortable—homey, even—and he knew exactly who was responsible for making it so.

There were not many men about, which given the late morning hour wasn't surprising. The warriors would already be hunting or practicing their battle skills, and the farmers would be tending their fields and livestock.

As Robbie and Hamish had been to see him earlier, he knew he would find his men with the other guardsmen, practicing their skills with the bow on the far side of the *barmkin*—near the terraced garden.

He noted a few raised eyebrows as he approached. "It's good to see you looking so hale, Captain," Robbie said, moving forward to greet him with an enthusiastic clap on the back. Patrick knew that his men had been more worried than they'd wanted to let on. They'd been through a lot together and weren't only kin but brothers by the sword.

"Aye," Finlay added before Patrick could respond. "With you taking up residence in the earl's chambers, we thought you'd take advantage of all the comforts of the keep for a wee bit longer."

It was an innocuous enough statement, but coming from the Campbell guardsman, it made Patrick's instincts flare. Advantage? Of *all* the comforts? There was a hard gleam in his eye that Patrick didn't like. He'd been right to be wary of this man. Nevertheless, Patrick feigned an ease he did not feel, not wishing to put the man any more on guard. "My place is with my men." He forced a relaxed grin to his face. "And from what I saw of that last shot," he said to Robbie, "I'm not a minute too soon."

Aware of the pretense, Robbie gave him a good-natured lopsided smile and a mock salute. "Aye, Captain."

"Don't you mean *my* men?" Finlay said. "I was told that you had decided to stay on. And I am captain of the castle guardsmen."

Patrick's face gave no hint of the reflexive surge of angry pride that he felt by the other man's blatant attempt to flex his muscles and intimidate him. It would take one move to wipe the smug smile off his face, but instead Patrick nodded. "Aye. I was told you could use some extra sword arms. Was I misinformed?"

They stared at each other for a long pause. Though he knew he should do what he could to appease the Campbell guardsman, Patrick could not force himself to stand down. It wasn't in his nature. They might have been stripped of their land, their homes, and their wealth, but the MacGregors were descended from kings—he bowed to no man. Pride was all they had left.

"Nay," Finlay admitted. "You were informed correctly."

Robbie moved in to defuse the situation. "We were just about to move the target back a few paces."

Grateful for the reprieve, Patrick said, "Maybe you better think about moving it forward."

The men laughed, and Robbie made a disgusted face.

"Perhaps your captain will show us what he can do with a bow?" Finlay said. There was no mistaking the challenge in his voice.

What Patrick could do was stick the arrow right between Finlay's beady eyes from one hundred paces away. MacGregors were the best bowmen in the Highlands, and Patrick was second in skill only to his cousin. But skill such as his would be noticed—and remarked upon. He didn't want to do anything to draw attention to himself.

A sudden silence fell over the men, but it was not for the reason Patrick thought.

"He'll do no such thing!"

He spun around at the familiar voice, surprised to see Lizzie fast approaching from behind.

He quirked a brow in question. As if she knew what he—and every other man—was thinking, she quickly explained her presence in the middle of the men's practice. "I saw you over here and"—her cheeks flushed prettily—"I wondered that you were out of bed. The healer said you would need a few more days to recover."

"Thank you for your concern, my lady, but Fionnghuala"—*the old biddy*—"is being overly cautious. I'm recovered well enough to resume my duties."

She bit her lip, looking as though she wanted to argue, and were it not for the crowd of men listening, she likely would have done so. He found it amusing that this wisp of a lass would tread where few others had.

"Very well, if you are sure—"

"I am."

Their eyes met for an instant before she suddenly dropped her gaze. For the first time, he noticed her clothing. She was wearing simple clothes—a rough woolen kirtle and plain linen sark. They suited her. Without the farthingale, he could see her trim waist and the slim curve of her hips. She was a tiny thing, and the stiff lace and layer upon layer of skirts drowned her natural willowy figure. A large basket was draped over her arm, and he noted the tips of her sturdy leather boots peeking out from below her skirts.

"Are you going somewhere, my lady?"

"I thought I'd collect some of the wildflowers that grow on the top of the brae."

He frowned, looking in the direction of the hill she'd pointed to. "You shouldn't go outside the castle gate without an escort." Particularly when his brother was likely lurking nearby, waiting to meet with him.

"It's no farther than a few hundred feet—"

"I will go with her," Finlay volunteered.

"That won't be necessary," she interjected, perhaps a little too quickly. "You are needed here with the men. But if you can spare Patrick for a short while, there is something I would like to discuss with him."

Patrick caught the flash of animosity directed his way before Finlay covered it with a sycophantic smile. "Of course, my lady. Though with his injury I'm not sure how much use he'll be to you. Maybe we should send another man along just to be safe."

Patrick's reaction was instantaneous. He stepped forward. The muscles corded in his arms and shoulders as one hand clenched in a fist as if he had it around the other man's thick neck. Finlay didn't know how close he was to finding himself flat on his back. Patrick had more strength in one arm then most men did in two. Weakened or not, if Patrick let loose, the square, heavyset guardsman would stand no chance in a contest between them.

Blood pounded through his veins. It was one thing to ignore a subtle challenge and quite another to ignore an outright slur of his warrior's abilities. Nor was he one to duck from a fight.

Sensing the dangerous undercurrent running between the two men, Elizabeth stepped between them, putting a staying hand on his chest. It proved surprisingly effective, the gentle touch more powerful than the edge of a *claidheamhmór*.

"I'm sure that won't be necessary, Finlay. Anyone who has seen Patrick fight would never doubt his abilities. You forget, he defended *all* of us admirably while injured. Should the need arise, he should be able to handle a bow well enough." She looked to Robbie for assistance. "Isn't that so?"

"Aye. Here, Captain," Robbie said, handing Patrick his bow. "Take mine. It appears I have little use for it anyway," he added with mock derisiveness.

The men laughed, welcoming the release of tension. Elizabeth took the opportunity to lead him away before Finlay could find more reasons to object or slurs to cast.

Patrick slung the bow over his shoulder and followed her across the *barmkin* and out the gate. She slowed to allow him to walk up beside her. They walked in companionable silence for a while, enjoying the sun and fresh air. It was a beautiful day. After so much rain, the colors of the landscape seemed even more vibrant against the clear blue sky.

It didn't take long to reach the top of the hill. Bending down, she began to collect the colorful bluebells. A corner of his mouth lifted in a wry smile as he noticed how much care she took in choosing each one, examining the petals and testing the strength of the stem before plucking the flower from the ground. He shook his head, wondering at the attention to detail and the obvious pride with which she attended even the smallest of her duties.

It wasn't that she was a perfectionist, but simply that she took pride in her task and possessed an uncanny ability to make everyone comfortable.

From the short time he'd spent in the keep, he'd noticed that very little escaped her attention. She took her role as lady of the castle seriously. It was also clear that she'd been groomed to the position from birth. Again, he thought of what she would be giving up. But the thought of Glenorchy's son was enough to keep any residual pangs of conscience at bay.

Seeing that this was going to take a while, he sat down, resting his back against a tree, content just to watch her as she flitted around like a wee sprite, her fair hair shining like white gold in the sun and her eyes sparkling with excitement.

It was rare to see her smile so freely, without restraint.

He'd noticed it the first time he'd seen her. Happiness tinged with uncertainty. The smile of a person who never knew when disaster would strike but knew that it would. Something he could understand, and one of the things that had drawn him to her. He assumed it was the result of her stammer and her previous romantic disappointments. And like him, she'd lost her parents at an early age.

From the furtive glances directed his way, he could tell that she was aware of his eyes following her.

"What are you doing?"

"Watching you."

"I can see that. But do you have to do it so . . . intensely?"

He cocked an eyebrow, enjoying her discomfort. "It's my job."

She scowled. "Well, if you are simply going to watch my every move with that enigmatic expression on your face, at least come over here and make yourself useful," she said, holding out the basket.

He chuckled and made a slow show of strolling to her side. But the obvious enjoyment she took in her task was contagious, and soon enough he found himself exclaiming over her finds with nearly as much enthusiasm as she did.

To a man forced to seek shelter in the wild, the Highlands were an inhospitable place. But through her eyes, he saw the beauty of the countryside anew.

"You mentioned something you wished to discuss with me?"

"Oh, I . . ." Two pretty spots of pink appeared upon her cheeks. "I can't seem to recall."

He gave her a look that said he knew exactly what she'd done. It seemed Elizabeth Campbell had no great fondness for her cousin's guardsman, either. "If you remember, let me know."

"I'll do that." She picked a few more stems and added them to the growing pile in the basket. "I was surprised to see you in the practice yard today." She paused, then added shyly, "I didn't mean to interfere with your duties."

Patrick gave her a long look, knowing she meant it as an apology. A lass had no business interfering in a warrior's work, but he could not muster the admonition. It seemed he'd developed an annoying proclivity for having her worry about him.

"You didn't interfere with anything. I'd only just arrived myself." As they started to walk back, he adjusted the basket, which had grown quite full. "I don't think your captain is particularly anxious to have us join his guardsmen."

She lifted her chin and looked him in the eye, a steely glint in her crystalline gaze. "It's not his place to decide." Her voice was every bit as hard and uncompromising as her brother's, and it took him aback. Her gentle, sweet disposition made it easy to forget the life of privilege and power from whence she came. But Campbell blood stirred in her veins, and he'd best remember it.

She smiled and the glint was gone. "My brother made his instructions clear enough. Finlay can be . . . difficult, but he is a good warrior. You'll let me know if—"

" 'Tis nothing I cannot handle." It would be a cold day in hell before he went running to a wee lass to fight his battles for him.

Her mouth quirked as if she could read his thoughts. "I'm sure there is very little you cannot handle."

Their eyes met. There was nothing suggestive in her voice, but her obvious faith and confidence in him had the same effect. It warmed a very cold part of his heart. He smiled wryly. "Oh, you'd be surprised."

She laughed and they continued down the hill. He studied her out of the corner of his eye, taking in the details that had become so fascinating to him: the delicate profile, the slim nose and petal-soft pink lips, the long lashes that fanned out at the edges, giving her eyes a seductive tilt, and the smooth, creamy skin flushed from exertion and the sun.

But it was her eyes that truly mesmerized, dominating her elfin face. Crystal clear and as blue as the sky was wide, set off by arched brows drawn with a faint hand.

Everything about her seemed so fragile, but he knew it was deceptive. She was stronger than she looked.

He couldn't understand how someone had not snatched her up by now, and he wondered if he'd been wrong about her—was it Elizabeth who did not want to marry? He spoke his thoughts aloud. "How is it that you have not yet married?"

She stiffened ever so slightly, a flash of raw vulnerability on her face. The same vulnerability that had drawn him to her initially, making him yearn to protect her and pull her into his arms.

The same vulnerability that he'd come to exploit.

It stopped him cold. In focusing on the plan to return his land to his clan, he'd failed to consider what it would do to Lizzie. Just when her feelings had become important to him, he didn't know—but they had.

His deception would hurt her.

Eventually, he would have to tell her his true identity, but he knew if she ever discovered why he'd targeted her, it would hurt her far worse. She would never forgive him.

She stopped and turned to face him, a wistful smile upon her mouth, and he felt like an ass for invoking the painful memories. "It's not for lack of trying. I'm surprised you have not heard of my marriage woes. Or, I probably should say, engagement woes."

He shrugged, despite the fact that he knew of them very well. It was the reason he was here. "Perhaps a word or two."

She sighed, taking a deep breath. "My cousin has arranged three betrothals for me, but none of them have ended in marriage."

"I'm sorry." He reached out and put a hand on her arm

and then didn't know who was more shocked by the gesture.

"I'm not. It was for the best."

"There is no one you have wished to marry?"

She hesitated. "Perhaps once, but that was a long time ago." The smile on her face was strained with the obviously painful memories.

He felt a primitive flare of anger, and a not insubstantial flash of what could only be described as jealousy. If Montgomery hadn't already paid for his sins, Patrick would have enjoyed making him do so all over again. "In any event," she continued, "it will soon be irrelevant."

His mind snapped back to his plan. Feigning ignorance, he asked, "What do you mean?"

"When we were attacked, I was on my way to Dunoon to discuss this very subject with my cousin."

"He has arranged another marriage?"

She shrugged. "Nothing has been formalized yet, but my brother informed me that one is in the works."

Good. She'd not completely resolved herself to marrying Glenorchy's son. If he'd learned one thing about Elizabeth Campbell in their short acquaintance, it was that she took her duty very seriously. It would be much more difficult for him to persuade her to run away with him if she'd accepted the match proposed by her cousin. "Do you know the man?"

She nodded.

"And he is acceptable to you?"

She fumbled with the lace at her wrist. "I do not know him that well," she hedged. "But my cousin would never force me to marry a man I could not abide."

He took a step closer. The faint floral scent in her hair was stronger under the heat of the sun. It filled his nose and clouded his head. "Abide? Is that enough? What of love?"

She wouldn't look at him, and he could sense her ner-

vousness, feel her response as her body flared with awareness. "I'm sure I will come to love my husband."

He laughed. "It's not as easy as that. Attraction and love
cannot be forced."

Two angry spots of color appeared upon her cheeks. "I
might not be as experienced as you are in such matters, but
you do not need to laugh at me."

He sobered, realizing that he'd struck a tender spot. The
incident that day at Inveraray had left a deep mark. "It was
not my intention to do so."

"Was it not? Not all of us are blessed with a face such as
yours."

He took her chin and forced her gaze to his. "I can assure you, my lady, that your countenance pleases me very
well. But what stirs between us is not as trifling as fairness
of face."

"There is nothing between us," she said, gazing into his
eyes. "Nor can there be."

Her crisp denial angered him, and not because of his
plan. Right now he wasn't thinking about his damn plan.
He wanted her to acknowledge what was between them.
That she could easily dismiss him when it was taking everything in his power to fight the urge to ravish her senseless
infuriated him. It also made him determined to prove her
wrong.

She tried to turn away, but he caught her up against his
chest. She was so tiny and soft, and with all those womanly
curves pressed tightly against him, it was all he could do
not to groan.

"Are you so sure of that?" The huskiness in his voice did
not need to be feigned. He slid the back of his finger down
the curve of her cheek. Her eyes widened, but she didn't
move. "If there is nothing between us, then why is your
heart fluttering like the wings of a butterfly?" His thumb
found the velvety pillow of her bottom lip. "Why is your

breath quickening?" He cupped her chin and lowered his head. "And why do your lips part for me?"

It was too soon, but he didn't give a damn. He kissed her, gently at first. A soft brush of the lips that made his chest tighten so sharply, it almost burned. God, she was sweet. An innocent lamb to his wolf.

He never thought someone like her could be his.

He might need her to reclaim his land, but there was no denying that he wanted her for himself.

The knowledge angered him. He knew better than to complicate retribution and vengeance with personal desire. It would only lead to trouble.

He lifted his head and looked deep into her eyes, seeing the surprise and passion shimmering in the crystalline depths. He gave her every opportunity to tell him to stop. To push him away. To refuse his kiss. To tell him he was wrong.

But instead she melted against him, twining her hands around his neck in silent surrender.

This time he did not hold back. The passion, the hunger, the lust, could no longer be held in check.

She was his—even if she didn't know it yet.

Lizzie's heart thumped hard in her chest. The brush of his lips over hers had ignited the ember smoldering inside her.

She could taste him on her lips, the hint of spiciness that made her mouth water with anticipation.

His eyes bored into hers, giving her no doubt as to what he intended. The sharp rays of sunlight cast his handsome features in hard angles. His black hair glistened like a raven's wing. He looked dark and dangerous and very, very hungry.

For me.

A thrill shivered through her, not in coldness, but in warmth . . . delicious warmth. A shimmery, tingly sea of sensation that threatened to drown her good intentions. She knew better. Knew better than to confuse lust with something more. But it felt like more. So much more. Strong and true and real.

His mouth lowered.

Her pulse jumped, and she froze like a deer caught in sight of the hunter—paralyzed not with fear, but with wanting. A wanting unlike anything that had come before. A wanting that made what had happened with John feel like child's play.

The force of it, the intensity with which desire came over her, took her by surprise.

It was like nothing she'd experienced before. This man was far more dangerous than John Montgomery, and look at what had happened with him.

She should stop him. She knew what he was going to do. Knew how dangerous playing with fire could be. But she was weak. Too weak to resist the strange pull that came over her, the heaviness, the bonelessness that made her body soften and flush with heat.

Desire was intoxicating. It simply felt too good.

She sank against him, her breasts crushed against the powerful wall of his chest. Safe, secure, and, for the moment, desired.

Was it so bad to want to feel like this? To crave the closeness? To know that she was a woman a man could want?

What if Patrick was the man she'd been waiting for?

She gasped, feeling the warmth of his breath sweep over her skin. His mouth was achingly close, but he was giving her time. Too much time. She didn't want to think, she wanted to feel. To take the moment of pleasure that he offered without thought of the consequences.

Desire warred with cold, hard reality. It was wrong. An impossible situation. A guardsman was not the right man for her. Her cousin and brothers would expect her to marry a chief, a laird, a man who would help foster the preeminence of clan Campbell—even an Englishman would be preferable. What good could possibly come of it? It would only make her yearn for something she could not have.

But her body wasn't listening. Her hands twined around his neck in silent invitation to take what he wanted. To give in to this fire that had been burning between them from the first.

Just for a moment, she vowed. *Just one kiss.* Ever since that day in her cousin's bedchamber, she could think of little else. The teasing brush of his lips had only made her hungrier to taste him fully. She would do her duty, but she had to know what it felt like to have his mouth on hers, to taste his passion—this man who made her knees weak simply from looking at him. From the first, this rough, dark warrior had intrigued her. She would simply appease her curiosity, that was all.

His mouth covered hers, and for an instant everything stilled. Every nerve ending that had been set on edge in anticipation exploded in a rush of pure pleasure. All that mattered was the exquisite feel of his velvety soft mouth on hers, of dissolving into warmth and heat. Of his firm lips possessing her. Of their breath melding together. Of the connection forged in passion and desire.

God, it was even better than she'd imagined.

Her body ached for him to touch her. Ached in ways it never had before. Lizzie felt the world spin under her feet, drowning in a sea of pleasure.

Her mouth opened against him, and he groaned. Sinking into her with an intensity that told her she was not the only one affected by this kiss. His fingers plunged through her hair to curl around the back of her neck, bringing her mouth more fully against his, as if he would devour her slowly and thoroughly. Very, very thoroughly.

His tongue slid into her mouth with long, slow strokes, fueling a hunger that she feared could consume her.

It came over her so fast, with such force, she couldn't have prevented it even if she wanted to.

She realized her mistake right away. The passion stirring in her blood was like nothing that had come before it. With John she'd felt a girl's curiosity, a girl's desire. But the intense emotion gripping her now went far deeper and was far more dangerous. Her desire for Patrick Murray was elemental. Like food and air, she *needed* him.

She couldn't get close enough. Wouldn't be close enough until her body melted into his. Until he was deep inside her, filling her and crying out her name. Loving her.

She sensed that he was holding back, having care for her innocence. How could she tell him that it wasn't necessary?

She kissed him back, sliding into the damp heat of his mouth. Meeting the thrust of his tongue instinctively with her own. Savoring the dark, delicious taste of him.

He growled and kissed her harder, bringing her body more fully against him, until it seemed that she'd melted into him. Chest to chest. Hip to hip. Soft curve to hard granite. He wedged her between his legs so that she could feel the heavy weight of his manhood straining against her.

God, he was big—and, like the rest of him, hard as a rock. The erotic knowledge settled somewhere low in her belly, clenching tight. And she was wicked, because she wanted to crawl over every inch of him. To feel him thrust up high inside her. To be connected to him in the most primitive, beautiful way.

Her body dampened with desire. She opened her mouth wider, taking him deeper, her tongue circling his in a frantic rhythm. His mouth moved over hers with less tenderness and more raw desperation, his hard jaw scratching the tender skin around her mouth until it tingled and burned.

No gentleman indeed. No gentleman kissed with such raw passion. Patrick Murray was a wickedly carnal man who wasn't afraid to let her see the depths of his desire.

He covered her breast with his big hand and she arched

her back, pressing into the hard curve of his palm. He dragged his mouth down her throat, sliding wet, hot kisses over her fiery skin as his hand gently plied the soft flesh of her breast. The raggedness of his breath on her damp skin sent shivers sweeping over her.

His hair was soft and silky under her chin, warm from the sun. She had to touch it, to run her fingers through the dark, silky strands.

She could feel his control wane. Feel as the smooth, deliberate movements dissolved into a frenzy that matched her own. His hands were on her back, on her hips, on her bottom. Lifting her and circling her hips against him until the sweet friction made her quiver with need. She moaned, gripping his shoulders to hold herself steady as her body was racked with desperate shivers.

Her breath came quick. Her heart pounded.

He kissed her again, more insistently. His hands were in her hair. His tongue was deep in her mouth, her throat. He kissed her until her head spun. Until her knees weakened. Until all she could think about was collapsing on the ground and feeling the weight of his hard, muscular body on top of hers.

Her skin felt too tight for the sensations erupting inside her. She felt anxious and restless—poised on the precipice of something strange and wondrous—but not sure how to reach it. Something well beyond the short-lived pleasure she'd experienced with John Montgomery.

"Your skin is like velvet," he murmured against her ear.

She froze; the words uttered once before penetrated the sultry haze like a splash of ice water.

What was she doing? It was only supposed to be a kiss.

Dear God, hadn't she learned her lesson the first time? Lust was not love. Sex was not closeness. No matter how good it felt, it would not make him care for her. Was she so starved for affection that she would forget?

She'd made this mistake before and would not do it

again. Not for a man who could never be hers. Not for a man still mourning the loss of his wife. She felt a twinge in her chest, realizing why he'd probably reached out to her—to forget. To take solace in oh-so-willing arms.

"No," she murmured against his mouth, twisting out of his arms and pushing him away with a ferocity that startled them both. "Let go of me," she choked, her chest heaving for air. "I told you this cannot be."

His eyes were dark and penetrating, piercing her with intensity. Despite the raggedness of his breath, his words held an edge. "It felt very much like it could . . . be."

"Have you forgotten your wife?"

A strange look crossed his face. "For a moment, I did."

She gasped, not sure what to make of his confession. He took a step closer to her, the hunger in his gaze sending a shiver of trepidation whirling down her spine. Never had she been more aware that he was no courtier, but a warrior—and a Highland one at that. He could take her whether she wished it or not. But strangely enough, she trusted him.

"Don't lie to yourself, Elizabeth. You want this as much as I do."

His hand slid around her waist. She could feel the subtle pressure on her hip bringing her toward him again.

Why couldn't he see that this could not be? Didn't he know what this was doing to her?

It felt as if she were swimming against a strong current, one determined to drag her under. But she was just as determined to learn from the past. She had to put an end to this once and for all.

Summoning what was left of her resistance, she wrenched free of his hold. "You forget yourself, sirrah." Lifting her chin, she gazed deep into his eyes so there would be no mistaking her meaning. He was a guardsman and not a suitable suitor. "It was a kiss, nothing more. A mistake, and one that will not be repeated. Do not touch me again."

*   *   *

Words, Patrick thought, had not the power to strike a blow. He was wrong. She didn't want him. He could see it in her eyes: He wasn't good enough for her. And she didn't know the half of it.

By all that was holy, if there were any justice in this world, they would be equals in every way.

He buried his resentment behind a stiff bow, his jaw clenched tight. "I apologize. I didn't realize it was so distasteful to you."

She reached out to grab his arm. "No, I . . ." But her words fell away as her hand dropped back to her side.

He could see the turmoil on her face, in her eyes, but it did not lessen the sting of her rejection. "You need not worry that I shall make that mistake again. I'll not press my attentions where they are so obviously unwanted."

It was clear that she didn't know what to say. "I'm sorry."

He watched the sweet red mouth he'd just kissed tremble. But nothing could stir the cold, hard stone in his chest. He was a fool to let her get under his skin.

He made no move after her as she turned and ran down the hill toward the castle. He watched her, though, bitterness and longing twisting seamlessly inside him. The smoldering resentment born in a man who wanted something desperately but knew that it didn't rightly belong to him. She was innocent—

Nay, not so innocent.

The knowledge clawed at him with a viciousness that surprised him. Elizabeth Campbell had been kissed before. Thoroughly kissed. And from the way she had responded to his touch, he suspected that she'd done more than kiss.

How much more?

The question ate at him unrelentingly, a primitive voice in his head that wouldn't quiet. Every instinct clamored with possessiveness.

He told himself it was because of his plan. She might not

be as easy a mark as he'd thought. Experience would make her less likely to fall into his seductive trap and perhaps even make her wary.

But the intensity of his reaction told him that it was more complicated than that.

Never had a kiss ignited into passion so quickly. He'd been a few minutes away from tossing her down on the grass and taking her right here—like some damn animal. Elizabeth Campbell was far more desirable than he'd ever anticipated.

Patrick's blood had cooled, but his body still teemed with restless energy, his lust far from sated. Lust that would make him lose focus if he didn't do something. Hell, he was already losing focus.

He needed to keep his mind on his goal, not on his rock-hard erection. This wasn't about bedding the lass, it was about getting his land back.

He needed to clear the haze, and there was only one way to do it.

Chapter 8

It was only a kiss.

A lapse in judgment. No reason to keep punishing herself for it.

But when Lizzie returned to the castle, the turmoil had not lessened. Her heart wouldn't stop racing, her mind was going in a thousand directions, and she felt perilously close to tears. She'd never felt more confused, more uncertain, in her life. All she wanted to do was forget about Patrick Murray and how incredible it felt to be in his arms. Forget the way his mouth felt on hers, the hot, spicy taste of him, the imprint of his big swordsman's hand on her breast.

Forget that it had ever happened.

But what if I can't?

She quieted the voice in her head the only way she knew how, by attacking the duties for the day with even more than her usual zeal. The remainder of the morning she spent changing the bed linens in each chamber, and fluffing and airing the pillows and hangings. Not hungry, she skipped the midday meal to polish the silver candelabra, and then the furniture. In the afternoon, she swept and mopped the floors until they sparkled. Usually the maids performed such tasks under her supervision, but Lizzie needed the distraction. It worked. The physical labor finally succeeded in clearing her mind.

Only when every muscle in her neck and back ached and she could no longer move her arms did she stop, collapsing in her room in an exhausted heap. So tired that had she not been covered in dirt, she would have simply gone to bed. But when her bath was brought up, she roused herself sufficiently to sink into the warm water of the deep copper tub.

She closed her eyes, wanting to drift away into nothingness, but the memories found her. The more she tried to push them away, the harder they came.

Even bone-deep exhaustion, it seemed, could not cure what ailed her: the knowledge that she'd acted disgracefully. Not just in allowing him to kiss her, but in her reaction afterward. It wasn't Patrick Murray's fault that she lived in fear of repeating her past mistakes. She'd welcomed his kiss, even encouraged him, and then when he'd taken her up on her wanton offer, she'd lashed out.

Though he'd covered it quickly, she'd seen it in his eyes—her cold rebuff had hurt him. He thought she'd rejected him because of his station. But it was much more complicated than that.

Patrick Murray was confident, powerful, decisive—a rock even in the most precarious of circumstances. The ultimate warrior. How could he ever understand what it was like not to trust yourself? To no longer have faith in your own judgment? To know how it feels when every instinct tells you something is right and then to later discover that it was wrong—terribly wrong?

She'd never told another living soul about the sheer depths of her stupidity with John Montgomery.

In the weeks following their engagement, he'd stolen kisses, a chaste peck here, a slightly longer kiss there. But one day—a few days before the gathering—she'd accidentally stumbled upon him in the middle of the night on her way back from the garderobe. He'd been drinking in the hall below and had only just come upstairs for the night. He'd kissed her. At first she'd giggled nervously and swatted him away. But then the kiss had turned more insistent, and she'd realized that she no longer wanted to stop. He'd pulled her into a mural chamber inset into the stone wall and down onto a cushioned bench. His hands stroked her body, touching her, awakening wicked sensations that she'd never imagined.

Your skin is like velvet.

He'd nuzzled his face in her chest.

Your breasts are so soft and round.

The things he'd whispered in her ear had excited her. She liked the way he made her feel. Loved. Protected.

Feel what you do to me.

He'd slipped her hand around his manhood, and she'd wondered at the solid strength of it.

Let me love you.

He'd told her it would be all right. That they were to be married. Told her that if she loved him, she would want to bring him pleasure.

Like a fool, she'd believed him. And truth be told, after an initial moment of pain, he hadn't been alone in his pleasure. She'd liked the weight of him on top of her, liked the way his hands caressed her breasts, the way he'd moved inside her. Except for the mess when he'd released himself on her stomach, it had been quite pleasant.

That night she'd given John her virginity, and two days later he'd broken her heart.

He'd found her after the fiasco at the gathering and apologized. Said he hadn't meant his cruel words—his laughter. She'd even believed him. A little. But by then it didn't matter. Her illusions of this handsome man loving her were gone, and in their place she saw the man he was—not the man she wanted him to be.

"Please, Elizabeth, you must reconsider. Think of the contracts. Of what this will mean to our families."

To his family. Hers did not need her tocher or his cousin's influence in a feud with the Cunninghams. "Nothing would compel me to marry you."

His handsome face turned as petulant as that of a spoiled child. "But you're ruined."

She despised that word. She wasn't ruined. She was different. Changed. No longer naïve. "I'd suggest you keep that fact to yourself," she said coolly. "You'll sign your own death warrant if either of my brothers discovers what you've done."

He paled. She didn't blame him. Jamie was well-known for his ruthlessness, and Colin, if not as skilled a fighter, possessed an edge of cruelty that made him equally terrifying. "Someone will find out eventually," he pointed out.

A husband. Her chest squeezed as she thought of all she'd wasted on a man who didn't care about her at all. Who didn't love her—not the way she deserved to be loved. The pleasure she'd shared with him should have belonged to her husband. She clenched her jaw. "That will be my problem."

Then, she'd still thought she would find a husband to love her. A man who would be able to overlook a foolish girl's mistake.

But time had run out. When she married, love would not be part of the bargain. She would have to tell her cousin what she'd done, and if Robert Campbell could not look past her loss of maidenhood, she was confident that her tocher would blind many an eye.

Crude, perhaps, but none the less true for it.

She dipped her head under the water and plunged her face through the glassy surface one more time, then stepped from the tub. Despite the steamy air, her teeth chattered as the young maidservant rubbed the gooseflesh from her skin with the swathe of linen warmed by a pan of stones heated in the fire. The soft scent of lavender, made more pungent from the steam, filled her nose. It was her favorite scent, and Lizzie saw to it that all the linens were stored with the dried flowers.

The maid started the long process of combing out her

hair, hitting a few painful snags along the way. In between the poor girl's horrified apologies, Lizzie thought how much she missed Alys. Donnan was recovering from his wound, but it would be some time before the older woman would chance to leave his side. Lizzie visited their cottage in the village when she could. With five children it was more than a bit chaotic, but she loved every minute of it.

It was everything she wanted and one day hoped to have.

The bath had worked its magic, and for the first time since their kiss, she could think rationally.

Patrick Murray's softly spoken words uttered in the haze of passion had brought all of it back to her. The uncertainty. The heartache. The knowledge that the next time she gave a man her body, she wanted to know that he loved her. Or, she thought sadly, that he would have a legal right to do so.

That was the cold, hard truth. No matter how much she desired Patrick Murray, it wasn't enough.

But . . .

Lizzie could not shake the nagging feeling that this time had been different. Patrick had roused all the same feelings in her, but so much more. Kissing him, with her body pressed up against his, had felt amazing. Perfect. Right.

A wry smile turned her mouth. Apparently, not all of her naïve wishful thinking had been lost two years ago.

After the maid had finished helping her dress and arrange her hair, she made her way down to the great hall for the evening meal. Although it was less involved and substantial than the midday meal, Lizzie made sure it was prepared and presented with equal aplomb. The tables were festively decorated with colorful cloths, flowers, and candelabra. A harpist sat before the fireplace, infusing music throughout the peat smoke–filled room. A handful of maids circled the tables with pitchers of the potent *cuirm* and claret, and platters stacked high with cheese, bread, and beef. The room was cozy, warm, and full of life.

Everything was as it should be, yet something was missing. Her eyes went to the dais. For a moment, she could
picture Patrick sitting at the head of the table, glancing up
to catch her eye and smiling to see her. The image was so
strong, she felt a wave of disappointment when it was
gone. He wouldn't be at the dais. He was only a guardsman. Hadn't she just told him as much? One kiss and she
was imagining things that could never be.

Perhaps it was because she'd just been thinking about
Alys and her family, but Lizzie suddenly felt very alone.
The cozy atmosphere she worked so hard to create was
only a thin veneer to mask her loneliness.

As she approached the dais, she noticed that the room
seemed quieter than usual. A quick glance around told her
why. Neither Patrick nor any of his men were here.

Dread coiled in her belly like spoiled milk.

Had she driven him away?

No. He wouldn't leave, she told herself. Not when he'd
promised to stay. Not without saying goodbye.

She took her seat beside the bailiff and Finlay, both men
offering her a pleasant greeting. As they'd been waiting for
her to start the meal, she raised her hand and the merrymaking began.

She made small talk with the bailiff for a bit before
broaching the question foremost on her mind.

"I don't see the Murray guardsmen in the hall. Were they
called to duty for some reason?"

The bailiff frowned, his eyes flickering over the tables
crowded with clansmen. "Not to my knowledge, my lady."

She heard Finlay snicker beside her; he'd obviously
overheard—or been listening to—their conversation. " 'Twas
not duty that called them away, my lady." He had a smug
smile on his face, as though he were thinking about a
naughty joke. "But a call of an entirely different kind."

"I'm afraid I don't understand."

Finlay sobered, but Lizzie caught the gleam in his eyes. "They went to the village to do a wee bit of celebrating."

Her brows knit together. "But why would they do that? We've food and drink aplenty here."

Finlay put on a show of looking uncomfortable, but Lizzie could tell that he was anxious to tell her what he knew. "We've not everything here that they have in the village."

Oh God. Lizzie sucked in her breath, feeling suddenly ill. Women. They went to find women.

A slim dagger slid between her ribs, pricking a tiny corner of her heart—the part that had believed for a moment that there was something special in the kiss she and Patrick had shared. She swallowed. "I see."

It shouldn't matter. Even if she had some claim on him—which she didn't—men often availed themselves of other women.

But knowing didn't lessen the kernel of disappointment aching inside her. Or the feeling that once again she'd seen something special where there was only lust. Lust that any willing arms would sate.

The comely, buxom lass perched on his lap did nothing to ease Patrick's restlessness. Still, cognizant of the tavern's patrons, he made a good show of enjoying himself as he tossed back another tankard of *cuirm*, letting the maid fondle him.

The needs of the flesh had provided as good an excuse as any for why he and his men sought to avail themselves of the village's offerings this night. Maybe a wee tumble was just what he needed.

But the smell of stale ale was not lavender. When her wet kisses on his ear and the press of her breasts against his arms did nothing to get a rise out of him, he gave her a pat on her round rump and ushered her away with vague promises that he had no intention of keeping.

He had business to take care of, and his reason for being here had just ducked through the front door.

Patrick almost didn't recognize him. Gregor had gone to great lengths to change his appearance from that day in the forest. His tattered *breacan feile* and *leine* had been exchanged for a leather jerkin and trews—no doubt obtained the way Patrick had secured his own new clothing.

It was the first time Patrick had seen his brother clean-shaven since Gregor was old enough to grow a beard. He'd trimmed his hair as well, and had it tied back in a short queue at his neck. Though Gregor's hair was lighter brown and his eyes dark blue, the resemblance between the two brothers had never seemed more marked. Patrick hoped to hell no one from the castle was around to take note.

He caught his brother's eye but gave no indication that he knew him. After a few moments, he moved back into one of the private "rooms"—a table and benches separated with a canvas curtain—offered by the alehouse for privacy in the back. Though the village of Dollar was small, it boasted a fine alehouse and lodging. If not as well maintained as a drover's inn, it would do for their meeting.

A short while later, Gregor slid onto a bench opposite him. Robbie and his other men would ensure that they were not interrupted and that no one drew close enough to overhear.

Patrick stared at his brother for a long moment but didn't say anything. He didn't need to. His anger was palpable.

To his credit, Gregor didn't back down or look repentant, trusting that the bonds of brotherhood would once again protect him from the full force of Patrick's wrath.

It would, but barely. Over the past few years, those bonds had frayed, and after the attack last week, they now hung by mere threads.

"I should cut your damn throat for what you did," Patrick said.

"You look *well*, brother."

Patrick gave him a sharp glare of warning, both for his recklessness in calling him brother and for the snide bite underlying his words. He reached across the table and grabbed his brother by the throat, hard enough to cut off his breath. "Don't fuck with me, Gregor. I'm of no mind for your subtle poison. If you've something to say, say it."

Gregor's eyes darkened and he jerked away, rubbing his throat until his breathing returned to normal. "You've lost none of your manners, Patrick. I was merely observing that you look well. Castle life agrees with you."

"What agrees with me is that my blood is running *in* my body and not out of it. For the first time in weeks I'm no longer plagued by an open wound." His eyes slid over his brother. "You don't appear to be suffering any from your . . . accident."

Gregor's face grew red with anger. "The bitch is lucky her blade did no lasting harm. But I'll bear a scar and the memory of the pain to remind me."

Patrick didn't like what he saw in his brother's eyes. He held his gaze with a look that brooked no argument. "Stay away from her, Gregor. Our fight is not with the lass."

"It's not? Then who is it with? She's a Campbell—or have you forgotten?"

"Leave it, I said. You've caused enough trouble as it is. You were supposed to wait until we were in position." He leaned across the table menacingly, daring his brother to ignore the ramifications of what he'd done. Of the men they'd lost. "No one was supposed to die."

"The men wanted a little fun. All those Campbells . . ." He shrugged. "It was too good an opportunity to waste."

"It wasn't your decision to make. I'd expect this from our uncle and from Iain—God knows not even our cousin can keep them in control—but not from you."

Gregor finally had the good sense to appear shamefaced. Even without land, Patrick was his chieftain. He also knew that Patrick would not allow his authority to be challenged. "I didn't think you'd mind."

"Not mind that you were trying to abscond with the lass I intend to wed?"

Gregor's face hardened. "It's not as if she means anything to you. The bitch made me angry. The way she looked at me. As if I were no better than a dog."

Had the situation been reversed, would she have looked at him like that as well? The thought was sobering.

Gregor might have deserved it, but it didn't mean that Patrick did not understand the source of his anger. Anger that he, in fact, shared. The king and his Campbell minions had stripped them of everything. Land. Family. Wealth. Position.

When Patrick looked at his younger brother, he saw himself untempered by responsibility, left to wallow in anger. After so many years as an outlaw, Patrick's sense of duty had been whittled away, but in Gregor it had all but disappeared. All pretense of civility had faded under the brutal existence of an outlaw.

He felt a strange urge to defend her, but he didn't think Gregor would welcome hearing Lizzie's finer points. "Leave the lass to me, and if you ever pull anything like that again . . ." He looked him straight in the eye. "Mark my words, kin or no, you will not live long enough to regret it." Gregor flinched, but it was clear that he understood. "Stick to the plan," Patrick cautioned him.

"It's working, then? The lass is taking the bait?"

Patrick thought about it. "Aye." Though she was fighting her attraction, Lizzie was far from immune to him.

"The pathetic little mouse played right into your hands, eh?" Gregor laughed. "She's itching for you, I'd wager. Or perhaps you've already given her a good scratching with your prick?"

Patrick gave no hint of the spark of anger that flared inside him from Gregor's coarseness. Usually it wouldn't bother him, but he didn't want to talk about the details of his seduction with his brother, and he sure as hell didn't want Gregor talking about Lizzie like that. But he knew Gregor would hang on to any sign that Patrick wasn't ruthlessly pursuing their objective.

"It's only been a week. This will take some time. The lass has been raised from infancy to do her duty. She'll not run off with the first man she fancies."

"I thought you said the gel was desperate."

Patrick bit back a grimace. Had he really said that? She wasn't desperate at all. She was sweet and kind and vulnerable, perhaps, but not desperate.

Still, it did not change the crux of what Gregor was asking. Though she might put up more of a fight than he'd anticipated, Patrick was confident that in the end Elizabeth Campbell would succumb. He could be just as ruthless as her black-hearted kin when it came to getting what he wanted. "Give it time, Gregor." He took a long drink of *cuirm*. "What news have you from our cousin?"

"They arrived safely at their destination."

Patrick nodded. "Good." The Lamont of Ascog must have agreed to protect them.

"Not good," Gregor corrected. "They arrived right before the gathering, and guess who should be in attendance but Jamie Campbell."

"He's not there now."

Gregor eyed him suspiciously. "How can you know that?"

"I saw him at Castle Campbell only a few days ago."

"You saw him and he did not leave with an arrow between his eyes?"

Patrick clenched his jaw. "There wasn't an opportunity. He was only at the castle for a short while before he was called away. I was more concerned with making sure our paths did not cross. I was fortunate not to be discovered."

Patrick didn't like the way Gregor was studying his face.

"With the Enforcer in your sight, I would have thought you would have found an 'opportunity.' "

Patrick tightened his hand around the tankard before him. "Are you questioning my loyalty?"

"Nay. Not that. But I do wonder what the lass has over you."

"She has nothing over me."

"She's a Campbell."

As if he could forget that fact. "She'll also be my wife," he said as a warning.

"We should have just taken her. You'd be married by now."

"But for how long? Nay, we'll do it my way. The prize will be worth the wait."

"Just don't confuse the real prize."

The land, not the girl. "I know well what I'm here for, I don't need you to remind me." Nor would he tolerate his brother's subtle threats. "And remember what I said, Gregor. Do not interfere again. I know what I'm doing."

Despite her protestations, he knew Lizzie had been just as affected by the kiss earlier as he. For whatever reasons, she was determined to fight her attraction to him, but he didn't intend to make it easy for her. Her brother had mandated that a guardsman be with her at all times, and from here on out he didn't intend to leave her side.

And if seduction didn't work . . .

He grimaced. He would do what he had to do to prevent her from marrying Glenorchy's son, including leaving her no choice.

Abduction would be the road of last resort, but if it came to it, he would not shirk from his duty.

Chapter 9

As the sun reached its zenith in the summer sky and the days began to shorten in their steady march toward fall, Lizzie had started to wonder whether her family had forgotten her.

It had been quiet—too quiet.

Except for a short missive from her cousin expressing his relief at her well-being following the attack and vowing retribution for the incident, she hadn't heard anything from Dunoon.

The prolonged silence made it easy to forget the plans for her future and to dream of other things. Things that, were it not for her lingering hurt, would be easy to believe possible.

Lizzie knew she had no cause to be distressed that Patrick Murray had sought his pleasure elsewhere, but it did not stop her mind from torturing itself with images of him doing so every time he ventured into the village. Images that were as sharp and cutting as any knife.

At first, she tried to avoid him. Every time their eyes met she would look away, the tightness in her chest nearly unbearable. But occasionally their gazes would snag for a long heartbeat, and she swore she could see pain that mirrored her own.

As the weeks passed, she found herself grateful for the pain. It was the only thing that prevented her from making a much bigger mistake.

Like doing something foolish and losing her heart.

Patrick had appointed himself her personal guardsman, and his constant presence had begun to fray the edges of her resolve. Whenever the opportunity arose, he was at her side, his intense, enigmatic gaze following where he could not. At meals, in the garden, in the *barmkin*, he was there. He'd invaded her home, her thoughts, her dreams.

She could not avoid him. Without her even realizing it was happening, a comfortable pattern had developed between them in the natural interweaving of their days. In the morning while she saw to her duties around the keep, he rode or hunted with the other guardsmen. While she tended the garden, he practiced his battle skills in the yard, often stopping on his way to and fro to exchange a word or help carry a basket. If she ventured beyond the castle gate for a walk to the village to visit Alys or for a ride, inevitably he managed to be in the group that accompanied her.

His attentiveness had been noticed, of course, but not remarked upon. Her brother had left instructions that she was to be well guarded, and Donnan, now recovered, had come to rely upon the skilled warrior almost as much as she did.

It alarmed her to realize just how accustomed she'd become to his solid presence.

Still, in many ways he was as much of a mystery to her now as the day she'd first met him. He did seem happier, but sometimes he got that faraway look in his eyes and she knew he was remembering. Her attempts to broach the subject of his past were met with silence or a swift change of topic.

Did the subject cause him too much pain, or was there another reason for his reticence? Lizzie couldn't help but wonder whether he was hiding something. Something was not quite right about him. A little too controlled. Always careful to mask his reaction. Maybe it was simply that she wasn't used to being around guardsmen.

Being so much in his company, however, did not come

without a cost. She alternated between not being able to imagine life without him and wishing him thousands of miles away. Her attraction to him had intensified to the point where it felt as if she were jumping out of her skin every time he entered the room.

Though he'd kept his word and not made any attempt to kiss her again, he touched her so often that she could think of little else.

Never had she been so aware of a man. Every detail seemed etched in her mind, from the lines that crinkled around his eyes when he let go a rare smile to the scar that bisected the edge of his right brow, to the way his eyes changed from mossy green to dark emerald with the falling of the light.

And his face. She'd looked for flaws—hoping to find something to bring him down to the level of mere mortal—but further inspection had done nothing to dispel her initial impression. Patrick Murray was simply the most handsome man she'd ever seen.

Her fascination, however, had begun to chafe. She didn't know whom she was angrier with: herself for wanting him or him for making her want him.

Lizzie was no fool; she knew what he was doing. The question was why.

She wiped her brow under the wide brim of her hat and stood up, her legs unsteady after being on her knees in the warm sun for so long. Though there was a small kitchen garden to the west of the keep, the formal—and unusual—terraced gardens to the south were where she spent much of her time. Today, rather than stroll around the grounds, she'd been pulling weeds.

As she walked past the rocky knoll known as "John Knox's Pulpit," since Knox's stay at Castle Campbell nearly half a century before, and up the path back to the inner yard, she kept her eyes fastened on the dirt and rocks at her feet, careful to avoid glancing in the direction of the practicing warriors. Her fascination with Patrick Murray had gotten so ridiculous that no longer could she watch his practice—*particularly* sword practice on warm days.

She'd almost reached the safety of the keep when a large shadow crossed her path. Her step faltered. The hair at the back of her neck stood on end, and her skin seemed to hum with the sudden spark that crackled in the air with all the subtlety of lightning.

She didn't need to look up to know who was standing before her.

"Will you be going for your ride as usual this afternoon, my lady?"

Gritting her teeth and willing herself to indifference, she lifted her gaze . . . and gasped. She couldn't help it.

Chest. All she could see was a naked wall of chest. A tanned, gleaming, naked wall of chest, with muscles rippling like sharp shards of stone chipped from the face of a rocky crag. She couldn't look away, momentarily mesmerized by the wide span of hard—very hard—male flesh. His body had been honed to steely perfection, as much a weapon as the sword he wielded with such ease. Built for battle . . . and female fantasies.

No man should look like this. Her eyes gorged on the taut, flat stomach and broad shoulders. On the arms as thick and powerfully wrought as any smith's. And on the trickle of sweat that carved a wicked path over the rigid bands of his stomach to disappear beneath the waist of his low-slung trews.

Trews that left very little to the imagination, displaying the powerful muscles of his thighs in formfitting leather. And the prominent bulge . . .

She shook off her stupor and snapped, "No."

He took a step closer and she could feel the heat radiating off his skin, mingling with the sultry masculine scent of toil in the sun.

"A walk, then?" His voice was low and husky, sending a

shudder of awareness down her spine. Warmth spread over her like molten lava.

Curse the blighter. He was doing this on purpose. Tormenting her. Making her want him. Eyes narrowed, she met his devilish green-eyed gaze. "You might think to don a shirt before addressing a lady."

The wretch had the nerve to grin. "My apologies. It must have slipped my mind—with it being so hot and all. If it makes you uncomfortable, I can return—"

"I'm not uncomfortable!" she shrieked like the madwoman he was turning her into. What had happened to the quiet, sensible woman she'd been before? Trying to calm the rising hysteria, she managed a smile, hoping her face didn't crack. "We wouldn't want to frighten the maids."

He laughed at her jest and eyed the group of serving women loitering around the well, doing a poor job of pretending not to stare. "I see what you mean," he said, folding his arms across his chest.

The muscles flexed and bulged to prodigious—to delicious—proportions. Her eyes widened, and her mouth went utterly dry. *Good God, he's magnificent.*

She pursed her mouth together like an old shrew and practically hissed, "If that is all, you'll excuse me. I've much work to do." She tried to push past him but miscalculated and instead came into full, sizzling contact with the wall of burning-hot skin.

Though they touched for only a second, it didn't matter. The effect, like that of a flame held to dry leaves, was devastating. Her body came alive; every nerve ending combusted with desire. Hot, heavy desire that washed through her veins in a flood of deep, insatiable yearning.

He grabbed her by the shoulders. "Whoa. Steady there. You'd best watch your step. There are quite a few rocks around to trip on."

Lizzie felt her temper blast hot on her cheeks. Frustration turned to anger at the sight of his knowing smile. Her hands balled into tight, rigid fists at her side. "There are very big rocks underfoot, and if they don't stay out of my way, I'll have to see about removing them."

And with that she spun around and stomped off toward the keep, intending to vent her considerable frustration on some very dusty carpets.

Patrick chuckled, watching her storm away, eyes blazing and face on fire, as prickly as a swarm of angry hornets.

God, she was magnificent. Spirited, passionate, beautiful. A lass any man would be proud to have at his side.

And in his bed.

His slow seduction was working, though he didn't know who was suffering more. Nor did he know how much longer he could be patient.

He spent the days hard as a rock and the nights with his cock in hand, trying to take the edge off his frustration. But erotic dreams were a poor substitute for the woman who inspired them.

His only consolation was that he was not alone in his sexual frustration. Did she touch herself and think of him? *Hell.* He adjusted the source of his constant agony and steered his thoughts from silken softness.

How much longer could she resist what was between them?

If her reaction today was any indication, he hoped it wouldn't be too long. Aside from his personal discomfort, his brother was growing impatient, and reining him in had become increasingly difficult as the weeks passed. Patrick was fortunate that Gregor had gone to the Lomond Hills to check on their clansmen—but he would return. Soon.

With that in mind, an hour later, after finishing his practice for the day, he washed and went in search of her.

Frowning, he wondered which of the many tasks left at her feet she was attending to today. Not only did Lizzie fulfill the usual duties of the lady of the keep such as overseeing the household servants and the numerous spinners and weavers tasked with clothing the clansmen, planning the meals, and seeing to the education of the children, she was also serving as lord in her cousin's absence, including arbitrating disputes, overseeing the accounts, and managing the castle affairs. If all that weren't enough, she'd been asked to supervise the large construction project under way to add a hall and chamber range to the existing keep.

Her family demanded too much of her.

Having lived in less-than-extravagant circumstances for much of his life, Patrick was surprised by the amount of work and responsibility in running a castle. After observing her these past weeks, he admired her—more than he should. His mouth fell in a grim line. But it also made him realize how ill prepared he was for such a life—and the birthright denied him. What the hell did he know about being laird?

When he didn't find her in the laird's solar poring over some dusty account ledger, or in the kitchen storerooms going over the week's menus with the cook, he headed toward the clamor of busy craftsmen.

On the south side of the existing keep they were attaching a new hall and then attached to that a chamber range that ran to the east. The structures were nearly complete, and when finished would be far grander than the existing tower house.

Hearing raised voices, he quickened his step. Finally, he found her in one of the small chambers at the end of the east range, arguing with a man he didn't recognize. Her back was to him, and she hadn't heard him approach.

"I'm afraid it cannot be done for less, my lady. The price of stone has soared in the past few months."

"How can that be when the stone is being quarried from my cousin's holdings?"

"It's the labor in getting it here, my lady. 'Tis not easy work."

"I fail to see how that has changed, sir. It has always been so."

He shook his head with exaggerated regret. "I need money to cover my costs. Three hundred more merks on top of what we discussed should suffice." He smiled. "For now."

She waved a piece of parchment in his face. "But we had an agreement."

He shrugged helplessly. "Circumstances have changed."

"Don't you mean that the supervision has changed? Would you be demanding more money if my cousin were here?"

The man looked shocked. "You do me a great injustice, my lady. It never occurred to me—"

"Didn't it?"

Patrick could hear the barely restrained fury in her voice. He wanted nothing more than to take the man and toss him against the wall for trying to take advantage of her, but he didn't want to interfere. Nor did he think she would welcome his coming to her rescue—not in this case, at least. He'd learned that Lizzie was more than capable of taking care of the duties that had been thrust upon her. Duties he might have shared under different circumstances.

Thus, he was as surprised as the workman when she said, "Very well."

The man broke into a wide smile. "I'm relieved that you have recognized the difficulty of the situation. When can I expect the money?"

"You can't."

The man's face fell. "What? I must have misunderstood—"

"You didn't misunderstand anything. If you do not fulfill the terms of the agreement, you and your men can pack up your belongings and leave."

Patrick grinned at the stupefied expression on the man's face. Good for her.

"But the earl—"

"As you've no doubt noticed, the earl is not here at present. He's left me in charge. I make all decisions. You can be assured that he will support me on this one when I explain—"

The man's face drained. "That won't be necessary." Obviously, he'd underestimated his opponent—a fatal flaw in battle as it was in any context. "There's no cause to bring this matter to the earl's attention. The stone will be here as we agreed upon by the end of the week."

He hurried away, brushing past Patrick with nary a glance in his eagerness to leave.

As soon as he'd gone, Lizzie sighed deeply, her shoulders sagging with weariness. Something inside him snapped.

Why was she doing this to herself? She was too young to be locked away in this grim castle, weighed down with responsibility that was not hers to shoulder. She should be at parties, being feted, dancing, and enjoying herself.

Or be surrounded by bairns. *My* bairns, he thought fiercely.

"Why are you doing this?"

She started at the sound of his voice. He hated the way her shoulders stiffened instinctively, as if to ward off attack. *From me.* The realization struck him cold. She turned her head just enough for him to catch her face unprotected and see the look of exhaustion on her face. It roused every protective instinct inside him.

"What are you doing here?" She looked at him imploringly. "Please, I've not the strength to do battle with you right now."

Her accusation was well aimed, and Patrick felt a hard stab of guilt. He'd wanted to press her, but not like this—not when she was vulnerable. Right now all he wanted to do was ease the worry from her mind.

He stepped behind her and put his hands on her shoulders. She tensed but relaxed as his fingers began to knead the tension from her neck. Her skin was warm and velvety, the tiny hairs at the back of her neck as downy soft as the top of a babe's head. She smelled like flowers, and if he dipped his head into her silky blond hair . . .

He straightened, reminding himself that he'd only meant to soothe her.

"They ask too much of you," he said in a low voice. He felt her stiffen. Before she could argue, he spun her around to look into her eyes. "You are doing the work of lord and lady with none of the reward. Does your family realize how much you've sacrificed for them?"

"You're wrong. 'Tis no sacrifice. They ask nothing of me that I do not wish to give."

He gave her a hard look. "I do not doubt that, Elizabeth. That's what you do: give and give."

She bristled. "What is that supposed to mean?"

"It means that you take care of everyone else before thinking of yourself. You think I don't see what you've done around here. Yet when is the last time you received even a word of thanks?"

Her mouth clamped together. He read the answer in her defiant gaze. "I do not need thanks. I'm happy to help my brothers and cousin where I can."

"They are taking advantage of you," he said bluntly. Though he admired her capability and the way she quietly attended to the needs of everyone around her, it was time someone looked out for her. "Of your kindness, of your skills, and of your strong sense of duty and responsibility. When is the last time you went to court or visited any of your friends?"

She bit her lip, looking troubled. "It's been some time, but the countess was ill."

"And after that? You've been locked away, taking care of your cousins and brothers when you should be enjoying yourself." He took her chin and forced her to meet his gaze. "Meeting people."

She turned away. "You make it sound much worse than it is."

Seeing her hurt, he softened his tone. "I'm sure they don't mean to, but it does not change the fact that they have taken advantage of you." He paused. "Haven't you sacrificed yourself on the altar of duty long enough?"

Lizzie's head was spinning. He was confusing her, making her see ambiguity where there was none. She enjoyed her duties. It was only sometimes, when she was tired, that everything suddenly felt so overwhelming.

"You act as if duty is a foul word," she said. "But it's not all about sacrifice, it's something you do for the greater good or because it's the right thing to do. My family is important to me. Is there nothing that matters to you?"

His eyes flashed, but he ignored her question. Patrick was unrelenting—in this as on the battlefield. He cupped her chin and stared deeply into her eyes. "Is it the right thing to do, Elizabeth? Do you not deserve to make your own choice?"

In a husband. She knew what he meant. She searched his face, heart pounding. "It is my duty to marry where my family wishes."

"Haven't you done enough? Or do you need to tie yourself to a man you don't want as well to satisfy them?"

She bristled. "You presume much. How do you know I don't want him?"

A dangerous glint fired in his gaze. She realized her error: He'd taken her words as a challenge. He stepped closer to her, moving her back until she was pressed against the stone wall. He braced himself over her with one hand on either side of her shoulders.

Her breath hitched and her pulse quickened, reverberating through her body until her skin seemed to beat with life. His heat warmed her. His scent intoxicated her—a heady combination of soap and freshly washed male skin with the faint scent of pine that made her think he bathed in a forest. He leaned closer to her, until only inches separated them. The look on his face . . .

He terrified her. But not with fear.

He's going to kiss me. She held her breath, knowing that she would not refuse him.

But at the last minute his mouth moved to her ear, his breath sweeping over her in a warm whisper. "Because you want me."

Blast the arrogant brute! And blast him doubly for being right.

But she couldn't forget the hurt. "And what of you, Patrick? Will you marry again? Or perhaps you've already found someone?"

His gaze burned into hers, knowing that something was behind her words. "What do you mean?"

Her eyes heated with the anger and hurt that had been held inside her for too long. "Your trips to the village have not gone unnoticed."

A look of confusion crossed his too-handsome face. "What does my going to the village have to do with us?"

"I know there are women—"

He swore and gripped her arm, jerked her up against his chest. "Who put such nonsense in your head?"

She didn't say anything, her throat hot and tight from the ball of tears constricting it.

"Finlay," he said flatly. She looked at him in surprise. " 'Tis no secret that he despises me, but I am surprised that you listened to his venom."

"It's not too difficult to believe. You are a man."

"Aye," he said softly. "But I've not had another woman, Elizabeth."

Her heart faltered. Her eyes shot to his, not daring to believe . . . He cradled her cheek tenderly in his big hand.

"How can I when I want someone else?"

He hasn't been with a woman . . . he wants me.

His thumb swept over her bottom lip as he contemplated

her mouth. He lowered his face to hers, their mouths separated by only a hairbreadth. Close enough that she could taste the spiciness of his breath on her tongue. Her body pulsed with need, desperate for the pressure of his mouth on hers. She could lift up and . . .

He pulled back suddenly—cruelly. His fingers cupped her chin, tipping her head back to meet his cool, piercing gaze.

"But it cannot be, isn't that right, Elizabeth?"

"I—" Her breath caught. Could it?

He gave her a long look. "Let me know when you decide."

She hated him for leaving her like this: heart pounding, body soft and heavy, drenched with heat . . . wanting.

But even though the effects of his touch faded, his question haunted her long after he'd left.

Could she ignore her duty to her family for the sake of personal happiness?

As she made her way back to the great hall, she contemplated the gauntlet he'd tossed at her feet.

There was no denying that on the surface, Patrick Murray—a simple guardsman with no land, wealth, or position to speak of—was an unsuitable choice of husband for her. Yet in the ways that mattered, he was everything she'd ever dreamed of—strong, handsome, honorable. A fierce warrior and natural leader who inspired devotion in his men. Perhaps he was a smidgen rough around the edges, but it seemed only to enhance his appeal.

She appreciated his blunt, straightforward manner, knowing that she could count on him not to hide the truth. She believed him about the village. He hadn't sought out another woman. And it was surprising how much that knowledge mattered. Her growing feelings, suddenly unhampered by doubt and hurt, had broken free of their moorings. She could admit to herself just how much she cared for her dark guardsman.

And just as important, he truly seemed to care for her.

From the first he'd singled her out, making her feel special, desirable. He'd never made her feel self-conscious about her stammer or lacking in any way. And no one had ever worried about her before. His protectiveness was nice—not smothering, but nice. She could get used to it.

Maybe . . . it was possible.

As she reached the hall, the sounds of a disturbance outside caught her attention. She intercepted the bailiff as he was making his way toward the kitchens below.

"What is it, Donald?"

"Ah, there you are, my lady. The Laird of Auchinbreck has arrived with some men."

Colin? What could he be doing here? She started toward the door, but the heavy footsteps treading up the forestairs from the *barmkin* below told her that it was unnecessary. A moment later, Colin and half a dozen men came bursting into the hall, and Lizzie came face-to-face with the explanation for her brother's unexpected arrival.

The blood drained from her face as she met the friendly blue-eyed gaze of the handsome blond giant standing before her.

It seemed she would not be able to ignore her duty; it had just arrived. For standing next to her brother was none other than Robert Campbell.

"Ah, there you are, Lizzie," Colin said, moving forward to enfold her in an awkward embrace. Physical affection had never come easily to her brother—actually, affection in general didn't seem to come easily to him. "I was surprised you did not come out to greet us."

Lizzie didn't miss the subtle admonition so typical of her brother. "I was in the east range and didn't hear you arrive." Remembering what Patrick had said, she added, "Overseeing the construction project that our cousin left under my supervision." Figuring that Colin could use a little admonition himself, she said, "If I'd known you were coming, of course, I would have been here to greet you and your guests myself."

Colin frowned, looking at her as if she'd just grown a second head.

But Robert Campbell chuckled. "She's got you there, Auchinbreck." He took her hand and gave her a short bow. "We apologize for descending on you unannounced, my lady, but there wasn't time to send a messenger."

"Aye," Colin said, recovering from his shock at her rebuke. "I met up with Campbell here a few days ago near the Lomond Hills. We decided to join forces, but the damn outlaws have vanished."

Lizzie swallowed hard. It seemed that the prospect of an alliance between the two warring branches of clan Campbell was already bearing fruit. The noose hanging around her neck tightened. Realizing that the men were staring at her, she asked, "So you've given up your search?"

"Nay, little sister, I'll never give up." Colin's eyes hardened. "After what they dared try to do to you, the MacGregors will pay. I'll see their heads on pikes—every last one of them."

Something in his voice made her skin crawl with fear. Colin was a hard man, occasionally even a cruel one. He was a difficult man to love, but as he was her brother, she tried to do so.

Though Lizzie had no wish to encounter the MacGregor brigands again, neither did she want any more bloodshed on her account. But she knew her brother well enough to know that nothing she said would change his mind. He cared for her in his own way. But of all her brothers, Colin valued her opinion the least.

"We decided to retrench for a few days and lull them out of hiding," Robert Campbell explained. "Your brother was kind enough to invite me and my men to enjoy the hospitality of Castle Campbell while we wait."

"I thought it was a good opportunity for you to get to know each other better," Colin said meaningfully.

Lizzie felt the heat rise to her cheeks. So much for subtlety. How like a brother to say something to embarrass her. "You and your men are most welcome, my laird," she said with a smile directed at Robert Campbell.

He returned her smile, and at that moment Patrick Murray walked through the door from the kitchens, holding an apple in his hand.

He stopped midstep, shock and something else crossing his face before he quickly covered it.

"Excuse me," he said with a short nod, heading immediately for the door.

Colin was studying him with a queer look on his face. "Who is that man? I don't recognize him, but he seems familiar."

"Patrick, wait," Lizzie said, stopping him just as he'd reached the door. He turned and looked at her, his face devoid of expression. "My brother the Laird of Auchinbreck has arrived."

"So I see, my lady." His gaze turned to Robert Campbell.

"And this is Robert Campbell," she said softly, the hint of an apology in her voice. His gaze chilled, as hard and black as coal. Something painful squeezed in her chest, and she had to look away. "This is Patrick Murray," she explained to Colin, "the man who rescued us from the attack. He and his men agreed to stay on for a while."

"Is that so?" Colin said, stroking his chin. "It seems we owe you a debt of gratitude, Murray."

"You owe me nothing, my laird. I was honored to offer the lady assistance." Patrick's voice was polite but empty. His gaze when he looked at her was that of a stranger, giving no hint of what had passed between them only moments ago. "If you'll excuse me, I must return to my *duties*."

She didn't miss his emphasis on the last word. A gauntlet indeed.

Chapter 10

To Patrick's mind there was no cause to celebrate, but the hall was filled to bursting with the sounds of the pipes and merrymaking as the *ceilidh* got under way. Highlanders welcomed any excuse to feast, and Campbells—Highlanders when it proved expedient—were no exception.

He kept his gaze fixed on the steaming pile of beef and vegetables in front of him and not on the laughing couple seated at the dais, but every inch of his body teemed with barely restrained fury. After a long week of being forced to stand in the shadows and watch his enemy woo the woman he wanted—and not being able to do a damn thing about it—Patrick was perilously close to losing control.

Every instinct clamored to storm over there and smash his fist through the too-damn-charming smile of his erstwhile cousin Robert Campbell, though to do so could be a disaster of deadly proportions. Patrick dared not do anything to draw any more attention to him and his men. They were treading on dangerous ground already.

The shock of walking into the great hall and seeing the Laird of Auchinbreck and Robert Campbell had yet to fade. Patrick knew he was damn lucky that neither of the men recognized him. He'd crossed paths with Elizabeth's brother a few times and Robert Campbell once or twice, but never close enough for careful study. Nonetheless, not even the knowledge of how close he'd come to discovery for the second time could temper the dangerous mix of emotions coiling inside him—anger, resentment, and what could only be described as jealousy—leaving him ready to strike at the barest provocation.

Indifferent? Hardly. No longer could he lay claim to that state, if he ever could. Discovery was not the only danger he faced; he was also in danger of becoming too attached. Something he'd carefully avoided.

Until now.

He glanced over at her again, but the picture hadn't changed.

As regal as any princess on a throne, she'd never looked more beautiful—or beyond his reach. She glittered like a diamond in the sun, her sky blue eyes sparkling and pale skin flushed pink in the candlelight. She wore an entrancing concoction of blue satin and some white gauzy material that floated around her like angel's wings. Her hair was arranged in a Grecian circle at the top of her head, secured by a wreath of diamonds and pearls. Long, silky strands of white blond curls cascaded around the creamy pale skin of her neck and shoulders.

She appeared as exactly what she was: the quintessential lady of the castle. A woman to be admired from afar.

Once again she'd worked her magic, turning the gloomy old hall into a glittering panorama of light and color that seemed to blaze with life—though he suspected that she would make a warm, comfortable home out of a hovel. He'd never seen so many candles—or so much silver to hold them. Evidence of the Campbell wealth was everywhere—from the colorful satin cloths dressing the tables to the precious metals and gemstones encrusting the tableware to the platters piled high with food and the overflowing casks of fine wine.

While his people were starving.

He should resent her, but it wasn't resentment that he felt when he looked at her laughing and smiling at Robert Campbell. It was something far more dangerous.

If only she didn't look so damn happy.

There was no denying that she had bloomed under the dueling attentions of two men. The new womanly confidence that mixed with her sweet vulnerability was irresistible—and he hadn't been the only one to notice. But as much as he wanted to, he couldn't fault Robert Campbell for falling under her spell.

The other man leaned over and whispered something in her ear that caused her to toss her head back and laugh. The sweet, throaty sound drove like nails into his chest.

"Have a wee bit of pity on the utensils, Captain."

"What?" he replied sharply, turning his anger from the laughing couple to the man who'd disturbed his self-inflicted torture.

As befitted their station, Patrick and his men had been seated at a table well removed from the dais, and with the music and loud voices they were in little danger of being overheard. Still, they spoke in low tones—out of habit more than anything else.

"Your knife," Robbie said, indicating it with a gesture.

Patrick looked down at the piece of twisted metal in his hand, bent without him realizing it while he'd been watching the dais. He tossed it down in disgust and exchanged it for his goblet, downing the contents in one long swig.

He needed to relax, but he doubted there was enough wine in the castle stores to take the edge off what ailed him. But it wasn't just sexual frustration tying him in knots. His plan had also been frustrated by the arrival of Auchinbreck and Robert Campbell; the opportunity for private conversation—let alone seduction—had been virtually nonexistent. The very real possibility of failure loomed.

He looked back to the dais, knowing he was glowering but unable to do a damn thing about it.

"Have care, Captain. Glenorchy's son has taken note of your interest in the lass."

Patrick muttered a curse and shifted his gaze. Robbie was right. He and Campbell had been circling each other for days. But Robert Campbell had the advantage of position, and they both knew it. "Patience is not one of my stronger virtues."

Robbie lifted a brow as if to question the others, but he refrained at Patrick's black look. Instead he asked, "How much longer do you think they will stay?"

Patrick shook his head. "Who can say? They were only supposed to be here a few days and it's been a week. But for our people's sake, the longer the better."

"You've sent word?" To Gregor, Robbie meant, warning him of the danger.

"Aye." His brother would see to it that the women and children were moved to safety, hidden deep in the wild, forbidding hills where only MacGregors dared to tread.

They ate in brooding silence for a few moments before Robbie added, "She won't accept him."

A wry smile turned his mouth. "I wish I shared your confidence." Though Lizzie might care for him, she was not as susceptible as he'd assumed. The deeply ingrained sense of duty that he'd come to admire just might prove insurmountable.

Nor had he anticipated competition.

His face darkened as his gaze flickered back to the dais. "She certainly looks to be enjoying herself."

"Aye," Robbie agreed. "She looks as bonny as a bluebell in spring. But Campbell's not the one her eyes follow."

Patrick's jaw flexed. "But she likes him."

Robbie frowned, not disagreeing. "He's not like his father."

"Nay, nothing like his father," he admitted with all the ease of having a tooth pulled. Black Duncan Campbell of Glenorchy was one of the cruelest, most ruthless men in the Highlands—ruthless enough to attack the castle of his own sister. And as much as Patrick would like to say the same of his son, he could not. Robert Campbell was witty, light-hearted, and from all appearances sincere in his attentions to Lizzie. And after watching him practice for a week, Patrick could also find no fault in his warrior's skills. Robert Campbell was a worthy opponent both on and off the battlefield.

She could do far worse.

Like marrying an outlaw—a man with nothing but pride and justice on his side. Marriage to him would be nothing like marriage to Robert Campbell, and the knowledge festered in his gut like a rotten piece of beef.

It was getting harder and harder to ignore the real cost his plan would exact on Lizzie.

It shouldn't be that way. By rights, he should be sitting in Robert Campbell's seat. Never had he so longed for the life denied him. The full force of everything that had been stolen from him hit him hard.

But not Lizzie. He'd be damned if he'd lose her, too.

Lizzie laughed until tears rolled down her cheeks. The room spun around her as she danced and twirled to the point of collapse.

"No more, no more!" she cried, breaking away from her partner. Cheeks flushed and chest heaving, she fanned her hand before her face as she fought to catch her breath.

Robert grinned, the dazzling white of his teeth matched by the dancing light in his deep blue eyes. A lock of blond hair fell adorably across his forehead. There was no denying his appeal. He was an incredibly handsome man. She should be giddy.

"But you can't stop now," he bemoaned woefully. "The reel is not yet over."

He reached for her hand to spin her back onto the dance floor, but she stepped away playfully, avoiding his capture. "You give no quarter, Robert Campbell." She put her hands on her hips and frowned at him with mock severity. "Show some compassion for the weaker vessel."

"Ha!" he exclaimed with a wicked gleam in his eye, taking a step toward her. He was tall and powerfully built, but she did not hum with awareness. "You'll not fool me with such an excuse. I've watched you around here for a week and there's not a weak bone in your body, Elizabeth Campbell."

She blushed, pleased by the compliment. And even more so because she heard the sincerity behind his teasing.

She looked up, met his gaze, and smiled, realizing how much she was enjoying herself. This past week had been . . . fun. For Lizzie, being courted by one man was a rarity in itself; two was unprecedented.

Even Colin had been more lighthearted than usual. She'd tried to question him about the disagreement with Jamie that had sent him riding hell-bent out of here a few months before, but Colin dismissed it as only a "misunderstanding."

Robert Campbell was everything she could have hoped for in a suitor: handsome as sin, intelligent, and charming. A perfect gentleman in every way.

As right as Patrick Murray was wrong.

"Very well, if you will not dance, then walk with me. A turn in the garden will refresh you soon enough."

"I can't," she said reflexively. "Not while the feast—"

He cut her off with a frown. "The guests will not begrudge their hostess a few moments. We will return before anyone notices we are gone."

"But . . ."

Someone would notice that they were gone. Her gaze instinctively searched for Patrick, though why she didn't know. He'd been avoiding her all week. With the arrival of Colin and Robert, the pattern of her day had changed; she missed their opportunities for private conversation.

She missed him.

She knew that something was wrong. All week he'd been as bristly as a bear, but today was far worse. She'd danced with all of his men, but not with him. Yet while avoiding her, he watched her with an enigmatic look on his face that made her uneasy. She could sense his brooding agitation and simmering anger. As the celebration progressed, the amount of wine he consumed increased, and his expression grew darker and darker.

Robert noticed the direction of her gaze. "It's only the garden," he said wryly. "No need for your watchdog. I've something I'd like to talk to you about—in private."

"Very well, a stroll in the garden would be lovely." With one last glance across the room, she put her hand in the fold of Robert's arm and followed him out the door, feeling Patrick's eyes boring into her back the entire way.

Once outside, the cool air was like a pleasant shock upon her flushed skin. She sighed deeply, inhaling a cleansing breath. It was later than she'd realized, the magical time between day and night when darkness closed in around the fading sun. The last orange embers of the day shone faintly on the horizon, creating a delicious swirling confection of pink and gray in the evening sky.

"It's beautiful," she said as they walked along the path.

"Aye," Robert agreed. "Beautiful."

Lizzie felt heat warm her cheeks, discerning from the huskiness in his voice that he hadn't been talking about the sunset. Perhaps this hadn't been such a good idea. She was enjoying herself and didn't want to think about anything beyond tonight.

They walked in companionable silence until they reached the iron gate for the terraced garden. A short stone wall encircled the gardens, decorative and not defensive. He opened the gate for her, and she passed through. He followed, motioning her to a stone bench along a hedgerow with a spectacular view of the Ochil hills and the village of Dollar below.

He took a seat beside her and after a moment gathered her hand in his. "I've enjoyed myself this week," he said.

"As have I."

He smiled, soft lines crinkling around his eyes. Smiling was something he was used to. "I'm glad to hear that." He was contemplative for a moment, as if searching for words. A bird sang softly in the distance. "Auchinbreck and I will be leaving soon."

"Oh." Her disappointment was genuine. "I'm sorry to hear that."

"As am I, but the outlaws must be apprehended. The king will not be mollified this time." He cleared his throat. "But that is not what I want to speak with you about. You are aware, no doubt, of the discussions between my father and Argyll."

She bit her lip and nodded, embarrassed. This was the first time the subject had been broached directly since they'd arrived.

"To be honest, an arranged marriage was not to my liking. I didn't know what to think at first, but after these past few days I've no doubt. I think we would suit in every way." She looked up at him, staring into deep pools of blue. "I would be honored if you would agree to be my wife."

She'd known it was coming, but the words were still a shock.

"I . . ." She didn't know what to say. She knew what she *should* say, but the words seemed to tangle in her mouth. Not in a stammer, but in uncertainty.

It was ridiculous. Here she was, sitting beside a handsome man in the moonlight, and all she could think of was someone else.

He must have read her hesitation. "I don't expect you to answer right now. Take some time. Think about it."

What was wrong with her? There was nothing to think about. Her duty was clear.

He watched her face, a faint smile lifting his lips, and she wondered if her thoughts were so transparent.

Robert stood up and pulled her into his arms. Tilting her

chin back, he forced her gaze to his. "I will do my best to make you happy, Elizabeth."

She believed him. He would make her happy. She would have a beautiful home, a wonderful husband, her own children, and the satisfaction of her family's approval. Everything she'd always wanted. It should be enough.

Then why, why couldn't she take it? Why did her heart cry out for more? For desire so strong, it swept away everything else in its powerful wake. For passion that consumed her soul. For everything she thought would not happen to her.

For love.

He dipped his head and his lips swept over hers in a soft kiss. It was sweet and tender, and she felt . . . nothing.

She wanted to cry out with frustration.

Lizzie willed herself to want him, this gallant man who looked at her with warmth and kindness in his eyes. She tried, tried with everything she had, but her body wouldn't heed the demands of her mind.

His hand fell from her chin. "Promise me you'll think about it."

She nodded, not knowing what else to say. Thinking wouldn't change anything.

"Good." He stepped back and offered her his arm. "Shall we return?"

"You go ahead." When it looked as if he were going to argue, she added, "I just need a moment."

"Very well," he agreed with an understanding smile. "But don't be long or I'll start to worry. It's almost dark and you'll catch a chill."

His thoughtfulness only made her feel worse. What was wrong with her?

Robert Campbell stopped suddenly as he was about to enter the keep. Standing stone still, he peered into the deep shadows created by the wooden structures erected along the *barmkin* wall. It was almost as if he sensed the danger.

He was right to fear.

Patrick stood in the shadows, possessed by a rage so intense that it took every ounce of his control not to kill the bastard.

He'd kissed his woman. Touched her. Held her in his arms.

Patrick's fists clenched at his sides. Rage seethed inside him, filling his veins. Building and building until his muscles flexed and burned with the pressure to contain it.

He wanted to be discovered. Wanted the excuse to vent his rage. Damn the consequences. After what he'd just witnessed, he'd probably lost what chance he had with her anyway.

But with one last glance in his direction, Robert Campbell strode back into the keep, not realizing how close he'd come to death.

Patrick's gaze turned back to the solitary figure shadowed in the moonlight, seated on the bench in the garden. He was filled with a yearning so intense it threatened to consume him. He was beyond reason, beyond caution, beyond any claim of indifference.

This tiny, serious woman had penetrated his defenses, revealing emotions he'd thought himself incapable of. His black heart, it seemed, was not completely dead.

Seeing her in the arms of another man had unleashed something primitive in him. Something wild and uncontrollable. Something that could not be denied.

He looked around the perimeter of the *barmkin* wall, checking to make sure the castle guardsmen were in their usual positions. He'd studied their routine—their movements—knowing that he and his men might one day need to make a quick escape.

I could take her right now.

She would be mine. No other man would ever touch her again.

The temptation to take what he wanted was overwhelming, warring with the tattered shreds of his honor.

Do it.

Hell, he was already an outlaw. He would only be fulfilling the destiny the Campbells had created for him. After everything they'd stolen from him, didn't he deserve a little happiness?

He'd stolen before. Food, clothing, whatever it took to survive.

But this was different. This wasn't about survival. He would possess her . . . but at what cost?

Not since his parents had died had someone looked at him as Lizzie did. In her eyes, he felt like the man he might have been had circumstances been different. If he took her, he would be no better than the lawless brigand they'd tried to turn him into. She would look at him the way he deserved to be looked at: as a thief, an outlaw, a man without honor.

Could he bear to see the derision in her gaze and know that it was warranted?

Nay, not that. Never that.

As much as he wanted to claim that this was all about the land, he could not. He was not indifferent—if he ever had been. He wanted her to choose him.

He wouldn't hand her over to Robert Campbell without a fight.

But not tonight. Tonight his anger was like lightning— wild and ready to strike at any moment in any direction.

Without another glance, he returned to the keep, intent on taming the beast writhing inside him with plenty of the Campbells' best claret.

Lizzie had lingered as long as she could to no effect; the answer to her dilemma still eluded her.

Who would have thought a few months ago that she would be faced with the problem of having two men pursuing her?

Her nose wrinkled. Though exactly what Patrick Murray wanted from her she did not know. He desired her, but he'd never made his intentions clear. In truth, he said very little at all. She was hardly an expert at decoding masculine motives. She'd thought John had wanted her, too. He had, but for the wrong reasons. And with the way Patrick was looking at her tonight, she was no longer sure of anything.

Had she done something wrong?

Her chest squeezed. Or maybe he'd reconsidered. Was that it?

She had to know. She needed to see what was behind that enigmatic shell of his. Why was he so secretive? What dark secret hung over him like a thundercloud ready to unfurl its destruction in its stormy path?

If she was going to make the right decision, she needed to know everything. It was well past time to clear the air between them.

She hurried up the path and across the *barmkin* on her way back to the keep, wondering when she'd developed this sudden streak of boldness. Something had changed in recent weeks, and she suspected that she had Patrick Murray to thank for it. He was right: She'd locked herself away— in more ways than one. Her quiet, serious nature had been exacerbated by stammering and fear of ridicule. After the disaster with John, she'd removed herself even further, hiding behind the wall of her duty. If her family had taken advantage of it, it was as much her fault as theirs.

The lilting sound of the pipes greeted her arrival back to the hall. Smoke from the peat fires swirled around the rafters and wound through the room crowded with throngs of dancing clansmen whirling by. She noticed more than one serving girl perched on the lap of a guardsman and felt a sudden pang for the simplicity of a life uncomplicated by duty. With privilege and position came responsibility, and she'd never felt more aware of that than right now. What she wouldn't give for the ability to choose freely.

She caught Robert's eye from across the room and smiled. He was locked in conversation with her brother and the Laird of Dun, one of their neighbors who'd come to enjoy the festivities.

Patrick, on the other hand, was nowhere to be found. His men were still gathered around the table drinking, but he'd disappeared. She contemplated asking after him but couldn't come up with a good reason for doing so. Frustrated that he seemed to be avoiding her once again, she was about to rejoin her brother and Robert when she saw Robbie duck out of the laird's solar, the small room located off the far side of the hall.

As inconspicuously as possible, Lizzie worked her way across the crowded room and slipped through the door, closing it firmly behind her.

Patrick sat sprawled out in a chair before the fireplace, his long, powerful legs kicked out before him, holding a large flagon of wine in one hand. By all appearances he was relaxed, but even with his back to her she could feel the tension radiating from him.

"God's blood, Robbie, I told you to leave me alone."

"What are you doing in here?"

He flinched at the sound of her voice, taking a long drag from the flagon before turning to face her. His eyes glinted dangerously, his expression dark and forbidding and tainted with drink. Every muscle taut, he seemed like a surging lion restrained by a silken thread.

"Trying to find some peace," he replied, then added, "without much success."

His rudeness took her aback. As did his anger. It seemed coiled in him like a snake, ready to strike.

He took another long drink. "So unless you'd care to bring me more wine, you'll leave me be."

Determined not to be intimidated, she forced herself to take a few steps into the lion's den. "I think you've had enough."

He laughed, a harsh, ugly sound bereft of humor. "There isn't enough."

She'd never seen him like this. He'd always seemed too controlled to lose himself in drink. "What's wrong, Patrick? What is bothering you?"

He turned away from her, gazing stonily into the smoldering fire, his jaw locked and unyielding in profile. "Return to your guests, *my lady*. I'm not fit for civilized company right now."

There was something behind his words, but she couldn't hazard a guess. Her instincts told her to leave, but instead she moved closer. Close enough to reach out and put her hand on his arm. It felt as yielding as stone under her fingertips. "Is it your wound?" she asked gently.

He wrenched away as if her touch had scalded him. "My wound is fine," he growled.

She swallowed the hot ball of hurt. Why was he acting like this? "Then what is it? I know something is wrong." His eyes met hers, dark and impenetrable. "Won't you tell me?" she implored.

His hand clenched the flagon until his knuckles turned white, but he didn't say a word.

Something was eating away at him, causing him pain. There could be only one explanation. Her heart went out to him, her only thought to try to ease his suffering. "Is it your wife? You must miss her terribly. Is there anything I can do?"

He muttered a crude curse and tossed the flagon into the fire, the jar shattering and claret spraying before bursting into a web of crimson flames. He was out of the chair and on her before she could react. He grabbed her arms, shaking her with the force of his anger. "God damn you, Elizabeth, always so bloody selfless! Trying to take care of everyone around you. Don't think to try to fix me. There are some things beyond even your considerable skills."

She shrank back instinctively from the vitriol; he'd never talked to her like this. Yet she realized this was the anger she'd sensed in him, lurking under the surface. The part of him he'd always kept hidden. Without the façade, she saw him for what he truly was: a man consumed by demons she couldn't begin to fathom.

But it didn't explain why all this rage was directed at her. He was looking at her as if he hated her. What had she done to provoke him so?

She'd thought . . .

Fool. She'd thought he cared for her.

Tears burned behind her eyes. "I was only trying to help. I just wanted to know what was wrong."

Something in his gaze seemed to snap.

She stepped back instinctively, but he caught her to him in his iron grasp, the hard-muscled arms closing around her like a vise. Her breath caught in surprise. For the first time, she felt the force of his strength. He could crush her without even trying.

"You want to know what's wrong?" He took her chin, forcing her to look at him. She could feel the angry pounding of his heart through the soft leather of his jerkin. "I'll tell you what's wrong. I want you so bad, I can't think straight. My body is on fire. I can't look at you without wanting to pull you into my arms. I can't touch you without thinking of running my hands all over you." Her eyes widened. The raw desire in his gaze shocked her. Never had she thought herself capable of driving a man to such extreme passion. "But that is only half the problem." His eyes had narrowed to slits, the lines around his mouth etched white. The dark stubble of his beard cast an ominous shadow along his hard, square jaw.

Whatever the problem, it didn't bode well for her. She tried to pull away, for the first time truly frightened, but he wouldn't let her go. His arms were like steel.

"You want to know what's really wrong, Elizabeth?" His face was only inches from hers. "I saw you kiss him." He spoke each word with damning precision.

She gasped. *He saw us.* He was angry with her because he was jealous. But it was the intensity that surprised her. One chaste kiss had driven him to the edge. "It was nothing," she said softly, trying to soothe his anger.

"Nothing?" He looked as though he wanted to shake her. "He asked you to marry him, didn't he?"

She didn't say anything. She didn't need to.

He swore and finally released her, raking his fingers through his dark hair. "God, you are actually considering him, aren't you?"

"Why shouldn't I?"

His fiery gaze pinned her. "Because you want me."

His flat tone infuriated her. "Wanting you isn't the issue." His eyes flashed, but she pressed on, heedless of the danger, needing to know his intentions. "If that is all that is between us—"

"Is that what you think?" His eyes locked on hers, his expression tight and fierce but brutally exposed. She could see the warning tic at his jaw and felt his body shudder with anger. "Did you think I would take you and not marry you? I might be only a guardsman, but I'm not without honor."

"I didn't mean to suggest—"

"Didn't you?" He gave her a piercing look. "I've no right, but I want you to be my wife more than anything I've ever wanted in my life. And the thought of you marrying him is tearing me apart."

Her heart slammed into her chest at the dark emotion in his voice. But before she could react, his mouth was on hers, claiming her, possessing her, giving proof to his words.

The dam had broken. All the pent-up anger, the pent-up emotion, the pent-up desire, rushed free with the force of a tidal wave, crashing over her and pulling her into the dark whirlpool of passion. Where the only thing she could think of was kissing him and drowning in sensation.

His mouth devoured hers with a hunger that could not be denied. As if she were the only one for him and he for her. As if he could claim her forever with the force of this one kiss.

It was a kiss not to persuade, but to compel.

She opened her mouth and he groaned, sliding his hand through her hair, cupping her head to bring her more firmly against him. And then his tongue was inside her, twining, demanding, urging her deeper and deeper. Harder and faster. Until his breath became her own.

The taste of him filled her. The wine. The spice. The heady masculine essence of him permeated her bones.

She melted against him, wanting to get closer, the power of his body a potent aphrodisiac. He was so tall and strong—all thick, heavy muscle and long, powerful limbs. A warrior. A protector. In his arms, she knew that nothing would ever harm her.

She trusted him. Completely.

The fierce pounding of his heart against hers drove her on. The rough stubble of his jaw scratched the tender skin around her mouth, but she didn't care. Her nipples hardened against his chest. His hand slipped around her bottom, lifting her to him.

She gasped, feeling the thick column wedged against her, and then moaned. Her body clenched hot with desire.

She kissed him with all of the emotion that she could not yet put words to. Kissed him with all she had, wanting it never to stop.

Patrick was mindless with lust, his hunger insatiable. The claret had dulled his reason. All he could think of was touching her, sinking into the heat, and making her his.

It was what she wanted, too. He knew it in the way her body went limp in his arms in sweetest surrender. She dissolved against him, warm and syrupy.

He lifted her in his arms and carried her to the large wooden table, laying her back so that her hips rested just on the edge. His breathing was as heavy as the pounding of his heart as his gaze swept over her flushed cheeks, her pink lips softly parted, her trusting blue eyes hazy with desire. Her skirts were tangled in glorious disarray, revealing part of one slim, shapely leg.

So beautiful. So ripe and ready for his touch. He'd never been more aroused in his life. He wanted to see her naked, splayed out before him. The only thing that prevented him from ripping apart her bodice was the crowd of people in the other room.

The possibility of discovery only heightened the urgency.

Slowly, he edged up her skirts and sucked in his breath. He jerked hard, the sudden pull in his groin almost unbearable.

She was naked from the waist down except for thin ivory stockings that stopped above her knee and pale blue stain slippers on her tiny feet. Her legs were exquisite—delicately shaped with flawless velvety ivory skin that he ached to touch. And between her legs was the sweetest soft pink flesh he'd ever seen. He couldn't wait to taste her. To slide his tongue between her honey folds, to take her shudders of pleasure against his hungry mouth.

His pause had given her time to be embarrassed, and she tried to push down her skirts.

He grabbed her wrist and held her gaze. "No. I want to see you. Don't you know how beautiful you are?"

Her cheeks flushed and he could see her uncertainty, but before she could protest he touched her, sliding his hand between her thighs. "God, your skin is so soft." He scraped his knuckles back and forth along the tender skin, and she shivered. "Like silk," he whispered huskily.

She tossed her head back, and the sexy little throaty sound she made told him that she'd forgotten her embarrassment. His fingers swept higher, closer, teasing her until she moaned. Until her body started to quiver. For him.

In their passion, if nothing else, they were equal.

He inhaled deeply, the faint feminine scent of her desire calling to him in the darkest, most primitive way. "Look at me, Lizzie," he demanded gently. "I want to see your face when I touch you."

Her eyes widened and her breath came quickly from between her lips in a little gasp, but she didn't look away. Her hips lifted reflexively against his hand.

It was he who closed his eyes with a groan of pleasure when he finally slid his finger inside her. The relief was too intense. She was so slick and soft. So hot. His finger dipped inside her, and she closed around him like a glove. He sank into her again and again as he pressed the heel of his hand against her mound.

The sweet little sounds she made forced his eyes open, and the look of utter rapture on her face nearly undid him. He was hard as a damn rock and ready to explode, throbbing to the point of pain. But he didn't stop.

He was going to make her come.

He watched her breath quicken, watched the confused restlessness cross her face, watched as her back arched and her hips started to press against his hand. He couldn't wait to get inside her. Couldn't wait to meet her passion with his own.

He could feel it come. Feel the pressure build and the need for release drown out everything else. Feel that sudden clench—the little pause at the very peak of pleasure—before she started to break apart.

It was the moment he'd been waiting for. He pressed against her mound a little harder, increasing the friction to make her pleasure more intense, and found the sweet little spot with his finger. Her eyes widened with surprise as the rippling contractions crashed over her. She cried out, and her sexy little sounds of pleasure made him pulse.

Watching her come was the most beautiful thing he'd ever seen.

He clenched hard to prevent himself from joining her. Not yet. . . .

He kissed her again, sliding his tongue deep in her mouth with long, demanding strokes as he fumbled with the ties of his breeches—not for the first time cursing the absence of his plaid—and positioned himself between her open legs.

The thick head of his cock nudged against her warm dampness, the contact almost shooting him over the edge in a burst of sensation.

He had her. All he had to do was close his eyes, toss back his head, and slide deep inside her. She was his for the taking, thoroughly seduced. If he took her, she would marry him. He knew it.

He didn't know what stopped him—perhaps the kernel of deep-seated honor awakened by Lizzie—but with a pained growl, he broke the kiss. His eyes searched her face. "Tell me not to stop, Elizabeth," he said tightly. "Tell me you want me."

She was still soft with her release, and confusion filled her eyes. "You know I do."

He looked right into her eyes, breaking through the haze, forcing her to think. "Then you'll marry me?"

"I . . ."

Hesitation was the only answer he needed.

She didn't want him. Not enough, anyway. What the hell had made him think he could compete with the likes of Robert Campbell? The moment was gone, fading into uncomfortable silence.

The fire in his veins turned to ice. He uttered a vile oath and pulled away from her. The pain in his groin was nothing compared to the tight burning in his chest.

She sat up, her face crumpled. "Don't you see? I'm trying to do the right thing."

He turned back to her, his face revealing no hint of the sting she'd given him. "So am I." And he was a fool. Honor had no part in his life—not anymore. This was about getting his clan's land back. Righting a grave injustice. He wasn't supposed to give a damn. His eyes narrowed on her. "But you had better make a choice soon, because next time I won't stop." He went to the door. "I hope your family realizes the sacrifice you intend to make for them. But if they love you as much as you say they do, I would think they would want your happiness."

She didn't say anything, just stared at him with a helpless look on her face. Achingly vulnerable. She appeared to be exactly what she was—a woman who had just come apart in his arms. She wanted reassurance, but he forced himself not to go to her.

He'd given her the best part of himself, and it hadn't been enough.

His eyes lingered over her swollen mouth, mussed curls, and disheveled clothing. "You might want to freshen up a bit before you return to Campbell," he said coldly. His eyes raked her face. "You have the look of a woman who has just been very thoroughly pleasured."

Chapter 11

❖

The next morning dawned cool and clear. The early mist had lifted, leaving a thick layer of dew clinging to the hillsides beyond the castle, shimmering in the morning sun like faerie dust sprinkled over a lush bed of emerald.

Like his eyes.

Lizzie shook off the image of his gorgeous face tight with passion as he'd stroked her. God, could she think of nothing else? Especially now, when her mind should be on other matters.

She stood in the *barmkin* with Robert, readying their horses for a hunt that Colin had organized for the handful of guests who'd remained after the feast. Colin had begged off at the last minute; apparently the ill effects of drink last night had yet to wane. In addition to Robert and herself, there was a handful of noblemen from the surrounding area and half a dozen guardsmen—they would take no chances. Patrick was in his usual place at the periphery, looking unbelievably handsome and completely unaffected by the events of the evening before.

His calm, solid presence proved an unexpected annoyance. If he was still angry, she couldn't tell.

How could he behave as if nothing had changed when it felt as if Lizzie's entire world had just been flipped upside down?

Never had she experienced anything like that. It wasn't just the closeness of their bodies, the intimacy of his touch, or the shattering pleasure he'd given her; it was something much more intense, much more powerful—the feeling of utter connection to another soul. For those few brief minutes in his arms, they'd felt as one. At least she thought so.

She was a romantic fool, always seeing things that weren't there.

Her eyes sought his again, but as he'd done all morning, he avoided her gaze. When their eyes happened to meet, he looked away. Her chest tightened with pain. His cold indifference stung even more than his terse words of the night before.

She'd angered him with her hesitation, but surely he had to know how difficult this was for her? He was asking her to put aside the learning of a lifetime. Duty had been ingrained in her from birth—it was part of who she was.

Instead, he'd looked at her as if she'd failed some unspoken test—as if she'd failed him.

Had she?

Every bone in her body had cried out to say yes to his proposal, to his body; only fear had prevented her. Fear of being hurt. She'd made the wrong decision once before based on passion, and she couldn't bear the thought of making another mistake.

Could she risk her heart again?

Her chest squeezed. She wondered if it was already too late.

Robert came up beside her. "Are you ready, my lady?"

She managed a smile. "Yes, if you'll help me up."

"Gladly," he said. Instead of moving the mounting block to her horse, he slipped his hands around her waist, lingering intimately, possessively. She caught a movement out of the corner of her eye. She didn't need to look to know that it was Patrick. She bit back a smug smile. Apparently he wasn't as indifferent as he appeared.

Robert must have caught it as well, because after he'd finished lifting her and settling her on her horse, he turned to address Patrick.

"You and your men are not needed today, Murray."
There was a note she hadn't heard in Robert's voice
before—a note of steel that belied his normally light-
hearted manner. "I will watch over the lady."

Patrick's face betrayed none of his resentment, but Lizzie
felt it fire the air between them. It was odd. Though Patrick
was as dark as Robert was light, there almost seemed to be
a resemblance between them.

"I'll be going along all the same," he replied matter-of-
factly. " 'Tis the laird's orders. The lady is not to be outside
the castle gates without her guardsmen."

Lizzie could sense the burgeoning tension between the
two men and knew that she'd better intervene before something terrible happened. She was painfully aware of the dif-
ferences in their station. Moreover, Colin would have
Patrick hung in chains for offending a guest—particularly a
guest of Robert's importance.

"I'm afraid Patrick's right, Robert. My brother was quite
clear about it." Her lingering anger at Patrick for his cold
treatment made her turn and give him a sugary sweet smile.
"But Patrick and his men won't interfere. I'm sure we'll
hardly know they are there."

She saw the sudden spark of anger in his eyes and knew
her barb had struck. Good. She was tired of being alone in
her uncertainty.

Her words had also served to mollify Robert. He spoke
to her, not to Patrick—a subtle reminder of Patrick's position. "Very well, but I hope they can keep up." He paused,
a sudden gleam in his eye. "As long as they are going along,
we might as well see what they can do with a bow." And
with that none-too-subtle challenge, they were off.

For the next few hours, they rode across the countryside
stalking their prey. But hunting deer and fowl soon became
secondary to the subtle battle being waged between Patrick
and Robert.

Lizzie felt as if she were at the center of a tournament

with two knights jousting for her favor. Each time Robert took a shot, Patrick would respond with one of his own. If Lizzie had been worried that Patrick would trounce Robert with his skill with the bow, it had been for naught. Surprisingly, they appeared evenly matched.

Appeared.

Though there was nothing Lizzie could point to, she had the distinct feeling that Patrick was holding back. But why?

As the unofficial competition continued, the tension between the two men mounted—as did her unease. She'd never seen Patrick like this before; he seemed not just dangerous, but unpredictable. There was a reckless edge to him that did not bode well.

Though she admitted a certain womanly thrill to have two fierce warriors fighting over her, she'd begun to fear that their game might take a very real turn. Thus, she was glad when the men decided to stop and water the horses at the edge of a narrow loch.

The break, however, would prove no rest for her unease. Indeed, the battle was only climbing toward its climax.

Patrick and a few of his men were sitting on a group of boulders nestled beside the loch, eating oatcakes and dried beef, when Robert ambled over toward them. Lizzie felt the back of her neck prickle. He was carrying his bow. He stopped right before Patrick, who looked up only when Robert addressed him. "You've fine skill with the bow."

Patrick nodded his head in acknowledgment.

Lizzie feared what was coming next. She hurried toward them, intent on intervening, but it was too late.

"But it's hard to measure the skill of a man in the wild," Robert said indolently. "I've always thought it better decided by contest, don't you agree?"

Patrick took a bite of beef, then chewed it slowly before responding, appearing to weigh his words carefully. "I find no better measure of skill than in the wild. Life or death seems a fair enough determinant. A contest serves no purpose but to satisfy pride."

Though there was nothing overtly wrong with Patrick's manner, it was also clear that he did not offer any deference to Robert for his station. He hadn't even bothered to stand up.

Whether it was because Patrick did not rise to the challenge or because he'd issued a subtle one of his own, Robert dropped the pretense of equanimity. His face turned florid, and the charming smile flattened into a hard, thin line. "Spoken like a man afraid to test his skill."

A harsh silence fell.

Lizzie sucked in her breath, not daring to let it out before Patrick responded. To a one, Highlanders were an exceedingly proud race, and Patrick, she knew from experience, was no exception. Inadvertently she'd pricked his pride before, but it was nothing like the blow just wielded by Robert.

Patrick's jaw flexed, the only outward sign of his rage. Though on the surface he was calm and controlled, Lizzie could tell that he was fighting to hold back some very fierce emotion. He stood to face Robert, a dangerous glint in his eye. "There is very little I fear, my laird."

The two warriors squared off against each other. Patrick held the advantage in size, though both men were tall and muscular. For a moment, she thought they might come to blows. She knew that this was about far more than skill with a bow and arrow; this was about her. Robert was trying to put Patrick in his place—force him to acknowledge that he reached too high.

Thinking to defuse the situation, Lizzie quickly stepped between the two men. "Should we start back?" she asked, her voice a tad too chirpy. "We've success enough for the day."

It was a testament to the dangerousness of the situation that both men ignored her.

She looked to Robbie, silently begging him to do something, but his face was every bit as implacable as Patrick's. Robert's challenge could not be ignored.

"We can't have a contest without a prize," Robert said. "Should we say a gold scepter piece?"

Lizzie bit her tongue to keep from objecting on Patrick's behalf. She knew he was not a man of wealth. A scepter was worth twelve pounds Scots, and more gold than Patrick might earn in a month. But it was also clear that the money was not the real prize. The real prize was her.

Obviously, they thought to leave her no say in the matter. As if she would let some ridiculous contest decide her fate. Her outrage, however, would have to wait.

Patrick shrugged indifferently. "It's your challenge."

Robert smiled. "Shall we say three shots, closest to the target?"

"What target do you have in mind?"

Robert turned to Elizabeth. "My lady, might we borrow one of your ribbons?"

She colored and lifted her hands to unwind one of the blue satin ribbons securing her hair, but Robert stopped her. "Please. Allow me."

His fingers brushed her neck as he carefully slid one from her hair, lingering for perhaps a moment too long. Had Patrick noticed? She peeked sidelong from under her lashes. The white lines etched around his mouth told her he had.

Ribbon in hand, Robert walked about a hundred paces away from their position and tied the length of blue satin around the nearest tree at about eye level. At that distance, only the thinnest line of color appeared around the tree. When he returned he said, "Any arrow that strikes blue will count as a point."

"And if they all land in blue?" Patrick asked.

Robert smiled. "A bold question, but I appreciate your confidence. In the unlikely event that all our arrows hit the ribbon, the closest to the knot wins. If you can see it from here."

Patrick's expression was grim. "I can see it."

Robert drew a line in the dirt with his dirk and then turned to Patrick. "We'll need a judge. Do you have any objection to the Laird of Dun?"

"Nay."

The Laird of Dun made his way down to the target, and both men took their positions behind the line. Robert would shoot first.

There was complete silence as he carefully threaded the arrow, lifted it to his eye, drew back his hand, and released it with a loud *swoosh*. It was followed seconds later by a solid *thump!* in the tree beyond.

Elizabeth could tell by Robert's reaction that it was a good shot.

Dun confirmed it. "Damn good shot, Campbell. Right through the ribbon."

Two more followed in quick succession, each better than the last. Of Robert's three shots, all had found the thin blue target.

His men cheered. It was an impressive feat of shooting. Robert didn't boast, but his eyes when he looked at her said it all: He'd won the prize—or at least he thought so.

Patrick's expression betrayed nothing of his thoughts as he strode to the line. But they were all well aware that if he missed the ribbon with any shot, he would lose.

He moved quickly and surely. With cool precision he prepared his shot, drew back his hand, the bulging muscles of his arms and shoulders the only indication of effort, and fired.

In spite of her unease, Lizzie was swept away by the excitement. Her heart pounded as she awaited the result. She could tell nothing from Patrick's stance.

Dun shouted excitedly, "Magnificent! A perfect shot, dead center, right through the knot."

The men cheered wildly.

Robert's face drained, along with some of his bravado. His gaze turned sharp as it fell on his adversary. "Impressive. A one-in-a-thousand shot."

More like one in a million, Elizabeth thought, staring at Patrick with unconcealed awe. She'd seen his presence on the battlefield and watched enough of his practice to know that he was an exceptionally skilled warrior, but nothing had prepared her for such a feat.

"I'd wager there aren't a handful of men in Scotland who can make that shot," Robert pointed out, echoing her thoughts.

It might have been an innocuous statement but for the effect it had on Patrick. If she hadn't been watching him carefully, she wouldn't have seen the muscles in his arms and shoulders tense slightly as his hand reached back to pluck his second arrow from the quiver. He threaded the bow again, but something had changed. His movements had lost their ease and grace.

Something was wrong. She was even more certain of it when he glanced in her direction, something he'd avoided most of the day. His eyes flickered with . . . regret? But why?

He lifted the bow and took steady aim. Right before he let the arrow fly, he made an almost imperceptible adjustment.

Her breath caught and her pulse raced. It felt as if she were standing in a dark tunnel where all she could hear was the sound of the arrow ripping through the air before it landed with a resounding thud.

She didn't want to look. She knew.

"You missed!" Robert shouted, unable to hide his glee.

And Robert had won.

"Aye," Patrick said, lowering his bow.

Disappointment washed over her. She was unable to

escape the feeling that he had just made some kind of choice. The pang in her heart throbbed. It didn't make sense.

She cast a surreptitious glance at him, but he'd already turned away, conceding defeat.

Whether it was just the contest or her, she didn't know.

Patrick hadn't missed a shot like that in years. But skill like his did not go unnoticed, and the last thing he needed was for Robert Campbell to start asking questions.

He'd sworn not to let himself be goaded by Campbell today, but he'd been unable to ignore the outright challenge. If Campbell wanted to let a contest determine the better man for Lizzie, so be it—he would damn well find out.

Patrick had wanted to win so badly, he could taste it. He'd allowed the thought of the satisfaction he would feel to wash over him—but only for a minute.

It had been one of the hardest things he'd ever done, but he'd forced himself to stand down. To do otherwise would invite too many questions.

But losing did not sit well. Pride warred with discretion. It was one thing to lose and another to do so purposefully. He told himself that it was only a simple challenge, that Lizzie had nothing to do with it, but he couldn't escape the feeling that he'd let her down. That in conceding the contest, he'd conceded much more.

That Robert Campbell was the better man.

Every instinct cried out to prove otherwise.

He dared not look at her. Weathering the wounded look in her eyes following his cold withdrawal last night was hard enough; disappointment would cut him to the quick.

He didn't know what the hell was wrong with him. He should have made love to her and had it be done. In allowing it to become personal, he'd lost focus on his goal. His moment of nobility had served only to give her the opportunity to reject him, making today's events even more difficult to swallow.

But he would have done just that if Campbell hadn't chosen that moment to bring up the one subject Patrick could not ignore.

The group had started to disperse after the anticlimactic end to the contest, but Robert, buoyed by his victory, had taken Lizzie by the arm and drawn her to the edge of the loch. Patrick was in no mood to hear the other man's subtle wooing and started to walk away, but one word stopped him in his tracks.

"Edinample is situated much on a loch like this."

Patrick's blood ran cold. *Edinample.* The castle built on the ashes of his family's old keep. His entire body drew tight with rage. Rage that boiled inside him with nowhere to go. He could feel it consume him. Hot and furious, it pounded in his head and roared in his ears.

Robert's voice carried toward him, every word fanning the flames. "I would like to take you there one day. My father only finished building the castle a few years ago, and it's quite beautiful. Though it could use a lady's touch."

Patrick snapped. The image of Lizzie making a home with Robert Campbell on Patrick's lands—the place where his parents had been murdered—was too much to withstand.

If Campbell wanted a damn contest, by Hades, he would have one.

Possessed by a recklessness more characteristic of his brother and rage born of resentment so deep that it seemed to penetrate his bones, Patrick pulled out his bow and walked back over to the line etched in the dirt.

"Campbell." His voice rang out like a thunderclap, drawing all eyes to him.

The other man turned, a puzzled expression on his face.

Patrick's mouth drew back in a feral smile. "You did say three shots, didn't you?"

Campbell's brows drew together. He eyed Patrick warily, as if it were a trick question—which it was. "Aye."

"Good." Patrick slid two arrows from his quiver. "I'll be taking my third after all." Carefully, he threaded both arrows on the string, aimed, and let them fly—two in one shot.

He heard the collective gasp, followed by a stunned silence.

"Jesu!" said one of the men, his voice tinged with awe.

God, it felt good. Too damn good.

The Laird of Dun rushed back toward the tree, the others trailing after him. Only Patrick, Lizzie, and his guardsmen stayed behind. His men didn't need to look—they knew what he'd done. And from the satisfied gleams in their eyes, he knew they were pleased with the result, no matter the increased risk to their safety. A MacGregor besting a Campbell was always a reason to celebrate.

Lizzie, however, was staring at him with a strange look on her face. Not surprised, but questioning—as if she were trying to put something together. He met her stare unflinchingly, part of him wanting her to know the truth. He was tired of deception. Tired of hiding, of being forced to live the life of an outlaw.

Would she understand? If it was only him to consider, he might be willing to take the chance. But his men's lives were in her hands as well.

The crowd had reached the tree. Loud cheers went up when they saw what he had done. Both arrows had pierced the piece of ribbon and landed on either side of his first.

He'd won.

But at what cost?

Chapter 12

❖

Patrick was about to find out.

Robert Campbell strode toward him, one of Patrick's arrows in his hand. From the rigid set of his shoulders Patrick knew he was furious, but the assessing glint in his gaze bothered him far more. The other man stopped before him, studying his face for a long time before saying anything.

"A definitive win," he conceded. Gracious, Patrick noted, even in defeat. Glenorchy's son was proving to be a difficult man to despise. *Hell*, the only mark against him that Patrick could find was that he was Glenorchy's son. A problem for a MacGregor, but not for a lass seeking a powerful alliance. "Next time I will have more care in choosing my words." He tapped the arrow in the flat of his hand a few times, the dull thud an ominous tolling. "Quite remarkable. I've only seen something like it once before."

Patrick held his body in check, though every instinct flared. He kept his voice politely questioning. "Aye?"

"Aye," Campbell repeated. He stared right into Patrick's eyes. "A few years back I saw the outlawed MacGregor chief shoot down two men with one shot. The Arrow of Glenlyon is regaled not only for his skill with a bow, but also for his unusual trick shots."

Patrick didn't betray a muscle at the mention of his cousin. " 'Tis no trick, just hours of practice. I've seen the MacGregor's skill as well—'tis where I got the idea."

Campbell's eyes turned hard and flat; perhaps there was

a bit of his black-hearted father in him after all. "You know the outlaw, then?"

He was treading disturbingly close to danger. Patrick figured that it was better to appear forthright and admit some familiarity. "We've met. My laird provided caution for him and his clansmen a few years back."

Campbell rubbed his chin thoughtfully. "Aye, I remember. I also remember that Tullibardine sheltered the scourge the last time the MacGregors were put to the horn."

"And was fined heavily for his actions," Patrick reminded him. " 'Tis not a mistake he will make again."

"Hmm . . ." Campbell weighed the arrow back and forth in his hands, then held it up to examine the shaft and fletching.

The feathers. Hell. The distinctive fletching was identical to that of his cousin. Patrick forced himself to breathe evenly. He noticed that Finlay had come up behind them and was following their conversation with keen interest.

Finally, Campbell handed it back to him. "The MacGregor is also said to have the finest arrows—he makes them himself."

"Is that so?" Patrick said with just the right amount of interest. His pulse raced, knowing the treacherous path this conversation was taking. "Then we have that in common. I make my own arrows as well."

Lizzie's interruption came not a moment too soon. "What are you suggesting, Robert? You can't think Patrick has anything to do with those vile men." She shuddered. "If not for Patrick and his warriors, I would not be standing here."

Vile men. He had no right to blame her after what his brother had done, but the revulsion in her voice ate at him nonetheless. What would she do when she found out the truth?

Could she ever accept him for what he was? A MacGregor. An outlaw. It was a question he'd never dared ask himself before, too wary of the answer.

Campbell gave him one more long look before turning back to Lizzie, apparently satisfied by Patrick's explanation. "Forgive me," he said. "Of course I've not forgotten the debt we owe to Murray here. I'm most grateful for his skills." A wry grin turned his mouth. "Even if it means I must lose a wager."

Lizzie, being Lizzie, immediately responded to his self-deprecating charm and moved to soothe his injured pride. "But you acquitted yourself quite impressively as well. I've never seen such exceptional shooting."

Bloody hell, Patrick thought with renewed irritation, staring at the hand she'd instinctively placed on the other man's arm. Even when he lost, Campbell managed to come out ahead.

The group of riders who made their way back to the castle was decidedly more subdued than the group that had set out a few hours ago. The dramatic conclusion to the archery contest seemed to have exhausted their excitement, and none more so than Lizzie. She couldn't believe what Patrick had done. Two arrows fired at one time and both with exceptional accuracy. Never had she seen anything like it.

He was magnificent. A champion to set any woman's heart aflutter—and she was certainly not immune.

From the first moment she'd met him, Patrick Murray had seemed an answer to her dreams. A romantic dark knight who'd ridden into her life slaying dragons. She wanted to believe in faerie tales, but her past had made her cautious. Part of her still couldn't quite believe he wanted her. Really wanted *her.*

But she knew that her time enjoying the attentions of two men was at an end; she had to make a decision before matters spun out of control. Next time, their confrontation might not be so civilized.

A contest to decide a lady's favor might make for a romantic story, but she had no intention of allowing her future to be decided by the vagaries of male pride. Just how she would decide, however, was equally unclear.

She felt a sharp tug in her chest. There was something else she'd been avoiding, but she owed her future husband the truth. Would either man still want her when they learned that she was not a maid?

She sighed, not looking forward to that conversation but knowing it must be had.

Having satisfied her obligations as hostess by conversing with each of her guests, she slowed her mount a bit to fall back with Patrick and his guardsmen, who were bringing up the rear.

Though he was often out of her sight, she knew the reverse was not true. No matter his brooding silence, he took his job as her protector seriously. The weight of his gaze followed her wherever she went.

If only she knew what he was thinking. Unfortunately, trying to discern his feelings was like trying to penetrate granite.

She drew up beside him. Robbie, who'd been riding on his other side, greeted her with a smile and then quickly fell back to talk with some of the other men, leaving them alone.

They rode in silence for a while. She eyed him curiously. He certainly was not acting like a man who'd won. But there wasn't much that made sense about his actions today.

"Are you going to avoid talking to me all day?"

He lifted one brow in a sardonic arch. "I wasn't sure you wanted to talk to me, after last night."

Her cheeks pinkened at his bold reference to the intimacies they'd shared. "If that's an apology—"

"I wasn't aware I had anything to apologize for. You didn't seem to have any complaints at the time."

Pink deepened to scarlet. He was purposefully trying to embarrass and discombobulate her. But she refused to be so easily diverted.

"That was quite a display today." He gave no indication that he heard her. "I've never seen anything like it. Your skill is remarkable." She pursed her lips together; his blank expression was infuriating. "That was a compliment if you didn't realize it."

His mouth twitched. "Thank you."

"It's strange, though . . ."

He turned to look at her. "And now I suppose you are waiting for me to ask why?"

She ignored his sarcasm. "It's strange that with skill such as yours no one has ever heard of you. Do you not participate in the Highland games?"

"As I told Campbell, skill is best determined on the battlefield. I have no use for contests."

"Hmm." He was unusually modest for a warrior. Most men weren't nearly so circumspect—particularly in the Highlands, where a warrior's reputation was as powerful a weapon as his sword and bow. Was there another explanation for his reticence? She straightened her back and looked him full in the eye. "Why did you purposefully miss your second shot?"

The dark slash of his brow cocked. "What makes you think I did?"

"I saw the small adjustment you made right before you fired."

"It's called aiming. Although I appreciate your confidence in my skills, I do occasionally miss the mark." He met her gaze. "What reason could I have to do so?"

She lifted her chin. "You tell me."

"There isn't one, but I thought—since you seem to be

doing such a good job of figuring everything out—that you might have something in mind."

His evasiveness left her even more convinced that he was hiding something. "Why would you want to conceal your skill?"

His mouth curved into a crooked smile. "I can hardly be accused of that."

She ignored his attempt to deflect the question. "That's just it. What I don't understand is why, after going to all the trouble to lose, you changed your mind."

He met her gaze, his green eyes hot with intensity. "Maybe I decided that the prize was worth the price."

Me. A shiver ran down her spine. The look in his eyes sent heat pouring through her veins. It was a look of possession. Of pure masculine desire. It claimed her so thoroughly that it took her a moment to find her voice. "What price? What would you possibly lose by winning?"

He didn't answer right away, turning his gaze back toward the path that wove through the forest, choosing his words with care. "I deemed it prudent under the circumstances."

Lizzie wrinkled her nose. "I don't understand."

His jaw flexed tight. He spoke through clenched teeth, extracting the words with difficulty. "Robert Campbell is a powerful man."

Lizzie tilted her head, studying the hard lines of his proud, handsome face. "And you thought besting him would bring retribution?" She shook her head. "You don't know Robert."

His gaze could have cut stone. "Not, apparently, as well as you do."

Her cheeks heated, though she'd done nothing to be ashamed of. But clearly he didn't like how readily she'd jumped to Robert's defense. "All I meant is that Robert is not the kind of man to begrudge another for winning. Surely you can see that now?"

He shrugged, his words pried reluctantly. "So it seems."

His explanation made sense but didn't ring completely true—not from what she knew of him. Patrick Murray wasn't the kind of man to back down from a challenge. "And that's the only reason?"

His gaze locked on hers. "I don't think I need to point out the difference in our positions."

The accusation in his gaze made her cringe.

She knew she should say something. She could see it in his eyes: He thought she was going to choose Robert.

Her heart tugged and then lodged in her throat. She wanted to say something.

But what could she say when he might very well be right?

It was past noon by the time they arrived back at the keep. Lizzie hurried inside to see to the midday meal for the guests, carefully avoiding Patrick's gaze.

He watched her go, anger and frustration simmering inside him like molten lava ready to explode. He didn't know whom to blame: Lizzie for her indecisiveness or himself for giving a damn.

He might have proved himself the better man on the battlefield, but it wasn't enough to change her mind. All he'd achieved was salving his own pride and making himself a target of unwanted attention. His skill had made the Campbells curious. And curiosity for a man at the horn could be deadly.

Danger lurked in every direction: from the surly guardsman Finlay to Auchinbreck to Campbell and now to Lizzie herself. It was only a matter of time before the truth was discovered.

He had to leave. Soon. He wouldn't unduly risk the lives of his men, not if it could be avoided. It was probably too early for Gregor to have returned from the Lomond Hills, but Patrick would make his weekly Saturday pilgrimage tonight nonetheless.

But first, he needed to clear his head. He was pulled as taut as a damn bowstring, besieged by conflicting emotions. His plan. Lizzie. Everything was unraveling around him, and he didn't know what the hell to do about it.

After seeing to his horse, he decided that a cool plunge in the loch would help cure what ailed him—in more ways than one. He was leaving the stables on his way to the barracks to fetch soap and a fresh shirt when the last man he wanted to see stepped in front of him.

"I was looking for you," Robert Campbell said.

"Apparently you found me." The flash of angry sarcasm was reflexive, if unwarranted. He sighed and then said more evenly, "What do you want?"

Campbell reached in the small pocket of his doublet and pulled out a gold coin. "I didn't get a chance to give this to you earlier."

Patrick shook his head. "Keep it."

The other man took umbrage at his refusal. "But you've earned it. I always pay my debts."

"I'll not take gold won by a play upon words. Consider us even."

Campbell studied him for a moment. "Are we even?" Patrick didn't have to guess what he meant. "I don't think so," Campbell said. "What can you give her?"

Patrick didn't want to hear this. He took a threatening step toward the other man and said in a low voice, "It's none of your damned business."

Campbell didn't move an inch, squaring off to meet his challenge. Patrick had to admire his courage—no matter how ill conceived. He didn't know what Patrick could do, and right now Patrick teetered close enough to the edge to show him.

"I'm making it my business," Campbell said boldly. "You reach too high. Elizabeth Campbell is cousin to one of the most powerful men in Scotland. What can you possibly think to give her?"

Patrick met the other man's gaze full force. "I can make her happy."

"Are you so sure of that? Look at this place. You would take her from this castle, to live where? In some small *bothan*?"

Patrick stared at him stonily. *If he only knew . . .* A hut would seem like a palace compared with some of the places he'd stayed.

"Elizabeth has been raised in luxury and wealth her entire life. She was born to be the lady of the keep. You are a guardsman. Do you realize what you'd be doing to her by marrying her? You'll be taking her away from everything she's ever known. Taking her away from this life. Taking her away from her family. Jesu, man, have you looked at her? She's a delicate rose, not sturdy Highland heather." He pointed to an old serving woman laboring with her buckets by the well. "Would you have her look like that?"

Patrick stared at the woman, feeling his stomach curdle. She wasn't old at all, he realized—probably of age with Lizzie—yet she looked ten years older. Her face was not creamy ivory, but freckled and leathered from the wind and sun. Thick boned and wide hipped, the woman had little trouble carrying the heavy buckets across her shoulders. How would Lizzie manage such a basic task? She was so tiny. So delicate. Her hands so smooth. Her skin so clear and unblemished. She'd never done menial labor in her life.

He swallowed the wave of bitterness that stuck in his throat. He had nothing to give her. He was an outlaw. A man without a home. Without land. Without a damn future.

Even if she could forgive him for the deception and accept his being a MacGregor, life at his side wouldn't be easy. If she suffered only a portion of the pain and hardship he and his clansmen had endured for years, it would still be too much.

A change of clothes and food in his belly did not alter the

fact that when he left Castle Campbell he would still be a hunted man. Her family would protect her, but he did not deceive himself that she would be completely insulated from the forces seeking to destroy his clan.

She would suffer.

Lizzie was wholly unprepared for the life he would give her. How would she survive? Too many of their women had died last winter—from starvation and an unusually harsh cold. Women who were much better prepared than Lizzie.

He would never let that happen. He would take care of her. Protect her. He met the other man's stare, feeling like a man grasping for a thread to save a sinking ship. "She will be well cared for."

Campbell studied him with an intensity that made his instincts flare. "What is it that you really want? You don't look like a man prone to tender feelings. Do you love her?"

He stiffened. That was none of his damn business. He cared for her. As deeply as it was possible for a man like him to care for anyone. But love . . . that had died in him long ago. What had started with the death of his parents had been completely destroyed by the years of seeing nothing but hatred, death, and sorrow. Patrick squared his jaw, feeling the tic at his neck jump. "Do you?"

Robert Campbell had seen too much. "I can."

Patrick flinched, unprepared for the force of the blow. Lizzie deserved someone who could love her. Not a man with scars too deep to heal.

He looked into Campbell's eyes, at his solemn, earnest expression, and saw what he'd been trying to avoid. Robert Campbell was a good man—the better man for Lizzie. He could give her everything Patrick could not. A safe home, a loving husband—the knife burning in his chest twisted mercilessly—a houseful of blond-haired, blue-eyed children.

"She deserves to be loved," Campbell continued. "Not

to be married for her tocher and advancement. You'll only bring her down."

He would give anything to be able to deny it. But it was the truth—partially, at least—no matter how ugly. "I care for her," Patrick said, unable to completely mask his bitterness. But it filled his mouth, his soul.

"Then don't make her choose," Campbell said softly, wielding his sword with deadly finesse.

"You're so sure she'll choose me?"

"Nay. But I'm not sure she won't, either." Campbell gave him a hard look. "Do what's right. Walk away."

"And what makes you so bloody sure that's the right thing to do?"

Campbell smiled, and it wasn't without sympathy. Patrick almost hated him for it. "I think you know it as well. It's what made you miss that second shot, isn't it?"

He turned and walked away. Campbell didn't say another word. He didn't need to. He'd said enough.

Patrick clenched his fists, his body tense with rage. He wanted to lash out. To strike at the truth that Campbell had forced him to confront.

He'd been living in a fantasy world. If he proceeded with his plan, not only would he be using her for his own ends, but in doing so, he would destroy her. If she married him, she would have nothing.

Part of him still didn't want to let her go.

Robert Campbell had everything that belonged to him. The injustice ate at him, but he wouldn't ruin Lizzie's life to save his own. She deserved better than to be the innocent instrument of his revenge. She deserved to be happy, in a warm, comfortable home, surrounded by the loving family she'd always wanted.

Innocent.

Like my mother.

The realization filled him with shame. His mother would be horrified to know what he was doing in her name.

Was he the kind of man to make war on women and children?

Do what's right. Walk away.

Patrick had made his decision. Campbell might have lost their battle, but he'd won the war. Patrick would leave. He cared for Lizzie enough to do what was right. He could not destroy her happiness for his own. His fight to restore his family's lands wouldn't end, but it would have to be won another way.

Though he'd known his plan was a gamble from the beginning, failure in any guise was difficult to swallow. But it was nothing to the pain that knifed through him at the thought of leaving Lizzie, forsaking the only woman he'd ever wanted for his own.

He felt as though he were being ripped apart. In giving Lizzie a chance at a happy future, he knew he was destroying his own and failing his clan. Doing what was right wouldn't put food on his people's plates or keep them warm in the dark of winter.

Was the happiness of one lass worth such a cost? He sure as hell hoped so or he would live with the consequences.

Chapter 13

❖

Alys removed a dark sapphire gown from the ambry and held it up to Lizzie, who was standing barefoot in her sark in the middle of her bedchamber, feeling quite superfluous. Making a face, the older woman tossed it atop the growing pile of discarded velvet and satin on Lizzie's bed—not that you could tell there was a bed under there right now.

Lizzie groaned, rolling her eyes with nonexaggerated hardship. "What was wrong with that one?"

"Too dark," Alys murmured, her head already burrowed deep in the ambry as she rifled through Lizzie's quickly depleting wardrobe. "All these deep jewel tones are harsh with your pale coloring."

"Perhaps you mean insipid?"

Alys's eyes sparked. "I mean pale. It is not the same, but you do need to be careful when choosing colors."

Apparently. Lizzie watched with bemusement as gown after gown was tossed out behind Alys, until she finally emerged holding a shiny satin gown of such pale blue, it looked almost like quicksilver. "Ah, let's try this one. It will be perfect with your luminous *pale* skin and eyes."

Lizzie shook her head and folded her arms defiantly—already anticipating the argument that was sure to follow. "I can't wear that. It was made for a masque at court a few years ago. I was supposed to be Demeter." The gown was cut in a simple Grecian style, with little embellishment and no ruff or lace to speak of. "It doesn't even have a farthingale."

"Bah. What care do Highlanders have for courtly fashion?"

Lizzie smothered a grin, observing the look of disgust on Alys's face. "In case you've forgotten . . . we aren't in the Highlands. *And* it's barely decent."

Alys stared at Lizzie with a devious smile on her face. "Not decent? Wonderful. Your braw laddies won't be able to take their eyes off of you."

Off quite a bit of her, if Lizzie recalled the tight, low-cut bodice correctly. She arched her brow. "Is that what this is all about?"

The older woman looked at her as if she were addled. "Of course that is what this is about. Time is a-wasting, my wee lassie. You'll not be able to keep those two dangling after you forever. Like two snarling wolves, they are. I heard what happened earlier on the hunt."

Lizzie blushed and quickly turned away to avoid the maidservant's eagle-eyed gaze. Instead she made a great show of yanking a brush through her damp hair. "They aren't dangling and nothing happened."

"Don't you play coy with me, Lizzie lass. Imagine," she said, sighing dreamily, "two handsome, strapping warriors like that fighting over you. It's so romantic."

Lizzie bit back a smile at Alys's expression. It *was* a wee bit romantic, but she didn't want to encourage her.

"Too bad you can't choose both," Alys said wickedly. "But I don't think Patrick Murray is of any mind to share." She shook her head. "Poor Robert will be disappointed."

Lizzie shot her a glare. "What makes you think I want Patrick? Robert Campbell is the man my family has chosen for me to marry."

Alys's eyes narrowed. "You don't love Robert Campbell."

"I don't love either—"

Alys's sharp gaze cut off her protest. "Elizabeth Campbell, I've known you since you were a wee lass. Don't try to deny that you are in love with that gorgeous man."

Lizzie blanched. *Am I in love with Patrick Murray?*

"You practically light up the moment he enters the room," Alys continued, unaware of how thoroughly Lizzie was reeling. "And he's every bit as much in love with you as you are with him." She shook her head. "Why is it that young people are so stubborn and foolish when it comes to matters of the heart?"

Lizzie didn't know what to say. Alys made it sound so simple. But it wasn't. It was complicated and difficult and tearing her apart. "Marriage has very little to do with the heart," she said softly.

"Don't be ridiculous. It has everything to do with it. Don't let what happened with that poppycock ruin your chance for happiness. Would you marry a man you do not love?"

Lizzie twisted her hands. "I have a responsibility to my family. I'm in no position—"

"You've done enough for your family," Alys said harshly. "They love you and want to see you happy." It was exactly what Patrick had said. There was a fierce look on the older woman's face that Lizzie had never seen before. "I've never regretted for a moment my decision."

Lizzie's brows wrinkled. "What decision?"

Alys pushed aside some of the gowns to clear a spot on the coverlet. She patted the space next to her for Lizzie to sit. "Did you know that my father is the Chief of Buchanan?"

Lizzie's eyes widened. "I knew you were a Buchanan, but you've never mentioned that the chief was your father."

"As a young girl, I was betrothed to Lord Aven, the Marquess of Hamilton's son." Lizzie let out an audible gasp, which she tried quickly to smother, but Alys only smiled. "Yes, he recently inherited an earldom, I hear. As you can imagine, my father was less than pleased when I decided to marry a young, landless Campbell guardsman instead. But from the moment I first saw my Donnan at court with your cousin the earl, I loved him." Her eyes sparkled. "Still do, as a matter of fact. And I've never regretted my decision for a moment."

Lizzie stared at her for a long time. It had taken some real courage to do what she had done. "And your father?"

Alys laughed. "Oh, he was angry at first, but he eventually recovered from the shock. My younger sister married well. He does still enjoy reminding me of all that I have forsaken, and I figure the least I can do for all the years of happiness he's given me is let him." Alys stood up. "Enough about me. That was a very long time ago. But if you aren't going to be late for dinner, we need to get you dressed. You'll need your pearls," she said, going back to the ambry. "And the matching circlet, I think." She pulled out a thin piece of gauze that matched the gown and could be worn in Lizzie's hair like a veil, then shook her head. "No. We want them to see your beautiful hair." Her hands lifted the heavy blond waves and then let them tumble down Lizzie's back. "Your hair is glorious, Lizzie. You must show it to your advantage."

"I'm not wearing that dress," Lizzie protested, but as before, her words fell on deaf ears. Alys was already searching for stockings and underskirts thin enough to wear under the gown.

"Try this," she said, holding out a thin satin underskirt. When Lizzie started to argue, Alys smiled sweetly. "Why don't we just see how that old dress looks on?"

An hour later when Lizzie left her chamber for the great hall, it was no surprise what she was wearing.

Patrick returned to the castle that night for the last time, his trip to the village having been for naught. Given what he'd decided, however, he was glad Gregor had yet to return from the Lomond Hills. He knew his brother wouldn't be as understanding as his men.

The guardsmen had taken the news of their leaving on the morrow with nary a word of protest. After today's events, they all realized they were living on borrowed time. Even Hamish had made only a halfhearted attempt to argue for taking Lizzie with them. It seemed the heart had gone out of their fight. Patrick was not the only one who'd fallen under the spell of Elizabeth Campbell. She'd charmed them all with her kind heart and serene beauty. He shook his head. Look at them now: a pack of ruthless MacGregor warriors brought to heel by a mere wisp of a lass—and a Campbell one at that.

His men had gone to the hall to join in the evening entertainment, but Patrick was in no mood for merriment. He returned to the barracks, welcoming the solitude. With only one more night to fill their bellies with food and drink their fill of the Campbells' wine and ale, it would be a while before anyone returned.

He started gathering his meager belongings in a pile and then fitting them into the leather bags he would tie to his saddle. He'd been a fool to reject Campbell's gold. Pride wouldn't keep him warm or his belly full in the coming winter. He would see about procuring some food from the kitchens in the morning. It would need to last them a while—the ride deep into the Lomond Hills to find the rest of his clan might take some time. Though his mind was already on the road ahead of him, he hadn't figured out how he was going to say good-bye to what he left behind.

No matter how tempting it might be to simply leave, he knew he could not do that to her. Lizzie deserved some kind of explanation—if only he could find the words to make her understand that what he was doing was for the best.

Leaving a note wasn't an option. An education was just

one more thing he'd lost when his parents had been killed and his clan broken.

He was still weighing what to do when the door opened and the decision was wrested from him.

Lizzie stood silhouetted in the doorway, the torch in her hand illuminating her stricken face as she stared at the bags and belongings strewn across his pallet.

Every muscle in his body went taut. He froze, as though he'd been knocked senseless, utterly transfixed by the ethereal beauty of the fey creature before him. She looked like a figment of a dream, her flaxen hair and silvery gown shimmering like quicksilver in the flickering flame. An angel.

His face darkened. Except that her gown was anything but angelic.

What the devil was she trying to do, drive him mad with longing?

His eyes slid over her and came back to rest where they had started: on the sweet round breasts displayed to mouthwatering perfection in a gown that revealed far more than it concealed. She might as well have been wearing a damn night rail. It was no more than a wisp of cloth; he could see the curve of her hips, the round of her bottom, the long, slim lines of her legs. Heat pounded through his body, surging hard through his veins. Lust. Hot, demanding lust throbbed in his suddenly too-tight breeches.

A wave of possessiveness came over him, almost frightening in its intensity. *Mine*. The thought of another man looking at her was almost enough to make him change his mind about leaving.

He turned his back on her as he fought to temper the instinct to toss her down on the rough pallet, rip that flimsy dress off her until she was naked beneath him, and ravish her senseless. And then hold her warm, soft body against his and drink in her sweetness.

"What are you doing?" she asked.

He flinched at the sound of her voice, hearing the disbelief tinged with panic. He wanted to go to her. To hold her in his arms and tell her everything was going to be all right.

But it wasn't.

He clenched his jaw, realizing that this was going to be harder than he'd ever imagined. He bent over the bed to continue his packing, his movements harsh. "What it looks like I'm doing, packing."

He heard the door close and then the tap of slippered footsteps approaching tentatively. His pulse raced as her soft feminine scent hit him, coiled around him, and wouldn't let him go.

"How long will you be gone? A few days?"

He took a deep breath and stood up, meeting her wide-eyed gaze, his muscles vibrating for want of her. "Nay, Lizzie, I'm leaving for good."

Her heart felt yanked out from under her.

"Leaving?" Lizzie echoed dumbly, her thoughts scattering like petals in the wind. *For good.* When he hadn't showed up for the evening meal, she'd been apprehensive, but never could she have anticipated this. "No! You can't go."

He arched a dark brow, an unspoken challenge.

"I mean . . . I . . . we need you here."

His face shuttered, and she knew she'd said something wrong.

"You have your brother"—he gave her a hard, penetrating stare—"and Campbell. It should be easy enough to hire more guardsmen. There are plenty of broken men to be found eager for work."

As if he were so easily replaceable.

This couldn't be happening.

"But what about us?" Her voice was barely above a whisper. "I thought . . ."

His eyes were hard and flat. They belonged to a stranger. "Campbell can take care of that as well."

Lizzie made a small choking sound, stunned by his coldness. How could he talk to her like this? After what they'd shared, he was just going to walk away and never look back. Was she so insignificant to him?

I thought he cared for me.

She put her hand over her mouth and tried to swallow. Dear God, had she made some horrible mistake . . . again?

His jaw was set in a hard, determined line. He looked so remote. So alone. As if he didn't need anyone in the world. Certainly not her.

Never had she imagined that the ruthlessness she'd witnessed on the battlefield would be directed toward her.

She turned away, unable to look at him any longer. She fought to breathe. *One. Two.* She forced air in and out and tried to prevent the hot ball of hurt from swallowing her up.

She had to get out of here before she disgraced herself by bursting into tears. And she would have done just that if she hadn't chanced to glance up at him one more time.

His eyes gave him away. Tormented. Pained. Filled with such naked longing, it took her breath away.

He *did* want her. With an intensity that matched her own.

In that one unguarded moment, she recognized the truth of her own heart. From the first moment he'd burst through the trees, she'd sensed something special. Not just physical awareness, but a sense of connection so strong and deep, it seemed as if it had always been there.

I love him.

This big, strong warrior whose implacable exterior masked a tortured soul.

She'd been attracted to his handsome face, to his strength, courage, and natural authority, but it was the wounded man inside who had captured her heart.

He needed her.

She yearned to soothe his sadness. To heal him with the balm of her love. Just as he had given her the courage to risk her heart again. John Montgomery was in the past. This was different. She needed to trust herself—and him.

Robert might be the "better" choice, but there was something about Patrick that could not be measured by objective criteria, it simply was. He might have been born a guardsman, but he had the makings of a fine chieftain. Leadership ran in his veins, and it was up to her to unlock it with opportunity.

Alys was right. She would never regret marrying the man she loved. Her family would understand. They would have to.

The unexpected news she'd received this evening gave her even more cause to hope. Jamie had written to tell her of his impending marriage to Caitrina Lamont. Though by the time she received the letter they would already be married, her cousin demanded her presence at Dunoon as soon as possible.

She still couldn't believe it—her brother . . . married. Colin had been furious. From what she could tell, the Lamonts had recently been accused of harboring MacGregors, and the poor girl had lost her entire family and been left virtually penniless. From Jamie's note, it appeared that he felt some sort of responsibility. But it also meant that she would not be the first in her family to make an inopportune match.

Now that she'd made her decision, she thought of all she might have unknowingly forsaken. This was what Meg and Flora talked about. Love so strong you would die for it—or without it.

Whether destiny or fortune, she didn't know, but she thanked God for having Patrick Murray appear on the road that day.

Even as the truth of her feelings became clear, however,

she could not savor the moment, not while he was trying to push her away.

She straightened her back and looked him square in the face. "So just like that, you are going to leave? No explanation. Nothing."

He stood stone still, but every inch of his body seemed set on edge. She crossed the room, stopping only when she stood right before him. Close enough to inhale the spicy masculine scent of him. He wouldn't look at her, but she could feel the tension radiate from him, hot and heavy. The air between them seemed charged, ready to fire.

She tilted her head back to look up at him. His chiseled features seemed even sharper, harder. The tic below his jaw pulsed. His fists clenched and unclenched, as if he were fighting for control. Danger swept over her skin in a prickly sheen of awareness. He looked every inch the fearsome warrior pushed to the edge.

But she did not heed the warning and leaned closer, allowing her breasts to brush his chest. "I thought you wanted to marry me?"

Every muscle tensed at her intimate touch. His eyes flashed shards of green fire. "What the hell do you want from me?" he growled through clenched teeth. "I'll not sit here and watch you marry another man. God's blood, Elizabeth, I'm not made of stone."

His very ferocity gave her courage. *He did care.* Boldly, she put her hand on his chest and felt him flinch beneath the soft leather of his jerkin. "You're not?" she asked, skimming her hands over the heavy slabs and sharply defined muscle that felt as unyielding as stone. "You feel like it." When she reached the opening, she slipped her hand beneath the leather to the thin linen of his shirt, breathing in the hard, warm skin underneath.

He practically hissed.

She peeked at him from under her lashes, wanting to press tiny kisses along the rigid lines of his jaw until his resistance softened. As she leaned against him to whisper in his ear, damp tendrils of slick dark hair brushed against her nose and mouth. The faint scent of soap and warm male cascaded through her in a heady rush. "I'm not marrying another man," she said softly.

His muscles flexed under her fingertips. She could feel the hard pounding of his chest, but he made no move to enfold her in his arms.

Lizzie felt a moment of uncertainty. She'd just as good as told him that she'd chosen him. Shouldn't he be holding her tight against his chest and pressing kisses on her head? On her mouth?

Instead, he clasped his hand around her wrist and forcibly set her away from him. "You should."

The look in his eyes pierced her newfound confidence. Stricken, she felt the happiness seep out of her. "What do you mean?" Her voice wobbled. *Please, don't stammer.* She took a deep, ragged breath. "Don't you wish to marry me?"

He swore, and the tiny lines etched around his mouth turned stark white. "God damn it, Elizabeth. You're not making it easy. I'm trying to do the right thing here."

"Right thing?" Her eyes raked his face. She could feel her chance at happiness slipping away. The prospect of unrequited love loomed like a dark cloud. "Why is it right that I marry Robert?"

He turned from her, taking a few steps away as if to clear his mind. "There are things . . . there are things about me that you don't know."

She put her hand on his arm. "Then tell me. I want to know everything about you."

He wanted to. She could see the turmoil on his face, but he shook his head. "I can't."

She dropped her hand. "Or won't," she said tonelessly.

"Or won't," he agreed.

Disappointment fisted in her belly at his rejection. But

she heard the sadness in his voice and knew that even if he would not tell her its source, she could not just walk away.

"It doesn't matter. I know all I need to know. All that is important. I know the kind of man you are: strong, kind, and honorable to the core."

A bark of pained laughter shot from him. "You don't know me at all. Would that I were half the man you think me." He shook his head, no longer fighting it, as if her words had made it easier on him. "No. Marry your Campbell, Lizzie. He will give you the life you deserve. I have nothing to offer you. No position, no wealth, no fine castles."

"None of those things matter."

He looked at her as if she were a fool. "Only someone who has never known otherwise would think that."

Her cheeks burned. "All I meant was that I have those things already. I do not need to marry Robert to get them."

He stiffened, and she feared she'd pricked his pride again. No man wanted to have his wife provide for him. How could she explain that without him by her side nothing else mattered? He started to turn away from her, and her heart dropped.

I'm losing him.

She clasped his arm again. "Please." His eyes met hers. She opened her mouth, but no sound would come out. She had to tell him how she felt, but the idea of leaving herself so exposed, so vulnerable, terrified her. A cold sweat dotted her skin. Fear churned in her stomach, and for a moment she thought she might be ill.

She was a coward. But if she didn't take a chance, she would never know, and that would be infinitely worse. "I can't marry Robert Campbell."

"Why?"

She wanted to close her eyes and hide, but she forced herself to say, "I don't love him." She heard his sharp intake of breath, and his gaze intensified. "I . . ." She took a deep breath and let it out in one fell swoop: "I love you."

The silence that followed was as loud as thunder and as painful as a thousand bolts of lightning striking her heart. She stared at him, willing him to say something—anything. But he stood motionless, as if turned to stone, and didn't say a word. Not one word.

Her heart started to thump and her breath quickened as horror slowly drained over her—as thick and heavy as the mud that she'd slipped in that hideous day.

I was wrong.

She looked away, wishing she were anywhere but here. In this warm, dark room, inches away from the man she loved who didn't want her.

"Lizzie . . ."

She tried to breathe through the knife plunged deep in her chest. "You don't need to say anything. I"—she choked— "just . . . thought. It seemed"—tears burned in her throat— "I thought you wanted me." God, it hurt. The pressure in her chest was unbearable. She couldn't breathe. Her voice came out in a ragged whisper. "Obviously I made a mistake."

He swore and grabbed her arm, pulling her against him in one harsh movement. More furious than she'd ever seen him. "You didn't make a mistake. God, can't you feel how much I want you?"

Shocked by the violence of emotion she'd unknowingly unleashed, she nodded and was suddenly very conscious of the hard column of steel thrust against her stomach. He *did* want her. And if the size of him was any indication, badly. But was it more than lust? She gazed up at him through blurry eyes. "Then why are you doing this?"

"For your own good. You'll be better off with Campbell."

Her heart soared. He wasn't rejecting her, he was only trying to do what he thought was best for her. *Honorable*

to the core. She lifted her hand and cupped his cheek, savoring the rasp of dark stubble on her palm. "Shouldn't I
be the judge of that? Am I to have no voice in deciding my
own future?"

"Elizabeth . . ." His voice sounded tortured.

"Do you still want to marry me?"

His smoldering green gaze burned deep into her soul.
"More than anything in this world."

In his eyes, she saw the truth. *He cares for me.* A wide
smile broke through her shimmery tears. "Then it's decided."

His gaze fell to her mouth, and she thought he was going
to kiss her, but instead he dropped his hold and took a step
back. "I can't do this," he said quietly. "It's wrong."

She saw the steely determination in his eyes and knew
that his mind was made up. A low rumble started from
somewhere deep inside her and built until her entire body
seemed to shake with it.

Just when she'd given up hope, she'd found the man
she'd always dreamed of, a man who wanted her for herself. She'd be damned(!) if she would let him walk away
out of some overprotective male sense of honor.

Lizzie had always been the quiet one. The serious, bid-
dable girl who did what was expected. Well, she was tired
of hiding in the shadows and letting life pass her by. Not
this time. This time she was going to reach out and take
what she wanted, to Hades (the blasphemies were really
flowing now!) with the consequences.

She met steel with steel, her gaze every bit as fierce and
determined as his. "I'm afraid I don't agree."

She felt a supreme moment of satisfaction at the slight
wariness that appeared in his gaze—wariness that turned
to full-blown alarm after she stormed back over to the
door, lowered the bar, and turned around to face him.

There was only one way to bend steel, and that was with
fire . . . lots and lots of fire.

"What are you doing?"

She arched a brow. "I would think that is fairly obvious to a man of your perception." She moved back toward him. "We appear to have a difference of opinion, and I think it is better that we are not disturbed while we sort it out."

She pulled off the thin beaded shawl she'd draped around her shoulders and dropped it on the pallet where he'd stacked his belongings. It seemed to land with the resounding thud of a gauntlet. To the winner went the spoils. And this was not a battle she intended to lose.

His hot gaze washed over her, soaking up every inch of bare skin—especially the bare skin around her breasts. Her nipples tightened under his scrutiny. His eyes flared. The pulse at his neck twitched dangerously.

This dress really was shameless. But from the way his eyes gorged hungrily on the round swells of flesh and the deep cleft in between, she had to admit that perhaps Alys was right. Lizzie would never be a raving beauty like her cousin Flora, but that didn't mean she couldn't emphasize her attributes.

"And how do you propose we sort this out?" His voice was wonderfully hoarse.

She smiled, a devilish glint in her eyes. "Oh, I'm sure we can figure something out." Her gaze dropped to the hefty bulge in his pants.

Dear God.

Her mouth suddenly went dry. Her bravado faltered. She wasn't nearly as confident as she pretended.

Unconsciously, she licked her bottom lip. If possible, the prodigious bulge seemed to grow a little bigger. He appeared to be in a great deal of pain, but Elizabeth was discovering that she had a rather ruthless streak when it came to this man.

She approached him slowly, enjoying the way his body tensed as she drew near, his intense, predatory gaze following her every move. She felt a rush of heat. For the first time in her life, she felt the power of being a desirable woman. It gave her just enough courage to go on.

She slid against him, molding her body to his. The sizzle of contact startled them both. She loved the hard press of his body against hers, feeling every bulge, every cord of hard muscle. Her body flushed with heat, concentrating in tingling awareness where they touched.

He made a choking noise in the back of his throat—half groan, half pain. "You don't know what you are doing."

His voice was tight—very tight. She could feel the pressure reverberating inside him. The powerful muscles in his arms and shoulders tensed.

She tilted her chin. "I know exactly what I'm doing."

His eyes bored into hers, hot and full of passion. "There will be no going back. Once I make you mine, I will never let you go."

Her heart clenched at the possessive tone in his voice.

She slid her hands around his neck and rose to her tiptoes—he really was frightfully tall—her body stretched against him. The evidence of their desire rose between them. It was impossible to deny in the hard peak of her nipples driving into his chest and the rigid length of his erection held taut against her stomach. And the heat. So much heat. It seemed to meld them together.

"Good," she said. "I don't want to go back. I only want you." She pressed tiny kisses along his jaw, savoring the hint of salt on his skin and the scratch of his jaw against her lips. She wanted to inhale him. Devour him. Lick every inch of his incredible body.

His heart pounded furiously against hers, and she knew he was holding himself on a very tight rein.

She trailed soft kisses along his jaw until she came to the sensitive place below his ear, and then she drew little circles with her tongue.

He started to shake but still would not touch her. His

will was formidable, but so was hers—and she'd finally found a weakness in the steely armor of this fierce warrior. She had no intention of relenting now.

She rubbed against him a little more, raking her nipples against his chest, the friction sending delicious little fissures of pleasure down her belly, concentrating between her legs. She closed her eyes, wallowing in the sudden rush of heat and dampness, feeling the insistent clench of desire.

His powerful erection pressed intimately against her, teasing her with possibility. Her mouth was right on his ear, and she spoke her wicked thoughts aloud. "I want you inside me."

That was it. With a violent growl, he snapped. "Damn you, Elizabeth."

His mouth fell on hers in a ravaging kiss. A kiss that reached down to her soul, claiming her completely. Not wasting any time, he scooped her up and carried her toward an empty pallet.

Chapter 14

❖

His body was on fire. Patrick had never been more aroused in his life. His shy, sweet little Lizzie had turned into a bold seductress. She could bring him to his knees like this. Hell, she already had.

All his honorable intentions were forgotten in the space of one long heartbeat.

I want you inside me.

He'd almost come right then, his body already pushed to the edge by the seductive press of her sweet little body against his. His ironclad control shattered into fragments. All he could think about was tossing her down, twining her legs around him, and thrusting up high inside her until the demons roaring in his head quieted. Until these powerful, terrifying emotions unleashed by her tender declaration let him go. Until the burning in his chest stopped.

She loves me. God. He didn't want her love. It was too great a responsibility. He would only hurt her. But for one reckless moment he'd been moved beyond words, humbled by her gift. Almost . . . happy.

His kiss was brutal, punishing, for making him feel like this. He was desperate. Out of control. Never had he experienced this kind of irrational urgency. He *needed* her. Like a starving man needed food. Like a dying man needed salvation. Now. Before everything went to hell. Before she could change her mind.

Though she seemed in no danger of that. She met him full force, plying his carnal strokes with thrusts and parries of her own. The sensation of her sweet, silky tongue sliding against his, delving in his mouth with eager abandon, drove him wild.

He drank her in. Her heat. Her sweetness. God, he couldn't get enough of her. His tongue circled hers, twining and probing in an anxious rhythm that echoed the pulsing of his erection as he carried her toward the bed.

Her soft little sounds of pleasure were only increasing his agony. Her bottom nudged the heavy head of his cock as he held her, and he thought he was going to explode. The temptation to wrap her legs around his waist and plunge into her heat was almost overwhelming. It would be so easy to lift her skirts and smooth his hand over the velvet softness of her naked bottom, lifting her over him as the weight of her body took him deeper and deeper.

Oh, God. The heavy tug in his groin was unbearable.

What the hell was the matter with him? He was acting like a damn barbarian.

He *was* a damn barbarian. He wanted to take her over and over. Make her come until she could think of no one else but him. Until he proved that she truly belonged to him.

He broke the kiss long enough to lower her to the pallet, forcing himself to slow, to tame the beast raging inside him. Cursing the absence of his plaid, he divested himself of his jerkin, shirt, and boots and lay down next to her.

The soft press of her body stretched out against his was too much. He wanted to sink into her, to feel all that softness envelop him in its healing embrace. Unable to keep his hands off her for a second longer, he slid his palms down her waist and over her hips, molding every sweet curve through the thin gauzy fabric.

He felt like a bairn with a roomful of sweets. He didn't know where to start, but he was going to eat every sugary piece. Would she melt in his mouth? Dissolve into a warm puddle of syrup?

He scooped up her breasts in his hands. The soft round flesh spilled over his fingers, more lush than he ever could have imagined—and he'd done plenty of that late at night when the discomfort in his loins became unbearable.

Did she touch herself and think of him? He clenched his jaw to fight the surge at the thought of her pale soft hands pleasuring herself while he watched.

Barbarian.

His mouth slid over her jaw and down her throat, her skin as smooth and sweet as cream. "God, you taste incredible," he murmured, his tongue sliding a teasing path along the edge of her bodice. "I want to lick every inch of you." He lifted her breasts to his face and nuzzled her lightly, inhaling the warm feminine scent in the deep cleft. His thumb grazed the turgid peak through the silky cloth. "Your tight little nipples." He looked into her eyes intently. "The soft skin above your thighs."

Her eyes lit with surprise and then with something far more dangerous . . . curiosity. This woman could unman him.

She squirmed a little in his arms, her impatience fueling his hunger.

His fingers worked the ties of her gown, loosening it enough to ease it down past her shoulders and lift her breasts over the tight confines of her stays, at last revealing her bare chest to his greedy gaze.

He sucked in his breath, letting it out in short, ragged gasps. He loved breasts—big, small, and everything in between—but Elizabeth's were nothing short of spectacular. Mind-blowing. Bury-your-face-and-never-want-to-leave. Every man's erotic fantasy. Lush and round, firm and high, topped by small nipples the same soft pink of her lips. "You're beautiful," he groaned.

He almost didn't want to touch her. The porcelain skin looked so delicate and unblemished—too fine for his big, rough hands. But he couldn't resist. He cupped her, and the sensation of all that warm, silky skin under his callused palms forced another groan as he caressed the velvety softness with his hands and fingers.

She didn't break, she shuddered. Arching into his hand, into his mouth, threading her fingers through his hair insistently. He kissed her gently at first, brushing his lips over the smooth, creamy skin, savoring the taste of her on his tongue. He flicked his tongue over her nipple, using the heat of his breath on her damp skin to increase her pleasure. She beaded and tightened, the petal-pink skin darkening to mouthwatering raspberry.

He tamped down the reflexive surge. Hell, he could come just looking at her.

He couldn't wait any longer and took the pink pearl between his teeth and tongue. She moaned, a low, throaty sound that called to him in the most primitive way. God, she was ripe. Like a juicy peach that he couldn't wait to bite into.

He sucked her harder. Deeper. Circling her nipple with his tongue as his hand eased up the edge of her skirt.

She was so incredibly responsive. His hand slid up the inside of her thigh. So incredibly soft. His finger swept her sex, and he jerked, his body weeping to feel the slick heat. So incredibly ready.

He wanted nothing more than to strip her naked and devour every inch of her. To press his lips and tongue against her until she shattered. But that would have to wait; they had a lifetime to explore their passion. Though she'd taken the precaution of barring the door, his men could return at any time or someone could come looking for her.

He teased her with his fingers until her hips began to press against his hand. Until the tiny whimpers increased in urgency. Her hands were on his shoulders, on his arms. Sculpting his muscles, clutching him wildly, begging.

She was going to come.

Oh, yes. He swelled hard and hot.

He circled her nipple with his tongue, and when he felt her start to break apart, he sucked her deep into his mouth and pressed his finger against her sensitive spot. She cried out, arching her back against his mouth as her body clenched around his finger with a wave of rippling contractions.

He couldn't take his eyes off her face. She was so beautiful like this, it made his chest ache. Head tossed back. Cheeks flushed. Lips parted. Her raw passion roused him to the breaking point.

He couldn't wait another minute. He needed to be inside her.

He unfastened his breeches, and his cock sprang free. Big and hard and thick with blood. A pearly drop glistened on the tip.

Her eyes widened.

Before she could think about it, he moved over her, rubbing his sensitive head in her damp heat. The groan that went through him shook his entire body. He gritted his teeth against the urge to plunge deep inside. To relieve the unbearable pressure. She was so wet that it was killing him to go slow. He'd been waiting too long for this.

"Please," she whispered, looking into his eyes, as if reading his mind. "I need you now."

The heartfelt desire humbled him as nothing before. He could feel something grip him. An emotion so unfamiliar, he didn't know what to call it. But he knew that the need he had for this woman had nothing to do with lust. She was hope to a dying man.

He looped his arms under her legs and positioned himself at her entry. Slowly, he began to push inside.

He groaned, the pleasure too intense. The tight clench of her body fisted around him like a velvet glove. "God, you feel incredible." So amazingly tight. The urge to thrust, to sink into her full hilt, teased the edges of his consciousness.

But he needed to have care for her innocence. Except

that nothing about her responses to him felt innocent. In-experienced, yes, but not innocent. No maidenly shock. No fear. No pain.

She lifted her hips, urging him deeper, and his entire body clenched with restraint. He was too big and she was too small. But nothing in her expression suggested that he was hurting her. Her eyes were half-lidded, hazy with passion.

"I don't want to hurt you."

Her eyes flickered open, meeting his gaze. He detected a flash of anxiety before she shook her head. "You won't hurt me, Patrick."

There was something in her voice . . . He eased into her inch by inch, until he reached the point of no return. Holding her gaze, he thrust, and her body welcomed him without resistance.

Her cry was one of satisfaction, not of pain.

He paused, feeling a moment of surprise, but when she circled her hips he was sucked into a vortex of pleasure so intense that nothing else mattered.

Lizzie was weak with pleasure, her body tingling from the force of the release that he'd teased from her with his skilled fingers—and his mouth. She'd never realized her breasts were so sensitive, but when he'd clasped his lips around her nipple, shards of white hot pleasure had shot through her in a hail of flickering light.

But it was nothing to the sensation of him pushing inside her.

She had to admit that she'd experienced a fleeting moment of doubt when he'd opened his breeches. He was a big man. Thick and long, the heavy round head stood a few inches past his belly button. He was at least twice as big as John—and that had hurt initially.

John. She should tell him. . . .

But the moment she felt him rub against her sensitive

flesh, all other thoughts were gone. She wanted to take him into her body. To love him. To give him pleasure and find it in return.

Her body dampened, beckoning him in the most intimate way. The concentration of sensation started all over again as his plump head caressed her, teased her, roused her passion to a frenzied storm.

Until her body was wet and hot with need.

And when she didn't think she could take another minute of his exquisite torture, he entered her, penetrating inch by incredible inch. Stretching her. Filling her.

And with one last plunge, completing her.

Her body sighed, taking him in as if she'd been waiting for this her whole life.

Perhaps she had.

God, she could feel him. Her body tingled around the rock-hard column that pulsed with life inside her. She was a puddle of sensation, ready to be swept away in a maelstrom of passion and desire.

Then suddenly he stopped.

He knew.

It had always been her intention to tell him, but there hadn't been time. A flash of panic penetrated the haze. What if he didn't want her? Their eyes met, and she saw the flicker of surprise. The silent question. But not blame. Not anger.

Relief crashed over her in a warm, shimmering wave of acceptance. The last barrier between them was gone, and Lizzie gave herself over to the power of their lovemaking.

She circled her hips and he started to pump. Slowly at first. Long, languid strokes, sliding in and out with deliberate purpose. Her body clutching around him the entire way—trying to hold on.

He kissed her again. Her mouth. Her breasts. He took one nipple in his mouth, dragging it between his teeth. She moaned at the sensation of his silky lips closing over her.

Laving her with the heat of his mouth and tongue as his arousal stirred her to a wicked frenzy. To a peak such as she'd never known.

She clutched him as if she would never let go, running her hands over his heated skin, over the slabs of tightly defined muscles in his arms and chest, feeling them taut and straining under her fingertips, loving the feel of his hard, powerful body on top of her . . . inside her.

Propped up over her, he was magnificent, his shoulders impossibly wide and powerful. Tight bands of muscle lined his stomach with every thrust. Just looking at him made her feel weak all over. His dark, silky hair slid forward across his handsome face, tight with the effort to control.

But she didn't want control. She wanted to see the depths of his need for her, the depths of his very soul. She wanted all of him.

"Harder," she urged him on. "Don't hold back."

His eyes were dark with passion. "I can't. I'll hurt you."

"You won't." Her hands gripped his hard flanks and pulled him forcefully against her, lifting her hips to take him even deeper. "Please . . ."

It was all the encouragement he needed. He let go, and she welcomed him with all the love and acceptance in her heart.

He sank into her again, holding her gaze as he touched the deepest part of her. Again and again. Harder and faster.

He was amazing. All his power, his fierceness, unleashed inside her.

She clenched him tighter with her body, dragging each stroke from him. Until the violent crescendo reached its highest peak. Until all the love she felt for this amazing man converged into one perfect moment of sensual bliss.

It was magic.

This was love. What had happened with John Montgomery paled in comparison with the breathless splendor she felt in Patrick's arms. Not just the pleasure that overwhelmed her body, but the closeness. The emotional connection that made everything so intense. Every touch. Every kiss. Every stroke reverberated through her like wildfire. She felt cherished. Protected. Loved.

And at that perfect moment—when her heart stopped and her body clutched in one last gasp—they touched heaven together.

Their shared cries of release tangled in the warm, sultry air of their pleasure.

The warm rush of his release was caught in the rippling tide of her own.

Their eyes met and wouldn't let go—not even when the last shudder of their bodies had ebbed. And what she saw there touched her soul.

Tears of happiness blurred her vision. Lizzie had found her heart's desire. She loved him, and he loved her. He might not be ready to admit it, but the truth was there in the emerald depths of his heated gaze.

Patrick rolled to the side so as not to crush her, feeling as if he'd just run into a stone wall. Every bone in his body crushed. Every muscle ripped to shreds. Once he'd spent almost a week on the run in the Lomond Hills, evading a score of Campbells, without sleep or food and very little water. He felt like that now. When it had all been over, he'd slept for two days.

What the hell had come over him? He'd never lost himself like that. He'd been wild. Out of control. Possessed by passion unlike anything he'd ever experienced. Passion that had consumed him, wringing out every last ounce of his strength.

His heart tightened, gazing at the woman collapsed beside him like a rag doll. He swept his hand over her flushed cheek. "Did I hurt you?"

Her eyes were bright with happiness, giving him an unwelcome twinge. "Do I look hurt?"

His gaze slid over her red swollen lips, her flushed cheeks, her adorably messed hair, and her ivory breasts rosy from his kisses. No, she didn't look hurt, she looked very thoroughly ravished.

And sensual as hell.

If he hadn't just had the most amazing orgasm of his life wring him dry, he would be tempted to take her again—just so he could see if it had been real.

"You look beautiful," he said honestly.

He saw the pleasure she took from his compliment, as if it were a rare treat, and vowed to tell her often so that she would never forget it. Her smile, bereft of its usual uncertainty, deepened to pure radiance. It hit him square in the chest. She should look like this always. Happy without restraint. Secure.

She lay in his arms for a moment, the curve of her body nestled intimately against his. Her cheek and the palm of one soft hand rested on his chest. Absently, her fingers traced the narrow path of dark hair on his stomach. Her hair was spread out like a flaxen veil on his chest, tickling his tanned skin.

So this was contentment. Would that they could stay like this forever.

When the pounding of their hearts had steadied and their breathing returned to normal, she propped up her chin on her hand and ventured a wary glance at him. "Are you disappointed?"

He stilled, not needing to ask what she was talking about. Lizzie hadn't been a virgin. Though part of him had guessed the truth, he admitted a moment of disappointment to have it confirmed. He was a man, after all, it was only natural. She was his woman, and he wished that he'd been the first. Irrational, unfair . . . definitely. But also honest.

That initial flare of disappointment, however, had fled when he thought of the hurt she must have suffered. He suspected the identity of the man she'd given herself to, and it shed an entirely new light on the events he'd witnessed—and played an unknowing role in—that day. His body clenched. How could the bastard make love to her and then treat her that way?

He'd taken too long to respond, and she misinterpreted his reaction. "I can understand if you wish to reconsider . . ." Her voice fell off unsteadily.

"Nay!" His reaction was swift and forceful; the swell of fierce emotion made him tighten his hold around her. "There is nothing to reconsider."

The loss of her maidenhead to him was nothing to what it must have cost her. If anything, it eased his own sense of guilt about taking her.

Holding her in his arms like this, just the two of them, he found it easy to forget the complications that awaited them beyond. Life married to a MacGregor would be nothing like what she knew. He had nothing to give her. But he would do everything he could to make her happy.

He ached to taste every delectable inch of her body, cover her creamy soft skin with his hands, and make sure she never regretted the decision to marry him.

But it was a battle he was doomed to lose.

How else would she react when she discovered the truth? He'd deceived her. And that deception, though necessary, had never weighed more heavily on him.

She tilted her head, her eyes scanning his face. "You truly aren't angry?"

He cupped her tiny chin. "Not with you." But he wanted to kill John Montgomery. If the man wasn't already living his penance, he would do just that.

She read him better than he realized and eyed him warily. "Do you want to know?"

He thought for a moment, then shook his head. "Nay." It was in the past. "Then I would have to kill him."

Her eyes widened, his blunt statement surprising her. "You would do that for me?"

The woman was daft. "I will kill anyone who harms you." He cocked a brow. "I hope that doesn't offend your delicate sensibilities?"

"No," she said hesitantly. "Though I'm not used to having such a fierce protector."

He kissed her forehead. "Get used to it." He paused. "Why didn't you tell me?"

"I never meant to hide it from you. I always intended to tell the man I married. But when I imagined an engagement, I thought of a nice quiet discussion in a hall, not . . . this." He chuckled, and she blushed. "There wasn't much time for discussion."

"No, there certainly wasn't," he said wryly. "Though had you told me ahead of time, it would have saved me a significant amount of pain and suffering."

She giggled and then said with mock seriousness, "Your control does you honor, my laird."

"Witch." He slapped her playfully on her bottom. He had no control with her. Heaven help him when she figured it out. "You'll pay for your insolence."

The wicked gleam in her eye stirred his cock from its sated stupor. "I'm looking forward to it." She leaned up and pressed a soft kiss on his lips. "Thank you."

"I aim to please, my lady."

She whacked him playfully. "Not for that, you arrogant beast. For being so understanding."

"That's the first time I've ever been accused of that."

She looked at him with those crystal-clear blue eyes that never failed to unnerve him. She saw so much more than he wanted her to. "You don't fool me one bit, Patrick Murray. You aren't nearly as cynical and impervious as you pretend." She tapped his chest emphatically. "Beneath that steely chest is a tender heart, and I intend to find it."

The playfulness fled, a sudden pall cast over the moment

of joy. "Don't, Lizzie," he warned, his expression as serious as his tone. "Don't try to find something that doesn't exist. You'll only be disappointed."

She shook her head. "I love you. You could never disappoint me."

But he would.

I love you. The words he'd been trying to forget but that seemed to be imprinted on his soul. A ray of light in a pit of blackness. Hope for a man who should know better.

His chest felt as if it were being squeezed in a vise of foreboding. He hugged her tight, savoring the moment of connection. The thought of losing her tore him apart.

He dropped a kiss on her nose. "Come. We need to get you back to the hall before someone comes looking for you."

"When they hear the news, perhaps they will understand." Excitement lit her eyes, making her look just like a bairn with a platter of sweets. "I can hardly wait to tell my brothers and cousin."

Which would be a disaster. Jamie Campbell and Argyll would recognize him. Marriage was only the first hurdle; he still needed to convince her to run away with him—without giving her cause to suspect the true reason.

He hated to put a damper on her excitement, but it was important that her brothers and cousin not learn of their marriage until it was too late to be undone. His voice, though grave, gave no hint of his unease. "Are you sure that is wise?"

Her brow furrowed. "What do you mean?"

"You know as well as I do that your brothers and cousin will not be pleased with your choice of husband. They want you to marry Robert Campbell, not a guardsman with little but his sword to recommend him. I don't want to give them an opportunity to refuse their consent."

She eyed him warily. "What are you suggesting?"

He held her gaze. "That we find a minister to marry us before we tell your family."

All of the excitement drained from her face. "You mean a clandestine marriage?"

He nodded. "Aye."

"No," she said firmly. "I'll not sneak off as if I'm ashamed of this marriage. I'll be proud to be your wife. My cousin will perhaps be disappointed, but with my brother's marriage—"

"What?"

She smiled. "I was just as surprised as you. It's the most amazing thing. I received a missive from Dunoon before the evening meal. It seems Jamie is to marry Caitrina Lamont."

The Enforcer and the daughter of the Lamont of Ascog— a MacGregor ally? There had to be a mistake. "You're sure the woman is Caitrina Lamont?"

She nodded. "Do you know her?"

He stroked his chin thoughtfully. "Aye."

"I hear she is very beautiful."

Patrick looked at her sharply, having heard the odd note in her voice. He studied her expression. She was doing her best to seem uninterested, but he could feel her hanging on every nuance of his response. He grinned. Lizzie was jealous. "She's not my type."

"What type is that, beautiful?"

He chuckled and dropped a kiss on her pursed lips. "Nay, spoiled and sharp-tongued. If this is true, your brother will have his hands full with that one." If he didn't despise the man, he would almost pity him.

She smiled but looked a bit shamefaced. "I should feel sorry for the poor girl. I'm sure she's not had an easy time of it these past few months." At his questioning look, she continued. "Apparently, the news my brother received all those weeks ago that drove him from here so quickly had to do with Caitrina Lamont. I don't have all the details, but from what I've been able to piece together from Jamie's missive and Colin and Robert's conversation tonight, the Lamont of Ascog and his sons were killed trying to protect the MacGregors."

Patrick's blood turned to ice. He grabbed her arm. "Killed?" Weeks . . . months ago? What the hell had happened to his kinsmen? "Are you sure?" he said intently. Too intently. She looked down at her arm, and he realized his fingers were pressing into her tender skin. "Sorry," he said, releasing his hold and trying to calm the race of his heartbeat.

"I'm sure. I didn't realize you knew him."

"Not well," he admitted. It was the implication for Alasdair and his brother Iain that worried him. Where the hell were they? Had they been taken? Was that why Gregor had yet to return? He should have come back by now. A heavy pit of dread lodged in his chest. "How did it happen?"

Lizzie shook her head. "I'm not certain. But from comments Colin made tonight and something Jamie said before he left, I think Colin had something to do with it. But don't you see what this means? If my cousin has no objection to Jamie marrying a destitute girl tainted by treason, he is not likely to object to my marrying you."

"Did your cousin have another bride in mind for your brother?"

"No, but—"

"Then the situations are not the same. I won't risk losing you."

"You won't lose me."

"You can be completely certain of that?"

She bit her lip. "Almost certain."

"Almost isn't good enough."

"But my cousin has sent for me—I cannot ignore his summons."

"No, but you can delay."

"I don't know . . . ," she hedged.

He took her into his arms and gave her a long kiss. She'd rearranged her gown to cover herself again, but his fingers caressed her breast through the thin fabric. When he finally broke off, her eyes were soft with passion again. His finger slid over her swollen mouth. "It will be romantic," he said huskily.

A wry smile played upon her lips. "It will be illicit. You'll not persuade me so easily. But I will agree to consider it."

That was good enough for now, but he would persuade her. "And you will say nothing to your brother and Campbell?"

She nodded. "It won't be too difficult, since they are leaving in the morning anyway. Now that Alasdair MacGregor has surrendered, Colin hopes it will be easier to round up the other outlaws."

"What!" he exploded, unable to hide his shock. Surrendered? Impossible. She was looking at him strangely, and he realized he'd betrayed too much.

Her brows knit together across her tiny nose. "Didn't I mention it?"

Patrick held his impatience in check. "Nay, you didn't. What happened?"

"I don't know all the details, but Jamie found the MacGregor and his men on the Isle of Bute and negotiated their surrender to my cousin. My cousin has agreed to take the MacGregor to England to have his case heard by the king. Jamie's marriage will seal the bargain."

Patrick rolled onto his back and stared up at the ceiling, trying to figure out what this could all mean.

"There will be peace," Lizzie said.

Peace. Was such a thing possible? Dared he hope . . . If this was true, it could change everything. Alasdair had talked his way out of trouble with the king before; could he do it again? It was obviously what his cousin was counting on.

If the MacGregors were pardoned, he would be able to tell Lizzie the truth. He would be able to explain to her

what the land meant to his clan and why it had been necessary to hide his identity. It might make it easier for her to
forgive him.

"Is everything all right?" she asked. "Why are you interested in the MacGregors?"

He saw the aversion in her gaze. "You've just surprised
me, that's all." And had given him much to think on. He
glanced down at her upturned face, seeing that she was still
studying him with far too much curiosity in those expres-
sive blue eyes.

His body stirred. The heat of their last kiss still lingered
on his lips. He knew just the way to distract her.

In one smooth move, he flipped her onto her back and
rolled on top of her.

"What are you doing?" she gasped.

He kissed her and rubbed his throbbing erection between her legs, letting her feel his arousal. "I thought that
would be obvious to a woman of your perception?"

She giggled to hear her words repeated back to her. "I
thought you said we didn't have much time?"

"We don't," he agreed, sliding his hand between her legs
and groaning. So warm and deliciously wet. He slid one
finger inside her, watching as her eyes grew hazy with passion. "But this shouldn't take too long."

Chapter 15

Lizzie settled onto the stool before the smoldering peat fire and wrapped her plaid a little tighter around her shoulders. Though comfortable and cheerful, Alys and Donnan's cottage was a bit drafty. Next week the villagers would be lighting the bonfires for *Oidhche Shamhna,* the night of Samhain. The days had shortened considerably, and the air had taken on a distinct wintry chill. Sometime next month the first snow would blanket the hills and glens, making travel much more difficult.

The missive that she'd sent to her cousin would not delay him for long; they needed to leave soon. She'd told Patrick as much this morning when she'd woken up snug and warm, cradled in his powerful arms.

Her heart pinched, thinking of the conversation that had followed. She hated arguing with him. But in the week and a half since Colin and Robert had left, it seemed when he wasn't sneaking into her room late at night to catch a few stolen moments of pleasure, they were disagreeing about their impending nuptials.

She'd thought finding a husband would be the difficult part. Never had she imagined how hard it would be to agree on how the wedding would take place.

Alys finished stirring the pungent, mouthwatering beef porridge in the fire and took a seat opposite her. After plucking some yarn from the basket at her feet, she went to work on a pair of wool hose with a large tear.

"So to what do I owe the pleasure of your visit today, my

lady?" Alys said, peering at her out of the corner of her eye. Even with that small glance, the older woman conveyed so much. She was not fooled by Lizzie's bright smiles and false cheer.

"I thought you might be lonely with Donnan away and wanted to see if you needed anything," Lizzie replied airily.

"Hmm," said Alys, not believing a moment of it. "Where is your fierce protector? I'm surprised that he let you go to the village alone."

Lizzie blushed. "With the MacGregor's surrender, there can be little danger. I've walked to the village thousands of times by myself. A great many of those visits to see you and the little ones." She looked around. "Where are they, by the way? They usually rush to greet me to see what I've got hidden in my basket."

"That's because you spoil them with sweets. They are fishing down at the burn, but I'm sure they'll smell those tarts you brought and be on their way soon enough." Alys gave her a hard stare. "But don't think to distract me." She made a short sniffing sound. "So you snuck away without telling him, did you?"

Lizzie lifted her chin. "I'm the lady of the keep, I don't sneak."

"Bah! Don't take that tone with me, little one. I know you too well. Here," she said as if to make her point, handing her a needle and some wool thread, "you might as well do something if you are just going to sit there with a long look on your face. Or do you want to tell me what is really bothering you?"

Lizzie picked up a pair of small trews that must have belonged to one of the boys and began to sew, finding the monotony of the work oddly calming. After a short silence, she said, "We had a disagreement."

Alys chuckled. "Is that all? Ah, child, there will be plenty more of those. What you need to learn is how to make up afterwards." Her eyes twinkled. "It can be worth every minute of the distress that leads up to it."

Lizzie blushed, and Alys raised an eyebrow. "Or maybe you've already discovered what I'm talking about? That braw lad of yours doesn't seem like the sort to wait for a minister to stake his claim."

Lizzie's face was on fire. "How do you know what I decided?"

"Anyone around here with two eyes in their head can see that." Lizzie's face fell. Was she really so transparent? "You wear your heart on your sleeve, my love. It's one of your most endearing qualities. So if you've made your decision, what is the problem?"

"We can't agree on the wedding." She took a deep breath. "Patrick doesn't think my family will approve the match."

Alys eyed her sharply. "He wants to marry without their consent?"

Lizzie nodded. "I've told him he's wrong, that my cousin and brothers will accept my wishes, but he doesn't want to risk their forbidding the match."

"He doesn't seem like the kind of man to run from a fight." Alys tapped her chin thoughtfully and then frowned.

"What is it?" Lizzie asked.

"I don't know," Alys said. "Something that Finlay said before he and Donnan left with your brother. I thought nothing of it, but he mentioned that he was looking forward to paying a visit to the Laird of Tullibardine and learning more about Patrick Murray. Do you think your Highlander is hiding something?"

Lizzie shook her head. "Nay, I think he truly fears that we will not be allowed to wed. But he doesn't know my family like I do." Tears filled her eyes. "He doesn't understand how important they are to me. How it wouldn't feel right marrying without my family around me sharing my happiness.

Missing Jamie's wedding was disappointing enough, but unlike him, we've no need to rush."

"You've told him how you feel?"

Lizzie nodded.

"Be patient, lass. The man loves you. He'll want to make you happy."

Loves me? She wanted to hope so. *Why was he being so stubborn?*

The sound of laughter outside drew her away from her maudlin thoughts. A few moments later, Alys's five children came bursting through the door and Lizzie found herself enfolded in a multitude of excited embraces, from her tiny Sari at her knees to not so wee Robin around her neck. Bombarded by questions and laughter, she found it impossible not to feel her spirits lifting.

This was why she'd come. Not only for Alys's counsel, but to immerse herself in Alys's crowded and noisy home, which teemed with the life and happiness she yearned for—and hoped one day soon would be hers.

Rather than barge in as he wanted to, Patrick waited—impatiently—for Lizzie to finish her visit. Arms crossed, he leaned against a tree and watched the chaos through the door left open by the arrival of Alys and Donnan's pack of unruly bairns. At the eye of the storm was his Lizzie—laughing and giggling like a girl as the children climbed all over her in an effort to get whatever was inside her basket.

He sniffed as the faint toasty scent of browned butter and sugar wafted through the air. Cakes or tarts, by the smell of it. An all too poignant reminder of the honey sweet taste of her skin.

Still, even angry, he didn't have the heart to disturb her when she was clearly enjoying herself. Indeed, except for her fine clothing, she looked right at home in the comfortable—though decidedly rustic, compared with the luxury of Castle Campbell—cottage. Not just comfortable, but happy. Maybe . . .

He allowed himself to hope that maybe life without all the luxuries she was used to wouldn't be as unpleasant as he feared.

Alys caught sight of him first and whispered something to Elizabeth. Her gaze shot to his, and he felt a certain satisfaction at seeing her face drain of color.

Good. She should be scared. Very scared.

Turning her gaze, she said her good-byes—making no effort to rush on his account, he noted—lifted her chin, and strode purposefully to the door.

Patrick's eyes narrowed. Readying for a fight, was she? Well, she wouldn't be disappointed.

His expression betrayed none of the fury raging inside him when she stepped outside and walked toward him, but he knew she could feel it thick in the tension between them.

Let her think about it for a while and stew, he decided. Just as he'd done.

Without a word he took her arm, his fingers clamping like a vise, and started to walk her back to the castle. His men flared out behind them, wisely giving them a wide berth.

She made a sharp huffing sound and marched along beside him in the damp, mossy ground, mud spitting from under her feet. Winter was in the air. The rain last night lingered as a fine mist. Living in the wild for so long, Patrick was able to sense the changing seasons. They needed to leave. Needed to find shelter for the coming winter. Shelter that would undoubtedly make Alys's cottage look like a palace.

Where in Hades was his brother? Nothing more had reached them about his cousin's surrender. He wanted to think there was reason for hope, but until he heard from Gregor he had to proceed with caution.

After a few minutes, she spun on him. "Are you just

going to glower or are you going to tell me why you are so angry?"

His eyes darkened. "I told you not to leave the castle by yourself."

Her blue eyes sparked with defiance that at any other time might be adorable. Right now, however, he wasn't in the mood to admire her spirit.

"I wasn't aware you had any right to give me orders."

His hands fisted into tight balls at his side, the haughty tone in her voice pushing him close to the edge. He wasn't one of her Lowland toadies. She didn't know how close he was to tossing her over his shoulder and showing her just exactly how far from civilized he could be. Hamish's method of wooing a bride was suddenly sounding very appealing.

"I have every right." He lowered his voice menacingly, each word laden with warning. "You will be my damn wife."

The stubborn lass didn't know when to retreat. She arched one delicate little brow. "Not if we never get married I won't."

With an emphatic toss of her head that sent her flaxen tresses flying, she started to spin away, but he pulled her harshly against him. His eyes narrowed to slits. "We'll be married, Elizabeth, if I have to tie you up and carry you to the kirk myself. You are mine." His gaze slid down to her belly. "Even now, you could be carrying my babe." He felt a twinge of satisfaction when her eyes widened and her hands clasped her stomach instinctively. "Surely you are aware that is a natural consequence of our nighttime activity?"

And a child would make it harder for her to undo their marriage. He hated himself for even thinking it.

She swallowed hard. "Of course I am. I'm not a child."

"Then stop acting like one." He gave her a hard look.

"Next time you are angry with me, don't do something foolish and risk your life."

She made a soft snorting sound that only enraged him further. "Don't be ridiculous. I don't need your protection to walk from the castle to the village. *If* there had been any danger, it is gone now that the MacGregor has surrendered. Do you intend to keep me locked up forever or just until we're married?"

Forever. So that he never had to experience that moment of icy fear again when he knew she'd gone—alone. He was being irrational, but rationality seemed to desert him when it came to her.

"I haven't decided yet," he snapped.

She gasped with outrage and tapped her finger on his chest. "I have three older brothers, so don't think you can bully me."

Unbelievable. He glanced out of the corner of his eye to see if his men were seeing this. They were, and even from a circumspect distance he could see that their amusement matched his own.

He frowned. "Three?"

She nodded but didn't elaborate. "You are the most infuriating, overbearing—"

"Enough." He cut her off the best way he knew how. He pulled her against him, their bodies sliding together with intimate familiarity, and kissed her. Deeply. Passionately. Until the heat of desire tamped down the heat of anger. Until nothing else mattered but the rush of sensation pouring through his body.

Soon he was lost in the soft warmth of her mouth. The silk of her lips. The languid stroke of her tongue against his. His hand slid down her back to the curve of her bottom, wanting to fit her more snugly against him.

"Your men," she murmured against his mouth.

He swore and broke off the kiss. He'd forgotten about

their audience, and from the smirks on his men's faces, they'd realized it.

He tipped her chin to look into her eyes. "We'll finish this tonight," he promised, before releasing her.

"The kiss or the discussion?"

"Both." He could see the worry in her eyes, and it clawed at him. Persuading her to run away was proving to be more difficult than he'd imagined, and it was wearing on them both. "It will be all right, Elizabeth."

She met his gaze uncertainly and nodded.

A movement in the trees beyond her shoulder sent ice shooting down his spine. With his senses honed from years of evading capture, a cursory glance was all it took to assess the situation: His brother had finally returned, the news was grim, and there was an arrow pointed at Elizabeth's back.

Patrick had her behind him, shielding her with his body, almost instantly.

"What are you doing?" she asked, shocked by his sudden maneuver.

He made a gesture with his hand, ordering his men into position. His gaze shot to Robbie. The silent communication was enough to convey the seriousness of the situation.

"What's wrong?" Lizzie asked again, looking around.

He grabbed her by the shoulders and stared into her eyes. "Do you trust me, Lizzie?"

Her brows furrowed. "Of course I do."

"Then don't ask me any questions right now and go with my men back to the castle."

"But what—"

He silenced her with a press of his finger on her lips. "No questions."

She looked as though she wanted to argue, but to his relief, she nodded. His men formed a circle around her and led her safely up the hill.

When she was out of sight and earshot, he turned to face

his brother, who along with half a dozen other warriors had emerged from behind the trees like bedraggled wraiths. All were covered in dirt and dried blood, their plaids hanging in tatters from their weary limbs like ghostly robes. They were in bad shape, but he was too angry to care. All he could see was the arrow pointed at Lizzie's back and the look in his brother's eye that said he intended to shoot.

"What the hell do you think you are doing, Gregor? I warned you to leave Elizabeth Campbell to me."

Gregor returned Patrick's rage in kind. "It's too late for that."

"You're wrong. My plan is working, the lass has agreed to marry me."

"Plan?" Gregor sneered. "I should have killed the bitch when I had the chance."

In two long strides, Patrick had his brother by the throat, holding him a few inches off the ground, eye to eye. "Have care how you talk about the woman who will be my wife," he said in a deadly tone, looking right into his eyes so there could be no mistake. But the hard blue gaze teemed with such hatred, there was little left of the brother he remembered.

Disgusted, he released his hold, pushing Gregor away from him.

"She'll never be your wife," his brother sputtered, clasping his throat.

Patrick ignored Gregor's taunts. "Where have you been? You should have returned weeks ago. I've news of our cousin."

Gregor stilled, and the look in his eyes cut Patrick to the quick. He felt a premonition. . . .

"Our cousin is dead," Gregor spat. "Murdered by the Campbells, along with our brother Iain, our uncle, and every other man tricked into surrender under the false terms of Argyll's promise."

Ice froze in Patrick's veins. It took a moment to absorb

the shock of his brother's words. A trick? Dead? A quick glance at the other men's faces told him every word of it was true.

He felt as if the blood had been drained out of him, his body sapped of life. He wanted to sink to his knees in an agony of despair and horror. Not since his parents had been murdered had he felt such a blow. It was almost impossible to conceive such a loss. "Dear God," he whispered.

"God?" Gregor roared. "He had nothing to do with this. It was the devil Argyll." His voice shook with rage and resentment. "Twenty-five MacGregors have hanged at Mercat Cross in Edinburgh this past week alone courtesy of the Campbells. Right now, our chief's head sits on a stake at the gates of Dumbarton beside our brother's." Something changed in Gregor's eyes, a flash of pain so acute that Patrick braced himself for what was to come. "And while you have been playing the fine gentleman with your lady, mooning after her like some lovesick pup, our sister was being raped by her brother's men."

"No!" The sound he made wasn't human. Raw pain tore through his chest like a ragged claw, splicing him apart. Not his sister. Not sweet, stubborn, beautiful Annie. He grabbed Gregor by the shirt and shook him as if he could clear away his words. "What the hell happened? I told you to hide them." His throat was tight and his voice raw. "You were supposed to keep them safe."

"I tried, damn it." Gregor wrenched away. "I had them hidden in the braes of Balquhidder, but they were betrayed for gold, and Auchinbreck exacted his retribution on Annie."

Auchinbreck was a dead man.

"Retribution?" Patrick growled. "For what?"

"When news reached us of Argyll's treachery—of the deaths of our chief and kin—there were risings from the braes of Balquhidder to Rannoch Moor. We burned a path of vengeance a mile wide."

"And you didn't think to let me know." All of a sudden, the ramifications of Alasdair's death hit him. He pinned his brother with his gaze. "I am chief."

Gregor's eyes flashed as if he wanted to argue, but instead he shrugged. "There wasn't time."

It was a damned insufficient excuse, and they both knew it. Did Gregor intend to challenge his leadership? Being chief was not a position Patrick had ever wanted, but he damn well intended to be a good one—certainly better than his brother. If the MacGregors had any chance of survival, it wouldn't be with the mercurial Gregor at the helm. He didn't want to think his brother could be so disloyal, but Gregor had changed. He'd always been able to placate him before. "And the resurgence of fighting is why Auchinbreck sought retribution?"

Patrick caught the flicker in Gregor's gaze. "The men were enraged, out of control. Thirsting for revenge." He shrugged. "A Campbell lass got in the way."

Patrick swore, guessing what had happened. "And our clansmen decided to take some of their rage out on a woman?" He looked away in disgust. Poor Annie had been caught in the crossfire.

I should have protected her. Could he have done something different? If he'd taken that shot at Jamie Campbell, would his cousin and brother still be alive?

It sickened him to think that less than two weeks ago, he'd sat across the room from the man who was responsible for the rape of his sister. His stomach clenched. He couldn't think about it. "I have to go to her," Patrick said. "Where is she?"

Gregor shook his head. "She won't see you. She won't see anyone. Not even Niall Lamont. I knew how Annie felt about him, so I fetched him from Bute. That's what delayed my coming here. But she sent him away."

"Where is she?"

"Molach, the islet in Loch Katrine, with some of the other women and children. She's safe for now."

Safe? Annie would never feel safe again.

Black. That was all Patrick could see, all he could feel. Cold. Empty. Dead. Any feeling left inside him had been destroyed by the news of the deaths of his kinsmen and his sister's rape. All that was left was a simmering rage. Rage that lashed inside him with nowhere to go.

He clenched his fists, his mouth pressed into a tight line. By all that was holy, Achinbreck and the Campbells would pay for what they had done.

Only moments ago he'd had hope for the future, and now everything had changed. His cousin and brother were dead, his sister raped; he was chief of a broken clan. . . .

And marrying Lizzie had become impossible.

The return of his family's land was secondary to saving his clan from destruction and his duty as chief. Any hope of a peaceable solution had vanished with Argyll's treachery.

The enormity of his responsibilities hit him hard. He'd been running his whole life, focused on surviving, but now he was responsible for the survival of his entire clan. His duty was clear. His clan would demand vengeance, and he would give it to them—gladly.

Ironic, he supposed, that at the moment he realized he could never have her, he understood Lizzie better. Understood her sense of duty and the struggle she must have gone through to decide to marry him.

He'd been a fool to think he could ever find happiness with a Campbell. With anyone. He should have known better.

"Where is Auchinbreck now?" he asked.

"I don't know," Gregor replied. "But we have everything we need to find him."

Lizzie. Patrick fought the urge to thrash his brother even for the suggestion.

I will kill anyone who harms you. He recalled his vow but had never anticipated that that someone might be his brother. "I won't let you hurt another innocent woman," he warned. "It's Auchinbreck who deserves our vengeance, not his sister."

But Gregor was beyond rationality, and Patrick's words of caution fell on deaf ears. Eyes wild, Gregor gave him a look teeming with scorn. "You've grown soft, brother. The lass has blinded you to what needs to be done. You have a duty to the clan—"

"I don't need you to tell me what my duty is." Patrick's voice held the edge of a razor. "I know exactly what needs to be done." And it didn't include harming Lizzie.

Gregor studied his face. "You'd put this Campbell slut above your own kin? She'll die, but first she'll suffer like our sister. If you aren't man enough to do what needs to be done, I will."

Every muscle in Patrick's body flexed, but he kept his voice deadly calm. "Raping a woman does not make you a man. Touch her and I'll kill you. I said to leave the lass be. I'm chief, I make the decisions."

"For now."

Patrick's gaze hardened. "Is that a challenge, *brother*?"

Gregor looked uncomfortable, proving that he was not completely without loyalty. "Not if you do what needs to be done."

"And by that you mean taking revenge on Elizabeth Campbell?" Patrick held his anger in check, though his first instinct was to take his dirk to his brother's neck and impress upon him the seriousness of what he was about to say. But one of them had to be rational. "Revenge on innocents isn't going to help our cause."

"Cause?" Gregor scoffed. "What cause? The Campbells won't rest until every one of us is dead. I for one intend to take as many of them as I can with me."

Patrick heard the murmurs of agreement from the other

men and knew he had to make them see beyond the thirst for revenge. It was a thirst he shared, but one he had to hold in check for the future of the clan. "So your answer is to give up? Go down in a blaze of glory? Don't you see that every day we survive is a victory? The Campbells have tried for years to get rid of us, but the fact that you and I are standing here shows that they've failed." He looked into the faces of the other men. Men with wives and families. "What about our women and children? Would you leave them unprotected, at the mercy of men like Auchinbreck? Would you see the name MacGregor die, never to be re-born?"

Gregor had a mulish look on his face. "The clan wants revenge."

"And they shall have it. Our murdered kinsmen and our sister will not be forgotten. But if you make war on Elizabeth Campbell, there will be no place for us to hide. Every Campbell will be hunting us, and the other clans will turn against us. Don't you see?"

His brother's eyes had lost a bit of their rabid glaze. Patrick's words appeared to have finally penetrated. He nodded. "Aye."

"Good. Then ride north and send out the *crann tara*, the fiery cross. I want every MacGregor from here to Rannoch Moor to gather at the kirk in Balquhidder a week hence."

Gregor frowned. "What about you? Aren't you coming with us?"

"Aye, but first I want to see what I can discover of the Campbell plans and Auchinbreck's movements. I'll follow in a few days."

"And the Campbell chit, you intend to just leave her?"

"Aye." The tightness in his chest nearly cut off his breath. Every instinct rejected what had to be done. His course had been laid out for him. To join his men. To fight. To punish those who'd murdered his kinsmen and raped his sister.

Only one thing stood in his way.

Lizzie. He was torn between his duty to his clan and his need to see her safe.

His brother's accusation rang in his ears. He wasn't putting her before his clan, but he couldn't leave her unprotected. He thought he'd gotten through to his brother, but with Lizzie's safety Patrick wouldn't take any risk. If anything happened to him . . .

There would be no one to keep a rein on Gregor.

Lizzie would be as good as dead.

Patrick formulated his plan on his way back to the castle. Tonight he would send a few of his men to follow his brother and ensure his return to the Highlands, and then tomorrow morning Lizzie would get her wish.

She must have been waiting for him, because as soon as he passed through the gate she ran toward him. "What happened? Why did you send me away like that?" She stopped in her tracks a few feet away when she saw his expression. "Patrick, what's wrong?"

Everything. He forced himself to look at her, wanting to see her for what she was—a Campbell, his enemy, the sister of the man who'd ordered the rape of Annie, and the cousin of the fiend who'd sent his brother and chief to their deaths.

He wanted to hate her.

But all he could see was guileless blue eyes set in a pale face fraught with concern. For him.

His chest twisted. Did she have to be so damn sweet? He wanted to grab her and shake her, lash out until she hated him. It would make leaving her so much easier.

He squared his jaw. "Go. Pack your things and be ready to leave at sunrise."

"Go?" she repeated, startled. "Where?"

He met her gaze, giving no hint of the turmoil raging inside. Heaven help him, he still wanted her. But he would see her safely to her cousin and be done. With the removal of him and his men and the conscription by Auchinbreck of half its already depleted fighting force, Castle Campbell would be left woefully undefended. He might despise Argyll, but he knew Lizzie would be safe with her powerful cousin, and he had no choice but to take her there himself.

"Dunoon," he said flatly. "Isn't that what you wanted?"

"Yes, but—"

"Then you shall have your wish."

And without another word, he turned on his heel and left her standing there, unable to look at her another minute.

He'd thought he was dead inside, thought that he'd lost the ability to feel.

He was wrong.

Letting her go would be like cutting himself in two, and he feared what would be left of himself when she was gone.

His brother's face flashed before his eyes, giving him his answer.

Chapter 16

After a sleepless night waiting for Patrick to come to her room and explain his sudden change of heart, only to be disappointed, Lizzie stood in the *barmkin* in the semidarkness of dawn, shivering, watching a stranger ready their horses to leave.

Her heart squeezed as she wrestled with confusion. This should be the happiest moment of her life, but he wouldn't even look at her. She'd gotten what she wanted, but she would run away with him right now if only he would stop acting like this. Too late, she realized that it didn't matter how they married just as long as they were together.

Never had she seen him like this. Patrick seemed a cold, angry shell of the man she loved. His expression was hard and implacable, his eyes flat. All attempts to question him were rebuffed with stony curtness.

What had happened on their way back to the castle yesterday? Was he angry because of her refusal to run away with him or was there some other reason?

Nothing made sense.

She listened as he gave orders to his men and the handful of Campbell guardsmen who would accompany them, and before the sun had crested the horizon, they were on their way to Dunoon.

They rode along the edge of the Ochil hills, then crossed the bridge over the Forth at Stirling. Instead of taking the main road to Lennox, they kept north of the river, following narrow paths across the moors and through woodlands that were at times difficult to make out.

For a man who hadn't wanted to go in the first place, he couldn't seem to get there fast enough. But he was being careful—wary, it seemed, of another attack. She sensed his vigilance in the intensity of his gaze and the way he reacted to every sound distant or near. He had men scouting ahead and behind them as an added precaution.

He pushed them at a brutal pace, traveling for hours—with only short water breaks for the horses—before finally stopping to rest. Though it was only a few hours past noon, with winter creeping ever closer the sun was almost gone.

It wasn't only the horses that were exhausted. Lizzie was a good rider under normal circumstances, but she wasn't accustomed to riding at this gait over difficult terrain for so long. Her legs, not used to such abuse, shook as she tried to dismount. She would have fallen if Patrick hadn't caught her.

Just the sensation of his strong hands around her waist was enough to make her heart clench—and then drop when he released her all too suddenly.

Dear God, what was wrong? He wouldn't even touch her.

Her legs wobbled, but she managed to stay on her feet. "Thank you." He nodded curtly and started to turn away. She grabbed his arm, the leather of his jerkin cold and stiff under her fingertips. "Wait."

His gaze met hers. He didn't bother to mask his impatience.

Her heart throbbed, not understanding his coldness. "Where are we?"

"East of Menteith."

Her brows drew together. "So far north? Shouldn't we be heading south?" Though it was possible to reach Dunoon over land by winding along the fingerlike coast, it was days faster to take a *birlinn* from Dumbarton across the Clyde. And this late in autumn, there was always weather to consider. They were fortunate thus far to have avoided rain, but the heaviness of the mist descending upon them did not bode well. Her cheeks were already numb from the cold.

"Aye. We'll turn south near Loch Lomond."

Loch Lomond. A veritable oasis. "Is that where we will stop for the night?"

He shook his head. "We won't be stopping."

She offered her protest with a groan.

Finally showing some sign of sympathy for her exhaustion, he explained, "I know you are tired, but as you well know, the roads can be dangerous."

A shiver ran through her. She remembered all too well.

His voice softened. "You are well protected, Lizzie. But it's best if we keep moving. Besides, your cousin is expecting you." He hardened his jaw. "If that is all, I need to see to the horses."

Dismissed. Lizzie suddenly felt her pulse spike with anger. She didn't know what was wrong, but whatever it was, she didn't deserve to be treated like this. "That is not all," she snapped. "I want to know why are you acting like this."

His eyes sparked with warning. "Leave it be, Lizzie."

She lifted her chin. "No, I will not leave it be. What have I done to earn your displeasure? I apologize for leaving the castle alone, but I honestly did not see the harm." He didn't say anything, just stared at her with that hard, implacable look in his emerald gaze. She took a step toward him and gazed up at him beseechingly, wanting to penetrate this mysterious barrier he'd erected between them. "I know you don't want to go to Dunoon, but if it means that much to you, I will go with you right now—wherever you want. It doesn't matter where we marry—"

He swore, cutting her off. Grabbing her by the shoulders, he shook her, his face tortured by conflicting emotions she couldn't even begin to comprehend. "Damn it, Lizzie! Don't you understand? There will be no marriage."

She recoiled as if he'd slapped her. A bolt of searing white-hot pain shot through her, cutting off her breath. If he'd turned around and shot her with a musket, she couldn't have been more surprised.

Her heart rejected his words even as her eyes confirmed them. One look at him left no doubt. Her eyes burned with dry tears of disbelief as she gazed up into the fierce, handsome face of the man to whom she'd given her heart, the man who now thought to crush it under his heel with all the significance of a bug.

She didn't beg, didn't plead, didn't burst into tears—though she wanted to. Instead, she drew up her shoulders and swallowed the thick ball of hurt, too outraged to let her emotions reign. She wasn't insignificant, and she deserved to be treated better than this. "Am I to be told the reason for this decision, or did you think to just drop me at my cousin's gate and leave with no explanation?"

The expression on his face made her step back in horror.

"My God," she breathed, gazing up at him as if she'd never seen him before. "That's exactly what you intend to do." Her throat was so hot and tight, she could barely get the words out. "Do I mean so little to you? I thought you . . ."

Her heart caught, the burning in her chest excruciating. *Cared for me—maybe even loved me.*

His eyes bored into her with brutal intensity. She thought she saw a flicker of regret before it was quickly shrouded behind the steely veil.

Once she'd admired his control; now she hated it.

"Circumstances have changed, making a marriage between us impossible."

"Circumstances?" she repeated. Her voice was beginning to rise, and the other men were glaring in their direction uneasily, but Lizzie didn't care. How could he stand there so calmly—with all the emotion of a rock—when her heart was breaking apart? His coldness infuriated her, making her lash out with haughty sarcasm. "Could you perhaps be any more specific?"

She saw the flash of anger in his gaze. "No, I can't. I told you before that there are things about me—"

"I'm tired of your secrets," she exploded, her voice shaking with outrage. "Whatever it is, just tell me. Don't I deserve the truth?" She gave him a look full of scorn. "Or do you often seduce women with promises of marriage and discard them when they no longer have use to you?"

"That's not the way it happened," he clipped, reminding her that she'd been the one foolish enough to seduce him. His eyes blared with something she'd never seen before—recklessness. He started to say something, but his words were cut off. If he'd meant to tell her his secret, she wouldn't hear it now.

"Chie—Captain."

Lizzie jerked around at the sound of Robbie's harried voice, breaking above the din of stomping hooves. The young warrior had been scouting behind them, and from the anxious look on his face, there was a problem.

Chief. He'd been about to call Patrick chief. That was a strange mistake to make. Her gaze shot back to Patrick, but he'd already turned away from her.

Robbie dismounted by jumping from the saddle and strode quickly to Patrick's side to confer with him. He spoke in a low voice, but she was able to make out one word. A word that sent chills sweeping across her already cold skin: followed.

Patrick knew it was useless to rail against the injustice, against the capricious fates that seemed intent on forcing them apart, but he couldn't prevent the anger. At her for being a Campbell, for being so damn sweet and trusting. And at himself for allowing himself to care.

And God, he cared about her. More than he'd imagined possible. Just looking at her, knowing that he couldn't have her, made him want to lash out wildly. Cruelly. What limited possibilities they'd had for a future had been all but extinguished by the executions of his kinsmen at the hands of her cousin and the rape of his sister.

He knew that she was confused, that she didn't understand his frustration, but it would be better for her to hate him. It would make leaving her easier.

There was one way he could ensure her hatred. And for one reckless moment—despite the danger presented by the handful of Campbell guardsmen that accompanied them—he contemplated telling her. *I'm a MacGregor. An outlaw. Chief of a broken clan since your cousin murdered mine.*

There was no reason to hide his identity any longer—only the need to get her to the safety of Dunoon without getting his men killed stayed his tongue.

Then Robbie arrived and the impulse was gone, his attention focused immediately on the threat at hand. The only question was who it was from.

"What is it?" he asked.

Robbie's voice was hard and succinct. "We're being followed."

Patrick's gaze darted meaningfully to Elizabeth, who was making no effort to hide her interest in their conversation. Robbie lowered his voice. "Campbells, Chief. The guardsman Finlay and ten other men, not two miles behind. I wanted to be sure, but they are definitely tracking us."

Finlay. And ten men? Hell. With the five Campbells he'd brought with him, that would leave him and his five men vastly outnumbered. Under normal circumstances, it wouldn't worry him, but he had Lizzie to consider. The threat he'd expected was from his brother, not from the

Campbell guardsman. Patrick's mind went to work with the possible explanations for Finlay's sudden arrival hard on their heels, but none of them boded well. "Tell the men to ready the horses."

"We will attempt to outrun them?"

Patrick shook his head. If it was just him and his men, it would be different. But Lizzie was already about to fall off her horse. "Nay, but I would like to be closer to the hills before we find out what they want." Though he'd picked a relatively protected area in which to rest, they were still in the valley of the river Forth—and a few leagues away from the forested hills and glens that separated the Lowlands from the Highlands.

If necessary, they could disappear into those hills.

Robbie nodded. "What about the lass?" he asked, broaching the question Patrick didn't want to contemplate.

What about Lizzie?

Though he'd wanted to see her to Dunoon himself, if Finlay had discovered who he was, they would part much sooner than that.

His chest pinched. Perhaps it was for the best. "She'll be safe enough with her clansmen." And if his fool brother was tempted to attack almost a score of Campbell guardsmen with only a handful of ragtag outlaws, Patrick would keep him at bay.

Surprisingly, Lizzie made no complaint when their respite was curtailed and once again they were riding at a hard—if not breakneck—pace across the moors. But her eyes haunted him, wounded and full of silent recrimination. Recrimination he could not answer for.

In spite of the circumstances, with each mile that brought them closer to the lush border of hills, forests, and secluded lochs that separated the Lowlands from the Highlands, Patrick felt his excitement grow. This was MacGregor land. His land.

And he'd been gone too long.

After an hour of hard riding, they reached the eastern-most edge of the forest just south of Aberfoyle and the great shadow of the mountain of Beinnmheadhonaidh; at last, they slowed. It didn't take long for Finlay and the other Campbell guardsmen to come into view behind them.

Lizzie, who'd been looking over her shoulder with enough frequency to tell him that she'd heard at least part of Robbie's report, saw them and pulled up. "Wait. They're Campbells."

Patrick made eye contact with Robbie and Hamish, giving them silent communication to be ready.

Lizzie was studying him suspiciously, as were a few of the Campbell guardsmen they'd brought with them. "Why are we running from my cousin's men?" she asked point-edly.

"We weren't running," Patrick replied. It wasn't an answer and she knew it, but the arrival of Finlay and his men prevented any further questions.

If Patrick's suspicions proved correct, her question would be answered soon enough.

"Finlay," she said, swinging her horse around and moving toward him, "what are you doing here? Why are you following us?"

"Move away, my lady," Finlay said.

Patrick and his men readied. One look at the triumphant expression on the Campbell guardsman's face was enough for him to know that they'd been compromised. But if Finlay thought he'd won, he was mistaken. They might be out-numbered, but they were MacGregors—and the Campbells were on his terrain now. If there was a fight, the only thing that worried him was ensuring that Lizzie stayed out of harm's way.

"Move away from what?" Lizzie asked, clearly con-fused.

"From me," Patrick said flatly, his gaze never once leav-ing the guardsman.

Lizzie looked back and forth between them. "What is this about, Finlay?"

"Aye," Patrick taunted, cocking a brow in a manner designed to get a rise out of the other man. "What is this about?"

Anger turned Finlay's already red and sweaty face scarlet. "This man is not who he says he is."

The pronouncement was met with dead silence. Lizzie didn't gasp or make any other sound of surprise, nor did she look at him, but Patrick saw the slight stiffening of her shoulders. "Then who is he?"

Her voice sounded hollow—empty.

Finlay scowled. "I don't know. But the Laird of Tullibardine has never heard of Patrick Murray."

Like a musket shot, the sound of a horse tearing through trees from the forest to the west was greeted with the steely sound of blades being drawn from scabbards.

"Wait," Patrick said. "It's my man." It was Tormod, the man he'd sent scouting ahead of them. "What is it, Tormod?"

The warrior looked around, grasping the situation. "MacGregors," he said. "Coming fast."

Patrick swore. Could this get any worse? Damn his brother to hell. He thought quickly and turned to Finlay. "Take the lady and make for the road to Lennox. I'll hold them off."

Finlay scoffed. "Think you I'm an idiot? This is just a ploy for you to make your escape."

Patrick wanted to grab him by the throat and shake him. He didn't bother to hide his rage. "This isn't a ploy, and if you don't leave right now, you'll find out soon enough that I'm telling the truth. But by then it will be too late. We can settle this later, but right now your duty is to the lady."

The Campbell guardsman was unmoved. Instead he said, "Arrest these men." The man at his side moved quickly to do as he commanded.

"No," Lizzie said, stopping him. "On what charge?"

Finlay frowned. "That will be for your cousin to decide when we reach Dunoon."

"And what if he's telling the truth? About the attack," she added to clarify. Lizzie looked at Patrick, and for the first time he could see the hurt in her eyes. The knowledge that he'd deceived her. She knew he was not the man he claimed to be.

But he wasn't deceiving her about this. "I'm telling the truth. I swear it on the souls of my parents. These men seek you harm."

There was so much more he wanted to say, so much he wanted to explain, but he would never get the chance. He stared deep into her eyes, saying a silent apology, begging her to forgive him, and then he broke the connection and turned back to Finlay. He would protect her with his life, but the idea of her getting caught in the middle of a battle—where he could not control the chaos—sent chills running down his spine. A stray arrow. A misfired hagbut. A wide slash of a sword.

"You bloody fool!" he shouted to Finlay. "Listen!" The unmistakable sound of horses resonated in the cold night air. "Get her out of here before it's too late."

Finally the truth seemed to have penetrated. Finlay's confidence was shaken, and he looked at Patrick uncertainly. "Maybe you're right—"

"Just go," Patrick said. And with one last look at Lizzie, a look that would have to hold him for a lifetime, he turned to face his brother.

But it was too late.

A hail of arrows broke through the canopy of trees and landed with deadly precision behind him. Patrick turned in time to see the stunned look on Finlay's face before he slid from his saddle and dropped like a rock to the ground, an arrow pinned right between his eyes. Two of the Campbell guardsmen he'd brought with him fell at his side.

Gregor and at least ten MacGregor warriors broke through the trees. In addition to the men with his brother yesterday, he recognized the others as some of the most dangerous, bloodthirsty, and savage of the lot—men who'd earned the MacGregors their outlaw name.

The Campbells under Patrick's command looked to him uncertainly—Finlay's pronouncement had not been without effect—wondering what to think.

Patrick was caught between two worlds—one real and one invented. He was a MacGregor, the blood enemy of Campbells. A few months ago, he would never have hesitated to lift a sword on a Campbell, but he'd lived among these Campbell guardsmen for months. Knew them. Ate with them. Drank with them.

He'd hoped to get Lizzie to safety without bloodshed, but Gregor had made it impossible.

When a Campbell guardsman next to him lifted a hagbut from his pack and took aim at his brother, the hesitation was gone. In one seamless movement, Patrick reached behind his head, grabbed the horn hilt of his *claidheamhmór,* and swung. The long steel blade slammed into the mail chest plate of the Campbell, knocking the gun from his hand and the man from his horse.

The battle lines were drawn.

He was a MacGregor. *The* MacGregor. For better—or worse—these were his men.

There was only one reality. All it took was one look at Lizzie's horrified expression to remind him of that.

Her face had drained of color. "My God, what are you doing?"

Patrick didn't have time to explain; he needed to get her the hell out of here.

The battle erupted around them like wildfire as his men joined Gregor's in battling Campbells—only the four Campbells he'd brought with him had yet to join the fray, momentarily stunned by his actions. Before they could turn on him, he stopped them. "Take the lady and go. Ride south for Dunoon as fast as you can."

One of the men reached for his gun, but Patrick was faster. The guardsman pulled his hand back in pain, cut from thumb to wrist by the swiping edge of Patrick's sword.

One of the other men called him a foul name and lifted his blade, but Patrick easily blocked the attempt.

Out of the corner of his eye, he could see the Campbells falling under the MacGregor blades—the fight inching closer.

"You can kill me later. Go. Protect the lady."

The men appeared to be reconsidering when Lizzie, who'd been conspicuously quiet, spoke. "Why should any-one listen to you—"

"If you want to live, you will do exactly what I say," he said fiercely. "I told you the truth, these men mean you harm."

"Then why did you . . ." Her voice dropped off as his brother drew close enough for her to make out his face. She gasped with recognition.

Her gaze shot to his. Confusion. Disbelief. Hurt. None of which he could explain or excuse.

A lifetime lost stretched between them in that one look. Of her eyes sparkling with merriment, of a smile no longer tentative, of holding her in his arms, of looking deep into her eyes as he slid inside her, of her cheeks pink with rap-ture as she came apart around him, of her sitting before the fire, her belly softly rounded.

Of everything that could not be. His chest cinched with pain, wishing . . .

Hell. "Go," he said roughly. Coldness was the only mask he could don to smother the pain.

If he'd wanted her hatred, he had it. The last look she gave him before turning her mount and heading south along the path through the trees left him no doubt. The accusation and betrayal pierced like a dirk in his chest.

His gaze lingered on her back, on the flaxen strands of hair loosened by the day's events and now flying behind her like a silken veil. *Farewell*. The heaviness pressing against his chest cut off his breath.

But before Lizzie and her guardsmen could pass out of sight, two arrows fired in quick succession hit the backs of two men riding behind her. One slumped forward, the other one fell to the side. His foot caught in the stirrup, and he was dragged for a few feet beside his horse before coming loose.

Gregor's voice rose above the din of battle. "Don't let them get away. I want the Campbell bitch."

The last guardsman with her had slowed to see what had happened to his companions, and it proved to be his death. Another MacGregor arrow fired and hit him in the neck.

Lizzie's cry was all that Patrick heard. He swore, knowing that his last-ditch effort to send her to safety with her cousin's men was not going to work. It would be up to him to keep her safe, but his options were running out.

Before he could go to her, two Campbell guardsmen rushed him on foot. He shouted at her to stay back—hoping that she would listen to him—and met them full force, wielding his sword with deadly precision and knocking them back long enough for him to dismount. His horse was only an encumbrance in the dense trees. They attacked him from both sides, but Patrick used his sword with one hand to hold one back as he dispatched the second with his dirk in the other. A few swings later, the second man lay beside the first.

A quick glance around told him that the day was almost done. Only a few Campbell guardsmen remained. His fury at Gregor rose as he noted that four MacGregors had fallen—

including two of the men with him at Castle Campbell—shot before they could reach the Campbells with their swords.

Gregor had stretched Patrick to the end of his brotherly compassion. He understood his brother's rage—his need for revenge and the hatred that blackened his soul that matched his own—but the challenge to Patrick's authority as chief could not be ignored. And the blind rage lashing around inside him was rooted in something far more elemental. Gregor had threatened his woman, and right now Patrick could kill him for it.

He glanced over his shoulder, relieved to see that Lizzie had followed his direction and stayed back, partially hidden in the trees. When he turned back around, his gaze met his brother's. Slowly they walked toward each other until they stood face-to-face a few feet apart.

Through the rage, Patrick felt sadness that it had come to this.

"I should kill you for what you've done," he said flatly. "You think you can be chief?"

Gregor's face was as hard and unyielding as his own. "A better one than you. I wouldn't put a lass before my clan. Before my own sister."

Patrick gritted his teeth, forcing himself to bite back the swell of rage. Gregor was just trying to make him lose control. There was only one way to settle this once and for all.

"If you want to challenge my authority, *brother,* do it as a man." He swung his sword around, holding it before him. "By right of sword."

If he lost, he'd be leaving Lizzie unprotected, at the nonexistent mercy of his brother.

But he wouldn't lose.

Gregor snarled, his mouth pulling back in a cruel imitation of a grin. "To the winner goes the spoils?" he taunted, glancing over at Lizzie.

When Patrick followed his gaze, Gregor swung his sword around in a violent slash that Patrick barely blocked. It was his answer to Patrick's challenge—a dirty move that would have made Arthur and his knights of the Round Table shudder in shame, but it set the stage for how this battle would be fought. Chivalry and the knightly code of honor had no place among hunted men. The MacGregors survived by ignoring the rules. It was one of the reasons they were prized by other clans as fierce warriors.

But Patrick could play just as dirty as his brother, and his next move proved it. He spun and snaked his foot around Gregor's ankle, knocking him to the ground. Gregor just managed to roll out of the way of the blow from Patrick's sword that followed.

Gregor righted himself, and the battle continued. They circled each other like gladiators of old, sizing each other up, exchanging swings of the swords, trying to find the weakness that would let them go in for the kill. Though Patrick had the advantage of height and build, Gregor was quick. They were well matched—always had been—but Patrick had one thing Gregor did not: Lizzie's life in his hands.

The battle continued, blow after blow, swing after swing, until sweat poured off his skin, and the muscles in his arms and stomach burned from exertion. He was tiring, but so was his brother. The violence of the blows increased as exhaustion and the urgency to see it done overrode patience.

Patrick blocked another blow to his head; steel clashed against steel, reverberating in his ears and the force of the blow shuddering through his body. He responded with one of his own, grunting as he swung his blade with two hands across his body in a wide arc. This time his brother was a fraction of a second slow, and Patrick's blow knocked him back.

It was the opening he'd been waiting for. With a fierce cry, Patrick swung his sword again and again, raining down on his brother blow after blow of powerful strikes.

Gregor couldn't withstand the force and started to fall back, blocking rather than fighting.

Patrick had him, and they both knew it.

One final blow brought Gregor to the ground. Patrick had the point of his sword at his neck before Gregor could recover. Patrick's heart was hammering from exhaustion and the rush of blood from the fight. He wanted to kill him, and the force of it shook him. He could see the rage he was feeling returned in his brother's gaze. And something else—hatred. Gregor wanted him to do it.

God, he was tempted. But this was his brother, the only brother he had left. Other than Annie, the last of his family. He'd won; that was enough. "Yield," he said softly.

Hatred blazed back at him, and Patrick knew that Gregor would not have shown him the same mercy. He pushed the blade a little deeper, drawing blood. "Do you yield?"

"Aye," Gregor grunted through clenched teeth.

"Say it," Patrick demanded.

"I yield, damn it."

After a moment, Patrick pulled back his sword, leaving Gregor seething in the dirt and mud. Gregor was furious, but he would get over it. His challenge had failed.

Patrick mounted his horse and swung it around, closing the short distance to Lizzie in a few moments. He dropped to the ground and approached her cautiously—walking past one of the men who'd fallen trying to protect her. The one who'd been dragged by his horse hung at a grotesque angle only a few feet ahead. She was watching Patrick with wide, terrified eyes, staring at his face as if she'd never seen it before.

"Are you all right?" he asked.

She took a few steps back. "W-who are you? W-w-what do you m-mean to do with me?"

Her stammer made something in his chest twist. *She's scared of me.* "I won't hurt you."

She gave a sharp cry of disbelief. The hurt swimming in

her eyes made his heart wrench. "God, how can you say that?"

Patrick was so focused on soothing her, he didn't notice the movement until it was too late. He heard Robbie's cry of warning behind him and looked up just in time to see the barrel of a pistol pointed directly at him.

The Campbell dragged from his horse was not dead.

Everything seemed to move in slow motion. He heard the blast. Saw the smoke. Then the force of the shot knocked him back. White hot fire seared through his thigh.

Robbie rode by and with the MacGregor battle cry ended the Campbell's life, this time for good. But the damage had been done. Only ill aim had saved Patrick's life.

His head cleared and the impact of his injury hit him hard—not just the lead ball, but the import. In showing his brother mercy, he'd allowed him an opportunity. One that Gregor would not hesitate to use. Patrick could not risk Lizzie's life on his brother's honor.

With a bullet lodged in his thigh, he would be no match for Gregor. And with only four of his own men against Gregor's ten ruffians, they would not be able to defend Lizzie should he die.

Gritting his teeth to bite back the cry of pain, he got to his feet.

"Hold them off," he said to Robbie, mounting his horse. The pain that shot through his leg almost made him keel over—only the knowledge of the ugly death that awaited Lizzie kept him seated.

Robbie nodded. "Aye, Chief."

"The cave," Patrick answered the silent question. "If you can get there tonight without being followed. Otherwise rally the men at Balquhidder Kirk as planned."

Robbie gave him a short nod, and before the others realized what he was going to do, Patrick snatched Lizzie off her horse, set her before him, and plunged into the trees.

Chapter 17

❖

Lizzie thrashed wildly against him as they raced through the trees in the darkness, the horror of the day finally catching up with her.

Patrick's arm jerked hard under her ribs, cinching her tight against him. The familiar muscled wall of his chest felt as yielding as granite.

"Damn it, Lizzie, stop," he said harshly in her ear, his voice rough with pain. "I'm trying to save both our lives, but if you keep hitting my leg like that, we're going to fall."

She stilled. His leg. God, he'd been shot. The moment of bloodcurdling panic when the ball had exploded was still etched on her foolish heart. Even after he'd discarded and betrayed her, she didn't want him to die. Not yet, at least. Not until she knew the truth. Then she might do the foul deed herself.

She remembered the shock, the hard slam in her chest, when he'd lifted his sword against her clansmen, preventing him from shooting the very MacGregor who'd attacked her. He'd joined the MacGregor against her clansmen and then turned around and fought him. It didn't make sense.

It was obvious that they knew each other—more than knew. Looking back and forth between them as they battled—there was something . . . She closed her eyes, fighting the sour taste that rose in the back of her throat. *No!* She didn't want to see it. Didn't want to even acknowledge the possibility. "Why should I go anywhere with you?"

"Would you rather I had left you back there with them?"

"So you are the better of two evils?"

He barked a sound like a laugh, but it was too filled with pain. "In this case, yes."

Though she wanted nothing more than to rail against him, to confront him and demand an explanation, the precariousness of their circumstances proved a temporary deterrent. One thing Patrick had said earlier she did not doubt: The MacGregor scourge meant to hurt her. And like it or not, all that stood between her and the vile beast was Patrick. A wounded Patrick. She bit back a wave of panic.

She fell silent as they careened through the forest, the pounding of her heart every bit as fast and furious as the clopping of the horse, until Patrick suddenly reined in the massive destrier, bringing them to a stop near a large rock.

"Why are we stopping?"

"We'll never outrun them on horses. We need to try to lose them, and I need to get somewhere safe to get this ball out of my leg."

"Where are we going?"

"North."

She froze. Dunoon was to the south. "But—"

"Going to Dunoon is no longer possible, Lizzie. Not now, at least. I'll get you there, but I can't do it alone. Not with them following us. We'd never make it."

He dismounted, careful to land on the rock so as to leave no footprints, and quickly lifted her down beside him. After removing the packs and plaid from the horse and tossing them over his shoulders, which were already laden with his bow and *claidheamhmór*, he slapped the horse on the flanks, shouting a command in the Highland tongue. The horse took off like a bullet, disappearing through the trees and darkness before Lizzie even had a chance to react.

It suddenly felt very quiet and very dark. The sliver of light from the moon was not strong enough to penetrate the heavy canopy of trees.

"With any luck, it will be some time before they catch up

with the horse," he whispered near her ear, then he dropped to the other side of the rock and held his hand up to her. "Careful where you step. They'll be tracking us."

Where were they? She'd lost all sense of direction some time ago.

Reluctantly, she slid her hand into his and leapt down next to him. Standing so close to him, with his familiar masculine scent wrapping around her, set off a tumult of conflicting emotions. She thought she'd known him so well. She could close her eyes and feel exactly what it was like to be held in his arms—to press her cheek against his incredible chest. To trace the layers of hard muscles with her hand. To look into his eyes when he pushed inside her, filling her inch by incredible inch.

Once again she'd confused sex with love.

Part of her wanted to catapult herself into his arms and burst into tears; the other part wanted to pound her fists against his chest and hurt him the way he'd hurt her. He'd deceived her—the extent of which she was almost too scared to find out. "Why are they tracking us? You know the men who attacked me, don't try to deny it."

"I won't deny it. You can question me all you want, Lizzie, but not now. We have to move fast."

"Wait." She looked down. "Your leg." Blood had saturated the brown leather of his breeches. A large stain had formed high on his left thigh, and the dark hole near the outer portion showed where the ball had entered. Quickly, she lifted the front of her wool skirt and ripped the bottom portion of one of her muslin underskirts. Holding it out to him, she said, "You'd better bind it with this."

He gave her a curious stare, before quickly doing as she bid. "Thank you."

She nodded, and then they were off. He pulled her through the woods after him, opposite the direction in which they'd been riding. Obviously, he hoped they would follow the horse. Even wounded, he wound through the trees with the agility and speed of a wildcat; she could barely keep up with him. The occasional grunt over uneven ground was the only reminder that he had a ball lodged in his leg. Despite the chill, sweat gathered on her forehead and between her breasts. Her breath was harder and harder to find amid the frantic pounding of her heart. They ran until she thought her lungs would burst.

She started to drag.

He slowed and offered her a drink of water from a skin in his pack. She took a deep gulp, thankful for the moment of respite.

"We can't stop, Lizzie. It's just a little farther."

She gasped, fighting for breath, unable to tell him that she couldn't go on. God, what was wrong with him? He was barely even out of breath. In the darkness, she could just make out his jaw clenched against the pain, which must have been excruciating.

"I can carry you, if you are too tired," he offered.

Her eyes widened. He was serious. She made a garbled sound, half cry and half laugh, and shook her head. He would do it, too. Even as angry as she was, she couldn't imagine what the added weight would do to his leg. Moreover, she sensed that she would need him as strong as possible for what lay ahead. Maybe his clansmen were right: Nothing hurt him.

Why had she ever thought he could care?

Taking a deep breath, she concentrated on putting one foot in front of the other and tried not to focus on her burning lungs.

After about another mile—though it felt like fifty—the sky opened up a little, the trees were not as close together, and the ground underfoot grew denser with bracken and heather. He let her rest for a few moments while he gathered an armful of fallen branches and moss, which she hoped meant a fire in the near future.

Once beyond the shelter of the trees, they were forced to move more slowly as the footing became more precarious. The footholds in the heather could be quite boggy.

A short while longer and she was looking up at an enormous rocky mountain. "What is that?"

"Beinnmheadhonaidh." Hill of the Caves, she translated. "Lowlanders call it Ben Venue."

He'd mentioned a cave to Robbie, so perhaps this was their destination? She hoped so.

He slowed their pace even further when the heather and bracken gave way to rock. "Careful," he warned, "the stones can be slick from the mist even if it isn't raining."

She was trying, but it was difficult to see.

They skirted around the base of the mountain until they got to a narrow, steep ravine. When she looked up, all she could see was the rocky face of the cliffside.

She stopped in her tracks. "You can't mean to climb up that?"

He chuckled. "Nay. You can't see it right now, but about a hundred yards up is an opening in the rocks. The cave is known as Coir nan Uriskin."

The Cove of the Satyrs. "Sounds idyllic," she said dryly. "I suppose it's haunted, too."

"Nay." She heard the amusement in his voice. "Though this area is supposed to be the meeting place for all the goblins in Scotland."

She shivered. Even though she wasn't superstitious, the place was eerie in the darkness. "Won't they know where to find us?"

He shook his head. "They should be traveling south for a while; this will give us a few hours."

"What about Robbie and your other men?"

His face was grim. "They can take care of themselves."

He would be with them if it weren't for me.

After a short but demanding climb, he tossed a few rocks deep into the cave—apparently to scare off any wild beasties using it for a home—then pulled her into the wide cavern of the cave. Once inside, she saw that it was about as big as her chamber at Castle Campbell—though decidedly danker. Heaving an enormous sigh of relief, she looked around for a place to collapse.

"Sit here," he said, spreading out the plaid he'd removed from the horse on the rocky floor of the cave. The thick wool provided little cushion to the hard floor beneath, but in her state of exhaustion it felt like a bed of feathers. "We won't be able to stay here long, but I need to get the ball out of my leg."

His matter-of-fact tone took her aback. "How do you intend to do that?"

"With my dirk."

My God, he was going to dig it out himself. "Isn't that dangerous?"

"I've done it before."

Not an answer, although she supposed in a way it was. He handed her a skin of water and a bit of dried oatcake, which she chewed slowly as he moved about the cave. She was hungry, and the oatcake barely made a dent; she hadn't eaten since they'd left early this morning. A lifetime ago.

Gradually, her breathing returned to normal, and her body began to feel the effects of the cold, damp night air, making her all the more grateful for the fire that Patrick had started to build.

He'd arranged some rocks near the back of the cave in a circle and laid the branches on top. After gathering some moss in a ball, he started to peel the outer layer of bark off a piece of birch with his dirk, then proceeded to crush it.

"What are you doing?"

"The wood and moss are too damp to catch a spark from my flint, but there is oil in this bark that ignites readily."

And after a few strikes of the flint, she heard the distinct

snap and popping of oil as the bark caught flame in the pile
of moss. He blew on it until a flame appeared, and then
carefully moved it to the pile of wood. Minutes later, a fire
crackled to life.

She studied his handsome face in the flickering light—the
hard angles of his cheekbones, the square of his jaw,
the straight line of his nose.

Her heart clenched as his face merged with another. She
couldn't ignore it any longer.

"You're one of them," she choked. "You're a . . ." She
could barely get out the words, the name fell so distaste-
fully from her tongue. "MacGregor." An outlaw, a scourge,
an enemy to her clan.

She could tell by the way his shoulders stiffened that he
didn't like her tone. He turned slowly to face her, his expression a mask of angry pride. "If you'll remember, I'm no
longer allowed to use that name." His gaze pierced her.
"But, aye, I was born Patrick MacGregor, eldest son to
Ewin the Tutor."

She gave a strangled cry. The crushing weight in her
chest was unbearable. Having the truth confirmed was a
brutal shock, her suspicions notwithstanding.

A MacGregor. He was a MacGregor. He'd tricked and
deceived her. But why?

Her heart pounded. She didn't know whether she could
withstand the truth, but she had to hear it all—every ugly,
hateful bit of it.

Her eyes didn't leave his face, looking for some sign of
emotion in that steely façade. *Tell me it's not what I think.*
"And the man who attacked me? The man who wants to
kill me?"

His mouth was pulled into a grim line and the pulse at
his neck began to tic, but he did not flinch from her gaze.
She braced herself for the worst. It came.

"My brother."

A choking sob tore from the depths of her shattered

heart with wrenching pain that dwarfed any that had come before. That vile, brutish man was his brother. She could only stare at him mutely as the ramifications tossed around wildly in her head. Of the first time she'd seen the MacGregor scourge. Of the first time she'd seen Patrick.

Her eyes burned with unshed tears, with the burgeoning realization that she'd been used. "Your appearing on the road that day was not a coincidence."

A flicker of regret passed over his face. She'd penetrated the implacable façade, but it was too late. "Nay, it wasn't a coincidence, though no one was supposed to be hurt."

Her chin quivered uncontrollably. "I'm to believe that? MacGregors are hardly known for their compassion and gentlemanly manner."

He ignored the barb, although his eyes flared. "As you no doubt realized by what you saw today, my brother and I are not exactly seeing eye-to-eye on things."

If she didn't feel as though she were dying inside, she would have laughed at the understatement. "You mean he wants to kill me and you don't?"

He grimaced. "Something like that. But I never thought he would take it this far. Gregor is hot-tempered and can be difficult to rein in, but he's always been loyal."

She stared at him, seeing him for the first time. Seeing things she'd never seen before. The strength and toughness had always been there, but now she saw the hard-edged ruthlessness. "God, I don't even know you."

He strode over and pulled her to her feet, forcing her to look at him. "I'm the same man I was before. The same man you said you loved."

How dare he throw that back in her face! Force her to see what a complete fool she'd been. "I loved Patrick Murray, not a ruthless outlaw. I loved a man who doesn't exist."

His jaw clenched. "I'm the same man. You know everything about me that is important."

"What? That you are an outlaw and a thief? A murderer—"

"Don't," he growled, his face taut with anger. "I'm no saint, but I've never taken the life of another not in battle."

"So what happened at Glenfruin, the murder of forty innocent boys, was acceptable because it happened during a battle?"

Her barb was well aimed; he stiffened. "Do not believe everything you hear, Elizabeth. Though my clan has taken the blame for that act, the killing of those boys was done not by a MacGregor, but by a rogue MacDonald. Our fight was with the Colquhouns—a battle that was fought at the urging of your cousin. Though the wily Argyll may claim otherwise."

His accusation took her aback. Lizzie knew there was no love lost between her cousin and the Colquhouns, but she could not believe her cousin was so devious as to use the MacGregors to do his dirty work and then hunt them down for doing it. And the killing of those schoolboys was only one of the atrocities leveled at the heads of the MacGregors. She thought of his brother. Of her dead guardsmen. "Are you suggesting that your clan's reputation is not well deserved?"

"Some of my kinsmen are wild and unruly, but could not the same be said of some of yours? Aye, I've stolen, but to keep my clan from perishing from starvation or the elements. Is that any different from the land your clan has stolen from me?"

Was that what this was about? Revenge?

Unable to hold them back any longer, she let the hot tears roll down her cheeks. "Why? Why me?" she choked, gazing up at him as if there could possibly be an answer that would make a difference, when they both knew there wasn't.

Patrick had never imagined that it would be like this. He hated hurting her. Hated making her cry. He wanted to pull her into his arms and kiss away her tears, but he forced himself not to move. She didn't want his comfort right now, she wanted an explanation. The truth. He owed her that, at least.

He met her gaze. "The Campbells stole my family's land. I sought to get it back."

"Land?" she said dazedly. "What land?"

"Near Loch Earn. Argyll has recently made it part of your dowry."

The blood drained from her face. She gazed at him in horror, all her emotions, all her heartbreak, revealed clearly in her eyes. She looked so fragile and vulnerable— like a kitten who'd just been kicked. By him.

He reached for her, but she twisted away. The rejection burned in his chest.

"So you used me for my land? For some petty revenge on my cousin and brothers?"

His anger sparked to hear her so casually dismiss the desperate situation of his clan. "I assure you, there is nothing petty in the enmity between our clans." He had plenty of cause for revenge. But not on Lizzie. "Initially I sought you out for your land, but that is not the only reason I wanted to marry you." He stepped toward her, the burning in his leg excruciating, halting when she retreated from him as if afraid. *Of me.* The burning in his leg crept up to his chest. "I care for you, lass," he said softly.

"You deceived me," she shot back at him, anger breaking through the sheen of tears. Her eyes glittered like sapphires. Perhaps there was more wildcat in her than kitten. "Why would I believe anything you say?"

"Because it's the truth."

"Truth? What about you is true? Not your name, not your purpose . . ." Her voice fell off and she looked at him with renewed horror. "Dear God . . . your wife and child?"

He met her gaze unflinchingly. "I have never been married."

She gasped and covered her mouth with her fingertips. "How could you lie about something like that? Was rescuing me from fake brigands not enough—did you have to invent a dead wife and child to earn my sympathy?"

He didn't shy from the scorn that he knew was deserved. "I needed a reason to explain our presence on the road. One that you would not question."

"Congratulations," she said, her voice dripping with sarcasm. "It was a brilliant plan. And successful, too. I fell right into your trap. Were you chosen for your handsome face or for your skills at seduction?"

"Damn it, Lizzie, it wasn't like that." But a small part of him cringed. He never wanted her to learn of their prior meeting or that he'd thought her an easy mark—susceptible to seduction. Now that he knew her, he understood how much it would hurt her.

"It wasn't? I'm surprised you even bothered with seduction at all. Why not just abduct me and force me to marry you? It seems more in keeping with the methods of your crude, bloodthirsty clansmen."

He bit back the flare of anger at her derisiveness—some of which he knew was deserved. " 'Tis not my way. I'd not want an unwilling wife. A forced marriage would be easily set aside."

"And you wanted the land." He could hear the unevenness of her breathing as she grappled with the implications. "You wanted me to fall in love with you." The hollowness in her voice cut him to the quick. "God, I'm such a fool."

He knew what he had done was unforgivable. He knew how she'd been hurt by Montgomery and thought he'd done the same thing. But what had happened between them was different.

"I wanted you to want the marriage. I make no excuse for what I did, Elizabeth. I hated deceiving you, but I had good reason for what I did. What happened between us was real. Can you honestly believe that I don't care for you? Everything I've done is because I care for you. I've fought my own men, my own brother, to protect you."

"All that proves is that you didn't want to see me killed before you could claim your spoils."

"Damn it, Lizzie, that's not true. If I cared nothing for you, why did I urge you to accept Robert Campbell's proposal? I knew I could not deny you a chance at happiness. I tried to walk away that night you came to the barracks."

"But I wouldn't let you," she said, her voice teeming with self-disgust. "Your conscience can be absolved, then—if you even have one. But thank God my mistake isn't irreparable. Thank God I didn't marry you. I'll be happy when I never have to set eyes on you again."

Her words stung more than he wanted to admit. How much of it was hurt speaking and how much was his being a MacGregor? "You will get your wish soon enough," he said harshly. He wished that it didn't need to be this way. Wished that he were begging her to understand instead of trying to make it easier for them to part. Wished that they didn't need to part.

Hell, he knew better than to wish.

His eyes met hers. Her cheeks were flushed and her eyes sparked with fire. "I hate you."

Her words unleashed something primitive inside him, the flare of emotion hot and quick. Anger. Frustration. And fear that it might be true. He didn't think, just reacted, pulling her into his arms. His heart pounded wildly, dangerously, with the primal need to prove her wrong.

She doesn't hate me. I won't let her.

He hardened against her, his body responding to the familiar feel of her pressed against him. Never had he felt so out of control. He wanted to ravage her senseless.

Kiss her.

Take her.

She gasped and tried to wrench out of his arms, but he held her firm.

He could feel the frantic beat of her heart, see her mouth tremble, her eyes wide and damp with tears. They stared at each other for a long moment, her soft mouth parted just below his. He could almost taste her sweetness on his tongue, calling to him.

His body hammered, the urge uncontrollable . . . almost violent.

The realization stopped him cold, and he released her as suddenly as he'd taken hold of her. What the hell was he doing?

What was between them could not be denied. But proving it would do nothing but salve his own male pride.

He dragged a hand through his hair, turning away from her and allowing his blood to cool. She eyed him warily.

Finally, he spoke. "You can hate me later. But right now, I'm all that stands between you and survival." He could just imagine her out here alone. A pampered girl brought up at court in the Highland wilderness. She wouldn't last a day. What the hell had he been thinking? "I don't think you have any idea of the precariousness of our situation, but if we are to have any chance, I need to get this ball out of my leg."

His body still teeming with violent emotion, he sat before the fire, pulled his blade from the scabbard at his waist, and went to work.

Lizzie watched Patrick wipe the flat of the blade of his dirk back and forth over his breeches—cleaning it, though the leather was caked with dirt and dust—her heart still pounding from the ferocity of his attack. No matter that for a moment she'd wanted his lips on hers.

I hate him. Never had she felt this kind of anger— irrational in its intensity. If he weren't already shot, she would have done it herself. She would rather be anywhere than here with him.

He was a MacGregor. Brother to the man who'd attacked her. He'd wanted her not for herself, but for her dowry. He'd used her like a pawn on a chessboard, deceiving her, making her fall in love with him, all for the sake of a few merks of land.

It was all a lie.

I'm such a fool. Actually believing that he cared for her. Of course she did, that's what he'd wanted. It was all part of his cruel plan. She crossed her arms around her waist as if warding off the attack, struggling to keep herself from falling apart. She'd thought she'd found happiness, but all she'd found was betrayal. How could she have been so mistaken? Again.

God, it hurt. The burning in her chest. The feeling that her heart had just been ripped out and stomped on.

I should be used to this. But it wasn't just disappointment. Her feelings for Patrick had gone so much deeper than anything she'd ever felt for John Montgomery.

Tears burned behind her eyes, anger and heartbreak converging in a powerful storm. Her mouth started to tremble. Her breath hitched.

Be strong.

She wanted nothing more than to bury her head in her hands and cry, but she would never let him see how much he'd hurt her. She closed her eyes and forced back the emotions, knowing this was not the time.

He was right. When this was all over she would never have to see him again, but right now she needed him. She hated it, but it was the truth.

She tried not to look at him. She shouldn't care about what he was doing.

She heard a tearing sound and knew that he was making the opening in his breeches bigger.

Dear God, he was actually going to do it. She felt a cold chill settle in her stomach.

Telling herself that it was only because she needed him to survive, she asked, "Do you need any help?"

He shook his head. "Nay, I've tended enough battlefield wounds to know what to do. It's not too deep—I can see the ball. If he'd waited a few more feet before firing we would not be having this conversation." He gave her a sideways glance. "You might not want to watch."

She pursed her lips. She wasn't some squeamish girl. But she found herself clenching the wool of the plaid between her fingers nonetheless.

After taking a long drink from one of the skins—which she suspected held something stronger than water—Patrick put the hilt of his eating knife in his mouth and used his dirk to dig into the soupy, bloody mess. The reason for the knife in his mouth became clear a moment later. His entire body tensed at the invasion—his teeth clamped down hard against the hilt, the muscles in his neck and arms went taut, and a guttural sound emitted from deep inside him. The pain must have been unbearable, but his hand showed no hesitation. In one smooth, determined stroke, he plunged the tip of the dirk deep into the hole.

He made another grunting sound as he appeared to maneuver the tip under the ball. The hand that held the knife pressed down, levering the ball up; then, using two fingers from his other hand, he dug it out.

Blood gushed from his leg—so much blood that she feared something must be wrong. Unwittingly, her heart fluttered wildly.

He used the cloth that she had given him bunched up in a square to press against the wound and took another long drink from the skin before he started to heat the blade of his dirk in the fire.

She might despise him, but she could not sit aside any longer. Without a word, Lizzie got up, walked over, and knelt beside him, taking over the stanching of blood with the cloth. The metallic scent mingled with the smell of whisky.

Their eyes met, and she read his thanks in his gaze.

He held the blade in the flames, turning it until it glowed. After removing the steel from the fire, he lifted her hand

and the cloth from his leg. Gesturing for her to get back, without hesitation, he placed the flat of the blade against the open wound.

His entire body clenched. The scent of burning flesh nearly made her gag, but she forced herself not to turn away. She put her knuckle in her mouth to keep from crying out. God, how could he do such a thing?

Having someone else do to him what he'd just done was bad enough, but doing it by yourself . . . took some kind of strength. Toughness that she couldn't even begin to comprehend.

Finally, after what seemed an eternity but was likely only a few seconds, he removed the blade from his leg and the hilt of the knife from his mouth.

Lizzie tossed up her skirts again and ripped a fresh piece of muslin from her underskirt, which now came down only to her knees. She handed it to him, and he used it to bind the seared wound.

They exchanged a long look. The lingering pain in his eyes made her heart twist, and she had to fight the urge to comfort him. He was so pale, with deep lines of pain and weariness etched around his mouth.

He seemed to understand her quandary.

"Go, get some rest, Lizzie," he said gently. "We only have a few hours. It's too dangerous to travel into these hills at night; we'll need to leave at first light."

She wanted to say something, but what was left that hadn't already been said? Instead she nodded and returned to her place on the plaid. Alone. She lay down and purposefully turned away from him, lest she be tempted to watch over him. He didn't need her; why had she ever thought he did? Closing her eyes, she let the pull of exhaustion take her under.

The crunching sound of someone walking quietly over rocks sounded in her ear where it pressed against the ground, startling her awake. Her eyes fluttered open in the semidarkness, and she was relieved to see that it was only Patrick. For a moment, her heart leapt with joy—forgetting where they were and what had happened—then the truth brought her crashing back to reality. Reality in the form of a dark, rocky cave, musty with animal scents, with more crevices than she cared to explore.

The fire had gone out, but surprisingly, she wasn't cold. She looked down to see the plaid wrapped around her.

"You can tend to your needs down by the loch," he said, raking his fingers through his still-damp hair. "I've left you some dried beef and a bit of oatcake. It's not much, but we need to ration just in case." He motioned to a rock near the saddlebags. "I'm going to climb up the hill to get a better vantage of the area before we go."

Lizzie felt an unwelcome pang in her chest. He looked horrible. Though if she didn't know him so well, she might not notice the lines of strain etched around his mouth, the flatness of his eyes, and the slight pallor of his skin. The signs of a long night spent in pain that no dunking in the loch could wash away. Her foolish heart went out to him. She'd be surprised if he had slept at all.

"Your leg . . . ," she started. "Does it hurt very badly?"

He shrugged. "I've had worse."

"But . . ." She bit her lip, unable to hide her apprehension.

"I'm not going to die, Lizzie," he said gently. "Not yet, at least. But my brother and yours, when they discover what has happened, will be doing their best to see otherwise. I'm going to need you to be strong if we are to have a chance. I won't lie to you, lass. The next few days are going to be difficult. Can you manage?"

"Of course," she retorted, annoyed that he thought her so weak.

Later, she would come to question that confidence.

Chapter 18

Lizzie was holding up better than Patrick had expected. Stubborn pride apparently had its benefits. He'd issued her a challenge, one that she would not easily forgo.

From the way she carefully avoided his gaze, he knew she was hurting. Her initial anger had turned to sadness— as if she were mourning the death of a loved one. And though she was not the sort to appear sullen or to mope, this quiet acceptance was almost more difficult to take. He wished she would lash out at him, but that was not her way.

He'd known it would be difficult when she discovered the truth, but seeing the betrayal in her gaze was far worse than he'd imagined. The only consolation was that at least he was not deceiving her any longer.

Their slow trek through the boggy pass between Loch Katrine and Loch Achray known as Bealach nan Bo, Pass of the Cattle, where his clansmen brought their cattle (some reived) from the Highlands into the Lowlands, had taken longer than he'd anticipated, complicated by his efforts to hide their muddy tracks and avoid dangerous bogs. But as they climbed higher and the ground became firmer, he was able to quicken their pace.

The low clouds and fine mist that descended as the day wore on did not bode well, and Patrick wanted to reach the edge of the tree line along the hill of Binnein before the rain came. There weren't any caves in the area, but he would be able to fashion some sort of shelter that would keep them dry enough while they waited to see if they'd eluded their pursuers.

He was used to being hunted and disappearing into the wild, but this time it was different.

He glanced over at Lizzie, noticing her flushed cheeks and heavy, uneven breathing. She wasn't used to this kind of exertion, and even with the aid of the walking stick that he'd made from a tree branch, she was struggling. But if they wanted to stay ahead of his brother, they had to keep forging along.

With the plaid he'd given her wrapped around her like an *arisaidh,* she certainly didn't resemble a Campbell heiress. She looked more like a bedraggled urchin. Her hair had long ago lost its bindings, and stray flaxen tendrils fell across her face and, more often than not, tangled in her lashes. Mud stained the bottom of her skirts up to the knee, and small droplets were spattered over the rest. At least she was wearing sturdy leather riding boots and not the flimsy slippers she often wore.

What the hell had he been thinking? This was after just one day in the wild. At times he'd lived like this for weeks. How could he have ever thought to bring her into this sort of life?

She wasn't the only one struggling. Truth be told, he was looking forward to reaching their destination as well. Each step he took sent a fresh needle of pain shooting up his leg that was becoming more difficult to ignore. He'd taken a risk in burning the wound closed and sealing in any infection. But that wouldn't come for days, if it did, and if he hadn't, he would have lost too much blood.

Sensing that Lizzie needed a rest, he stopped on a small rise and offered her a drink of water from the skin that he'd refilled at the loch. She accepted it eagerly, taking a long gulp before handing it back to him.

There was a break in the trees affording a breathtaking view east through the mist of the loch beyond.

"Is that the loch where we were earlier?"

She'd been silent for so long, it was a surprise to hear the sweet melody of her soft voice. "Aye." He pointed a little farther south. "The cave is on the side of the mountain there."

She nodded. "The loch is beautiful. What's it called?"

"Loch Katrine," he said, his voice forbidding. He'd been doing his best not to think about it all day. To think how close they were.

He saw her eyes scan eastward and then stop. Her eyes sparkled with the first glimmer of excitement he'd seen from her in days. "Is that an island?"

He stiffened. "Aye. Molach." The islet where his sister and some of the other MacGregor women and children had taken refuge. Only the knowledge that it was one of the first places his brother would search once he realized they hadn't gone south prevented him from going to see Annie. He didn't blame Lizzie for what had befallen his sister, but he was trying not to dwell on the events that had separated them. As soon as Lizzie was safe, he would find Annie. And then he would find Auchinbreck.

"It's charming," she said. When he didn't respond, she asked, "Do you think they are following us?"

"Aye. My brother will not give up that easily." He saw the fear in her eyes and instinctively sought to reassure her. "I chose these hills for a reason, Lizzie. No one will find us if I don't want them to."

If he'd intended to allay her fears, his words seemed to have the opposite effect. Her cheeks paled beneath the flush. "We're going into the hills?"

"Not unless we have to, but I need to get to Balquhidder to gather my men." It was too dangerous to try to get her to safety on his own. He hoped to hell that Robbie and the others had gotten away without a problem. He pointed in the direction of the hill where they were heading. "From up there I will have a clear view of the surrounding area. If my brother has picked up our trail, I will see him. If there is no sign of him, we will follow the lochs and rivers north and get my men, then I will take you to your cousin."

She looked at him as if he were mad. "To Dunoon? Won't that be dangerous for you? What if my family has already discovered that I'm missing and have learned who you are?" She paused. "What if I decide to tell them?"

He peered down into her tiny upturned face, seeing the challenge in her gaze and in the hard set of her chin. "Will you?"

Her mouth pursed together. "I just might."

His lips curved in a half-smile. "I suppose 'tis a chance I'll have to take."

They both knew his secret was safe with her. No matter how angry she was with him, Lizzie did not have a blood-thirsty bone in her body. Hers would not be the hand that spelled his doom. But she was right. When it was discovered that she was missing, there wouldn't be anywhere in the Lowlands for him to hide.

"And what if your brother has picked up our trail?"

"We'll take the high road through the hills. Gregor won't be able to track us as easily over the rock, and we've enough of a head start to stay well ahead of him. But at this time of year, venturing into the mountains can be dangerous."

"Why?"

"The weather changes quickly." At least it was still too early for snow. He slung the skin back around his shoulder. "Which will work in our favor today. The rain will slow them down."

"Rain?" Lizzie looked up to the sky and frowned. "What rain?"

Lizzie swore she wouldn't complain. No matter how exhausted, no matter how hungry, no matter how miserable she felt. She would prove to him that she was not some fragile piece of porcelain ready to crack at the first sign of difficulty.

And then as he predicted it started to rain.

Not a light, misty rain, but a full Highland downpour with icy gusts of wind that cut to the bone.

So now in addition to being tired, hungry, and cold, by the time they reached the area where Patrick decided to shelter for the night, she was also drenched.

And when she realized there would be no cozy cave to sleep in this night, she wanted to cry.

But it appeared she had underestimated Patrick's resourcefulness. He showed her to a fallen tree for her to sit on while he set about gathering the materials—tree limbs, pine bows, and moss—to build a shelter. Using part of the fallen log she was sitting on for a base, he cleared away the ground of leaves and rocks and built a tentlike structure with branches. Then he wove the bows between the branches to create a roof and laid moss on the ground to provide a buffer from the wet ground.

At the open end of the shelter, he built a small fire. It would be smoky, perhaps, but warm. And a few minutes later, when he settled her underneath, she realized it was also dry.

"You've done this before," she said wryly.

His mouth twitched. "Perhaps once or twice." He paused. "It's not what you are used to."

"No," she admitted. Far from it.

"Are you hungry?" he asked.

"Famished," she replied before she could think to lie.

"I might be able to catch a mountain hare. I can try to fashion some twine from vines or . . ." He gave her an odd look—almost as if he were embarrassed.

"Or?" she asked.

"If we had some kind of string."

She tilted her head, perplexed.

"Such that might be a part of a lady's undergarments."

"You want the tie from my stays? Why didn't you just say so?" He'd seen her naked, but he was flustered by talk of undergarments. It was . . . adorable. If a heavily muscled Highland warrior of well over six feet could be characterized as such.

He turned to give her privacy, and she quickly went to work removing the plaid that he'd given her and the heavy woolen jacket that she wore underneath, then loosened the ties of her kirtle enough to slide it down to her waist. With all the walking and climbing they were doing, it would be nice to be able to move a little easier. When she got to her stays, however, she had to stop. She'd forgotten. They tied in the back.

She bit her lip and looked at his broad back, debating.

"Is everything all right?" he asked.

"I'm afraid . . ." She took a deep breath and started again. "I'm afraid I need some help."

She covered her breasts, fully visible beneath the damp linen of her sark, with her arms as he turned. His eyes heated for an instant, lingering on the bare skin of her arms and neck, before he bent and placed his hands on her back, slowly working the ties of her stays. She held her breath, painfully aware of the warmth of his hands, of every stray brush of his fingers on her back. Of his breath on her neck. Of his body so close to hers.

It was an altogether too familiar intimacy that her body remembered well. Her skin prickled. From the cold, she told herself. But then why was she so flushed?

God, did he only have to touch her for her to fall apart? Did she so easily forget that he'd lied to her and deceived her from the first moment they'd met? That his seduction had been coldly calculated with one purpose—her dowry? That he was a MacGregor—her clan's enemy and an outlaw?

She straightened her spine and forced herself to ignore him and not let his touch affect her.

He must have felt her resistance, because he finished

quickly, murmured a brusque thanks, and said that he would return soon, leaving her to dress in peace.

Being alone in the forest at dusk, however, even with a fire, was not conducive to a state of peace. Frankly, it was terrifying. She jumped at every sound, imagining all sorts of horrible creatures lurking behind the trees. Time passed slowly, tolled by each rustling leaf, each snapped twig, and each oddly timed raindrop that splattered on a nearby rock. By the time he returned, her nerves were frayed raw and she would have welcomed the devil himself with open arms.

He took one look at her face and apologized. "It took longer than I expected. With the rain, there aren't as many hares venturing from their holes." He set down his bow and sword and sat opposite her. After putting the dead animal in front of him, he took out his dirk. "I hope you weren't frightened?"

"Of course not," Lizzie said automatically, before seeing his teasing expression. "Well, maybe a little," she conceded. "I kept thinking of that wolf. Are there any other wild beasts that I should be aware of?"

She turned her gaze as he started to skin the dead animal. Not normally squeamish about such things, she was nonetheless usually more removed from the preparation of her meat.

"You mean other than boars and wildcats?"

Boars and wildcats, dear God! "Aye, other than those."

He appeared contemplative and then shook his head. "Nay, nothing else I can think of."

"I'm greatly reassured," she said dryly.

He chuckled. "I don't mean to make light of your fears, lass, but it's not the wild animals we need to worry about. They're just as scared of you as you are of them."

"I doubt that."

He laughed again. "I won't let anything harm you, Lizzie."

She peered up at him, gazing at the hard angles of his handsome face flickering in the firelight, and could almost believe him. There was very little, she suspected, that this man could not do. His strength had always impressed her, but she was only now beginning to learn of its depths. She'd never met a man like him—tough to the bone, resilient, and resourceful. He would protect her with his last breath. Even against his own brother.

She'd been too angry to think about it at first, but she was glad Patrick hadn't killed him. The thought of him killing his brother for her . . . She shuddered.

"How is your leg?" she asked.

He shrugged. "A bit stiff."

An understatement if there ever was one, she would wager. "That's right, I forgot. Hamish said that you don't feel pain."

He gave her a long look. "I feel pain, Lizzie. I've just learned not to show it."

Their eyes held, and she wondered if maybe he wasn't as unaffected by what had happened between them as she had thought. It was some time before she looked away.

The smell of roasting meat a short while later was surpassed only by the first succulent bite. It was the first real meal she'd had in almost two days, and not knowing when she would have another, she ate her fill. It was some time before she stopped eating long enough to speak.

"Good?" Patrick asked, a wry smile on his face.

"Delicious," she said enthusiastically.

He handed her the skin of water. "If we had something to boil water in, I could make you a hot drink with pine needles."

"Hmmm. I didn't realize you were such a talented chef."

"Necessity breeds many talents."

She heard the underlying truth behind his jest, a reference to his life as an outlaw, she realized. What must it be like? A little like this, she'd wager. Hunted, living on the run, forced to find shelter in the wild. She felt a moment of compassion before she shook it off with the memory of how he'd gotten that way.

But now that the initial sting of his betrayal had dulled, she was left with many questions. "There's something I don't understand."

He nodded for her to continue.

"I thought the MacGregor had agreed to surrender."

Something in his gaze hardened. Or perhaps it was just the light from the fire?

"He did," he said carefully.

"Then why did your brother attack my guardsmen, and why did you change your mind and decide to take me to Dunoon?"

He didn't say anything, the silence punctuated by the crackle and pop of the fire and the slowing plop of rain on the bows overhead.

"What is it? What won't you tell me?"

His jaw clenched. "You won't want to hear what I have to say."

His forbidding tone gave her a moment's hesitation. "Yes, I do."

He took a deep breath, fixing his gaze on hers. "You know that Alasdair MacGregor surrendered under a promise from Argyll to see him safe to English ground—the deal brokered by your brother Jamie. Well, your cousin kept his promise, transporting the chief to England and setting him down upon English soil, only to immediately arrest him and return him to Edinburgh. Alasdair was executed along with twenty-four other of my clansmen a fortnight past."

Lizzie gasped with horrified disbelief. "You must be mistaken!" Her cousin wouldn't do something so dishonorable . . . would he? His hatred for the MacGregors made her pause. But even if Archie were so inclined, Jamie would never be a part of it.

Patrick's gaze was hard as steel. "I assure you, I am not mistaken. My cousin's and brother's heads sit over Dumbarton gate right now."

Her heart plummeted. "Your cousin and brother?"

"Aye, Alasdair MacGregor was my cousin—twice over. Our fathers were brothers and our mothers were sisters. My youngest brother, Iain, died at his side."

Lizzie felt ill. She could not doubt him—the ravaged sadness on his face couldn't be feigned—even if she couldn't believe the part he'd attributed to her family. "I'm sorry," she said.

"I do not blame you."

"But your brother does?"

"Aye. I erred in trusting Gregor, but always before I could convince him to see reason. I thought he'd understood. I was wrong."

She could see something in his expression. "What are you not telling me?"

His gaze was flat as he stared into the fire. "There were risings after the executions. My sister . . ."

He had a sister. God, she knew nothing about him.

He stopped and cleared his throat. Lizzie felt her heart start to hammer with trepidation. "My sister, Annie, was rap—" His voice cracked, and she put her hand on his arm.

Her stomach turned. He didn't need to finish. "I'm so sorry."

He gazed down at her hand and then back up at her face. His expression was as grim as she'd ever seen it. "At Auchinbreck's orders."

She pulled her hand away as if she'd been scalded. "No!" Tears sprang to her eyes. "That's a vicious lie! How dare you make such an accusation!"

He didn't say anything, just stared at her—almost as if he felt sorry for her.

Lizzie was not naïve. She knew that men often violated women in the name of war—as a means to humiliate and attack the pride of their opponent. But the thought that her brother could do anything so vile—so cruel and despicable . . .

God, was it possible?

There had to be an explanation. She needed to see Jamie, he would clear things up.

Lizzie was reeling from what Patrick had told her. No wonder he'd changed his mind about marrying her. If even a small portion of it was true, he had every reason to hate her.

Instead, he'd saved her life and battled his brother to do so.

Her eyes flew to his, suddenly recalling Robbie's hastily spoken word. "My God. You are chief."

"Aye, though it's clear that my brother means to challenge me."

Patrick Murray, simple guardsman, was really chief of the once-proud clan of MacGregor. The irony would have been laughable if it hadn't been at her expense. He was every bit her equal in position and in another time might have been a suitable husband for her. "Can he do that?" she asked.

"If the clan thinks I am unfit."

"But why would they . . . Oh." *Because of me.*

"I didn't say they would, just that they could. Gregor will try, but I will be able to convince them otherwise."

In her heart, she hoped Patrick succeeded. He would be a good chief. The qualities that had made him seem like a good husband also made a good leader: smart, strong, controlled, calm under pressure, and a fierce warrior. The type of man others looked to.

But she also knew the danger that position would put him in. It would also make him the most hunted man in Scotland.

He moved away from her toward the opening of the shelter. She noticed that it had stopped raining. "That's enough talking for tonight. Get some rest. You will have need of it."

She lay down, using the plaid as a blanket, her head resting on a surprisingly pillowlike pile of moss. She closed her eyes, but they wouldn't stay shut. Her gaze kept drifting to the large solitary figure shadowed in the flames. Finally she asked, "Aren't you going to sleep?"

"Later, lass. Later."

Later never came.

The sun had risen an hour ago, and still there was no sign of Gregor. Patrick wanted to be relieved—if his brother had picked up their trail, he should have been here by now—but the heavy sense of foreboding that had shadowed Patrick all night would not be so easily persuaded.

He'd kept watch by the fire all night, not simply because he feared an attack, but because he didn't trust himself. The shelter was barely big enough for both of them to fit under; he would be lying too close to her. And she was too damn tempting.

Now he stood just below the summit of Binnein, his gaze sweeping from east to west. The rain had cleared, leaving gray skies but a clear view of the surrounding area. If his brother was heading this way, Patrick would see him.

He'd woken Lizzie just before dawn and told her to tend to her needs and be ready in case they needed to leave quickly. He didn't like leaving her alone, but these slick, steep rocks were far more dangerous than anything she was likely to encounter in the forest.

The climb up the hill, normally done without thought, had been agonizing, taking far longer than he'd expected. At least he could be grateful that there were no signs of infection. So far. Little good he would be to Lizzie if infection set in.

He had to admit, she'd surprised him. She was holding up much better than he'd expected. She was tougher than she looked. Though tired and weary, she'd adapted to the situation, accepting what had to be done with fortitude and without complaint.

It almost made him wonder . . .

Nay. Even if she could forgive him, he was chief now. He had a duty to his clan. A duty that put him at odds with her family—he'd not ask her to choose.

He'd wanted to keep the details of her family's treachery from her—knowing it would be difficult for her to accept coming from him—but even if she didn't believe him, at least now she understood.

He watched the lochs, the pass, and the forest beneath him for any sign of unusual movement. A few fishermen were scattered on the water, but this was wild, inhospitable land, and inhabitants were few and far between.

Had Gregor decided not to pursue them? Had he lost their trail?

Though neither scenario sounded like his brother, Patrick knew that they needed to leave soon. If Campbells weren't already blanketing the area, they would be soon.

An eagle cried and soared overhead. It dipped, and Patrick's gaze lowered. And there, in a clearing in the trees below—two miles, maybe three, away—he saw a movement. Then another.

His instincts went on full alert, and he watched as a group of five men on foot followed the exact path he and Lizzie had taken yesterday. He couldn't see the men's faces or plaids from this distance away, but he knew: It was them.

Damn. There was only one road to Balquhidder open to them now—the high one through the hills. Lizzie was going to be seeing more of the Highlands than either of them had bargained for. He hoped to hell she was up to the challenge.

Skirting around the north side of Binnein to avoid being seen, he raced back to camp—the pain in his leg dulled by the knowledge that every second counted. They had a good lead, and they needed to keep it that way.

When he arrived back at camp, he didn't need to say anything.

She paled. "They're coming this way."

"Aye. But we'll lose them in the hills."

She nodded, unable to completely mask her trepidation. He almost reached for her, but she turned away. His chest tightened. She didn't want comfort from him, not any longer. Now that she knew the truth.

He looked around, intending to start getting their things in order, and realized it was unnecessary. Everything had already been packed neatly away in the bags. She'd even had the foresight to refill the skins from the small burn nearby that he'd told her to wash in this morning. In these hillsides water was never hard to find.

He quickly smothered the fire but didn't bother to hide the evidence of their encampment. It would only take time they didn't have, and his brother was too good at recognizing the signs to be fooled. But once they were in the hills, it wouldn't be so easy.

Within five minutes of his arrival, they were off. He kept them moving at a brisk pace—if not a run, then not quite a walk, either. He wanted to put as much distance as possible between them and Gregor before nightfall. With any luck, they would spend one cold night in the mountains and be at Balquhidder before dusk tomorrow.

The woodlands soon gave way to the strath. They followed the curve of Binnein north to the higher hill of Meall Reamhar. As they made their way up, bracken, heather, and grass gave way to rockier paths and Patrick was able to easily hide their tracks.

In addition to keeping an eye on the landscape behind them, he kept constant watch on Lizzie, slowing every so often to allow her to catch her breath. Only when they crested the hill did he stop. Stretched out before them, from east to west, was a panoramic vista of burnished brown hilltops—broken only by the occasional glimpse of a loch or small copse of woodland nestled in the deep corries.

Lizzie made a sound beside him that might have been a gasp, had she breath to lose. "It's magnificent." Her eyes met his. "Hills as far as the eye can see." She bit her lip. "Are you sure . . . it would be easy to get lost."

"We won't get lost."

"How can you be so sure?"

"These are MacGregor lands. I was raised in these hills."

She flushed. "Of course. I didn't think. Is your home near here?"

His gaze hardened, her innocent question hitting a nerve. "What home? I've had no home since I was a boy."

"I'm sorry, I—"

"We've tarried long enough." Turning his back to her, he started down the hill. He didn't need her sympathy.

They walked for hours. He pushed her as hard as he could without risking her collapse. The same could not be said of himself. Each step caused an explosion of pain so blinding, he wondered how much longer he could stand it. Steely determination and the knowledge that it was not just his life on the line kept him forging ahead.

Once he thought he'd caught sight of figures cresting a hill in the distance behind them. But as often happened in these hills, the clouds proved an expedient cover, descending like a curtain to hide them from view and further hampering his brother's ability to track them.

But it wasn't just his brother they had to worry about.

As the day drew on, the low clouds, once friendly, took on an ominous change. They thickened, turning heavy and dark. The weather in these mountains was like quicksilver, changing without warning. But it wasn't just the prospect of rain that worried him. It was the sudden drop in temperature— the unseasonable sudden drop in temperature.

This high in the hills, with little to protect them, the cold was bone-numbing. With the plaid wrapped around her and her heavy wool skirts, Lizzie was better protected than he was with only a shirt and leather jerkin, but neither of them could stay out here for long, and they were still a good distance away from the place he'd hoped to shelter for the night.

Realizing they weren't going to make it before the storm set in, he knew he had to find someplace closer. He changed direction, heading due east, making for a copse of trees in one of the gulleys on the other side of the mountain ridge.

Every time he looked at Lizzie, exhausted, shivering, trying bravely not to show her fear, he felt a stab of guilt so sharp that it felt like a dirk twisting in his gut. He urged her on with words of encouragement, but she was flagging.

This was his fault. He never should have gone to Castle Campbell in the first place. Why had he? Land, yes, but also because from the first moment he'd seen her, he'd wanted her. And look where it had brought them: running for their lives in one of the most dangerous places on earth to be caught in a snowstorm—early or not.

For the first time in his life, Patrick felt real fear. Not for himself—he'd weathered storms before—but for Lizzie. He didn't know how much more she could take.

His fears were well-founded when moments later the snow started to fall—hard and fast, as if it had been waiting months for the opportunity to let go, instantly covering their footsteps in a heavy white blanket and making each step over icy rock and dense heather more treacherous than the last. But worse was the wind. Blowing in hard gusts, it blinded, preventing him from being able to see more than a few feet in front of them.

And ever present was the growing threat of darkness.

"Patrick, I . . ."

He turned, holding his arm against his face to ward off the icy wind. He was just able to make out her tear-filled eyes beneath the edge of the plaid that covered her head.

His chest squeezed, seeing her cheeks wet and red from the cold.

"I'm sorry," she cried. "I don't think I can go on."

He pulled her against him, tucking her under his arm as if he could protect her from the brutal elements by the shield of his body alone. She let him hold her, and though he knew it was for his heat, for the moment it was enough.

"Come, love, you've done wonderfully, don't give up now. It's not much farther," he lied.

He could hear the rising panic in her voice. "But how do you know? How can you see anything in this?"

He pointed to a rock. "By the direction of the snow on the rocks." The wind had been blowing from the east.

"Is there nowhere we can rest, just for a few minutes?"

He didn't need to look around, he knew the answer. There was no place for shelter—there were only high moors and rock with occasional patches of heather. "I know you are tired, Lizzie, but we need to keep moving." If they stopped, they would freeze, and there was less than an hour left of light.

She looked up at him, eyes wide with concern. "I've taken your plaid. You must be freezing."

"I'm used to the cold." He looked down at her tiny hand on his arm. The tinge of blue on her fingertips struck him cold. Quickly, he took from his bag the pelt he'd kept from the hare. "Use this to wrap around your hands." She did so without argument, though it hadn't been tanned. "We need to keep moving. I'll help you, all right?"

She nodded and allowed him to lead her on. He kept her tight against him, bracing her from the wind with his body as they slowly wound their way through the maze of rocky hills. But as the snow got deeper, her skirts started to tangle, impeding her steps even further.

He was literally dragging her, and when she tripped, almost falling headfirst down a steep crag, he picked her up.

"What are you doing?" she said weakly, delirious with exhaustion and cold. "Your leg. You can't carry me."

He was so damn cold that he didn't feel anything—he just knew that he had to do something if they were going to have a chance. He ignored her protests and, cradling her against his chest, plowed forward through the storm.

But as he approached the summit of the last big hill before they descended toward the copse of trees, the light dimmed to almost nothing and the snow started to come down even harder. He couldn't see two feet in front of him. They weren't going to make it. He looked around for anything that might help shelter them from the full brunt of the storm.

Once before when he'd been caught in a storm, he'd been able to stay warm by using the carcass of a deer that had fallen down the steep mountainside into the corrie. The vile, nauseating stench was not one he'd soon forget, but right now he would welcome it.

A few feet away, he saw the dark gray top of a large rock just breaking through the snow. It wasn't much, but it would have to do. But when he reached it and tried to set Lizzie down, his heart plummeted.

Her eyes were closed, and glittering crystals of ice hung from her lashes onto her bloodless cheeks. "Lizzie!" he cried, gently slapping her cheek when she wouldn't wake. "God damn it, Lizzie!" He felt as if his heart were being wrenched from his lungs. "Don't you dare leave me now!"

She was deathly cold.

Knowing he had to work fast, he set her down and began to dig furiously, tunneling a small cave of snow next to the rock. When it was just big enough for them to squeeze in, he hugged Lizzie tight and pulled her inside, nestling her against his chest and enfolding her in his arms as he fought to warm her shivering body with his. But he had little heat to give. He swore one minute and prayed the next, having never felt so bloody powerless in his life.

Take me, but don't let her die.

Not this sweet girl who'd done nothing but make the mistake of giving her heart to a man who didn't deserve it.

God, what have I done? "I love you, Lizzie," he said, speaking the words aloud for the first time.

His chest burned, the ache in his heart so profound that he could deny it no longer. The truth had been there all along: He loved her. Loved her as he'd never loved a woman before. He'd thought himself impervious, no longer capable of feeling these cruel emotions. But he was wrong. His love for Lizzie was too powerful to be denied.

But the realization was tinged with despair. He pressed his mouth against her head, the cold clamminess of her forehead sending ice through his already-frozen veins.

The snow and wind howled as night closed in around them like a shroud.

Chapter 19

Lizzie woke slowly, groggy with the effects of a heavy sleep. Her head throbbed, as if she'd drunk too much claret. And she didn't think she'd ever been so cold.

Her eyes fluttered open and she felt a moment of panic—seeing nothing but icy white snow all around her.

Her heart stuck in her throat. *I've been buried.*

But almost immediately, she became aware of the strong arms held tight around her and the steady beat of his heart behind her. Instinctively, she relaxed.

"Lizzie." Patrick shook her gently, and she could hear the urgency in his voice.

"Where are we?" she croaked.

"Thank God," he said. "You're awake."

She tried to wriggle out of his arms, but there was nowhere to go.

"Careful," he warned. "You'll bring the roof down on top of us."

"What roof?"

"I dug a snow cave. It was the only way to get out of the storm."

Memories of the day before came rushing back full force, and she immediately became aware of his injured leg and the painful blisters on her feet.

"Is it still snowing?" she asked.

"I don't think so, but I'll go outside and make sure."

She wanted to cry out when his arms unwrapped from around her and the warmth of his body left her backside.

He kicked a hole with his feet and scooted out carefully. Moments later, he reached back in to help her out. "Come outside and see."

Unnaturally stiff with cold, she struggled out of the small hole, but with his help a few minutes later she was rewarded with the gentle warmth of the morning sun on her face. Dawn was just breaking over the horizon, spraying soft rays of gold over a glistening carpet of white.

Lizzie sucked in her breath. "It's beautiful."

"Aye," Patrick said harshly. "But it could have been deadly."

She turned to him, realizing that she had no idea how she'd gotten into that cave. The last thing she remembered was him picking her up and carrying her.

"Thank you," she said softly.

He turned to look at her, surprised. "For what?"

"For saving my life."

His expression hardened. "I could have killed you," he said stonily. "It's my fault you are out here in the first place."

"You couldn't have known it was going to storm."

"Nay," he admitted. "Even with the unaccountably cold winters we've been having the past few years, 'tis early for a snowstorm of this magnitude. But I never should have brought you into this." It wasn't the storm he was talking about. His eyes met hers. "I never meant to hurt you, Lizzie. I want you to know that. I hope one day you will be able to forgive me."

Lizzie stared into those familiar green depths, searching for signs of deception but finding only sincerity. Her heart tugged, and she was plagued by the confusion of conflicting emotions. The experiences of the past few days had thrown her feelings into a turmoil.

He'd deceived her and lied to her in every conceivable way for a few merks of land. She should despise him. Part of her wanted to. Hatred didn't hurt.

But she couldn't ignore what he'd done for her—protecting her from his clan and battling his own brother to do so. He'd chosen her even when it would have been easier not to. These were not the acts of a cold, ruthless man. He might be an outlaw, but he was not without honor.

An honorable MacGregor. Was such a thing possible? Her family might not think so, but Patrick made her wonder.

Here, in the primitive, unforgiving Highlands, Lizzie felt as if she were seeing him for the first time, and it was impossible not to admire what she saw. This rugged, harsh landscape helped define him. In the hard angles of his handsome face and the granite strength of his body, she saw the beauty of the hard, uncompromising countryside. Like the sturdy heather on the hillsides, he was resilient. Like the power of a sudden storm, he could be deadly. And like the Highlands, he was tough to the bone. Hunted, with a bullet hole in his leg and little more than what they had on, he'd kept them alive.

If the past few days were any indication of the challenges facing his clan, it was a testament to their strength that they'd survived as long as they had. It also gave her a better understanding of the difficulties he faced as the leader of a broken clan—a clan without land.

Nor could she ignore the strange pull she still felt when she looked at him. Not just physical attraction, but something far deeper and far more elemental.

She wanted to believe that he'd cared for her, that it hadn't all been a lie. That she hadn't confused lust with love. That what they had was worth fighting for—even against the horrible events that had conspired to separate them. She swallowed, her throat suddenly tight. "My forgiveness is important to you?"

"Very." He gave her a long look, clearly debating whether to say something further. When his hand closed around hers, her chest gave an involuntary squeeze. With that simple connection, she felt the force of a far larger and more powerful one.

And she felt a little piece of the wall between them crumble. He was right: His actions were not those of a man who didn't care.

"Come," he said. "On the other side of this hill there is a burn where we can wash and have something to eat. Later there is something I want to show you."

She had to wait hours to find out what he meant.

Walking in the hills was difficult enough; trudging over them in snow was even worse. She followed the path Patrick cleared for her as best she could, but her skirts made it slow going. When they reached the small copse of trees and the burn, she was at first skeptical and then grateful for the funny treads he'd fashioned for her from branches and pieces of the string from her ever handy stays. The branches gave her traction and kept her from sinking into the soft, wet snow.

But as they descended farther down the hills, they became unnecessary. The deep snow at the summit lessened to mere inches and then to only patches, as the sun—all but forgotten yesterday—worked its magic. When they entered the forest for what he assured her was the last few miles of their journey, she was warm enough to remove the plaid. They walked through the trees and along a burn for a time, finally coming to a stop just before dusk at the head of a charming loch. It was perhaps only half a mile wide at its mouth, but it was miles long. On her right, on the south bank, a few hundred feet away stood a small, stately castle—newly constructed, from the looks of it.

She gazed at Patrick, but his face was inscrutable as he intently scanned their surroundings. Her heart tugged. If anything, the past few days had only made him more handsome. His skin was rough and rugged from the wind and cold, his hair silky and tousled, and the dark shadow of a beard emphasized the hard lines of his jaw.

"What is this place?" Lizzie asked.

"Loch Earn." He turned to her, his face solemn. "It used to be my home."

She sucked in her breath. This was the land her cousin had added to her dowry. The land that Patrick wanted to get back. His sole purpose for wanting her. Her chest tightened. "Why have you brought me here?"

"I don't really know." He paused thoughtfully, his gaze returning to the loch. "I wanted you to see it. To know what happened here. To know why I did what I did."

"What happened here?" she asked gently, sensing the importance.

Patrick didn't answer right away. He couldn't stop gazing out over the loch, at the castle. It was as if something—the memories, perhaps—had overtaken him.

His face was ravaged with raw emotion, and Lizzie realized she'd never seen him look so exposed. Usually he kept himself remote, detached, but at that moment she saw it for what it was: a façade. The lines etched on his handsome face and the sorrow in his eyes revealed a man who'd suffered deeply.

His voice held no emotion as he spoke, but it was there—simmering under the surface—and she felt it wrap around her. "This land belonged to my clan for hundreds of years, but we had not the paper to prove it. The Earls of Argyll turned us into tenants on our own land."

Lizzie knew something of the MacGregors' history. In the dispute of the claim to the throne between the Bruces and the Balliols, they'd chosen the wrong side, and when Robert became king, he'd made them suffer for it. Without charters to prove ownership, the MacGregors had been divested of their land. That the Campbells had benefited was the source of the feuding between the clans in the years that followed.

"But that was hundreds of years ago," Lizzie said softly.

"Aye." He met her gaze. "But time does not correct a

wrong." His face hardened. "For years my family held this land as vassals of Argyll—never content, but accepting. Almost twenty years ago that relationship, however tenuously held, was severed. Argyll illicitly sold the tenancy of our lands to Glenorchy, and the black devil did not waste time in asserting his ill-gained 'rights.' "

He paused, and Lizzie couldn't tell whether that was all. "So Glenorchy evicted your family from this land?"

"Evicted?" He made a sharp, pained sound. "That's one word for it. Glenorchy's methods were more akin to extermination. When my father refused to cede our land, Glenorchy decided to burn us out. I was ten when the soldiers came. I remember looking out my window and seeing the fire and thinking it was Armageddon."

Lizzie's chest pounded as she waited for him to continue, her heart going out to the terrified little boy he must have been.

"My mother sent me and my brothers into the forest. Annie was just a babe, and my mother thought we would be safe—she was Glenorchy's sister, after all." His face twisted, and Lizzie felt her heart twist along with it. "I didn't want to leave her, but she insisted."

He stopped, and Lizzie put her hand on his arm. "I'm sorry." She had guessed what was coming.

"But you don't know what happened," he said harshly, his face tortured. "I'd left something behind, something my father had trusted me to keep safe, so I went back." His voice was hollow. "It was so hot. Hard to breathe. Everything was burning. I thought I'd walked through the gates of hell—but it was worse. The dead bodies of my clansmen lay scattered across the *barmkin*. My father was among them."

Lizzie squeezed his arm. He was so taut, every muscle clenched, she could almost feel the incredible tension running through him under her fingertips.

"A couple of Campbell soldiers found me at his side and decided I was better off dead."

"But you were only a boy!"

"Aye, but they were right. I would have hunted them down." His eyes were stark when he turned to her. "My mother saw what was about to happen and rushed out to stop it. Instead, she took the blade that was meant for me. She died in my arms." His voice was wooden. Emotionless. But it no longer deceived her.

Lizzie felt the tears burning in her eyes. She'd lost her parents at a young age but couldn't imagine seeing them murdered before her eyes.

"It wasn't your fault. Your mother was only trying to protect you."

"I know, though it took me years not to feel to blame. Glenorchy murdered my parents and built his cursed castle on the ashes of my home and the blood of my parents and clansmen. Their deaths lie at his feet." He held her gaze. "You see, Lizzie, it wasn't just about a few merks of land. I've been fighting ever since to get back part of what was taken from me that day. All my legal claims had failed. When I heard that your cousin had added the land to your dowry, I knew the opportunity I'd been waiting for had arrived. I just hadn't counted on one thing."

The look in his eye took her breath away. Her heart pounded. "What's that?"

One side of his mouth lifted in a wry smile. "You. I knew I couldn't tell you the truth, but I hated deceiving you. I told myself I would make it up to you, but it all changed when Robert Campbell arrived."

Lizzie sucked in her breath, realizing how horrible that must have been for him, seeing the son of the man who'd taken everything from him wooing her. All of a sudden, her eyes shot to his face. "You wanted me to marry him."

He tensed, his expression once again unreadable. "I knew he would make you happy and give you the life you deserved. With me you would have been . . ." He let his voice trail off as if he'd said too much and then straightened. "Until the king decides otherwise, I'm an outlaw."

My God, he'd cared about her enough to sacrifice everything he'd been fighting for since he was a boy—to the son of the man who'd killed his parents.

She didn't know what to say. What to do. Too stunned by all that he'd told her and suffered at the hands of her clan. "Thank you for bringing me here."

He met her gaze and nodded, looking a little embarrassed. Shifting his gaze, he lifted his eyes to the sky. "There isn't enough time to reach Balquhidder before it gets too dark. Come, I think I know a safe place we can stay for the night."

He led her along the shore of the loch. There were a few small cottages along the way, but she was surprised to see that the castle appeared to be virtually deserted.

"The castle," she said.

"Edinample," he supplied.

"Why is it so deserted?"

"It's cursed."

At first, Lizzie thought he was joking. "You're serious."

"The villagers believe so. Glenorchy is said to have tossed the architect off the roof when he found out that the parapet he'd requested had not been built. The ghost is said to walk the roof at night, cursing the laird."

Lizzie grimaced. From what she knew of Glenorchy, it was entirely believable. "How horrible."

Patrick nodded. "The black devil is said to have used gravestones of MacGregors to build it—to save him money and the trouble of bringing in more stone."

Lizzie shivered. If the place wasn't cursed, it deserved to be. They walked a little farther, and Patrick left her for a moment while he went to speak with an old man, his leathery face battered by years of sun and wind, who was pulling a small skiff out of the loch.

Patrick returned after a moment, a smile on his face. "We are in luck. Not only shall we have a warm place to sleep for the night, but you might even get a bath and a meal as well."

Lizzie sighed dreamily, unable to mask her excitement. It was amazing how what had seemed basic only a few days ago now felt like the most wonderful treat. "Where are we going?"

"There," he said, pointing into the loch. "It's an old crannog—an island built by our Highland ancestors hundreds of years ago—there is a small stone dwelling on the other side. Basic provisions are kept there in case it needs to be used as a refuge in an attack, though it hasn't been used for such in years. There used to be a wooden walkway to the island, but it sank long ago."

It didn't look to be more than a tree-covered rock, but Lizzie took his word for it.

Patrick helped her into the small skiff, and the old man rowed them out to the crannog. It was bigger than she'd thought—perhaps fifty feet in diameter. As promised, a small building stood—shakily, by the looks of it—on the far side.

Patrick thanked the fisherman, gave him a coin from his sporran, and secured a promise to return for them at dawn. As he left, the old man murmured something to Patrick and then snickered.

When the old man was out of earshot, Lizzie asked, "Why, what did he say?"

"Nothing fit for your ears."

Her eyes narrowed. "What did you tell him about us?"

Patrick looked mildly uncomfortable. "That we've just been married and are fleeing from your father, who doesn't approve."

She lifted her brow skeptically. "And he's a romantic?"

Patrick laughed. "Not quite. He's a MacLaren, and I mentioned that your father is a Buchanan."

"And let me guess, they are feuding?"

Patrick grinned devilishly. "For years."

Lizzie's heart stopped as for a moment she caught a glimpse of the happy, carefree man he might have been had fortune and not tragedy defined him. Yet even with everything that had befallen him, he was still amazing. A man to admire.

A man to love.

The realization took her aback. *I still love him.*

Perhaps even more so. For now she knew what drove him, finally understanding the darkness that she'd always sensed lingering just beneath the surface.

She hated that he'd lied to her, but no longer did she think he didn't care for her. His actions spoke the truth. Murray or MacGregor, his name didn't matter. What mattered was the man inside, and he hadn't changed.

She knew what this would mean. Knew what she'd be giving up. He was an outlaw, being hunted by her own family. If she went with him, she could lose everything. Her home, her comfort, her security.

But she also knew that without him she would never be happy.

She wanted him.

Her heart clenched. But did he want her?

Patrick frowned. Lizzie was being unusually quiet. He glanced across the small table, watching as she popped the delicate morsels of fish into her mouth, savoring each bite as if she'd never tasted anything more delicious. The tiny sounds of enjoyment teased his memory, driving him mad with lust, reminding him of very different circumstances where she'd made such sounds.

Her damp hair glistened in the firelight, and springy flaxen tendrils had started to curl enchantingly around her face.

His body heated as he grew painfully aware of the intimacy of the moment. Perhaps this place had been a bad idea. It was too small. Too cozy. Too hot and steamy from the water he'd heated to fill the small wooden tub—actually more of a large bucket, but it had sufficed under the circumstances.

With little space for privacy and not trusting himself to avert his gaze, he'd left her to her bath while he went outside to douse the sudden throbbing in his loins in the cold loch. He'd washed away the dirt and grime of the past few days, but his body would not be so easily tamed.

He was hard as a damn rock and painfully aware that beneath the plaid she'd wrapped around herself, only a torn thin sark covered her nakedness.

She took a nip of the last of the *uisge-beatha* that he'd poured in two tin cups, catching a drop of the amber liquid that dribbled down her lip with a flick of her pink tongue.

The bolt of raw desire went straight to the head of his cock.

He turned away with a sharp sound of annoyance. If he didn't know better, he would swear she was purposefully trying to torture him.

"Is everything all right?" Lizzie asked.

"Fine," he said tightly.

She stood up and walked around to stand beside him. She'd wrapped the plaid around her like a shawl slung low on her shoulders, emphasizing the lush, round curve of her breasts. Tiny bare toes peeked out below.

She was standing too close. Her soft feminine scent wrapped around him like a sensual vise from which he could not break free.

"You don't seem fine," she said, putting her hand on his shoulders. "You seem tense." She started to knead the tight muscles in his shoulders and neck. "Are you sure you don't want to take off your jerkin? It's nice and toasty in here."

With intimate familiarity, her hands moved around to the front of his chest and her nimble fingers started to work the buttons of his jerkin. During the course of their all-too-brief affair, she'd become amazingly proficient at undressing him. When her hands dipped too low on his belly, her wrist brushing the plump head of his erection, he knew there was no mistaking her overtures.

He grabbed her hands, clasped them around the wrists, and pulled her in front of him. Jaw clenched, he said tightly, "What are you doing, Lizzie?"

Her cheeks flushed pink. She looked like a naughty bairn who'd just been caught with her hand in the biscuit jar, but her eyes did not shy from his. "I want you."

Blood surged through his veins. The pulse at his neck started to tic furiously. Her words reverberated through his body, the devil's own temptation.

He stood up, releasing her wrists, but she did not move away.

Maybe it had been a mistake to bring her here. He'd wanted her to understand, but nothing had changed: They couldn't be together. "It's not a good idea."

Her face fell. "Why not?"

"Nothing has changed, Lizzie. I cannot marry you. Making love to you now would be wrong."

She flinched from the harshness of his words. He thought she'd turn away, but instead her chin edged up and she looked him right in the eye. "Why?"

"Isn't it obvious? With what has happened, there is too much between our clans."

"But not between us."

"What are you suggesting? Surely you know your family would never allow us to marry."

She took a deep breath. "Not right away, perhaps. But they love me—they'll come around . . . eventually. You know you can't run forever. Let me help you."

"Like your cousin helped Alasdair and Iain?"

She dropped her hands from his. "You do blame me for

what happened to your cousin and brother. And to your sister."

He could hear the hurt in her voice but forced himself not to react. This was for the best. "I don't blame you. But others will."

"Being hated for my name is nothing I'm not familiar with. I'm willing to brave it if you are." He read the challenge in her gaze. "Have you so easily given up on your vow to return your land to your clan?"

"Damn you, Lizzie." His eyes narrowed. It was a low blow. She knew now how hard it had been for him to give this place up—and how much he still wanted it. It was part of him. "I will get it back," he said, and his voice held a dangerous edge. "But I won't use you to do it."

"If you truly want to do the best thing for your clan, don't you have a better chance with me on your side?" She paused, giving him time to consider her words. "My family will listen to me; let me help plead your case."

She was right. Her influence with her family was the best option—the only option—the MacGregors had right now. But he didn't want to listen to reason. He was trying to protect her. "And if you are wrong about your family's acceptance? What then?"

"I want to be with you, Patrick. Wherever you are."

His heart hammered. He was so damn tempted, but then he remembered the past few days and how she'd looked last night in his arms—cold and lifeless. "More caves in the snow, is that what you want? God's blood, Lizzie, you could have died out there." He couldn't hide the raw emotion in his voice as the memories assailed him. He'd never felt so helpless in his life.

"But I didn't," she said quietly.

Her calm certainty angered him. "Not this time, but what about the next? Because there will be a next. I'm an outlaw. You've no idea what it's like to live on the run. To be without a home. To not know where your next meal is coming from. This isn't the life for you."

"Am I not allowed to make that decision?" She put her hand on his chest and gazed up at him, her mouth so soft and tempting. He wanted her so badly, he couldn't think.

Patrick's blood pounded; he was holding himself by a very tight rein. It scared him how much he wanted to take up her offer. But he loved her too much to do that to her. She had no conception of the life she would be thrown into, the desperate situation of his clan, and what she would be giving up. He couldn't allow her to make such a sacrifice for him.

His face turned hard, his mouth twisting in a sneer. "You've been raised in the finest castles in Scotland, surrounded by servants who tend to your every wish, you have never wanted for anything. Can you imagine what it's like to go to bed with nothing in your belly? To hear your babe cry with hunger? To go for months being so cold you can't move your fingers? This isn't some romantic girlish fancy—something you can end when you get tired of it. It never ends."

Her face flushed. "I won't pretend that it will be easy."

"Easy?" He laughed harshly. "You wouldn't last a month."

Her eyes flashed, and he knew he'd gone too far. "How dare you condescend to me like this! Have I in any way proved myself less than any of the women in your clan? I am not some pampered princess, and I will not be treated as such. I can make my own decisions, and I certainly don't need some overbearing, overprotective knight in shining armor who thinks he knows what's best for me doing it for me. What you describe is horrible, and I won't make light of the situation of your clan or pretend that I know what it is like, and God knows why with the way you are acting right now, but for some reason *you* make me happy. I love you and I'd rather endure hell with you than hell without."

Jesu, he thought, taken aback. She had a feisty little temper beneath that sweet façade.

"If you don't want me for your wife, just say so, but don't try to scare me away because it won't work."

He swore, standing stone still, willing himself not to pull her into his arms and ravish her senseless. He was only trying to save her from herself. "This has nothing to do with what I want." His eyes met hers. "God, Lizzie, you're killing me. I'm just trying to do the right thing."

She leaned toward him. Her soft breasts pressed against his chest enticingly, but it was the flash of hope in her eyes that proved the death knell of his resistance. "Then stop. This is the right thing." She reached down and clasped his hand in hers. Her soft, warm fingers entwined with his. "Give me a year to prove it to you. If I'm wrong, you can walk away with impunity."

He stilled, understanding exactly what she was proposing. A handfast. The old Highland custom was frowned on by the Kirk, but not as uncommon as it would like. A year? Hell, once she was his, he'd never wish to let her go. But it would give her a way out.

Gazing into her big blue eyes, he knew that he couldn't fight destiny. He loved her, and he was done trying to find reasons for them not to be together.

He lifted her hand to his mouth and kissed her fingers. "Here, before God, I, Patrick MacGregor, do pledge to you, Elizabeth Campbell, my troth. I agree to be bound to you for a year and a day under the ancient custom of handfast."

"Here, before God, I, Elizabeth Campbell, do pledge to you, Patrick MacGregor, my troth. I agree to be bound to you for a year and a day under the ancient custom of handfast."

When she was done, a wide smile broke across her face, unleashing a swell of something inside Patrick that he hadn't felt in many years—happiness.

His mouth brushed over hers softly, tenderly, sealing their vows with a reverent kiss. The poignancy of the moment was forever etched on his soul.

He swung her up in his arms and carried her over to the pallet near the fire.

"Your leg," she protested.

"It doesn't hurt." In truth, right now he was so happy that he could feel no pain.

He set her down and removed the plaid from her shoulders, arranging it on the pallet as a covering. He shirked off his unbuttoned jerkin and removed his boots, but when he started to pull off his shirt, she stopped him. "Let me."

The soft huskiness in her voice filled him with heat, but it was nothing to the incredible sensation of her hands on his body.

She slid her hands under his shirt, skimming her palms over his belly and chest, lingering, exploring the ridges of muscle with her fingertips, driving him mad with her feather-soft touch. His skin heated, and every nerve ending flared at her delicate caress. She drew out every movement, taking her time in lifting the linen shirt up and over his head.

She knew what she was doing to him, the little minx, and when her hand dipped to play the same game with the ties of his breeches, he clasped her wrist. "My turn."

He knelt before her, running his hands up her calves and looping his thumbs under the edge of her torn sark. He raised the fabric inch by inch as his hands stroked her long, shapely legs. Her skin was like velvet—so incredibly smooth and creamy under his rough fingertips. The contrast between them could not be more profound, but it no longer worried him. She might be tiny and delicate, but she'd been made for him. She wouldn't break—he smiled wickedly—though he intended to make her shatter.

When his hands had finished exploring every inch of creamy smooth skin, he used his mouth, pressing soft kisses on the curves of her calves, her tiny knees, the tender insides of her thigh, pushing the fabric higher and higher as his mouth climbed toward her petal-soft sex. The scent of her filled him, seeping deep into his bones, arousing dark, primitive yearnings.

His staff pulsed against his belly. But it would have to wait.

Her legs started to shake and her breathing hitched as he slowly approached his destination.

He wanted to bury his head between her legs and taste her hard and deep, but he forced himself to go slowly—to drag out every moment of her pleasure.

Her legs pressed together reflexively, her body tightening with resistance, but he forced them apart.

"No," she protested. "Surely you can't mean to—"

She gasped. Her words turned into a moan as his tongue flicked over her slick womanly core.

He closed his eyes and groaned, savoring her taste and the feminine scent of desire, before pressing his mouth fully over her.

Her legs wobbled and she had to grab his shoulders as he slid his tongue deep inside her, probing intimately. She was so warm and soft. So deliciously wet. And tasted as sweet as honey.

Her fingers dug into his shoulders as he increased the pressure, increased the pleasure. Stroking. Flicking. Sucking. Bringing her to the brink and then easing her down.

Her moans turned frantic. "Please," she whispered, threading her fingers through his hair.

Her passion undid him. He grabbed the soft curves of her buttocks and lifted her fully against his mouth, thrusting deep inside her with his tongue, the stubble of his beard scraping her gently as he gave her the relief she desired. And when he felt her body clench, he sucked, right as the spasms of release crashed over her.

He jerked, having to hold back his own release as the soft cries of her pleasure echoed in his ears.

Only when the shudders had ebbed from her body did he finally lift the sark over her head and lower her to the pallet. Naked. Sated. Her gaze soft and her cheeks flushed with pleasure. Never had she looked more beautiful.

My wife.

His chest burned with emotion and wonderment. Moved beyond words at the poignancy of the moment, the most perfect of his life.

Unable to wait a minute longer, he quickly divested himself of his breeches and moved between her legs.

She grabbed his shoulders, holding him with her loving blue-eyed gaze as he entered her.

He loved to watch her face, watch the erotic way her eyes widened and her lips parted with soft gasps as he pressed inside her, inch by inch.

Her body clutched him like a warm glove. He shook with the effort of restraint. She was so small, so incredibly tight. It felt too good.

He thrust, groaning at the sensation of being deep inside her, filling her. Loving her. The pressure in his groin was intense, but he wanted to prolong every moment of this—to show her with his body all the love and tenderness in his heart.

Cradling her face with one hand, he kissed her gently, twining his tongue with hers in a slow, delicious dance. Only then did he move inside her with long, deep strokes, drawing out every inch of pleasure.

He couldn't get enough of her, couldn't get close enough. He wanted to feel every inch of her soft skin pressed against his.

He could feel her restlessness, feel as her passion built. Her hands roamed his back, his arms, clutching harder and harder as their bodies climbed together in perfect step to the peak of pleasure.

He'd never felt like this in his life. So completely attuned to another person. Feeling her pleasure as surely as if it were his.

His chest pounded. The pressure in his loins was tight and hot. He pumped harder and faster, her hips rising in perfect synchronicity to meet him.

Warmth washed over him in a heavy flood. Pleasure intensified and tightened at the base of his spine.

Oh God, yes.

He was going to come. Her breath quickened. And so was she.

Their eyes met and the world exploded, shattering into a kaleidoscope of spine-tingling pleasure. She cried out, her body contracting tight around him like a fist. He thrust one more time, high and deep, roaring with the force of his own release. He gave himself to her completely as he was sucked into a vortex of pleasure so intense, she claimed not only his body, but his soul.

Forever.

Chapter 20

Lizzie pressed her hips back against him to take him deeper, in the throes of the most wildly erotic dream of her life.

Patrick's big, hard body was pressed against her back. God, she loved the feel of all those muscles surrounding her. His thick, strong arms, his heavy, powerful thighs, his incredible granite-hard chest. He was warm, his skin so hot that it sizzled. She sizzled.

He was kissing her neck, his warm mouth and wet tongue making her skin prickle and shiver with heated awareness. His big hands, rough with calluses, cupped her breasts, squeezing and caressing her as if he couldn't get enough of their weight.

She'd never felt so naughty or so desirable. She felt beautiful. Sensual. Free. She didn't think, didn't allow embarrassment or self-consciousness to hamper any of her movements. She took what she wanted, and that was him. All of him. As deep and hard as he could go.

She arched her back, pressing her breasts deeper into his palms as he thrust and churned inside her. The sultry masculine scent of him, of their lovemaking, infused her senses with a primal need.

She moaned, the tingling heat between her legs incredible. Pleasure washed over her in a hot, heavy wave, drenching her with sensation. She was so wet. So incredibly aroused. Every nerve ending flared, awaiting his touch.

She never wanted to wake up.

Her moans became frantic cries as their movements grew more frenzied—more intense. More focused on one goal.

Her pulse raced as the road to paradise opened up in front of her—beckoning. "Oh, God . . . yes."

Sensation built in a focused center between her legs. She arched back to take him deeper. He was so big and thick, wedged up high inside her. She could hear his harsh breathing and his hard grunts of pleasure in her ear.

His kissing grew rougher, more urgent, sucking, nipping, the roughness of his unshaven stubble scraping against the sensitive skin of her nape.

One hand plied the rigid peak of her nipple, twisting it gently, as the other hand slid down between her legs. His fingers caressed her from the front as his erection filled her from behind. And when his thumb found the most sensitive spot . . .

It was too much. Her heart slammed into her chest. Her breath caught. Sensation splintered and she started to shatter.

"That's it, love," he whispered. "Come for me." His voice was low and ragged. "God, you are so hot."

Her mind went blank as white hot pleasure exploded inside her. She cried out with the force of the spasms that rocked her from head to toe. No part of her was left out.

He thrust one more time, holding himself deep inside her, and then began to circle his hips, the pressure and friction taking her even higher—to a peak she'd never climbed.

And then he started to come, the hot rush of his seed joining the warm flow of her cresting release, drawing out the pleasure even further.

When the spasms at last began to ebb, he wrapped his arms around her, snuggling her against the warm, protective shield of his chest. They were still connected, her body tingling from the effects of their lovemaking.

She sighed against him with utter contentment. She could stay like this forever.

"You're awake," he murmured near her ear.

She laughed. "I am now."

"I'm sorry, I couldn't resist." He reached down and lovingly cupped her bottom. "I woke and this was pressed temptingly against me. Your skin is so soft." He stroked her gently, his hand caressing the curved flank. "I hope you aren't too sore."

Though they'd made love most of the night, surprisingly she wasn't. Or if she was, she was too exhausted and well sated to feel it. "No. Though at first I thought it was a dream."

He pressed a kiss on the top of her head. "Not a dream, Lizzie."

She turned around and smiled at him, emotion at what had happened last night tugging at her eyes and throat. "No, not a dream."

They'd handfasted. He was hers for a year. She would never let him go.

If there had been a smidgen of doubt in her mind that he didn't care for her, it was gone now. She thought of how despite his own desires, he'd tried to resist her last night, just as he'd tried to urge her to marry Robert Campbell. To the last he was honorable to the core, trying to save her from the hardship that marriage to him might entail.

And the affection in his eyes right now . . . he didn't just care for her.

He loves me. She knew it in her heart.

Some of the softness slipped from his face as reality intruded. "I wish we could stay longer, but it's not safe. We need to get to Balquhidder so I can join my men." His body slid from hers, and she felt an immediate chill. "It's almost dawn. Our ride will be here soon."

Sooner than he realized.

They'd barely had time to wash and dress before Patrick heard the sound of an approaching boat. His senses were uncanny; she hadn't heard anything. After he'd donned his

weapons and gathered their belongings, they hurried outside to meet the fisherman. Lizzie was surprised to see a
sheen of water clinging to the rock and trees. It had rained
last night, and she hadn't even noticed.

As they approached the boat, she knew something was
wrong even before he spoke.

"Hurry," the old man said. He gave Patrick a knowing
look. "Men are coming this way."

"Did you see them?" Patrick asked, the tenderness gone
from his voice—as if it had never been. Once again he was
the hard, implacable warrior.

The fisherman shook his head. "Only from a distance.
But since they're coming down the hills, I figured they were
after you."

The short ride to shore seemed interminable. Lizzie
could see Patrick scanning the trees and hills to the south—
the direction from which they'd come.

When at last they'd reached the beach, Patrick thanked
the man and gave him a few more coins. "If they do come,
I'd appreciate it if you keep our presence here a secret."

The old man put a coin between his teeth and bit it. Apparently satisfied, he broke into a wide-toothed grin, the
weathered ruddy leather of his skin crinkling into hundreds
of lines. "They'll hear nothing from me," he vowed.

Without wasting any more time, Patrick took her hand
and led her along the shore, back in the direction from
which they'd come. When the loch was behind them, they
continued west. "Do you think it's your brother?" she
asked.

"Or yours," Patrick answered. "Either way, we need to
reach Balquhidder first."

They ran for a while, perhaps a mile, but the ground was
slick and Lizzie was having a difficult time keeping up. The
challenges of the past few days had taken their toll; her legs
were like jelly.

But she bit her tongue, refusing to complain. This was

the first day of the rest of her life, and she'd better get used to it.

The outcropping of a few buildings came into view, and she knew they must be close. Patrick was a few feet ahead of her, when all of a sudden the ground slipped out from under her feet and she landed backward in a puddle of mud. The impact took her breath away, and a jolt of pain radiated up her spine. The shock of the fall jarred her, and it took her a few moments to realize that she was unhurt.

Patrick ran to her side. "Are you all right?"

She nodded. "I think so. It's my pride that's hurt most of all." She smiled. "I'm not usually so clumsy."

The smile slid from her face. *Except for once.* She looked up at Patrick's face, seeing his concern but also something else. He reached down his hand to help her up, and she took it, sliding her hand into his as he lifted her to her feet.

She felt a jolt of recognition. Something clicked together in her head, like two pieces of a puzzle snapping together.

She jerked her hand away with a gasp, the shadow of a memory hitting her. Of a gallant knight who'd helped her at one of the worst moments of her life. Her gaze shot to his, and her mouth went dry.

"My God, it was you," she whispered. "That day at the gathering."

"Aye," he said softly. "It was me."

For a moment, she was overcome. Overwhelmed with the realization that her knight in shining armor and the man to whom she'd given her heart were one and the same. She took a few steps forward, catapulting into the waiting shelter of his embrace and letting out a deep sigh of contentment when his strong arms enfolded her against him. She pressed her cheek against his chest, savoring the discovery of a connection that extended further than she'd ever imagined.

It was him. She couldn't believe it.

Was it fate that had brought them together?

It took her a moment to find the words she'd dreamed of someday saying, if ever given the opportunity, to the man who'd been so kind to her. She smiled, sheer wonder making her eyes shimmer with tears. "Thank you."

Her praise seemed to make him uncomfortable. "It was nothing."

But they both knew it was much more than that—he'd risked his life in helping her. He'd stood beside her when no one else would. How could she be anything but eternally grateful? Gazing up into his handsome face, she shook her head. "I don't understand. Why didn't you tell me?"

"I couldn't. You would have known I was a MacGregor."

She nodded and then frowned. "But why not after? Why not tell me once I discovered your identity? You must have known how grateful I would be." His gallantry had been the only bright spot in that horrible day.

"I thought the memory might cause you pain—I thought it better left in the past."

She winced, suddenly picturing with embarrassing clarity the scene he'd witnessed. Tripping and landing in the puddle on her backside. Sitting there, dripping with mud, utterly humiliated. No one coming to help her.

Had he heard what John and his friends had said?

Her cheeks heated with mortification. *Of course he had.*

She dropped her gaze, too embarrassed to look at him, scared that she would see pity on his face.

He tipped her chin in his strong fingers and forced her gaze back to his. "It's their shame, not yours, Lizzie." He pressed his lips on hers in a tender kiss. "Forget about it. That day was a long time ago and means nothing to us now."

He was right. What happened then was the past and he was her future. The memory would always be a painful one, but now perhaps knowing his part would make it a little more bearable.

She covered her embarrassment with a wry smile and a self-deprecating attempt at humor. "What must you have thought of me? I must have looked quite the pitiful sight." She laughed self-consciously. "Not exactly a good first impression. I can't believe you would even want to try tricking me into marriage after that. I suppose you drew the short straw."

The jest fell flat in a thud of uncomfortable silence.

She looked up at him expectantly, waiting for reassurance, surprised instead to see a flash of something akin to guilt.

Her poor attempt at eliciting a compliment had misfired—badly. The smile slid from her face and she stepped back, eyeing him uncertainly.

"It wasn't like that," he said an instant too late. "I'm the one lucky to have you, Lizzie. I never thought I could have a woman like you and jumped at the opportunity. I wouldn't hear of it being anyone else."

All of a sudden, the implication of what he'd seen—and then done—hit her with enough force to take her breath away. He tried to pull her into his arms again, but she backed out of his reach. "Patrick"—her eyes locked on his taking in every facet of his reaction—"did what you saw that day play a part in your decision to pursue me—to seduce me into marrying you?"

Her heart thumped wildly as she guessed the answer.

The look in his eyes said it all.

Please, anything but pity. Her insides curled. She wanted to crawl into a tight ball.

She took a step back, the burning in her chest excruciating. "God, it did," she said, her voice hoarse with pain.

"It's not what you are thinking," he said fiercely.

He couldn't imagine what she was thinking. He'd probably never felt a moment of self-doubt or insecurity in his life. Her eyes raked over his too perfect face, her heart straining to beat in her tight chest. Tears swam before her eyes. "P-p-poor, pathetic Elizabeth Campbell." She took a deep breath, forcing the stammer from her voice. Could she be any more humiliated already? "A plain girl with a stammer and three broken engagements would be grateful for the attention of any man, let alone a sinfully handsome one like yourself. Did you think me so desperate that I would fall at your feet?" The memories stabbed. She would lap it up like a grateful pup. And she had. She'd fallen right into his seductive trap. But look at him—she'd never had a chance. A sob tore from her chest. Eyes wide, she gazed up at him and asked in a tiny voice, "Did you laugh at me?"

He pulled her fiercely against him in a tight embrace, not letting her push him away. "Never! Don't ever think that. Aye, I admit I thought you might have been left vulnerable by what had happened, but that is not the reason I wanted to marry you. I wanted you from the first moment I saw you, and it had nothing to do with pity."

She heard the vehemence and sincerity in his voice, but it couldn't completely pierce the veil of hurt or repair the damage to her pride. Pride that had taken years to rebuild. "I'm to believe that?"

"It's the truth."

She wanted to believe him, and perhaps deep down she did, but she couldn't get the images out of her head. Had they laughed at her? Made fun of her?

She cringed, unable to think about it. He'd thought her an easy mark—a scorned woman who'd be only too grateful for his attentions. She'd thought she'd put that day behind her, but perhaps there was still a part of her that believed that her deep-rooted desire to fall in love made her susceptible to being taken advantage of—just as John had done. "I don't know which is worse," she said miserably, "to be pursued for my land or for being an easy mark."

But certainly not for me.

"Stop." His expression was as hard as she'd ever seen it. "I will not let you think that way. You are making more of this than there ever was. Even if I suspected you would be susceptible to seduction, I quickly learned that I was wrong. If anything, you had been made more wary by what had happened before. My motives for finding you again might have been ill conceived, but I'll never be sorry that I did. I wanted to marry you because I fell in love with you. Not for your land, but for you." His thumb swept over the curve of her cheek, wiping away a single tear. He looked right into her eyes. "I love you, Elizabeth Campbell, with all my heart."

For an instant, happiness broke through the pain. *I love you.* Words she'd dreamed of but never heard. Not until now. *Why now?* "You don't need to say that just to make me feel better."

His jaw flexed, and pride radiated from him. "I've never said those words to anyone before." His penetrating gaze moved over her. "Nor do they come easy for me."

Lizzie heard the censure in his voice and understood— he'd held himself apart for so long because of all that had been taken from him. Relinquishing that control over his emotions would have not come easily. Those words had cost him a lot. "I want to believe you."

He took her chin in his hand and turned her face to his, his gaze tender and . . . loving. "Then do. Does knowing I was there that day really change anything, Lizzie? However it started, I do love you. That isn't a lie. After all we've been through, all that we've shared, can you really doubt my feelings for you?"

She looked up at him with watery eyes. Could she? She knew the answer in her heart.

A sound in the distance behind them, however, drew his immediate attention. He swore and grabbed her hand. "I will prove it to you if it takes me a lifetime, but the rest of this discussion will have to wait. They're coming. We have to go. Quickly."

She nodded, not wasting any time arguing, and ran.

After a few minutes, an old stone church—now a kirk—came into view on the other side of a small hill. What looked to be a small waterfall ran alongside it. A large crowd of men and horses filled the yard.

Patrick turned to her with an encouraging smile. "Not much farther. My men—"

He stopped in his tracks and swore.

"What's wrong?"

He turned to her, eyes blank. "Those aren't my men."

"Then who?" Her gaze shot back to the kirk, and she easily recognized the man who was mounting his horse, obviously intending to give them chase. "It's Jamie!" Her heart gave an involuntary lift before she realized what it meant—if her brother was here, that meant Patrick's men were not.

She put a restraining arm on Patrick when she recognized the man at Jamie's side. *Colin. Dear God.* Patrick's entire body went tight as a whip. His face contorted with hatred—and she knew that if he had the opportunity, he would kill Colin without a second thought.

She would never know what might have happened, because at that moment a hail of arrows flew from the trees behind them, one landing not three feet from where she was standing. Patrick shouted a warning and pulled her around in front of him. She felt the frantic pounding of his heart at her back. The arrow could have killed her.

She didn't need to look to know that it had come from his brother.

They were trapped, literally caught in the middle between two worlds: hers before them and his behind.

With nowhere for them to go.

With only an instant to decide, Patrick knew he had no choice. Escape would be a long shot at best, and he would not risk Lizzie's life—not again.

Even if it meant his own.

He started to walk forward, but she stopped him. "What are you doing? You can't do this," she begged, her eyes filling with fear. For him. "Colin . . . I don't know what he'll do. You have to try to get away."

Patrick didn't say anything, just kept pulling her forward. He wouldn't leave her unprotected, not until she was safe with her brothers—not with Gregor within arrow's shot.

"Patrick, please. Don't do this. You need to run."

Her cries tugged at his heart, but he let them wash over him. The Campbells were mounted and riding toward them at full speed. They broke off into two groups—the larger party led by Colin headed into the trees behind them after Gregor. Jamie Campbell was riding right for him, his sword raised high above his head.

Patrick pulled his sword from the scabbard at his back and, ignoring her cries, pushed Lizzie out of the way.

He stood his ground . . . waiting.

It didn't take long. Campbell's face was filled with fury, but Patrick kept his eye on the blade. The sound of horses pounded in his ears. Almost there . . .

He braced himself but was still unprepared for the force of the blow. Jamie's sword descended in a high arc, and Patrick raised his sword with both hands to block it. The pain shot right to his injured leg. He wobbled but recovered quickly.

Campbell dismounted, his sword lifted high above his head.

Patrick could hear Lizzie begging her brother to stop. She would have run between them, but thank God a few of her clansmen were holding her back.

Jamie fought with a vengeance—his rage his only weakness. They exchanged blow after blow, and with each swing Patrick knew he was weakening. He managed to land a blow on Jamie's shoulder, and he heard Lizzie scream. His gaze shot to her, and he knew he couldn't do this. Even if he could kill Jamie Campbell, he wouldn't.

His blood pounded. Every instinct clamored against it. The rush of battle was still upon him. But he let it go.

He met Campbell's gaze, and when the Enforcer swung his sword around and tried to use his elbow to knock Patrick to the ground, instead of evading the blow, he took it full force in the temple.

Lizzie's scream rang in his ears as blackness crashed over him.

Chapter 21

He wasn't dead. That was the first thing Patrick realized when he woke. The next was that his head felt as if it had exploded and been put back together in a jumbled mess; and the third was that he was not alone.

He was lying on a bed in what appeared to be an old stone *bothan*. He could see a fireplace for heating and cooking, the bed, a few tables and chairs, a cupboard, and sitting on a chair in the corner of the room, watching him with a black look on his face, was Jamie Campbell. Though he appeared to be relaxed and not an immediate threat, Patrick did not fool himself. Argyll's Enforcer was one of the fiercest and most deadly men in Scotland—Highlands or Lowlands.

Still, he was alone, and for a moment Patrick contemplated escape.

Reading his mind, Jamie smiled. "I wouldn't advise it," he said. "Even if you could get past me, which I doubt given your current condition, my men have surrounded the building. This time, they will not hesitate to shoot."

Patrick realized that his nearness to Lizzie when they were taken was likely what had prevented them from using their guns before. He was immediately conscious of his disadvantage. Hell if he would lie here like some damn invalid. Gritting his teeth, he sat up slowly. His head exploded in fresh pain, and nausea crashed over him. Biting back the urge to empty his stomach, he rode out the wave. Then, seeing a flagon near the bed, he helped himself to a long drink, welcoming the fiery taste of the crude whisky—ambrosia to a starving man.

"Patrick MacGregor," said Jamie, tapping his fingers on the arm of the wooden chair. "It's been a long time."

Not as long as you think. Jamie was referring to the time they'd spent—briefly—fighting together on the Isle of Lewis, but Patrick had seen him much more recently than that. He'd had an arrow pointed at Campbell's back only a few months ago.

"Not long enough," Patrick replied dryly, given his current state of imprisonment. "How did you find us?"

"We learned of the attack on Lizzie almost immediately—one of the guardsmen managed to escape. Then, while we were searching the area, one of my men chanced to be nearby when the fiery cross passed through Callander. We took a chance that you were headed here."

Patrick swore at the bad luck. "And my men?"

Jamie gave him a long look. "We'd seen neither hide nor hair of anyone until you arrived." His expression hardened. "The outlaw Gregor and his men, however, were taken not long after you fell. They will be executed in Edinburgh for their crimes."

Patrick felt a stab in his chest. Not for the brother he had, but for the one he'd lost before circumstances changed Gregor into the bitter, hate-filled man he'd become.

"And your brother's crimes?" Patrick said cuttingly. "Will Auchinbreck be executed for his?"

Campbell's mouth tightened into a grim line. "I'm sorry for what happened to your sister."

The concession surprised him. Jamie Campbell seemed honestly repelled by his brother's actions. "Yet Auchinbreck will not pay for what he's done." It wasn't a question, but a statement of fact.

"In the courts . . . nay." Campbell met his gaze. "But I've no doubt that one day there will be a reckoning."

Patrick studied him carefully, knowing there was something Jamie Campbell wasn't telling him but also realizing he'd told him all he would.

But if Gregor had been taken and was already on his way to Edinburgh, as was likely, why was he here? "Where's Lizzie?"

Campbell gave him a hard look. "Somewhere safe."

"I want to see her."

"No."

If Campbell thought he would accept that, he was sorely mistaken. The first thing he would do when he got out of here was find her. She might hate him right now, but she was his wife.

Jamie rubbed his shoulder in the place Patrick had landed a blow with his *claidheamhmór*. "You've improved since last we met."

Patrick examined the knot on his head, his fingers skimming over the bloody, tender flesh. "So have you."

They'd both been young on Lewis. Now they were men—warriors in their prime.

Campbell met Patrick's gaze with a knowing look. "You're too good a swordsman not to have avoided the blow to your head."

Patrick didn't say anything, looking away from the other man's piercing stare. They both knew he'd stood down, but damned if he'd explain himself.

"My sister told me an interesting story," Jamie said casually, though Patrick could tell it was an act.

"Is that so?"

Campbell's eyes simmered with rage. "Give me one good reason why I shouldn't kill you right now."

Patrick met his anger with his own. "Because your sister insists that you believe in justice, and the only crime I've been accused of is one that I did not commit. The atrocities done at Glenfruin were not the work of the MacGregors."

Campbell's eyes narrowed dangerously. "I'm talking about what you did to my sister. Lying and wheedling your

way into Castle Campbell to convince her to marry you—
not to mention putting her life in danger, even if, as she
says, you did save it more than once."

Patrick wondered how much Lizzie had told him. The
basics, probably. If Campbell knew the worst of it, Patrick
wouldn't be sitting here right now.

There was nothing Jamie Campbell could say to him that
Patrick hadn't already said to himself. "I imagine the only
thing staying your hand is the same thing that stayed
mine—killing me will hurt her."

Jamie didn't appear very happy about it, but he reluctantly appeared to accept the truth of the observation. Two
enemies bound by the happiness of the woman they both
loved. "Mine is not the only hand itching to strike," Campbell warned him, referring to Argyll and Auchinbreck.
"Lizzie's feelings will not keep you alive forever."

Patrick's head hurt, and he was tired of Campbell's subtle interrogation. "What will, since I assume that is your
purpose for being here?"

Jamie smiled, though it lacked any pretense of friendli-
ness. "Cut to the quick, is it? Fine. My sister might claim to
care for you, and given what you did out there today, I'm
willing to concede that her feelings are reciprocated, but I
want you out of her life. Though I am not without sympathy for the plight of your clan, it doesn't mean I want my
sister tied to an outlawed MacGregor." His gaze turned
shrewd and unyielding. "You will have your freedom and
the tenancy of the land near Loch Earn, which I understand
was the reason for this pursuit of my sister in the first place.
I will find a way to mollify Glenorchy. In return, you will
repudiate the handfast and never seek her out again."

"No," Patrick answered without hesitation. Jamie Campbell was offering him the two things he thought he'd
wanted most in the world, but Patrick had been wrong. Lizzie had given him something much more important. She'd
brought him back from the very edge of darkness. Without

her, he would be the empty, cold shell of a man he'd been before.

He would be like his doomed brother.

Patrick's fight to reclaim his land would never end until once again it belonged to the MacGregors, but it would not be won at the cost of the woman he loved.

Wincing, he thought of the argument they'd had before he was captured. He might not yet have had the chance to convince her of his love, but he'd spend the rest of his life proving it.

He thought of all Lizzie had been willing to give up for him; he would do no less for her.

No smile marred the hard set of Campbell's jaw. "Even if it is the best thing for Lizzie?"

"Who are you to judge what is best for your sister?"

"Apparently," Campbell intoned darkly, "I'm the only person thinking rationally around here. God's blood, did you see her? Gowned in rags, bedraggled, weary to the point of exhaustion, looking as if she'd been through hell the past few days?"

Patrick clenched his jaw against the accusations, but she had been through hell.

"If you care for her, you will not drag her under with you. You will not see her denied the life that should be hers."

Patrick could see where this conversation was going, but damned if he would give her up without a fight. "It's her choice to make."

The other man was fast losing his patience. He stood up from the chair and strode toward the bed, all pretense of equanimity gone. But if Campbell thought to intimidate him, he was dead wrong. Patrick stood and met him eye to eye.

"You might make her happy now," Campbell thundered. "But how happy will she be in a few years after hardship has worn her down? I don't know what my cousin will do, but would you have her risk losing everything?"

Patrick stiffened, knowing he'd argued much the same to himself. "Is this what she wants?"

"She's confused right now. She doesn't know what she wants. But if you walk away now, she will recover."

Patrick flexed his jaw. "Let me talk to her."

"You'll only make it harder." Campbell paused and then said quietly, "If you truly care for her, as I think you do, you'll do the right thing. Doesn't she deserve better?"

Truth twisted like a knife in the gut. Campbell was only saying what Patrick already knew and had tried to ignore. She deserved everything, and a man who could give it to her. But he was so damn tired of trying to do the right thing.

Lizzie . . .

His heart cried out for her. She was all he wanted.

"Even if I agreed, what makes you think she will accept it?" Patrick was grasping, but if there was anything he'd learned about Lizzie, it was that she had a mind of her own.

"If you know my sister as well as I think you do, you will know the answer to that."

The land. Jamie would make it look as if all he'd wanted had been the land. Patrick wanted to think that she wouldn't believe it of him, but after their last conversation, when she'd discovered that he'd witnessed her humiliation, she was vulnerable. Maybe even vulnerable enough to believe it. "She'll hate me," Patrick said dully.

For a moment, he thought he saw a streak of compassion in Campbell's granite gaze. "Aye, but it's for the best."

It might be for the best, but it didn't stop Patrick from feeling that he'd just had his heart eviscerated from his chest with a rusty, jagged blade.

Never had he felt so empty. It was as if the last light had

gone out of him—and the hope that something good might come out of this bungled situation, extinguished.

Chest burning with emotion and not trusting himself to speak, Patrick nodded.

"I'm sorry, lass, but he's gone," Jamie said.

No. Every instinct rejected what her brother was saying. *It can't be true.*

Lizzie sat in an upstairs chamber of the drover's inn near Callander, where she'd been awaiting news of Patrick since Jamie's men had pulled her off him on the field near Balquhidder. Stunned, she stared at her brother. "Tell me again—everything—that he said."

"I offered him the tenancy of the land near Loch Earn and his freedom if he would repudiate the handfast," Jamie repeated. "He accepted."

"Just like that?" *He wouldn't have left me without saying anything.* Though her pride had been wounded by what she'd discovered, his last words had resonated: *Can you really doubt my feelings for you?* Deep in her heart, she couldn't. Lizzie shook her head, refusing to believe it. "You must have misunderstood."

Patrick would never give up that easily, unless . . . *No. He cares about me.*

Poor, pathetic . . . She wanted to close her eyes and put her hands over her ears to block out the memories. But there was just enough doubt lingering from the discovery that what he'd seen that day might have caused him to target her as an easy mark.

Jamie gave her a sympathetic look, though he would never understand the pain he'd just unwittingly inflicted. "I'm sure he cares for you, lass, but the land was what he wanted—isn't that what you told me?"

Unable to speak, she nodded. She'd told Jamie what had happened, how Patrick had sought her out for her land. *But I didn't mean it. I thought . . .*

She looked to her brother, hoping to find a kernel of hope to hold on to, but the sympathy in his eyes only made it worse.

Jamie loved her too much. He was so overly protective of her. Her eyes narrowed. "You didn't force him to agree to this, did you?"

Jamie arched a brow, a wry look on his face, as if he wanted to be offended but knew he couldn't be. "I didn't need to."

Her heart squeezed at the blunt honesty. It hadn't been only about the land . . . had it? To the last, she'd wanted to think she'd been wrong about his motives. But he hadn't stayed to convince her or make her forgive him. "Why didn't he come see me and tell me himself?"

"I'm sure he thought it would be easier this way. A clean break."

She made a sharp scoffing sound. A clean break? As if it were something as inconsequential as a bone and not her heart that had been broken. "What if I don't want a clean break? I have a year—"

"Is that what you want, Lizzie? To drag this out? To run after a man . . ."

Lizzie sucked in her breath. She gazed up at her brother, horrified. The blood drained from her face. *To run after a man who has made it very clear that I'm not important enough to him.* That was what Jamie was trying to say. Humiliation crawled over her in a mottled flush. Was that what she'd been doing, throwing herself at a man who didn't want her?

She'd practically asked him to marry her. Looking back at it now, she saw that her well-constructed argument had been just as much about what she could bring him as it had been about her.

But he said he loved me.

The cold, hard truth hit her square in the chest. Even if he did love her, it hadn't been enough. He'd taken the land

and his freedom and left her behind with nary a fare-thee-well.

Jamie came over to stand beside her, placing his hand on her shoulder consolingly. "With what has happened between our clans, I can't say I blame him, Lizzie. Can you?"

Tears blurred her eyes, and she shook her head. She'd been thunderstruck to learn the truth from Jamie. Patrick's accusations against her cousin and Colin had been horribly accurate. Though Jamie had no idea of their cousin's intentions when he'd negotiated the surrender of Alasdair MacGregor and his men, Archie had played them false and sent them to their deaths. And just as horribly, Colin was indeed responsible for the rape of Patrick's sister.

The thought that her own brother . . .

She shuddered, utterly repulsed and shamed.

The actions of her kinsmen were appalling. After what they did, how could she blame Patrick for not wanting to tie himself to a Campbell?

"You won't pursue this, will you, Lizzie?" Jamie asked.

Lizzie's heartbeat drummed in her ears. Everything she'd always wanted was slipping through her fingers like rain through a sieve. A husband. A family. A dream lost. For having been in love, she knew marriage without it would be impossible.

She gazed at her brother through watery eyes, knowing what she had to do. Even if they couldn't be together, she couldn't bear the thought of anything happening to him. She would do what she could to keep him safe. "On one condition," she said thickly.

Jamie eyed her warily. "What's that?"

"He won't just have his freedom for now, I want Archie to see to it that he is pardoned in full."

Jamie gave her a long look and then nodded.

It was done.

Her chest, her throat, and her eyes burned with the knowledge that it was truly over. With a Campbell and a

MacGregor, how could any ending other than heartbreak and disappointment ever be possible?

The pain was unbearable: Tears streamed from her eyes, and her shoulders were racked with heart-wrenching sobs torn from the depths of her soul.

Jamie pulled her from her chair and held her against his chest, stroking her hair. "Come, lass, I'll take you home. You'll see, you'll forget about him in no time."

That's where Jamie was wrong. Lizzie would never forget about him. She would love Patrick Murray, née Mac-Gregor, for the rest of her life.

Chapter 22

From the window in the small seating area off her bed-chamber, Lizzie gazed out at the Kyle below, her eyes scanning the icy gray waters and snow-covered banks, and then, unwittingly, they turned north. Though the hills she'd traversed with Patrick couldn't be seen from Dunoon, she knew they were there.

He was there.

The sharp pang of longing had yet to dull. The tightness squeezed her chest and cut off her breath. She fought back the viselike grip of loneliness and despair.

Unconsciously, she wrapped the plaid she wore around her shoulders a little tighter. It was the same one pulled from Patrick's horse before their flight into the wilderness all those weeks ago. Though winter had set in all around the Highlands, it was not the cold she sought to ward off. Somehow, the raggedy plaid made her feel closer to him.

She lowered her head to her shoulder and nuzzled the scratchy wool against the side of her cheek. Every now and then, she would catch the faintest scent of pine and spice lingering in the rough woolen threads. She inhaled deeply and sighed with disappointment. Not today.

The memories were painful, but she held on to them because they were all she had.

A whisper of a smile lifted the corners of her mouth. Her hands dropped to her belly. Perhaps not all.

Lizzie closed her eyes and prayed that her suspicions

were correct. The subtle roundness and the fact that she hadn't bled in weeks gave her every reason to hope.

A child.

His child.

The part of him that she carried around in her heart would not be left alone to die and wither into bitterness and regret but would blossom with the new life she carried inside her.

For the first time since that horrible day four weeks ago when he'd left her without a word, Lizzie felt a ray of happiness slice through the miserable shadows of darkness.

She turned at the sound of a door opening, surprised to see her brother entering the room, and not far behind him, his furious, albeit stunningly beautiful, wife.

Jamie hesitated at the door, and with two hands pressed against his back, Caitrina pushed him unceremoniously into the room. Hands on her hips and just noticeably pregnant belly jutting forward, she glared at her husband and then back to Lizzie. "Your brother has something to say to you."

Though Lizzie had been at Dunoon with Jamie and Caitrina for over a month, this was the first time she'd caught a glimpse of the Caitrina Lamont of the infamous spitfire reputation. Lizzie had been charmed by the sweet girl who'd lost so much and yet had loved Jamie enough to forgive him for the destruction wrought on her clan. But there was no sign of that forgiveness right now. With her flashing eyes and furious expression, she looked part wildcat—ready to tear him apart with her tiny claws.

Lizzie frowned, wondering what Jamie had done to provoke such a reaction in his wife. It amused her to see Jamie so disconcerted. Caitrina was good for him. The changes in her brother had not gone unnoticed. He seemed lighter now—not so serious and unyielding.

Lizzie also had Caitrina to thank for Jamie's apparent softening of his stance against the MacGregors. So caught up in her own pain, Lizzie hadn't thought about what her brother had actually done in allowing Patrick—*chief* of the outlawed clan—to go free. Initially, Colin and her cousin Argyll had been furious, but after a few hours in the laird's solar with Jamie, her cousin had changed his mind. Argyll had traveled to London not long after they'd arrived at Dunoon (much to Caitrina's relief), and Colin had returned briefly after the short trial where Gregor and his men had been sentenced to death then disappeared.

If she'd needed any further proof of the love Jamie bore his wife, however, she'd received it when she heard what he'd done in allowing Caitrina's outlaw brother Niall to "escape." No one escaped her brother—ever. That he'd allowed Niall to do so demonstrated Jamie's fair-mindedness to the plight not only of the Lamonts, but of the MacGregors as well.

With Niall Lamont on the loose, Lizzie could understand why Colin had made himself scarce following the executions. If her brother wasn't worried about Niall or Patrick exacting revenge for what Colin had done to Annie MacGregor, he should be. The irony wasn't lost on her—the hunter would learn what it felt like to be hunted.

Lizzie dropped the book she'd been reading—or trying to read—into her lap and gazed up at her brother with a questioning look on her face. "What is it, Jamie? Is there news of Duncan?"

She'd been shocked—but enormously pleased—on her return to Dunoon to discover from Jamie that their brother Duncan was rumored to have returned to Scotland. She smiled. Perhaps the blatant nudge in her note about Jeannie Gordon's recent loss had helped. Jeannie was the woman Duncan had once loved who'd betrayed him— though Lizzie was no longer so sure.

Despite the treason hanging over Duncan's head, he'd made quite a name for himself as the leader of a fierce group of warriors on the continent. It was about time he returned and proved his innocence. She'd missed him.

Jamie shook his head. "Nay. I've sent out scouts, but there's been no sign of him. It's probably nothing more than rumor."

"Then what is the problem?" Lizzie asked.

Her brother gave his wife an angry glance, to which Caitrina responded immediately with one of her own. "I swear I will give you nothing but daughters," she warned, her voice heavy with foreboding. "So that all of your over-bearing, overprotective male 'wisdom' can be put to good use." She smiled wickedly. "Girls. A whole bevy of them. Just like me. For you to worry about and fret over"—her eyes gleamed—"forever."

Lizzie could have sworn she saw her fierce, not-scared-of-anything brother pale. "What is this about, Jamie?" she asked.

"Tell her," Caitrina ordered.

Lizzie's pulse spiked as she waited for him to continue.

Not one to be intimidated, even by the wife he loved, Jamie drew himself up to every inch of his six-foot-plus frame, towering over his petite wife. "I'll not be raked over the coals, *wife*, for doing what I think is right. Nor will I apologize for trying to protect someone I love." Looking none too pleased, he turned to Lizzie. "I was only thinking of your happiness."

Caitrina's mouth quirked, and Lizzie could see that she was softening. For all her brother's fierce overprotective-ness, it was difficult to stay angry with him in the face of such equally fierce emotion.

"Does she look happy?" Caitrina asked softly.

Jamie gave Lizzie a long look. Though she'd been trying to hide it, her unhappiness was palpable. "What I told you about Patrick MacGregor was true," he said. "However, I did neglect to mention one thing."

Her eyes narrowed with suspicion. "And what was that?"

"When I first offered MacGregor the land and his freedom, he refused. Quite adamantly, actually."

Lizzie felt as if a weight had just been lifted from her shoulders. *He did care for me. I knew I couldn't have been that wrong. It wasn't just about the land.*

"Then how did you convince him to take the offer?" As if she needed to ask. She glanced at Caitrina in shared understanding.

"We thought—" Jamie started, but was cut off by a sarcastic scoff from his beautiful wife.

"That was your first mistake."

Lizzie had an inkling of the source of her sister-by-marriage's irritation and felt her own temper rise. She'd warned Patrick not to make decisions for her, but it seemed he—and her interfering brother—couldn't resist. *Men.* Was there a more protective breed around than a proud Highland warrior? "Let me guess. You and Patrick decided that I would be better off not married to a MacGregor—"

"An *outlawed* MacGregor," Jamie clarified.

"Not any more," Lizzie quipped back. "So you decided to make me believe that he didn't want me."

Jamie shrugged uncomfortably. "Something to that effect."

Lizzie felt her face flush with anger. She rose to her feet and crossed the room to stand toe-to-toe with her overbearing lout of a big brother. "How could you! How could you let me sit here in misery for weeks believing that the man I loved cared so little for me that he turned his back on me at the first opportunity? How could you both be so high-handed and cruel? I love him, Jamie. And if that means I live in a hovel, I will gladly do so. Wouldn't you do as much for your wife?" He had the good grace to grimace guiltily, but Lizzie wasn't finished. "How could you let my child grow up without a father?"

Jamie swallowed hard with a wince. "Child?"

"Oh, Lizzie, that's wonderful!" Caitrina exclaimed, rushing over to give her a hug. "When?"

Lizzie smiled, the excitement contagious. "I'm not sure. I've only just suspected. Perhaps a few months after your babe."

Jamie started to slink back, obviously happy for the change of subject, but Lizzie stopped him. She crossed her arms over her chest and arched a brow. "Where do you think you're going? I'm not finished with you yet. I'm not a girl anymore. I don't need my big brother to fight my battles." She shook her head. "I should have said something and put a stop to this interfering after what you did to John Montgomery."

Jamie smiled. "I'd like to take credit for that, lass. But someone beat me to it."

Lizzie frowned. "But if you didn't, who . . ."

Her gaze shot to her brother. *Patrick.* It amazed her to think that he'd felt enough of a connection even then to exact vengeance on her behalf. The knowledge soothed her lingering hurt and made her even more certain that she hadn't been completely wrong about his motives and feelings. "Did you know it was him?"

Jamie shook his head. "Nay. I'd recognized him at the gathering, and knew he'd come to your assistance, but that was all. Though after what happened a few weeks ago, I suspected."

Lizzie swallowed. *I will kill anyone who harms you.* John should be glad he'd only suffered the loss of an ear and part of his arm—if Patrick knew then what he did now . . . She shivered.

Though there was a certain poetic justice to it, Lizzie wasn't sure she liked the idea of such violence in her name.

"He's a Highland warrior, Lizzie. You can't make him something he is not," Jamie said, reading her thoughts.

Jamie was right. Patrick had been fighting for survival

most of his life. Like most Highlanders, he was used to exacting vengeance and solving problems with his sword. "Do harm to mine and I'll do worse to yours" was part of the Highland credo. Barbaric? She supposed some might think so, but it was the way of it. Not to say that she didn't plan to work on his skills at diplomacy.

"You must have made some impression on him," Jamie said. " 'Tis a lot of trouble to go to for someone he barely knew."

I wanted you from the first moment I saw you. His words that day when she'd realized that he'd been her gallant knight came back to her. He *had* cared about her, even from the beginning.

"What will you do?" Caitrina asked.

Lizzie thought for a minute. She was tired of being the one to fight for their happiness. If he wanted her, he was going to have to decide on his own—perhaps with a bit of prodding so he didn't wait too long.

"After all the effort my brother and Patrick went to just to see to my happiness, I hate to disappoint them." She smiled. "Now that I am free to marry, I think I shall do so. Perhaps I shall send him a wedding invitation?"

Caitrina's eyes went wide with admiration. "You wouldn't."

Lizzie smiled. "Oh, I just might."

Jamie looked back and forth between them. "I never thought I'd say this about a MacGregor, but I almost feel sorry for him."

Patrick might be going to hell in the form of the Campbell's dungeon for this, but he didn't bloody well give a damn.

He rode through the gates of Dunoon ready to do battle, barely heeding the formidable stone walls of the impenetrable fortress or the mass of equally formidable warriors lining them.

"Are you sure about this?" Robbie asked in a low voice. "Riding into the devil's lair is hardly the best way to test your newfound freedom."

Patrick gave him a sharp look. "It's you who insisted on coming along. I told you to stay back with Annie."

Robbie locked his jaw and shook his head. "Nay, she has Lamont to watch over her."

Because Patrick knew a little something about jealousy, he added gently, "She won't talk to him."

"Aye, but it doesn't mean that she doesn't love him."

Patrick couldn't argue with that. But in this case, love didn't seem to matter. It broke his heart to see how the life had been sucked out of her. Annie was a shell of the happy, spirited sister he remembered.

But one thing hadn't changed: She was still the most stubborn woman he had ever met. Patrick didn't know whether his sister would ever forgive Niall Lamont for not returning her love until it was too late. He could commiserate with Lamont—*what if I'm too late?*

Every instinct had told him he was making a mistake as he was riding away from the kirk. But he hadn't listened until he'd seen his sister and Lamont; it was then that he knew he had to do something.

But his duties as chief—trying to instill order in a clan dispersed by chaos after the death of so many of the clan elite—had interfered, and he hadn't acted fast enough.

Married. His stomach turned. It still seemed incomprehensible.

Word of her marriage had filtered up to him in Molach a few days ago, but he hadn't wanted to believe it. But when the missive from Campbell had arrived with his pardon, mentioning a wedding feast . . .

He'd never forget the shot of searing pain that knifed through him.

How could she think about marrying someone else? It had been only thirty-six bloody days!

The worst part was that it was his own damn fault. He'd had her, and like a fool, he'd let her go. But if Patrick knew anything, it was how to fight for what was his. And Elizabeth Campbell had belonged to him from the first moment he'd held her in his arms. Hell, from the first moment he'd helped her out of that damn puddle.

As his arrival at Dunoon had been announced at the gate, Patrick wasn't surprised to see Jamie Campbell coming out of the keep to meet them. He wore a grim look on his face when he saw Patrick, but he actually smiled when he noticed Robbie at his side. If there was any MacGregor who need not fear the Enforcer, it was Robbie. Campbell would never forget Robbie's loyalty to Margaret MacLeod, an old friend of the Enforcer's, during some trouble they'd had at the hands of Dougal MacDonald back on Lewis.

"Robbie, lad, 'tis good to see you." He checked Patrick with a hard look. "MacGregor. I thought you agreed not to seek out my sister."

Patrick met the other man's challenging gaze, cold steel on cold steel. "You know damn well why I'm here. I'm afraid I can no longer abide by the terms of our agreement, so if you intend to arrest me, you better do it now." When he didn't move, Patrick said, "Where is she?"

Campbell had a strange look on his face—almost pitying. "I'm not sure she wants to see you."

"Too bloody bad, because I'm not leaving until she does."

Patrick knew he was acting irrationally, but he didn't give a damn. They were meant to be together, and if she didn't listen to reason, he was going to do what he should have a long time ago—carry her away and make love to her until she did. Even if he had to defeat an entire Campbell garrison to do so.

He was done trying to do the right thing. Honor was overrated.

Jamie led him up the wooden staircase and into the great

hall of the keep. It was near dusk and the servants were preparing the evening meal, but otherwise it was quiet. He'd expected Jamie to have him wait and thus was surprised to be led immediately into the laird's solar.

Half expecting to see his nemesis, Argyll, Patrick heard the door close behind him and instead found himself alone with the very person he'd ridden hell-bent for leather to see.

His heart stopped when he saw her. She had her back to him. She loomed so large in his mind, he'd forgotten how tiny she was. She wore a dark blue velvet gown encrusted with tiny seed pearls. Her long flaxen hair tumbled down her back in silky waves, set off by a diamond-and-sapphire tiara as fine as any royal crown.

For a moment he hesitated, the disparity between their circumstances as sharp as ever. Wealth, power, privilege, she had it all. And though his situation was much improved— he was no longer being actively hunted, he had land to work and a place to live—it would still be a long time before his clan recovered from the destruction wrought by years of abuse and persecution.

But if she was willing to have him, he would cherish her and not look back.

She turned. If he'd hoped for a sign that she was happy to see him, he was to be disappointed. As smooth and expressionless as alabaster, her face betrayed no emotion.

Never had she looked at him with such . . . nothingness. Dread sank like a heavy stone in his stomach. He felt a prickle of uncertainty.

What if I'm too late?

Their eyes met, and still nothing. Were her feelings so shallow that they could be changed so easily? So damn quickly?

She arched a delicate eyebrow. "Did you come to offer me congratulations?"

Her cool, even tone and blunt question sent his already

hammering chest into a violent spin. Anger surged inside him, and he could barely restrain himself from crossing the small room and venting his frustration in an altogether less civilized manner. "Nay, I didn't bloody well come to offer you congratulations."

"No? Then why, may I ask, are you here?"

He took a few steps toward her and forced himself to stop. The muscles in his arms flexed and unflexed. *Be rational, not a barbarian.* "You can't marry someone else. You are bound to me for a year. The handfast can't be repudiated until then."

"Oh, that." She waved her hand dismissively. "My brother assured me that since there were no witnesses, it would be difficult to prove valid."

Patrick's fists clenched at his side. The little wave almost pushed him over the edge. His body tightened with anger, and it took every ounce of his strength to rein it in. "It was valid to me."

"Is that so? Strange way you have of showing it." She smiled. Actually smiled. "In any event, it was for the best. It was so lovely of you and my brother to see to my happiness like this. I don't know what I would have done without you two looking after me."

The lack of sarcasm in her voice was the first inkling he had that something wasn't right. Uneasy, he studied her face, not exactly sure what he was looking for.

"If that is all that you have to say, I'm afraid I'm quite busy." She turned to dismiss him, but he had his hand on her arm before she could move away.

"That is not all that I have to say. You can't marry someone else, because you love me, and I love you."

Tiny white lines appeared around her mouth, the first sign that she was not as unaffected as she appeared. "Love? You certainly have an odd way of showing it."

He cupped her chin in his hand and forced her gaze to his. The raw emotion radiating from her pale, upturned face socked him right in the gut. He'd hurt her terribly. "I love you with all my heart. It's because I love you that I left. I thought I was doing what was right. I thought you would be better off without me."

Her eyes searched his, probing. "What changed your mind?"

"I realized that if you were half as miserable as I was, there was no way you would find happiness with someone else." His heart pounded with dread, with fear. "Was I wrong?"

Tears blurred her eyes. And his chest squeezed with hope.

"How could you leave me like that? After what we'd shared?" The tiny fist of her hand slammed against his chest with surprising force. "You wanted me to believe that you didn't care about me."

He pulled her into his arms and smoothed his hand over her silky head. "I'm so sorry, love. My only defense is that I love you so much, I only wanted what was best for you."

She whacked him again.

"Ow," he said, rubbing the spot. His wee kitten had a bit of a vicious streak.

"*You're* what's best for me, you overbearing oaf."

Sweeter words had never been spoken, though he would have to work on her vocabulary. He pulled her into his arms again and squeezed her tightly. "Does that mean you won't be marrying someone else?"

Lizzie pulled back to look into his eyes, a mischievous twist to her sensuous lips. "Don't you want to ask who it is that I'm marrying?"

He frowned. "I assumed it was Robert Campbell."

She shook her head.

His face hardened. "Then who is it? Tell me so I can kill him."

"Another 'random' attack on the road, perhaps? Thank you, but there will be no more severed limbs in my name."

He lifted a brow. She'd figured it out, had she? Since he had none, he didn't bother feigning remorse. "The bastard is lucky I didn't know the extent of his blackguard behavior. Now tell me."

"I don't know," she hedged. "I haven't decided whether to forgive you or not."

His lips covered hers in a soft, coaxing kiss, his heart soaring with happiness when he felt her sweet response. He pulled his mouth away and gazed into her eyes. "Name your price, my love. I will do whatever it takes to win you back, even if it means getting down on my knees and begging."

Her nose wrinkled, as if she were seriously considering it. "Sounds intriguing. I recall the last time you were on your knees." He met her amused gaze and a bolt of hot lust went straight through him. "But I don't think that will be necessary. I'm thinking that what Caitrina threatened my brother with will be enough."

He hated to ask. "And what's that?"

Lizzie moved his hand to cover her stomach. "She swore she would bear him only girls."

His heart plummeted, the blood in his face draining at her words. He suddenly felt unsteady on his feet and had to brace himself against the wooden table beside them. "A babe?"

She nodded.

He sat on the nearest bench and sank his head into his hands, emotion overtaking him, overwhelmed by all that he could have lost. She sat beside him, and when he looked up, his eyes burned. "God, Lizzie, I'm sorry."

Her eyes shone with tears. "I take it you are happy?"

The lump in his chest was hot and thick as he gathered her into his arms. "I didn't think I could ever feel this happy."

He'd sought Lizzie for her land, but never could he have realized all that she would bring him. With her he would have a home—a family. And the love and happiness he'd known so long ago.

He kissed her again. Softly. Tenderly. With a poignancy that would mark this moment forever.

All of a sudden, he pulled back as the truth finally dawned on him. "There was never anyone else you were intending to marry. It was me."

Lizzie broke into a wide smile. She pressed her cheek against his chest and sighed. "It's only ever been you."

The heart he didn't realize he had seemed to become too big for his chest.

And this time when he kissed her, he didn't stop.

Author's Note

❖

The persecution of clan Gregor (or Clan MacGregor) by the Campbells is well-known. The Campbells—and the 7th Earl of Argyll in particular—have gone down in history as the "bad guys," and the MacGregors have been romanticized as outlaws in the vein of Robin Hood, no doubt in large part thanks to Sir Walter Scott. As with most things, I think the truth is much more complicated. As I mentioned in the author's note of *Highland Warrior*, it was clear that atrocities were committed by both sides. Errol Flynn the MacGregors were not, and I certainly wouldn't have wanted to be walking the moors at night and run into one of these guys. Even MacGregor historians conceded that there were some rough and wild men in the bunch,[1] although perhaps, given their history, this is understandable.

The downfall of the MacGregors stemmed from their landlessness. By the fifteenth century, the ancient fiefdoms of the MacGregors had all been forfeited, leaving the clan "without an acre of land held free of the crown."[2] The MacGregor alliance with King John Balliol led to the subsequent forfeiture of much of their land under King Robert the Bruce.[3] Not surprisingly, clan Campbell, with its close alliance to the Bruce, was the beneficiary, acquiring superiority over the MacGregors.

[1] Ronald Williams, *Sons of the Wolf* (Isle of Colonsay: House of Lochar, 1998), pp. 54–55.
[2] Donald Gregory, *Inquiry into the Earlier History of the Clan Gregor, with a View to Ascertain the Causes Which Led to Their Proscription in 1603* (Edinburgh: Society of Antiquaries of Scotland, Archaelogia Scotia, 1857), vol. 4, pp. 130–159.
[3] Ibid., p. 133.

But the MacGregors continued to occupy many of these lands by *coir a glaive*, the right of sword, giving rise to deadly feuds. As I alluded to in the story, this situation became even more complicated when Glenorchy purchased the superiority from Argyll (making Glenorchy and the MacGregors *both* vassals of Argyll) and refused to recognize the MacGregors as tenants.[4] By the end of the sixteenth century, the situation was desperate. Alasdair MacGregor did attempt legal means to secure possession, but his efforts were effectively thwarted by Glenorchy.[5] But the MacGregors were renowned warriors, and plenty of men, including the Campbells, were willing to make use of them.

The character of Patrick MacGregor was based loosely on Duncan MacEwin MacGregor, the Tutor of Glenstrae. As the hero of my next book is named Duncan, I borrowed the given name of his nephew (and future chief). Ironically, in writing novels based on actual historical figures, I find that one of the most frustrating things is trying to keep all the genealogy straight with the propensity for clans to use the *same* names over and over. Within and between generations, the MacGregors had numerous Iains, Alasdairs, Duncans, Gregors, and a few Patricks. Coupled with my effort to use historically accurate names for the period (of which there are a very limited number), it makes naming characters extremely difficult. Where I could, I tried to use different versions of the same name (for instance, John versus Iain).

The battle of Glenfruin, the Glen of Sorrow—or "the Field of Lennox," as it was known then—actually occurred on February 7, 1603 (with Argyll's "Highland promise" and Alasdair's execution occurring in early 1604). Four hundred MacGregors defeated the Colqu-

---

[4] John L. Roberts, *Feuds, Forays and Rebellions* (Edinburgh: Edinburgh University Press, 1999), p. 177.
[5] Ibid.

houns, killing one hundred forty, including (according to Sir Walter Scott) schoolboys from Dumbarton who'd come to watch the battle. The MacGregors claimed the killing was done on the orders of a rogue MacDonald. But rumors of MacGregor atrocities abounded. On his death, Alasdair, who could not write but dictated his final words, laid the blame for the attack at Argyll's feet. You can find a link to his last testament on my website.

After the battle, the Colquhoun widows went to Stirling Castle, parading the blood-soaked garments of their dead on pikes before the king. Exhibiting quite a flair for the dramatic, the widows were reported to have dipped the "bludie sarks" in sheep's blood for effect.

The MacGregors did take refuge on an islet in Loch Katrine, albeit in 1611, not following Glenfruin.[6] The island is referred to as "Mharnoch," but I think it must be Molach. Today, Molach is better known as the "Ellen's Isle" made famous by Sir Walter Scott in his *Lady of the Lake*.

Alasdair MacGregor, known as "the Arrow of Glen Lyon" for his skill with a bow, was executed with ten of his men on January 20, 1604. But over the course of two months, twenty-five high-ranking MacGregors were killed in Edinburgh. You can find a link to the list of the executed MacGregors on my website. Alasdair's head, along with that of his cousin Iain, was hung on the gates of Dumbarton.

After Alasdair's execution, the clan leadership was thrown in disarray. From what I could determine Alasdair's heirs, his nephews Gregor and Patrick Roy (sons of Black John of the Mailcoat), were just three and a few months old, respectively. Duncan MacEwin MacGregor, Alasdair's fierce cousin and the inspiration for Patrick, was named "tutor" (a kind of guardianship) of the

[6] Ibid., p. 182.

young chief, acting as laird until his young nephews reached their majority.

Interestingly enough, following Alasdair's death there was reputed to be a challenge to the leadership by yet another "Gregor," an alleged illegitimate son of Alasdair.

"Black" Duncan Campbell of Glenorchy died at eighty-one and was succeeded by his nearly fifty-five-year-old son, Colin, and nine years later by Duncan's sixty-year-old second son, Robert. The exact date of the building of Edinample Castle is unclear, but it was built by Black Duncan sometime at the end of the sixteenth century, supposedly on the site of a former MacGregor stronghold. Thus, it didn't seem too far-fetched to tie the retribution against the MacGregors to the murder of John Drummond (the king's forester) in 1589, which was said to have been particularly severe in "the braes of Balquhidder especially, and around Lochearn."[7] The connection of Edinample with my hero and his family, however, is fiction. The castle abounds with plenty of old ghost stories and curses, including the two I mentioned in the story.

If anything, I probably understated the desperate situation of the MacGregors during the time immediately preceding Alasdair's capture. In part, "the relentless persecution took a terrible toll on the women and children, the old and the helpless. With winter approaching, Alasdair's people were destitute. This year there would be no harvest; no Gregarach cattle driven to the fair at Crieff; no salted meat for winter provisions; no cows to keep for lifting into the pastures in the spring. Their settlements were burned out; what little they had was pillaged or destroyed. Their position became steadily more desperate."[8]

[7] Gregory, p. 145.
[8] Williams, p. 70.

Those of you who watch the television show *Man vs. Wild* will no doubt recognize many of the survival techniques Patrick employs on their foray into the hills north of Lochs Katrine and Achray. Bear's show on the Cairngorms definitely inspired this section of the book. When he mentioned how incredibly tough Highlanders were supposed to be, I knew he could have been talking about the MacGregors. The storm that hits Patrick and Lizzie so unexpectedly might seem heavy by today's standards, but this period of history was part of the Little Ice Age, and winters in the early 1600s were particularly severe.

As in my first book, *Highlander Untamed,* I've decided to go with the more romantic version of handfast marriages being sort of a "trial" marriage, although many scholars now believe that handfasts were more accurately a type of betrothal and became a marriage upon consummation. The issue of what constituted a marriage in Scotland after the Reformation is extremely complicated. For centuries, the idea of a present statement of intent to be married (that is, by declaration) was enough—with or without witnesses. Of course, there were problems of proof with this method that led to many cases of "he said, she said." Clandestine or irregular marriages were common but frowned upon by the Kirk, which increasingly tried to ensure that marriage was institutionalized (banns and performed by minister) by payment of fines and/or forcing the couples to get married again—even though recognizing the original irregular or clandestine marriage as valid.

Looking for more sexy Scottish adventure?

Turn the page to catch a sneak peek at the
next pulse-pounding book in
the Highland series

❖

Highland Scoundrel

❖

by

Monica McCarty

The guardsman never saw it coming.

Engrossed in ogling the woman swimming in the loch, he crumpled at Duncan's feet like a rag. Out cold, blood trickled from the gash at his temple.

Duncan could almost feel sorry for him. It wasn't the first time this woman had been the cause of a man's fall from grace.

Not that it was any excuse for such an egregious failure in his duty. If he were one of Duncan's men, there would be severe consequences beyond a knock on the pate for the lapse. His men were revered for their discipline and control, as much as they were feared for their dominance on the battlefield.

Bending over the prone man, Duncan quickly divested the fallen warrior of his weapons, and then returned his own dirk to the gold scabbard at his waist. The blow from the heavy, jewel encrusted hilt wouldn't do any lasting damage, but the pain in the man's head when he woke would give him something to think about. But that wouldn't be any time soon, buying Duncan time enough to complete his unpleasant task.

This was a meeting better had alone—and without interruption.

He heard a splash coming from the loch, but resisted the urge to look at what had so enthralled the guardsman. He knew. Instead, the man feared from Ireland to across the Continent as the Black Highlander—dubbed thus not just

for the color of his hair but for his deadly skill at warfare—
motioned for his men positioned at the edge of the tree line
to keep an eye on the guardsman in case he stirred, and circled around the loch to the place where she'd left her belongings.

If leaving the castle with such a paltry guard to frolic in
the loch was any indication, Jeannie Grant hadn't changed
one whit. He'd half-expected her to be meeting a lover for
a tryst, and had waited before approaching her just to
make sure. But she was alone—this time at least.

He moved through the trees as soundlessly as the wraith
some thought him. He'd been gone a long time.

Too long.

Only now that he was back did he allow himself to acknowledge it.

Ten years he'd bided his time, forging a new life from the
ashes of his old life to replace the one denied him by birth
and treachery, waiting for the right moment to return. Ten
years he'd waged war, honing his skills and laying scourge
across countless battlefields.

Ten years in exile for a crime he didn't commit.

For so long he'd forced everything that reminded him of
the Highlands from his mind, but every step that he'd
taken across the heathery hills, grassy glens, rocky crags,
and forested hillsides of the Deeside since he'd landed in
Aberdeen two days ago had been a brutal reminder of how
much he'd lost.

This place was in his blood. It was part of him, and he'd
be damned if he was forced from here again.

Whatever it took he would clear his name.

Duncan flexed his jaw, steeling himself for what lay ahead.
His controlled expression betrayed none of the fierce turmoil
surging through him as he neared the reckoning ten years in
the making.

Anger that had taken years to harness returned with
surprising force. But emotion would never control him

again and he quickly tamped it down. For many years now, Jeannie Grant—nay, he reminded himself bitterly, Jeannie Gordon—had been nothing to him but a harsh reminder of his own failings. He'd put her out of his mind in the way that a man wants to forget his first lesson in humility. Rarely did he allow himself to think about her, except as a reminder of a mistake he would never make again.

But now he had no choice. As much as he would like to keep her buried in the past where she belonged, he needed her.

The splashing grew louder. He slowed his step as he wound through the maze of trees and brush, taking care to stay well hidden as he drew closer. Even in the heavy thicket of trees, his height and breadth of shoulder should make hiding impossible, but over the years he'd become adept at blending into his surroundings.

He stopped near the rock where she'd left her clothes, keeping hidden behind a wide fir tree.

Every muscle in his body tensed as he scanned the dark mossy-green waters of the loch . . .

He stilled. *There.* The pale oval of her upturned face caught in the sunlight, illuminating the perfectly aligned features for only an instant before she disappeared under the water.

It was her. Jean Gordon, nee Grant. The woman he'd once been foolish enough to love.

He felt a hard jerk in his chest as the memories flooded him: the disbelief, the hurt, the hatred, and finally, the hard wrought indifference.

His name wasn't all that she'd destroyed. She'd taken his trust, and with it, the idealism of a lad of twenty and one. Her betrayal had been a harsh lesson. Never again would he trust his heart.

But that was a lifetime ago. The lass wielded no power over him now; she was merely a means to an end.

His gaze intensified on the stretch of water where she'd

disappeared. A frown betrayed his unease. He knew she was a strong swimmer, but she'd been under a long time. He took a step toward the loch, but was forced to step back quickly when she suddenly exploded out of the water like a sea nymph in a spray of effervescent light. She'd surfaced near the shore, perhaps only twenty feet separated them now, enabling him see her clearly.

Too damned clearly.

Hair slicked back, and water dripping from her face, she emerged from the loch like Venus rising from the sea and headed straight toward him. He'd forgotten how she walked . . . the gentle sway of her hips seduced with every step. The air between them fired with a familiar charge, the sharp, full-bodied awareness that he'd felt from the first moment he'd seen her across the crowded hall of Stirling Castle all those years ago.

His entire body went rigid. The sark she wore was completely transparent, clinging to breasts fuller than he remembered, but just as tantalizing. The cool air against her wet skin only made things worse. Her nipples beaded into two tight buds like berries waiting to be plucked.

He swallowed, trying to clear the taste from his mouth. Ten years and he could still taste her on his tongue, still remember the sweet press of her breast against his teeth as he'd sucked her deep into his mouth. His nostrils flared. He could still smell the fragrant honeysuckle of her skin.

Not even his steely control could prevent the sudden rush of blood surging through his veins. He swore under his breath, his lack of control infuriating him. But the vile oath didn't begin to summarize his anger at the realization that no matter how he felt about her, he was only a man, and for all his vaunted control, a hot-blooded one at that.

And Jeannie had a body that would tempt a eunuch.

But his earlier allusion to Venus—the Goddess born in

sea foam from the castrated genitals of Uranus—was a well-placed, brutal reminder of what this woman could do.

Even as an innocent girl she'd possessed an undeniable sensuality. A primitive allure that was deeper than the mere physical beauty of dark flame-red hair, bold green eyes, ivory skin as smooth as cream, and soft pink lips. It was something in the tilt of her eyes, in the curve of her lush mouth, and in the ripe sensuality of her body that spoke to a man of one thing: swivving. And not just any swivving, but gritty, mind-blowing, come-until-you-pass-out kind of swivving.

With her youthful curves ripened into the full blush of womanhood the effect was even more pronounced.

Worse, he knew from experience it wasn't all for show. She was every bit as wanton as she looked.

Jeannie was one massive cockstand—sex and carnality personified.

He knew seeing her again after all these years would be unpleasant, but he was unprepared for the fury of emotions unleashed inside him by the undeniable pull of the very thing that had been his downfall . . . desire.

He didn't know what he'd expected to feel: anger . . . hatred . . . sadness . . . indifference? Anything but lust.

Years ago he'd wanted her, had been foolish enough to think he could have her, and had been firmly put in his place.

But he wasn't a lovesick lad anymore, seduced by words of love and a body more deadly than any weapon he'd ever faced in war, he was a man hardened by the harsh blow of disappointment.

The sharp edge of lust dulled.

And then she removed her sark.

His stomach clenched and his breath came out in a hiss. Every muscle in his body went taut with the strain of curbing his reaction. Heat and heaviness tugged at his groin. His body wanted to thicken, but he fought it back. He had only one use for her now and it wasn't to satisfy his baser urges.

Lust and emotion would never defeat him again.

To prove it, he forced himself to study her—coldly, dispassionately, as a man might admire a good piece of horseflesh. His gaze slid down the curve of her spine, over the soft flare of her round bottom, and down the firm muscles of her long, shapely legs, taking in every inch of creamy bare skin.

Aye, she was beautiful. And more desirable than any woman he'd ever known. Once he would have given his life for hers. Hell, he had. Just not in the way that he'd ever anticipated.

His eyes lingered and then shifted away, satisfied. Whatever it was that was once between them had died long ago. Her considerable charms were no threat to him now.

Focused on the task at hand, Duncan realized that he could turn her nakedness to his advantage. He had her on the defensive and he knew that with Jeannie that was a good place to start.

Eyes hard, steeling himself for the unpleasantness of what was to come, he stepped around the tree.